'Elaine Graham-Leigh has a remarkable talent for placing the reader in the middle of the crisis and making us care about it. This serious sf novel, about rebels who have gone too far locked in a death struggle with an oppressive government that matches them in brutality, is political, thoughtful and clearly draws upon a rich understanding of similar conflicts on our own world. Our time with each character shows us another link in the chains of violence that keep people trapped in these conflicts. It's also a thriller, with shoot-outs, assassination attempts, incognito cross-country trips, and, about two-thirds of the way in, a murder mystery element that leaves the reader genuinely curious as to the assailant and their motives. It's an entertaining and exciting book about a serious subject, with a female hero whose optimism gives us everything to root for, and it has a keen eye for the small kindnesses that people do for each other, even in the most rotten of situations.'

STEPHEN THEAKER, *THEAKER'S QUARTERLY FICTION*

The Caduca

The Caduca

Published by The Conrad Press in the United Kingdom 2021

Tel: +44(0)1227 472 874
www.theconradpress.com
info@theconradpress.com

ISBN 978-1-913567-48-4

Typesetting and Cover Design by: Charlotte Mouncey, www.bookstyle.co.uk

The Conrad Press logo was designed by Maria Priestley.

Printed and bound in Great Britain by Clays Ltd, Elcograf S.p.A.

The Caduca

Elaine Graham-Leigh

For Dominic

'I set neither boundaries nor time to their fortune;
to them I give empire without end.'

VIRGIL, 29-19BC

'We are just civilians.
We are like citizens of any European city.'

MIROSLAV BETIC, TELEPHONE INTERVIEW TO BBC RADIO 5,
4AM, 24TH MARCH 1999, BELGRADE

Part 1

Mara

In Chaireddan, in the hot weather, the day begins long before the light.

In the market square the stalls glimmered with yellow-flaring lamps, enclosed in mesh against the insects. The women pushed through the folds, batting them down like swimmers. On their heads they carried wicker baskets, so that the leaves of their next dinner hung round their ears like ladies in Airdrossa wore jewels. The stalls were sparsely set so close to harvest, but still the crowds were thicker than usual, fingers flicking urgently among the vegetables. There had been no hint, no clue or proclamation; no one had said that day out of all others would be the day. But early that morning the women of Chaireddan piled their baskets high, then turned their black-coated backs and hurried away.

It was Na'Stelfia, Ar'Quila's mother's friend, who gave her the first picture of Mara; a threshold gift for when she first went away to school on Chi!me Two. Mara hadn't been fashionable then, but Aunt Stelfia was IntPro, as Ar'Quila had always sworn she would be when she grew up, and they were always one step ahead of a trend. When Stelfia wasn't at home at the

IntPro central office on Zargras, the once uninhabited planet where the United Planets was based, she was travelling the galaxy on missions as daring as they were secret. The Office of Interplanetary Protocols was the enforcer for the United Planets galactic government; staffed largely with Chi!me, there was always something thrilling to do.

Once, when Quila was very small, Aunt Stelfia had come home from a posting with a small, round, burnt hole in the brim of her hat. She had shown it to her, tipping back her seat and tossing it to her with an idle gesture, as if she didn't much care.

'Was it a hydrogen blaster?' Quila had asked, wide-eyed. 'Did someone *shoot* you?'

It had seemed unbelievably exciting to her, so amazing, so lucky.

'Did someone *shoot* you?'

Aunt Stelfia had crossed her boot heels on the hearth circle and laughed.

A picture from Aunt Stelfia was worth casting with respect. Quila had dutifully given it pride of place on the wall opposite her bed and, after a while and some appreciative comments from her age-mates, had even been moved to look its subject up on her terminal. She had barely heard of Mara Karne then, though the exports of Benan Ty figured in her galactic geography lessons all through her years at school. The sparse information available taught her only a little more. A guerrilla leader, she read, the daughter of Benan Ty's deposed president. A hero or a villain, freedom fighter or murderer, champion of peasants or destroyer of cities, depending on your point of view. A thin, white-faced girl with an ancient gun, a skein of

12

blowing hair; eyes that looked right out of the image at her.

She collected other images where she could, from fan outlets on esoteric places or in-depth reports on our primitive cousins in the old Terran space. A shot from a security surveillance recording, Mara with her hair bundled under her hat, marching down a corridor deep in conversation with an older man, her famous old Terran gun slung casually over one shoulder as if she had forgotten it was there. An old image from an article, Mara at her father's graveside, still and straight with a black lace veil pushed back over her hair. A police photo for a wanted poster, her mouth quirking at the thought of how she would shortly fight her way out.

And the last, dubious snippet, from a Terran who claimed to have been allowed into a ViaVera base, of a camp fire in an evening field, a blur of faces singing and Mara in the centre in a long flounced skirt, dancing with a young man as if she was just an ordinary girl and not a killer at all.

It was the birds that made her late. As she always did in a provincial base, Terise had gone down to the market early that morning. The sky was just starting to pale and she was heading back when she saw them. She knew the animal stalls well; usually in the narrowest entrance to the market, on bad days the stench from the frilleh cages would follow her all the way round the other booths. At least the frilleh sold, they were good for catching the rats the first human colonists had inadvertently introduced.

The frilleh always found a buyer in the end; what she had really learned to hate were the two moth-eaten jeebas that were brought out again and again and taken away each time without one. Ladies in Airdrossa, she had heard, would wear brightly coloured jeebas on their shoulders as pets, but it was not a fashion people had any truck with in Chaireddan. The jeeba would reach out with clutching paws as she passed them, as if they could feel her pity. When it was possible she always took another way.

She would have done so today, but the song called her. Just the littlest thread of a tune, a little high piping her grandmother had once said would be the music of the gods, if only it weren't for free. She hurried over, pushing through the clouds of mesh with the flats of her hands. There on the biggest stall, taking up almost all the room, was a cage of tarnished metal and inside, perched all in a line on a single loop of dead branch and singing their hearts out as they had always done, were six pietera.

The dawn light caught their dark plumage into purple and gold like the definition of beauty. At home they had nested in the trees all around the village; the girls had collected their discarded feathers to wear in their hair. Such small, round birds they were, with their purple feathers and bright eyes and no good eating on them at all. No one would ever harm a pietera.

Looking at them now she thought she could buy one for Ladyani. He was from her village, the only other in the inner circle who was even from the east coast. They could listen to it sing together, remember all the things from their shared childhood they could not speak of to anyone else, and when they had heard enough, they could open the cage up and let it go. He would like that, she thought, it would be a poetic gesture and a fit one for a revolutionary. More importantly, it would be theirs alone. She tried to find things to have with Ladyani.

She prodded one finger at the bars of the cage and one of the birds bounced along the branch towards it, cheeping hopefully. They were so friendly, so lacking in predators that they were always sure of their welcome. She saw Ladyani thinking of their village, his thrust-out lip and hard, red-rimmed eyes as clear as if he was standing before her. The bird fluttered up to her finger and cheeped again.

'Would Madam take a bird this morning? A nice little bird, very cheap, for pet or food? Come all the way beyond Camino, these do, I do you very good price?'

The stallholder was almost as mangy as his jeebas, another one in this poverty-stricken province hanging on beyond the point when there was nothing left to hold on to. Every time she came to the market she was reminded of how much the people needed them, even if they didn't know it. She wriggled her finger out of the cage, dislodging the bird.

'No,' she said. 'Not today.'

The carriers edged along the narrow streets of Chaireddan lower town, their engines straining at the slow speed. Ahead of them the crowd of dark, carapaced figures pulsed and shifted, full of scurrying motion. In the first carrier, the police chief sniffed at the faint bitter smell, the suggestion of fuel cell catastrophe building somewhere beneath him. It was as much as he could do not to accelerate and sweep them all out of the way; in moments like this, even the inevitable criticism seemed almost worth it. Almost, but not quite. He had always been good at controlling himself, it was what had got him where he was today. Self-control and hard work, against those who knew the meaning of neither.

Once they were out of the warren around the market, the

road was clearer, climbing between dust-hued walls up the hill to the old town. Fewer people lived up here; the rambling buildings on the summit were mostly a motley collection of religious missions, student hostels and sinking, threadbare charities. All sorts of organisations had a forsaken outpost in this forsaken outpost of a town. The police chief squinted into the rising sun. The tower of the building called the Adicalan Charitable Mission rose ahead against the skyline. He felt himself beginning to smile. There was only one woman with them now, a short, black figure climbing up the street ahead. For a moment he stiffened, but it was all right; everything this morning, he knew suddenly, was going to be all right.

He stood up in his seat, noting with surprise how his legs seemed to tremble beneath him, and gave the signal. The carriers behind him stopped. The men leapt over the sides and fanned out around the sides of the building. From his own carrier, his crew got out the heavy equipment. It had been years coming, this moment, years when he had planned and schemed and ignored everyone who had said it couldn't be done, years when he had been laughed at and worse and only endured it because he had known one day it would be different.

There was nothing worse than to be powerless, despised. He had learnt that, and today was the day he was done with it. There were all sorts of organisations up here, any number of which might be other than they seemed. Yet for them the law was nothing, ruling by violence they were themselves inviolable. There were many like that, many fronts for the teeming multitudes of his enemies, but after today, one less. One less. Petrus Desailly, the youngest chief the Chaireddan police had ever had, tasted the phrase on his tongue and waited for his battle.

It was fully light and she was halfway up the hill when Terise heard them behind her. She knew, sickeningly, that there was only one place they could be going. She wanted to run, but she couldn't. Couldn't run, couldn't shout, couldn't do anything, not even reach into her robes for her communicator to say goodbye. If she had been closer, close enough for a sprint to take her to the gates…They would not even know who she was; in her traditional black dress and head scarf, she could have been anyone, just another townswoman dragging her shopping home.

The carriers were drawing level now, she could feel them at her shoulder, breathe their fumes. She kept her eyes on the ground, bending her head as the local women did when they didn't want to be seen. She reached the top of the hill as they passed her and took the left fork around the front of the mission building. She was still walking but quicker now, the bones in her calves aching with the effort of inconspicuousness. Just a woman hurrying home with her shopping, just a woman with the sweat springing under her black coat and her breath hoarse against the edge of her headscarf.

A little way along there was a passage on the left-hand side, a set of steps leading steeply upwards to a cluster of houses perched on the escarpment above the mission. She turned into it, sprinting. Halfway up the steps, a path led off to the right into a garden. Gracious once, it was overgrown and neglected now, a riot of shrubs and tall, dry ferns lining the wall above the road. She flung herself down and wriggled along through the undergrowth until she was overlooking the road. She couldn't see anyone. She ducked back down into the bushes and pulled the communicator out of the waistband of her skirt.

'Mara? Can you hear me? Mara?'

No reply but the hiss of static.

'Mara?' *Come on*, she breathed to herself, *please answer*.

The communicator crackled, too loud. She slapped her hand over the speaker to muffle it and, at last, heard the voice she was waiting for.

'Hi, Terise,' said Mara Karne. 'Trouble?'

Even then, it made her smile. 'Trouble. You've seen them?'

'Two carriers out the front, nothing else. How many more?'

Terise parted the leaves in front of her face.

'There's five…no, wait, six men coming round the west side now.'

'Weapons?'

'Only that Espada crap, I think, I can't see any Chi!me blasters.'

Espada was the Ty weapons company, the official supplier of the government, whose blasters were so liable to jam or explode in your face that Mara said you might as well throw them at the enemy and duck. ViaVera favoured Gargarin hydrogen rifles, which were cheap and easy to source when they couldn't get Chi!me, but even Terran guns were better than Espadas.

'There were more of them, but I couldn't stay to watch. I expect they're working round the other side. They're not making a perimeter, my guess is they'll wait till they've got enough grouped, then storm front and back.'

'Hmm.' There was a pause as Mara digested this. 'Who are they? Army or CAS?'

The CAS paramilitaries would have been the worst, Army perhaps what they would have expected. This was almost embarrassing. 'They look like police. The locals.'

Mara snorted. 'Like being savaged by a flower. Alright. This is what we'll do. I'll get the ship underway, that gives us twenty minutes to hold them off and get to the roof when it comes in. You said they don't have Chi!me blasters? You don't think they'd have anti-aircraft?'

'I can't see any. I don't know what's in the carriers, but I don't see why they would. They don't know we have the ship, after all.'

'Or so we hope. We'll assume the ship can take care of whatever they throw it; we don't have a lot of choice, anyway. Where are you, you in the garden?'

'Opposite the kitchen window.'

'OK. You stay there, keep watch as long as you can. I'll pass you over to Michel, you can talk to him if you see anything. Give it 15 standard, then get yourself up to the roof. You should be able to take the side escape stairs if they're not cordoning the place, but if that changes, let Michel know. Can you do it?'

Terise had her doubts, but she wasn't going to share them. Below, another three policemen thudded past.

'Course I can,' she said, brightly. 'I'll be fine.'

'Well, don't miss the flight. You know I can't do without you. Who'd nag me to eat and sleep like my old granny, if not you?'

'I only do it for the appreciation.' With an effort, she kept the fear out of her voice. 'See you later, then,' she said.

'Yeah,' said Mara. 'Here's Michel.'

A buzz of her voice, receding: 'Shut up, you lot, we've got trouble…' Drowned out by Michel, tense with excitement. He had been with them two years, but by the Terran reckoning they still used on Benan Ty, he was only seventeen. Terise pulled herself together.

'Michel. What do you need to know?'

'Well...,' he began, and the world dissolved into noise. Terise found herself face down on the ground. She raised her head, gingerly, and saw that where the main gate of the mission had been, there was now only white dust.

'Fuck! Michel! Michel, can you hear me? Michel?'

The communicator sang in her hand.

'Terise? You there? That was the main gate, and half the front with it. All the windows have gone and the wall in the mess hall's shot. It got Çeru, he's still here but I don't think he's going to make it. Jesus, Terise, you should see his leg, it's gone, it's just...'

She kept her tone level, cutting across his panic. 'Where are you now?'

'In the salon, above the courtyard. We can hold them off here, they'll have to come through one at a time, the way it's fallen. We can hold them.'

'Of course you can.'

'Of course we can. Of course...' His consolation ended in a yelp. 'They're coming through! There's one!'

A crackle of rifle fire drowned him out.

'Michel? Michel? Come in!'

His voice in the background was jubilant.

'We got him! We got the bastard!'

Another crackle. She heard him shouting into the room.

'Take that, you fucks! Cesna, give me that charge pack. Come on!'

'Michel? What's happening?'

Belatedly, he remembered he was supposed to be talking to her. He breathed heavily into the communicator.

'I can't fire a rifle one handed. I have to go.'

'But…'

There was a clunk as his communicator fell to the floor.

It was fair enough, she couldn't tell them anything. She couldn't help, couldn't do anything except sit safe in her grassy hideout and listen to the shouts, the bursts of rifle fire and the deeper thuds of the blasters coming from the wrecked, burning building that had been their base in Chaireddan. Counting down the minutes to their rescue, ten minutes, five minutes now. She scanned the sky for the ship, fixing her hope on every dot that might be a bird, or might not.

Mara shouted something, too far from the communicator for Terise to make out. Footsteps crossed the floor towards it.

'Terise?'

'Michel? Are you alright? What's happened?'

'We're pulling back,' he gasped. 'You have to get to the roof.'

'OK, shouldn't be a problem. But tell Mara I don't know where the other policemen are, they might have got up the back, might be on the roof. I can't see from here.'

'I'll tell her. I have to go. Get to the roof.'

'Wait, Michel, where's…' The line clicked off. 'Ladyani,' she finished to the empty air. He would only have laughed at her anyway.

One of the dots was coming closer, definitely too big for a bird. The firing was at both gates now, but the policemen didn't seem to be watching the sides. Terise slipped down the escarpment into the road and ran, bent double, across to the door to the fire escape. In the stairwell, the blasters were louder and the air was hazy with distant smoke. She could hear shouting, but nothing very close. If she met a policeman coming down she knew she didn't have a chance, but neither would she have one if she were left behind. Terise pulled her headscarf over her nose, breathed once or twice into the folds for courage, and galloped up the stairs.

She stopped at the top and peered out round the door. The ship was just coming in to land, wings folding, bolts richochet-ing off its armoured sides. A group of four policemen, one with a leader's red trimmings in a fringe on his shoulder, were sheltering behind the power cell block on the west side of the roof. They were doing most of the firing. The crew of the flyer opened up on them, but the cell block was proving to be good cover. The main stairs from the building came up on the east side of the roof, slightly further along than the power cells. On these stairs, Terise guessed from the firing, the surviving group members were gathered, holding off more policemen following them up from inside. No one, it seemed, had seen her, yet.

After a minute, the fire from the ship increased in intensity. The policemen on the power block cowered back into cover and, in that moment, Michel sprinted across the open space and galloped up the flyer ramp into safety. He was followed by Cesna, Çeru's brother, his shirt flapping open and bloody. After him came Marius with something tied round his thigh and scorch marks all down one side of his jacket. Lander went with him, taking the left side so that Marius would have a better chance, firing one-handed while Marius leant on him. A bolt grazed his upper arm; he staggered, but kept on going.

Terise watched them cross. The need to shoot someone was so strong, she had to dig her nails into her palms to contain it. In the stairwell, she spotted thankful tufts of Ladyani's red hair as he fought to give them time. He was next to go, sauntering across the roof so slowly she would have hit him if she had been able to reach. Only Mara to come now, only Mara who had naturally insisted on being the last, and Terise herself should be making her move. Tensing her shoulders against the blaster bolts, she ducked her head and ran towards the ship.

She pounded in under the folded wings, swung herself round the rail on the side of the ramp. Ladyani was crouching at the bottom with one of the flyer crew. Then Mara came up the last step and started to run. Terise stopped, one foot on the slope. She saw the sweat on Ladyani's upper lip as he shot, the way his fringe got in his eyes because he would not let her cut it, felt the reverberations of the ship beneath her feet, the engine noise filling her head so that even the fury of fire from Ladyani was silent.

Mara was almost halfway across now, shooting over her shoulder as she ran, laughing, her hair flying out behind her like the sun trailing clouds. The man with the red trim on his shoulder stood up. Ladyani went on firing, bolts droning insectile past the man's head. Mara turned. The red-trimmed man lifted his blaster. Ladyani took one, half step forward, his hand stretching out as if he could touch her. Terise let go of the rail. Mara opened her arms out wide, like greeting an old friend, and the man fired.

The bolt took her right in the chest, lifting her up and back with the force of it, crumpling her into a heap of old clothes, a charity not worth the trouble of keeping. No one could survive a hit like that, no one who did not have the armour that cost money that could be better spent on weapons. No exemptions, no special protection. No one could survive it; not even her. Terise thought for a moment that she saw her hand flutter, then there was no movement but her hair, blowing in feathers around her face.

It was very quiet. From the trees beyond the rooftop, birdsong flickered above the crackle of the flames. The red-trimmed man stood still, staring at them, while the fringes on his shoulders ruffled in the breeze. Behind his head, the sun hung crowned in smoke. Everything was frozen; there seemed no reason why any of them should ever move again, why they should not be held in that moment forever. Then, slowly, the man lowered his blaster, and Ladyani started to scream.

It was Terise who pulled him back, Terise and the crewman who got the rifle off him and pushed him up the ramp.

'You know we can't lose both of you,' she cried, shaking him. *I can't lose both of you.* 'She told us what to do, we have to go on. No gestures, no throwing yourself away for nothing. We have to go on. Nothing else matters, not even revenge, not even for her. You know that's the first thing she'd say.'

He knew she was right; he must have done, or he would never have allowed her to force him on board. He knew she was right but, all the same, as Terise watched his face in the gloom of the hold, she wondered if he would ever forgive her for it.

The image of Mara dancing was always Quila's favourite, even though she never cast it up with the others. It was Terran and sentimental, probably faked, inappropriate for a political figure. Still, in the nights after she heard Mara had been killed, it was that picture she cried over, shielding the light from her ring terminal with her palm. It was such a personal image; it was as if they had been friends, as if she had known her. For a few days she walked the halls pale-faced, her age-mates shadowing her

24

as if she really had been bereaved. Then, when the mourning period finished, it was important that she should not seem to be holding on to it. She stopped casting all save the first of the pictures.

She was getting too old in any case for heroes. Any aspiring IntPro recruit had to know that the galaxy was too complex than that. At her first Academy interview, they asked her if she thought the idolisation of other planets' terrorists was a healthy trend among the Chi!me young. She managed an acceptable answer and took the warning for what it was. In her Aunt Stelfia's day, ViaVera had been the cause with which the young and daring would flirt. It had fitted, then, with a form of IntPro politics. The war on Terra changed that, as much as ViaVera themselves. So you had change too. IntPro was a life-filling commitment. If you were serious, you couldn't prepare yourself too soon.

She would still call her pictures up sometimes at first, in the rare moments when she could count on being alone; run her fingers along the contours of cheeks and chin as if by doing so she could make them unlock some mystery. But she never did. Half a cycle after Mara Karne died in Chaireddan, Stelfia went into seclusion on faraway Herantive. Quila was accepted into the Academy and put the last picture away.

Part 2

Quila

1

Quila stood on the gallery of the flyer as it came in over Zargras. It was clear for once, the dust clouds only a haze on the horizon. She could see the mirrored hump of Dome One in the middle of the plain, the ruins outside it where the original settlement had been, even a cluster of coloured tarpaulins where a contract worker camp had not yet been cleared out. The lower slopes of Dome Two had acquired a new outgrowth while she had been away. It had been barely half a cycle, but Zargras was always changing. The city is a flowing river, they were taught back home on Chi!me One.

It was most true here, which was officially not part of Chi!me at all. It was a base to the many officials working for the United Planets organisation, for IntPro, for the Chi!me civil service, for diplomats from Gargarin, Zhairgen, Terra and all the rest of the galaxy, but the bare rock, uninhabited before UP came, was permanent for no one. For a moment as the flyer decelerated, the domes seemed to wobble, as if the Zargras wind could bowl them over. It was a familiar illusion, Quila knew; after a day or so, they would look reassuringly rooted again.

The lights came up on the gallery as the landing preparations started. Superimposed on the approaching bulk of the Dome One station, her reflection looked back at her, her face above the familiar IntPro jacket, with the lapels of a Special Envoy and the new gold lacing on the shoulders. No one was watching, so she allowed herself to finger it briefly, smoothing it flat along the line of her collar.

It was deserved, of course it was deserved. Iristade had been her first posting as a lead envoy, her first chance to prove that she had fulfilled the promise of all the long cycles of her training. It had not been an easy posting, either. True, much of the negotiation had been handled before she arrived, but it was still an ex-Gargarin colony, with all the difficulties that implied. There might have been peace for generations, there might even be the odd Gargar in IntPro now, but dealing with Gargarin had been renowned as tricky since long before the great Chi!me-Gargarin war.

She had faced all those complexities and she had done it well. She had seen the new President acclaimed, the threat of civil war averted, the will of the people made into political reality. That would have been worth doing without thanks, of course, for its own sake. That was what IntPro did, what she was proud to do, spread truth and freedom throughout the galaxy for no better reason than that everyone should be able to have what the Chi!me had by right. The knowledge of a good deed well done was sufficient, but still…

She remembered the dinner, after the new President's inauguration. She remembered how he had praised the Chi!me for putting a democrat on the throne, how he had thanked them. She had kept her expression solemn, as befitted the occasion, sitting there at the top table under the brightest lights, as if she had done this many, many times before. And then, he had turned to her.

'And so we drink a toast to you, Ar'Quila of the Chi!me, for all your services to us and your great kindness.'

She remembered how the faces all turned towards her, the whites of a hundred Gargarin eyes shining over the room like stars. She'd got to her feet, allowing herself to smile, and 'Ar'Quila,' the speaker said, and the voices echoed, 'Ar'Quila,' her name filling the room. She had stood still before her chair while they drank to her, drank to *her*, feeling already on her shoulders the weight of the lace to come.

That was what she would remember from Iristade, not the annoying interlude with Terrenkomo, the Gargarin Ambassador. He was the first Gargarin she had known to talk to, and he was as disconcerting as everyone said they were; needling, pricking at her assurance like an insect on her skin. She supposed that Gargarin were all so thick-hided that they could learn to ignore it.

She had slipped away from the dinner when they had started the maze dances. They might be a Gargarin tradition, but she could never see that being lost and trapped was anything to celebrate. She had gone out to the night garden. It was famous in a small way, for Iristade: a palace garden planted entirely with flowers that bloomed only in darkness and visited by clouds of silvery-winged moths. There were booths where you could sit and watch them, without having to pluck them out of your hair.

She hadn't seen him coming until it was too late to hide, and that would have been an unworthy impulse, anyway. It was not a night for solitude, she told herself. No night was. He had lowered himself, creaking, onto the stone seat beside her.

'This is a good day for you, and your people. You must be very proud.'

He reached out and crumpled a purple flower in his large hands.

'I am. But it is a good day for Iristade as well.'

'Of course.'

She waited for him to go on, but he did not.

'We try always to learn the lessons of the past,' she said. 'We have a long history and we listen to it, we let the garnered wisdom of the ages guide our choices now. We give them the trappings of the monarchy because it is their history, but we do not allow them to be imprisoned by that. The people are ready for democracy now and we give it to them. It's a wonderful thing, to help them like that, see a people grow to maturity and freedom, move forward to more representative forms of government. They are following in your footsteps; I would think that all of Gargarin would rejoice to see this day.'

As the Chi!me had, many times, with worlds of their own. They were old peoples, their two, she wanted to say to him. They should understand each other.

'Ah, yes,' replied Terrenkomo, 'and we have once made this journey, as you would call it, ourselves. It is not only our colonies. Once we too had kings, and now we have…'

He shrugged.

'Freedom, Democracy, Responsibility. A place in the galaxy.'

'Yes.'

He threw the crushed flower into the bushes behind the seat.

'So, Ar'Quila of the Chi!me, now you have had your

triumph, what will you do? Will you stay here in Iristade, to savour it? Surely you will stay close at hand, I cannot believe they will let you go far.'

There was something in his tone she did not quite understand, something that made her pause and say, rather more stiffly than she meant to, 'As to that, I go where I am sent. I am a servant, I do what I am told, as you are, as you do.'

Their eyes met, soft deep blue against hard white, and as his narrowed she felt a challenge in them, a flicker of enmity far down in the depths. Then Terrenkomo blinked, leaned back and the moment, whatever it was, was past.

'You Chi!me work so hard,' he said. 'You work and you study and you never stop doing your duty. You never take any time for pleasure.'

'That's not true, I enjoy myself all the time. Anyway, doing worthwhile work is pleasurable, what greater pleasure could there be than helping someone?'

'Ah, that is your Chi!me training. My people, we know that true pleasure can only come from knowing you do no good to anyone at all. Many of us work for you now, but we still remember the old ways. We serve and we do good, as you say, and then when we are tired of working, we withdraw to our country estates and write stories, very long, bad, miserable stories that no one ever reads, and go out and paint the peasants working in the fields and hang the pictures where no one will ever see them, and make songs about the harvest and the trees that we will never sing, and when we have finished doing all these things we decide we have had enough of relaxation and return to the city again.

'We know that you cannot work all the time, we know you

30

must know when to stop. But you Chi!me, you never stop, you work and you work and that is why you win, but you never think, we have won enough for today, and stop. It is always on to the next task with you, looking to the next horizon. My people, we are an idle people. We have always a spare moment to look around our feet.'

He was smiling, but she couldn't help knowing she was being criticised somehow. It was better not to react. She said, lightly, 'but then we have a saying, spend too long looking at your feet and you'll find someone has made off with your hair. Perhaps you've heard it?'

He made a strange sound, halfway between a bark and a laugh.

'We have no need to hear it,' he said, 'not with teachers like you.'

2

Quila raised her loaded spearer for the third time and, for the third time, lowered it again untasted.

'And then he said, "When we've got you to teach us, we don't need to hear it." Can you imagine that? I was so angry, I didn't know what to do with myself. I mean, you just don't say things like that.'

Fe'Ceronodis spread her hands indulgently. 'Eat your food, it'll get cold. If you don't want those peroi, I'll have them. So, what did you do?'

'I'm eating, I'm eating.' Quila shoved a spearful of peroi threads into her mouth and spoke thickly round them.

'Well, I didn't know what to do. For the longest time I think I just sat there and stared at him, I just couldn't believe he'd said that, you know? All that talk about friendship, co-operation, after everything I'd done for them on Iristade, to come out with something like that! But, well, you can't react to things like that, it's what they want, isn't it? I just went in.'

'And that was the last time you ever saw him?'

Quila spread her hands 'yes', palms up. 'The orders came the next morning and I was gone before half the guests had even woken up. It's probably for the best, I didn't want to cause a diplomatic incident. I don't expect he even thought he'd said anything wrong at all. They're funny people, Gargars. However much time I'd spent on Iristade, I don't think I'd ever have got used to them.'

'Well, now you won't have to. It's such an honour as well, a real step up. Are you excited? I know you don't know where you're going yet, but another posting, so soon, it's unheard of. Everyone was talking about it, you know, even in our dining room and you know how no civil servants ever spread IntPro gossip if they can help it. It must be something really big and important and it's such an honour! When I heard, I was just so excited for you. You are excited, aren't you? You must be.'

Quila smiled at her best friend. 'Terrified,' she said.

Quila and Ceronodis had met on their first day at school on Chi!me Two. Although the moon was famous for its healthy atmosphere, the cycle-round population was small. Most of the girls were off-worlders, from Chi!me like Quila or from further-flung parts of the Chi!me influence; Ceronodis, a native of four generations' standing, was an oddity.

No one had needed to tell the new girls that natives were

despised, but Quila, puffing at the air clear as needles in her throat, had watched Ceronodis unloading her bags from her transport and been filled with envy. She had seemed so comfortable, so at home, easy with everything so that everything was easy for her. Quila, already in training for a lifetime of strangers, had studied her wistfully and Ceronodis, as if feeling her gaze on her back, had turned round with one bag hanging from her elbow, and smiled.

Chi!me children were taught to form networks, not pairs, but although they had both been careful not to exclude other friends, they had always been close. In their classes their marks were always together at the top of the chart; in, as their teachers put it, their co-operative striving for excellence, it was natural that they would be drawn to each other. Who else, after all, could keep up?

It was this closeness that kept them in touch after Quila went up to the Academy: Ceronodis did not share her interest in the military and had won a place instead at the civil programme on Chi!me One. They had kept in touch through messages and real-time conversations when they could and after two cycles, when Quila had still half a cycle to go, Ceronodis graduated to a posting in the UP bureaucracy and came to join her on Zargras. Now she looked after Quila's home when she was away on a posting and Quila in her turn gave her first pick when it was time to lend it out again for the duration of her absence. They were both a long way off having children, there was no way Quila would be allowed to for another cycle at least, but they had agreed that, when the time came, they would bear them in each others' houses.

Ceronodis smiled back.

'You know you like it really,' she said, chiding. 'The honour, the chance of serving, walking in tomorrow to Ai'Amadi's station with that gold lacing and seeing everyone falling over themselves...'

'I don't care about that! It's...' She shrugged. 'It's just a mark, it's nothing special.'

Ceronodis waved a dismissive hand.

'We wouldn't have this table without it.'

Quila looked around. The restaurant was one she had haunted since her Academy days, when it had been reserved for special occasions and visits from her mother. It was simply designed, with tables grouped in a courtyard in concentric rings around a central fountain. The edges of the courtyard were lined with trees and the roof left open, so that the diners could look up through the roof of the main Zargras dome to the distant stars. Their table that night was set aside in an alcove, raised onto a dais and looking down over the heads of the other diners to the fountain. Quila had to admit it was better than anything she had had before.

'Maybe,' she conceded. 'Possibly.'

'Oh, you know I'm right!'

'I suppose it was nice when they all drank to me.'

'There you are, you see? I told you you liked it really.'

'Alright, alright! I have to think of something else to say now, before you start gloating.'

She looked at her smiling, to show she didn't mean it.

'Umm...I know, how's the house?'

'Oh, it's fine. Heo had to go back home to Teyro, some family crisis or other, but I found another cleaner and she seems alright. She's got a whole cycle permit, the agency told me, so hopefully you'll be able to hang on to her for a bit longer. She's called Kera, or Kaiyro, was it? Something like that. Of course, I can hardly understand a word she says and she's got about ten children back home, but don't they all? So you owe me for the agency bill, but,' smiling sweetly at her friend, 'if you buy me dinner I might forget about it.

'Du'Kushkan's living there at the moment, I told you that, didn't I? He sits at the next table up from mine at lunch, he's very nice. He was thinking of moving out to Genoholdis, but he's not sure about the travelling time, so I told him he could stay at your place until he made up his mind. I know what he means, it would be nice to be out in the small dome with all the trees and flowers, but I don't think I'd volunteer for a tube trip every morning, they get so crowded now. You don't mind, do you? I thought, since you'd only be back for such a short time, it was hardly worth moving him out.'

'No, that's fine. You're right, I might only be here a few days, I'm just as happy to stay with you. I'll have to go and get a few things, but I'm sure he won't mind that.'

'No, of course not. He's not there at the moment, anyway, he went to Terra.'

'Really? To work? I heard there was a new office, there was something while I was on Iristade about the Terran dictator opening it. I have to admit, despite all the horrors of the civil war I would love a posting to Terra. Don't you think getting in on the ground like that, being involved in real rebuilding would be so exciting?'

'More your calling than mine, I think. I don't know about Du'Kushkan, I think it's just a holiday. You remember Cenna, she was that new girl with the really light hair when we were

35

in the top class? He went with her and Va'Caris.'

'Caris? The one whose mother…?'

'That's the one. She works in my section now, she's very nice too. It must be tough on her, having a mother everyone knows had to be put away. And an old IntPro hand, as well. You must know people who worked with her, don't you?'

'I suppose so, but it's not really something you ask people, is it? You know what it's like once people leave. At the time you talk it out, then it's done. No one wants to rake it all up again, after that.'

Unbidden, she had a brief memory of Stelfia, of whom she had hardly thought in four cycles, and pushed it away.

'So how's your mother?'

'Oh you know, still the same. Visiting Zhairgen the last I heard, though that was a while ago now. You aren't going home to see yours this trip?'

Quila spread her hands 'no', palms down on the table.

'It's too far, I'm tired enough coming from Iristade without trekking all the way to Chi!me. It's less than a cycle since I saw her, anyway. She's probably too busy to see me! I told her about the commendation, though. She was pleased.'

At least, she thought she was pleased. She had made all the right noises and, if she had sounded a little unfocused, well, that was mothers. She hadn't spent more than five days at a time with her since she went away to school; her mother was a remote, disinterested figure compared to Ceronodis. She remembered how her mother and Stelfia had laughed and laughed over nothing when Stelfia came home. It was natural, they were taught, to put your own generation first.

Quila sighed, pushed her bowl away.

36

'Do you want to finish these?'

'Are you sure?'

'Really. They'll just go to waste if you don't, I couldn't eat anything more.'

She watched the stars as Ceronodis chased the remaining threads around the bowl. The evening cleaning shift would just have finished and the glass above them was clear for the moment of the red dust that enveloped it every day. The stars were very bright tonight, she had forgotten just how bright they were on Zargras.

She wondered which one was Iristade's system; she had looked it up on a chart once, before she went, but she couldn't remember now how to find it. Somewhere out there, the place of all her work and triumph was nothing more than a tiny point of light on black, and here she was back at IntPro, at the centre of the universe, where all of the millions and millions of lives from Gargarin to Terra could be wiped away with one hand before her eye.

'Well,' said Ceronodis, dropping her spearer on the table, 'shall we go?'

Quila blinked, and pulled herself upright.

'Alright. But let's not take a tube, it will be too full this time of the evening. I fancy a walk, anyway.'

Cerondis sighed, deeply.

'You always fancy walking. You're the most tiresomely active person I know.'

Quila stood up, straightening her tunic.

'Well, you know what they say…'

'…if you don't like it, blame IntPro! As if that would make any difference. Come on then, pest, let's get the walking over and done with.'

She slid her arm through her friend's, and together they stepped out of the restaurant into the empty street.

3

Quila sat on the hardest seat outside Ai'Amadi's station and tried not to tap her feet. The representatives of the Chilme, and therefore UP and IntPro their servants, were supposed to be still and forbearing, showing no emotion but calm. It had always been difficult for her, who as a child had only to stop for a moment to be picking at loose threads on her coat or chewing the ends of her hair. They had trained it out of her in the end at the Academy, though it was the nearest she had come to not passing her first cycle, and her hair was always pulled back now from her face.

It was natural now, most of the time, when she was being professional. When she was out in the field it was not a problem, nothing she had to consider at all. It was when she was back here on Zargras that the old habits came rushing back to claim her, so that she had to breathe deeply and tell herself that she was not a little girl but a diplomat, a great diplomat with gold lace on her shoulders, and she did not have to be afraid of any of these people any more.

She waited, folding her hands in her lap, and listened to the chirrup of terminals from the clusters set around the wide room, between the occasional circles of the closed stations for the more senior officials. She remembered the days before her first posting, when she had worked in this room, carrying her tasks from office to home and back again, hurrying up the stairs to bag her favourite spot before anyone else could. It was strange to come back here after so long away and find it all the same, the deep blue carpet on the floor for stillness, the wafting draperies on the walls for spirituality and for clarity of thought, the great sphere in the centre that took an extra cleaner the whole of every evening to polish. All the same.

It had always had that effect, she remembered, the whole compound did. The moment you walked in, you ceased to think that anything outside it could be quite real. But she was glad she didn't work here any more, gladder still she was not expected to return. A woman walked up carrying a crystal storage box, slowed to stare. Quila saw her take in her dress and the greenish cast she knew a cycle of the Iristade sun had given her skin. She returned the gaze steadily and the woman dropped hers.

'Ar'Quila,' she mumbled.

Quila remembered her, faintly, though she couldn't summon up the name. Fa' something, she thought. Fa'Heradine? Fa'Gerondine?

'Greetings to you…,' she began, formally, but before she could finish the door to Ai'Amadi's station swung open. The woman, Fe'Ferada, that was it, looked, gasped, and scuttled away.

A man came out, passing Quila with a single curious glance. He was about her age, quite good looking in a pointed-nosed sort of way, his skin a blue so dark and matt it looked like the sky. He must be an outworlder, with that shade. Unsurprisingly, she didn't know him.

'Ar'Quila,' said Ai'Amadi behind him. 'Won't you come in?'

39

Ai'Amadi's station, as fitted someone in his senior position, was set into the outer wall of the IntPro compound, looking out over the tangle of tube tracks and power lines to the edges of the dome. It was on the fourth floor, a compact bubble of plain curved walls and a clear opening so that you could see all the way to the horizon. To one side of the door, a large terminal screen stood on a low table, switched off. He ushered her in and sat her down on one of the three piles of cushions, facing the view. The sky over the dome was as blue as the sphere lighting the station, but far off over the mountains grey clouds were piling.

'There's a storm coming, I think,' Ai'Amadi said. 'Look there, under the edges of that cloud, can you see that blurring? That's the dust, stirred up by the winds. They'll have to put the shutters up before long.'

'Do you think so?' The dome was strong enough on its own to withstand the worst of the weather, but the fiercest storms were too unsettling, it had been found, for those inside to watch without the semblance as well as the reality of protection.

He stared out at the planet. 'I've watched for enough storms,' he said. His face in the glass was sombre as she glanced at him, unsure whether or not to reply. He stood still for a moment then shook himself, smiled disarmingly, and sat down on the cushion opposite her.

'How are you, Quila? Are you glad to be back?'

'Of course. And I'm very well, thank you.'

'Not too tired after Iristade? We all heard about your triumph, never was gold lace better earned. After work of that kind, if you decided you wanted a break, no one would blame you in the slightest. Our best and brightest are an important resource, we need to conserve them. Don't think anyone will think any the less of you, if you feel you don't want to take another posting on now.'

He was still smiling at her, in reassurance, she supposed, that weakness would not be held against her. Well, she did not believe that, whatever he said. She had not got her gold lace by being naïve. (He called her the best and the brightest, he spoke of the best and the brightest when he meant her).

He had to try to convince her, of course, she was his junior, his responsibility since she had been an intern a month out of the Academy. If orders had come from higher up that she was not to be rushed, he would have to do his best to obey them. Quila knew little besides the rumours about the upper echelons of IntPro, though she had sworn she would know a lot more one day. She imagined Ai'Amadi being ushered into a station like this, being sat down and talked to very gently, having it explained to him what he had to do.

'You know you don't have to do anything you're not happy with doing,' he said.

She could see the reasoning, but she was the best and the brightest, wasn't she? She had joined IntPro to serve, not to sit around at home on Zargras getting the best tables in the restaurants. How could she face everyone who had been impressed by her gold lace if she did nothing to seem to have earned it? He could keep his discouragement, she knew where her duty lay.

'That's alright, Ai'Amadi,' she said, firmly. 'I'm not at all tired and, if there is a mission you would like me to undertake, I am ready for it.'

'Are you sure?' He didn't look very happy about it. Perhaps he had some other protégée he wanted for the post, someone he had taken on when she was on Iristade. Another bright young trainee, eager to make their mark…there was a lot of that sort of thing at IntPro. She was shunned if she was going to let them get hold of a posting that was rightfully hers.

'I'm certain. And I'm looking forward to hearing all about it.'

He studied her for a moment, but he could obviously tell she meant it.

'Very well then,' he said heavily. 'We'll need you to leave almost immediately, within the next few days. And you'll need plenty of supplies, it's a long trip. I'll have We'Carita look you out a list, but you might want to check it over, see if there's anything we've missed. I think the climate is fairly similar to Iristade in essentials, so you can probably advise us better than we can advise you. Are you ready to go?'

She was concentrating so hard on looking alert and obliging that her face hurt. 'Of course. But it would help if I knew where I was going.'

'Oh, I'm sorry, didn't I say? Benan Ty. The smaller planet in the Benan system, where that guerrilla was killed. I don't suppose you remember, it was a long time ago.'

Dark hair, pale skin beneath the graininess of a cheap picture.

Eyes that saw right through you and a Terran gun.

'Mara Karne,' she said. 'I remember.'

'Oh, you do? That's very impressive, but of course, you specialised in Terran planets, didn't you? I remember now. I think we've all thought you our resident Gargarin specialist for so long, we've forgotten your first love. Well, in that case, this might be a little superfluous, but you may as well have it anyway. Feel free to skip through the bits you know already.'

On her hand, her ring terminal buzzed in receipt of a message.

'Data on Benan Ty,' he explained to her inquiring look. 'A short history, thoughts on the current situation, hopes for the future, that sort of thing.'

'Thank you.'

'Come in when you've viewed it all and we'll talk in more detail about your mission.'

'Yes,' she interrupted. 'About my mission…'

'Well, in practical terms, we expect you to be on Benan Ty upwards of a Terran year. You will have all the assistance we can give you, both before you go and by terminal, and we're also sending you with an aide.'

'Really? I've never needed an aide before. Who…?'

'We thought Du'Fairosay, the young man you saw leaving just now. He's very much looking forward to going, but of course, if you…'

'Oh no, of course not. I don't know him, but I'm sure he'll be a great assistant. I just meant I wasn't used to having one, that's all.'

'I think the seriousness of the mission demands it. Did you know it's been thirty years, in Terran terms, since the beginning of the Benan Ty insurrection? Twenty years since Mara Karne was killed? It's been too long. The people of Benan Ty have the right to look to UP for assistance in this and the Benan Ty government have generously accepted our help. We'll discuss the details when you've assimilated the information, but this I can tell you now. Your mission is the single most important thing to happen to Benan Ty in all its history, because you will be the one who will bring them peace. As you did so well on Iristade.'

'Peace and Prosperity'. It was the official IntPro motto. She

43

had been away too long to know the current unofficial versions. It was customary sometimes to deride the earnest goodness of the IntPro mission, but although she had followed the fashion dutifully enough, it had never been to Quila's taste. Peace, she thought, bring peace to people who have spent their whole lives without it. What more worthy goal could there be? In her mind's eye she saw again the dinner tables in the palace on Iristade, candlelight glinting on raised glasses, heard the voices crying her name.

'It sounds inspiring,' she said. 'I'll do my best to be worthy of it. I'll come back when I've studied the data.'

They stood up together. He took her arm to usher her towards the door. It was such a wonderful opportunity, such a golden chance from this man who had been at the centre of her career ever since she came to IntPro. He had always been there, always on her side, and it seemed to her suddenly that she had never thanked him for it. It was not done to be demonstrative to a superior, but she couldn't resist.

'Thank you, Ai'Amadi,' she said, and reaching up, rubbed her nose briefly against his cheek.

It was something you only did to your peer group, an expression of informal affection you would only make to older relatives on great occasions, if at all. If she had stopped to think, the reaction she would have dreaded would have been affront, but it was not quite that. His eyes flickered, as if wincing. He dropped her hand like a stone. If she wanted to come in on the next day to discuss the cube, he said, she would be most welcome. But now he had another appointment, so...

His voice was stiff, his face blank. Before she knew it, she was standing out again in the office, with only the closed door of his station behind her. It was familiar somehow, like when she was an intern and he asked her a question on something her courses had not covered, that sense of disappointment, that he did not think as much of her as he might have done. It made no sense, but it stayed with her, shadowing, all the way down the stairs.

She viewed the data late that evening, after Ceronodis, who had her own work to finish, had gone to bed. She knew less of it than she would have admitted to Ai'Amadi, with his flattering assumption that all things Terran were familiar to her. It was Terra itself she had studied, and the earlier period at that. It was what had always interested her most, the establishment of the empire when the Terrans were first leaving their planet and emerging, blinking and strange, into the light. Benan Ty she had done at school but never since.

She had kept a lookout for news of ViaVera at first, if she could do so without anyone noticing. Whenever the name caught her eye she would read the article, aware of her pleasure at their continued existence and determined not to admit it even to herself. It was the train to Santos that had changed that, and for almost four cycles now, ViaVera had been as dead to her as the people they killed. So she had work to do, and she did not mind if she had to stay up all night to do it. After a little, she was so absorbed she even forgot to feel tired.

Benan Ty was the second inhabited planet in a system settled by Terra two hundred of their years before. The colonists had come to Benan, the larger planet first, only venturing onto Ty some thirty years later. The name was severally lesser, satellite and ruler in the Benan tongue. Which of the meanings was intended for the small shining planet that loomed so brightly in the Benan sky was lost: on Benan, there were no indigenous people left to ask.

The Ty colony had been ruled from Benan for the first seventy or so years of its existence, though if this rule amounted to merely the support of a colonial governor and the dispatch of valuable trade to the mother planet, no one on Benan was complaining. In the aftermath of the collapse of the Terran empire it had been set free, and though it had remained economically dependent on its neighbour, it could still go its own way.

'These are exciting times for Benan Ty,' one narrative had opined, 'if it can seize the opportunity of greater galactic contact to move out of the shadow of Benan and take its own place in the wider community. There have been hopeful signs over the last few cycles that this is what it is beginning to do, and it must be given all the encouragement of which we at UP are capable.'

The pleading tone was typical of a UP unsure of the outcome, she had seen it so often she had learnt to recognise the signs. The current government was co-operating with UP and had allowed the opening up of Benan Ty markets to the Chi!me, but they were not enthusiastic supporters. The pro-Chi!me party among the business community was much smaller than that of the Benanists. The situation could worsen at any moment, even when it seemed secure.

It was that kind of place, Benan Ty, a place where hopes could always, even in the very last moments, be dashed. Like the poem said, the only thing about Ty that everyone knew, it was 'a swelling breast of tears'. Everyone on Benan Ty apparently was a poet, of a pessimistic kind. Certainly, she thought as she scrolled on into their recent history, there was plenty to be pessimistic about.

The civil war after independence had ended when troops from Benan had installed a government, and since this government had been regularly re-elected every five years with a near unanimous majority, no one could argue it was not popular. The existence of a ruling President was primitive to Chi!me eyes, of course, but the Benans had done a reasonable job according to their lights, ensuring that he ruled only with a party in the parliament, never on his own, and insisting on regular elections.

The Catholic Socialist People's Party had ruled for almost forty years with the support of the army, the religious leaders and the major landowners, and in Benan's shadow, Benan Ty had prospered. Then, thirty years ago, something had gone wrong. Whether the elections were no longer managed, whether the Catholic Socialists had really started to believe themselves to be the people's party, or whether they had simply been outplayed, no authority she had could say. They could only repeat the startling truth, that the election was held and in the morning, when the votes had been counted, the winner was not the President but an outsider, a university professor from Santana called Sept Karne.

Sept Karne had made himself notorious in Santana for the reform he preached, for his association with the extremists who exploded the occasional shop window in Airdrossa in support of the poor and the landless. His own politics were well known and bad enough: redistribution of all the cultivated land; justice and equality for all. Before his election you would have thought they would have barely heard of him, but the people loved him, surrounding the new President with cheering crowds everywhere he went. Others, less so.

He had only been President for six months when the army retook the Presidential palace and installed General Juan Gutierrez in his place. They had not wanted Sept dead, in after years they had been very clear on that. *They* were not extremists, they did not want to kill anyone, least of all ex-President Karne. But they had to act to save their planet, and having acted, they could not think of anything to do with him. They did not know how to deal with him, either free or imprisoned he was a threat to them. They could not cope with him, so, wanting no violence, they shot him.

His family were a different matter. His pregnant wife, Harana, and his teenage daughter had been placed under house arrest in Airdrossa. Harana committed suicide five years after her husband died, but by that time, the daughter was not there to see it. Mara Karne, Sept's sixteen year-old daughter, had escaped her house arrest in less than a year and gone to join the nascent rebel groups in the hills.

The story that followed was more familiar to Quila; she skipped through, letting her eyes run down the screen. How Mara built the rebels into a movement capable of fighting for their world, how in less than ten years they had controlled almost the whole of the north province and the northern islands, and stretched their influence beyond. How they had successfully disrupted the government so that no department could feel itself safe from bombs nor store of funds from raids. How the people apparently had loved them.

It was from those stories, the Chi!me thought, that the name came: ViaVera, in the old Terran tongue revived under the

Terran Empire, the True Road. It must have meant something to those who called them that. It was so hopeful, so full of belief, not like the UP prose that bent over backwards to seem measured and detached. Those Ty peasants had known they were righteous, once; in the days when their cause had been just and even young IntPro officers like Stelfia had supported them.

Quila turned off the terminal and sat, staring at the dim room. The light in the street outside shone full in the main window; in Ceronodis' house it was never quite dark. It had not really been all that long ago, though it seemed a lifetime. Only five cycles, or a little less, since she had been a girl mourning for Mara, but ViaVera were no one's heroes any more.

She returned to Ai'Amadi the next morning for her mission and, in less time than anyone not accustomed to IntPro would have thought possible, found herself in a top-tier window cabin on the first leg of the long flight to the Benan system. Special Envoy Ar'Quila, sent to Benan Ty to arrange the first peace talks for thirteen years between ViaVera and the government. Sent to do the impossible as she had done before on Iristade, and bring peace.

Part 3

Terise

1

Terise, carrying a basket of hebas from the orchard, stopped on top of the ridge to watch the tax party coming in. She let her eyes run over the blue and green scarves the younger men tied over their hair, her heart clenching as it always did until she made out Ladyani safely bringing up the rear. He had a strip of bright blue cloth bound round his forehead to keep the sweat from his eyes, and the red and grey tufts of his fringe poked up above it like weeds. He was senior to be going out on missions, but not even Issa dared to suggest that he should stop. He swaggered along behind his young troops, his rifle slung negligently over his shoulder as if it was just another Terran piece of rubbish and not the best weapon in camp. He looked happy, as if he was still fighting. It must have gone well.

She couldn't tell how much tribute they had collected, but she could see that as usual they had picked up some new recruits. Boys, six or seven of them, tall and lanky like all the eldest sons in the villages, where even the lion's share was not enough food to grow plump on, stumbling along blindfold in the middle of the group with their hands tied behind their

50

backs. They herded them past her, along the road to the square in the centre of the camp.

The square was bounded on three sides by the oldest huts and the church and on the fourth by the largest building they had, which doubled as their headquarters and Issa's own house. They called it the government building and, when Issa was not listening, the Palace. They got the boys in a line facing it, pushed them to their knees before they took the blindfolds off.

This was always the crucial moment, the instant when you knew. They were a long way away from Terise now, but if she narrowed her eyes she thought she could still see them. Most of them looked just frightened, bewildered, peasant boys far from home, but a couple stared around boldly as if they wanted to be there.

'They look likely, don't they?' said a voice at her elbow.

She turned and saw Jaiyro, who had been helping her with the picking, limping up the slope behind her with a basket of windfalls under his one arm. Half his left foot was buried in an army carrier with the last three guards he'd killed; though they'd saved his life, he would never be fit for anything but camp duties again. His fighting days were past, and Terise had enough of a fighting past of her own to disagree with his verdict on the new recruits.

'Those two do,' she conceded. 'The others,' she shook her head, miming doubt, 'I don't know.'

'They'll knock them into shape. God knows we need all the men we can get. Father Ignatius told me we lost Donatello, did you know?'

A smiling, curly-haired young man, with a gap where his front teeth would have been...or was that someone else? There had been so many of them, she could never remember them all.

'No. I didn't know. Look, she's coming out.'

They would have called ahead when they were getting near, to give her time to prepare herself. It was what they always did. The priest came out first, to bless them, and in all this unfamiliarity even the young revolutionary ones who had no truck with that kind of thing at home would be comforted by it. Then, when the priest had finished, the door to the palace opened and Issa stepped out.

She was wearing green today, a long green robe that clung to her body and made her look tiny, almost inhuman, as if she really was a Jeban god and not a woman at all. She stood and looked at them in silence, studying them as if she could see their souls. They knelt with their eyes on her and slowly she raised her hands. She held her hands out over them like blessing, small and green and still, while the crowd held their breath and even the birds were silent. Then, without a word, she backed swiftly into the palace and disappeared.

Jaiyro pulled out a chewing stick and bit off the end. In the square, Sario was taking them through the oath of allegiance: after Issa, it was never the interesting bit.

'Brings back your first time, don't it? Just a stupid boy, I was, never been further than ten miles in the whole of my life, and here I was in the middle of the camp with ViaVera. I was so afraid, so afraid they would just kill me without even asking me what I wanted, or worse, when they found out how young and useless I was. If I'd only known, huh? I thought it would be like one of your exams, like, you study and you bring the right answer. I was such a stupid kid, just a silly boy who'd walked all the way from the other side of Ultima, and then they took

52

the blindfold off and she came out.

'Do you remember, how she used to do it? She came out from between the huts over there and she looked at my feet and she said, "You've walked a long way on those soles, brother. We'll find you some shoes and you can march a little further with us." That was all she said, and I thought, "No one's ever called me brother before." I promised her, I said, "I'll remember this for the rest of my life." And I have.'

'I know,' Terise said, as she did every time he told the story. 'That was what she was like.' Jaiyro stuck the stick into the corner of his mouth.

'Ah, well, it was a long time ago and it won't get the pies made. I'll take these along to the kitchens. Are you going to bring those, or are they all for *la dona*?'

'Not all of them, there's so many. I'll take them in, I'll have to sort them anyway and I'll need the table to do it. You go, I'll catch you up.'

'Alright.'

She watched him hobble away. He'd never been a leader, Jaiyro, never more than one of the soldiers even though he'd been one of the first to join up. He'd teased her, when she came, because she was a girl and she'd been to college. Dottore, they'd call her, he and his friends, the professor. She remembered the harsh smell of them, swaggering boys circling round her in tattered shirts: 'Teach us, Dottore! Tell us something we don't know!'

It had made her angry, work twice as hard to prove herself. She'd always worked her hardest at whatever it was given her to do, even if the task was not the one she had chosen, even then. Like picking the hebas, and they would be waiting in the kitchen for the best ones. She hitched her basket higher on her hip and hurried after Jaiyro.

The kitchen was a long, low building up the hill behind the palace, joining onto the dining hall at the east end. The inner circle all still ate together there, just as they had done in the early days when they had been just a collection of rebels in the forest; even Issa joined them sometimes, on the top table, although everyone knew she would rather take her meals alone in her palace when she could. Mara had always dined with them in the hall, but she had so hated to sit over her food that she was often finished and out again before half of them had even been served. At least with Issa you could take the breath to chew.

Terise pushed open the kitchen door, and stood back as a gale of steam rushed out past her.

'Who's that?' a voice cried from inside. 'Don't just stand there like a lemon, idiot, this dough will never rise with all the cold air you're letting in. Come in or fuck off, but whichever it is, be quick about it.'

'Sorry, Elenore, I just like my eyebrows where they are.' Terise stepped into the gloom and closed the door behind her. 'I didn't know you were baking.'

A shape rose from the long table in the centre.

'When do I ever do anything else? Bread, bread and more bread! Sometimes I think I'll have the holy father order a bread fast, just to give my arms a break. And my eyes.'

All Elenore's dough was made in the dark, she said the lights dried out the atmosphere too much. She waved her hand now in the direction of the lamp hung above the table, tapping it irritably as it flickered slowly into life. A wiry woman about the same age as Terise, she had grey hair pulled tightly back from her face and arms on which the tendons stood out like ropes. She and Terise had joined within a month of each other. Almost twenty years ago, in a village two days west of Ultima, they had saved each other's lives.

'Are those the hebas?' Elenore asked. 'Can I have some? It would give me a break from this damned bread, at least.'

'Of course you can, why do you think I brought them in here? I've just got to sort some out for Issa, then the rest are yours. Can I put them out on the table, or will I get in the way of your dough?'

'Ha!' Elenore rolled her eyes. 'Be my guest. But you don't have to do that yourself, Carmelita can take care of it. Sit down, take the weight off, tell me what's happening. I feel as if I haven't put my nose outside the kitchen for weeks. Carmelita!'

Over in the far corner, a group of younger girls were clustered around the heating element, talking in low voices. At Elenore's call, one of them detached herself and came slowly over. Terise didn't recognise her. Elenore's kitchen assistants changed so quickly it was difficult to keep track of them, and they always looked the same. Black hair, sun-burned skin, impassive faces above breasts straining the buttons of their shirts and a square of black cloth over their heads. She stood before them, expressionless.

'Take these over there. Pick out the best ones and bring them back,' said Elenore in dialect. 'Hurry now.'

The girl took the basket and did as she was told.

'She's new?'

'She's Allonso's, I think. From that village with the three trees, what's it called?'

'Three Trees?'

Elenore shot her a sharp look.

'Possibly. She's shy, like they all are, I think, but she seems happy enough with the others. She's quite a good cook as well, but as soon as I start training her up she'll start a kid and I'll be left with no help and it all to do again.'

'Tough,' Terise suggested slyly, 'being a boss.'

Elenore laughed. 'I know! I sound like my father, who would ever have believed it? The old boy must have got so used to spinning in his grave, these long years, he's probably just as put out now he's stopped.'

Elenore's father had owned a small factory in a town near Biterra and had died shortly after his only daughter had joined ViaVera. Terise didn't know how.

She watched Carmelita and the other girls in the light from the heater, talking softly in the northern dialect that was only spoken here in the remotest villages as they bent their heads over the hebas. It seemed a shame, sometimes, that she had never been able to make friends with the younger women. It was not that she didn't want to, but they seemed so alien to her. When she had been their age, all she had cared about was the fight, not even Ladyani had come close. She had gone out every day, risking her life for the cause, like Jaiyro she had walked her feet to ribbons to be there. But the young women now stayed in the camp. Girls, for the most part, from the villages ViaVera protected, they didn't care about the cause in the same way. They didn't come to fight, but to live with some man...

'Stop glaring at Carmelita, you'll make her nervous.'

Terise, taken aback, blinked.

'Huh?'

'You were miles away, weren't you? I said, stop glaring at

Carmelita, she already thinks you're about to attack her. Tell me interesting news instead. I take it Ladyani got back alright, or haven't they come in yet?'

'Oh, yes, they've come in, and he's fine. Well, he looked it anyway, I haven't spoken to him. He had the new boys to see to, and the tribute. I didn't want to bother him. But he's back safe.'

'That's good.' Elenore's voice was deliberately even, the days when they would argue over Ladyani were long past. 'So, anything else happening?'

'Not much. We had a new shipment in, Terran stuff mostly, contact explosives and things.'

'I know, I heard the boys playing with it. Is there any left?'

Terise laughed. 'Just a little. Lad started out furious with them and in ten minutes he was setting off charges and running like the rest. They're just...'

'Children.'

'Exactly. And the word is that we might be getting some of those new Gargarin blasters, but Terono isn't sure. He was up here until yesterday, talking big, but he didn't have the contacts in place, you could tell. He's supposed to be "seeing what he can do."'

Elenore groaned; it was a familiar catchphrase. 'Meaning, when you're down to your last charge pack he might come wandering back. I don't know how that man has kept his head all these years, the promises he's broken to us.'

'He thinks it's his charm.' They both laughed at that, so loudly that the girls in the corner raised their heads from the hebas and stared.

'So they're supposed to be good then, these new blasters?' Elenore asked, when they had calmed down.

57

'Up to Chi!me standards for accuracy, Terono said, but not with the same charge, so they last longer. He said they were pretty impressive.'

'That wasn't just him, talking up a sale?'

'Issa said not.'

'Oh, well,' Elenore shrugged. You did not disbelieve Issa on such things. 'If Issa said not…Well, I'll look forward to seeing one, or,' she twisted her lips, 'seeing someone else shoot one.'

Terise grimaced in response. Elenore, sitting up straighter, changed the subject.

'Oh, I remember what I was going to ask you. I heard the oddest rumour the other day, they said that Issa was talking to the Chi!me! Honestly, Allonso and that mate of his, what's his name, Mario, were in here seeing the girls and they said Issa had had a message from the Chi!me, that they'd seen it. It seemed such a strange thing for them to invent, but I couldn't believe it. Have you heard anything?'

Gently, firmly, Terise said, 'You know I can't talk about things like that.'

'You mean it's *true*? She's talking to the Chi!me? What about? Are they coming here? That's it, isn't it, they're coming here, they're coming here and they want to talk to her, because…'

'I can't tell you. You know I can't tell you.'

'Yes, I know. You have a privileged position, you get to sit at *la dona*'s feet and find out all her secrets and you have to keep them from the likes of me because what do I know? I might have an opinion, and what would we do then? Why's it such a secret, that's what I want to know. Anyone would think she was planning to sell us out.'

Terise got to her feet.

'She's not. She'd never do that. I have to go, I'm late.'

'Well, of course you have to believe that, but I tell you this, this wouldn't have happened like this in the old days. Mara never kept anything from us. She'd have told us, straightaway, and we would have fought it together, none of this, "I can't tell you" crap.'

'I know.' She shrugged. 'What can I say? This isn't the old days.'

'No.' Elenore's voice as she called across the kitchen was heavy with sarcasm. 'Carmelita! Bring the Caduca's hebas. The Caduca's servant is leaving.'

'Elenore, don't be like that.'

'You'd better hurry, hadn't you? You'll be late.'

Terise took the hebas from Carmelita.

'Alright. I'll come by tomorrow, when you're in a better mood.'

She hoisted the basket onto her hip and stepped out.

Turning to close the kitchen door behind her she almost fell over Ihanakan, crouched in the shade of the wall. The Jeba had his knees drawn up under the voluminous folds of his cloak and his head lowered onto his crossed hands, making himself nothing more than the brown shadow behind the opening door.

'Sorry, Ihanakan, I didn't see you there.'

He waved a hand, showing the dappled green skin of his underarm. His eyes, solid black and so large they seemed to spill over his pointed face, studied her.

'You were in too much hasste to look, I think,' he said. He spoke, like all the Jeba, with a hissing sibilance that gave his most banal utterance the sound of profundity.

The Jeba, the indigenous inhabitants of Benan Ty, had been

59

the friends of ViaVera since Mara had led her movement to the northern forest almost thirty years before. Once they had lived all over the continent, but they had been pushed off the best land by the Terran settlers and now they only had their villages in the north.

They scouted for ViaVera, sometimes, brought them rumours of soldiers or CAS actions that no one could tell how they knew but always turned out to be right, and for as long as anyone could remember, Ihanakan had wandered in and out of their camp at will. His village was two days' walk away, he had said once, northwards into the mountains. They didn't know why it was he who came, whether he had been chosen by others or if it was simply because he was the one who of all his village most wanted to come. All ViaVera knew was that sometimes you would be hurrying out of a door, down an alley and he would be there.

'I was annoyed with Elenore, that was why I was rushing,' Terise admitted. 'I'm sorry if I hurt you. Is there any word you would like me to take to Issa? I'm going there now.'

'She sayss what you don't want to know'.

It wouldn't have happened like this in the old days… You didn't ask how Ihanakan knew the things he did, any more than you asked how Issa knew the arms trader wasn't lying about the Gargarin blasters. He just knew, and you just accepted. What else could you do? Terise pulled her mouth into a rueful smile.

'Something like that. Is there anything you would like me to say to Issa?'

The Jeba didn't shake their heads, for them any movement of the head at all was a sign of submission. Stillness was the aim, the dignified option; Terise thought that at home in his

60

village, Ihanakan would probably use no body language at all. But he had learned to accommodate. He spread his hands out wide, green palms down, in a gesture she recognised as meaning negation.

'Not now,' he said. 'It iss too late, now.'

2

Terise found Issa in front of her mirror. She had changed out of the green dress and was now wearing trousers and a khaki combat jacket, watching herself as she swung her blaster from side to side. Terise put the hebas on the table beside the bed. Without looking round, Issa said,

'I think I'll make this the compulsory dress, what do you think? Everyone will have to wear it all the time, on pain of death, conductors on the tubes, doctors, teachers, government officials, everybody. Everyone wearing all the same thing...of course, no one will look as good in it as me. But everyone will wear it. What do you think?'

Terise regarded her calmly.

'You couldn't make the Jeba wear it. It wouldn't fit.'

'No, that's true. Not the Jeba then.'

She studied her reflection, flicking her hair back and forth over her shoulder.

'Council meeting soon, they'll all be coming. Will you braid my hair? Is there time?'

'Of course there's time. It's not for half an hour, and anyway, they'll wait, won't they?'

'That's a point. They have to wait for me.'

'Sit still then, and let me do it. You really should comb this more often, Issa, it's all in knots.'

Issa giggled. 'I like making you do it.'

Terise suppressed a sigh.

'I know. Now, stay still.'

When the first councillors arrived and took their places in the outer room, Terise passed the hebas around as they seated themselves and then withdrew back into Issa's bedroom to let them start. She wasn't allowed at council meetings, not being an official member. She had eavesdropped from behind the bedroom door for close on ten years; she was sure the councillors knew and did not mind, and whether Issa knew or not, she had never said. She supposed she could take that for assent.

She watched them through the crack between the door and the frame. Roberto, their quartermaster; Marius, stocky and powerful, who was responsible for everything to do with weapons. On his left, Sario, who'd set up the cells in Airdrossa twenty-five years before and who knew more than anyone else about covert operations; Wolfram, the son of a politician who'd been Mara's father's friend. And Ladyani. Ladyani, with the sun catching red lights in his hair and the satisfied smile his face always wore when he had seen action. Ladyani, the general.

There had been others once, empty chairs where Carlucci, shot in Biterra or Piero, in prison on Worm Island had been, but these five were what remained of the core of ViaVera, the heart of the organisation they'd given their lives to follow. Except they were not young men any more, and it seemed to Terise harder and harder that the lives that were given and taken still might be their own.

Roberto opened, as he always did, with a summary of their

stores. A brown, careful man, Roberto, a little dull perhaps, but dutiful, sensible. It was odd to remember that he'd once killed two CAS men with his bare hands and teeth, that once those teeth had shone in the light of the fire they'd started, and the screams...but that was the train to Santos, and she didn't think about that.

'...was good, and the fruit crop better than last year, so we can be confident that we will not have to exhort contributions over and above the norm from the villages this winter. I would recommend though that we acquire more livestock. We've been heavy on the meat this spring and unless we recoup those losses, we will find ourselves short when the salt pork runs out in the rainy season. I note that Dark River has been less than generous recently and it's good grazing land down there. I would suggest that's worth thinking about. Moving on, the cereals position is less good, but I think...'

He went on, all the time keeping a weather eye on Issa. Her patience for administrative detail was limited at best, and she had been known to leap to her feet and start screaming, 'I won't listen to this, I'm too busy to listen to this! Why must you bother me with this shit?' She had even gone for him once, he had borne the marks of her nails round his eyes for three weeks. What he had thought of it, he had not said.

Marius gave them a brief report on Terran sources for the new Gargarin blasters, so reliable they should have some in their hands before the rains, and Wolf another on the trouble-makers in the villagers.

'There's a man in Santa Maria says we carried off his daughter. He's been going around telling people they should turn us out, and he's got the priest with him, preaching in the church against us. No one's been listening. They say.'

It always happened, probably it always had. Some girl left home, some father to whom she was property looked for revenge.

'So, did we take her?' Mara would ask. 'Who is she? Does he want her back? Does she want to go?'

They spent two nights over it once in a great council in one of the villages, with the headman and Mara presiding and the father sobbing as he gave the girl in marriage at the end of it. Terise had sat with a young farmer called Juan, who'd said it was the best show they'd had in years. She'd almost slept with him.

'So,' said Issa. 'A problem. Ideas?'

Wolf leant back, examining his nails. When he was fresh from his father's house, he'd said the role of those born into the elite was to do the will of the people. He would report and execute, he always said, but the decisions in between were nothing to do with him.

'Shoot him,' said Sario.

Issa pulled a face. 'Too easy. Marius?'

'Shoot him and shoot the priest.'

'Better, but still it's not much of a deterrent, is it? What do you think, Lad?'

Ladyani, his chair pushed a little back from the group, had been sitting slumped with his eyes shut since Roberto had started on root vegetables. Without moving he said, as if it should be obvious, 'Rape his wife, kill his children, burn his house, *then* shoot him. Somewhere slow.'

'What would you do with the priest?'

Ladyani considered. 'He wants to be a martyr, doesn't he? So crucify him.'

Nobody moved. Issa smiled, like a child with a present.

'There you are, Wolf. You have your orders.'

Terise, behind the door, let out her breath in one long run.

Wolf waved his hand in the traditional salute. 'Yes, dona.'

'Alright, then,' Issa went on, 'there's nothing else, is there? Sario, I'm sure the cells can wait, since you're obviously not in a very imaginative mood.'

She got to her feet.

'But I have something to say. Some of you may have heard, in fact, if you're doing the jobs I ask of you, you should have heard the rumours about the Chi!me. You'll be wondering who's been spreading them, and I think it's time to tell you.'

Terise could almost see her timing. Pause, beat, wait for them to wonder. Keep them wondering, Issa, just like we taught you.

'It was me. I spread the rumour about us contacting the Chi!me, and for one good reason. It's true.'

'What!' That was Marius, leaping up. 'You've been talking to the Chi!me? Without informing us? That's…'

'How can you stand there and say…?' Sario was on his feet now as well, chair crashing behind him to the floor, and Roberto, 'I don't like this…'

'How can I? How dare I, you mean! This is what it comes to, is it? After everything, after all we've done, finally it comes to this. Have you forgotten everything?' Her voice, always shrill, was rising to a scream. 'Have you forgotten who I am?'

'Who you are?' Marius yelled back. 'You never stop…'

Now Ladyani was shouting, too. 'Listen, will you? Shut the fuck up and listen to her! There's a reason for this, a good reason, and good reasons why she didn't tell us until now.'

'You knew? You knew all about this?' Marius' hands were

shaking, like they wanted someone's throat. 'You son of a bitch, you...'

'I knew since just before we came in this room, just time enough to know this is worth listening to. For fuck's sake, give it a chance.'

His tone was level and it sounded sense. Everyone knew Ladyani, straight as a train tube, the last person who would ever let them down. He stared at them, searching their faces, waiting for a defiance he knew wouldn't come. In the surly quiet his was the voice of reason.

'Alright then. Let's listen.'

It sounded convincing, Terise thought. It would have been convincing, if she hadn't known that Issa and he had been plotting something for months and every word he said was a lie.

The wet season in the mountains was colder than her home; even after so many years, it still surprised her. The wind had been icy all that day, she remembered, the dark drawing in from the early afternoon. Issa had had the bath filled in the room they were sitting in now and Terise had been attending her while she soaked in the scant hot water, clouds of steam rising into the chill air. The bath had been liberated years before from a merchant's house in Ultima; around its rim, cherubs frolicked in stained brass. She remembered how the golden reflections had danced on the water, the light and the steam and the patter of the rain on the roof.

Terise had trailed one idle hand in the water and Issa, not moving, had said:

'You remember the blue people, don't you?'

'The Chi!me?'

'Yes, the Chi!me. I had a message from them the other day. They're coming here. I'm going to talk to the blue people. They're coming all the way across the stars to see me, and I'm going to talk to them and make them do exactly what I want. Coming across all those stars…If we took the roof off, we could see them. Do you think we should? It would be rude not to be watching for them, not when they're coming all this way to see me. Do you think we should?'

You never contradicted Issa, never if you could avoid it. 'It would be a bit cold,' Terise had offered, and Issa had looked at her in puzzlement, as if she had already forgotten what she'd said.

Her eyes were very wide, dark as her hair curling in the steam, flecked with points of gold like staring into the sky. You could look into them and lose yourself, lean so far down you'd fall and never find your way back, sunk in her vision, you and everyone with you. Terise had gripped the edge of the bath till it cut into her palm. Issa had leaned back into the shimmering water and repeated to herself and the ceiling, 'They're coming.'

'The Chi!me are coming here, to make peace,' Issa proclaimed to the group.

Sario snorted. 'Peace! Kill us all, that's what they mean.'

He thought he was expressing the common reaction, but Issa glared at him, chilling.

'No, Sario. I don't think they do mean that. They've said they want to help us, and I believe them. Anyone who thinks he knows better can say so. Anyone who thinks I'm wrong, can speak up. *Now*.'

Silence, while the circle of wanted men looked at their shoes.

'Alright then,' said Issa. 'There are no firm plans so far, just that they are sending an envoy to start negotiations and they should be landing any day. Once they're here, they'll make contact with us and we'll take it from there. We'll see what they can offer us, and if we don't like it, well…' She smiled, a sweet smile. 'Let's just say we'll encourage them to make us a better offer. Agreed?' Released, the council chuckled appreciatively. 'You can tell anyone you like, it's not a secret. Any questions, send them to me. Alright, well, if there's nothing further…? Good. I'll see you in a few days, gentlemen. Lad, a word in private, please?'

Terise watched them as they walked together to the far side of the room, standing before the window with their heads so close they almost touched. The councillors trooped obediently out of the room. Issa whispered something, smiling slyly at Roberto's back as the door swung behind him. Ladyani threw back his head and laughed; she patted him on the arm. Terise, abruptly, remembered something she should be doing and turned away.

3

Ladyani lay on his back in the middle of the bed, snoring, and Terise watched him. Whenever he was away she would be wakeful, thinking to herself how she could not rest unless he was beside her, but the truth was that she had never learned to sleep well in his presence either. More than twenty, almost twenty-five years now, and she was still not used to it. The first time had been in a copse beside the river Kerro, with the curve of the Biterra-Chaireddan tube glinting with starlight in the distance, and after that too she had lain awake, watching him sleeping, making herself believe he was real.

She told herself it was a good thing, this continued wonder; a romantic thing that showed that part of her was still alive. She had even said as much to Elenore once, and although she had not accepted it, Terise still tried to convince herself she had been right. She didn't want Ladyani to be relaxing; from the day he had first sat on the school bench behind her he had never been that. Ladyani snorted and wriggled, flinging out his elbow. If she hadn't ducked she would have been sporting a bruise in the morning, like the old days had returned. But he didn't wake, he never did. His face looked softer in sleep, younger; like a man who had never dozed half alert with one hand on his blaster, like a man with nothing to fear and no memories.

Unlike the others, he never had nightmares. Sario might watch as the soldiers shot his brother, Elenore might run from her house with her father shouting and her mother crying behind her, Issa flail in confused half-recollections of blood and flames and screams, but Ladyani in sleep was the mechanic in a village two days from Camino, a man with a smiling wife and children beside him in the workshop, a man who woke every day to the smell of the sea in his nostrils and the reed-pipe pietera outside his window. In a world where everything that happened, had happened to other people, far away.

When they first came to ViaVera, she had said they were led there, despite everything, she had even said that they were lucky. She had studied, she told Mara, she knew that the worst thing in the world was to have no power and no way of taking it. She'd never been more sure of anything, she'd never forgotten the way the revelation had burst in on her, *this is my work*. She remembered how she'd listened to her voice, pronouncing it, as if she was already old and looking back on the most important moment of her life. To her twenty-year old self she would be old now, but then, she had never really expected to see thirty.

Ladyani grunted again and turned away from her, pulling the sheet with him. Something buzzed drowsily for a moment at his ear, she flicked at it, and it flew away. He didn't stir. He didn't have nightmares, always slept well, with no horrors. He saved them for when he was awake.

The thought came to her around dawn and stayed with her all day. As she moved through the morning routine, tidying Issa's room, checking the cleaning girls, sewing up a tear in her shirt, it was there, lurking behind her shoulder, in the corners, just out of reach. Even the sky as she walked through the camp to the lower field was coloured with it, the branches of the trees standing out from the leaves like bones.

Pedro had asked her to come down to help with explosives training; she had been a neat hand with the hydro gel when she was younger. It must have been a year since she had had any, she realised, feeling it gloop cold on her fingers. The trainees, a circle of eighteen-year old eyes, watched her warily.

'You mustn't be afraid of it, but you must treat it with respect. This is hydrogen, remember, the same as in the blasters, and there's a lot more of it here. Throw it around, mess about with it, and it won't just be you we'll be picking out of the trees in bits.'

The same speech that had been given to her, long ago.

'So, you take your box, your inner casing, and you put the

gel in like this, just a handful at a time, and each one you just shape, like this, into a circle, leaving a small hole in the middle. Anyone tell me why?'

Blank looks. Pedro, small and round and conscientious, smiled apologetically. 'They're only beginners.'

'Because if you pack it too tight, there might not be enough oxygen to let the explosion happen. Stabilised hydrogen doesn't just go up on its own, does it, or I wouldn't be sitting here holding it. You need to give it room to breathe. So, you fill your case, and you close it, and then you're going to take these wires and put them...where?'

They looked, if possible, blanker than before. She supposed all new recruits were the same, but she still couldn't quite believe that she had been this dense. Patience, patience was the thing. She took a deep breath.

'Alright,' she began. 'So, what you want to do is...'

A shout from the rampart above interrupted her, someone's voice crying excitedly:

'We're on screen! Everyone, we're on screen!'

Pedro and Terise looked at each other, his solemn face bursting into an unaccustomed grin.

'We're on screen!' He seized her hands and they twirled around, giggling like children.

The recruits watched them, wide-eyed. One of them raised a trembling hand. 'Er...sir? What is...' He paused, searching for the word. They would have spoken dialect at home, it would take them a little while to learn Ty Terran. 'What is happening?' he managed.

Terise stopped midstep. 'Oh, of course, you don't know. Come on, all of you, come on and follow us. We'll show you.'

Terise and Pedro charged up the path from the lower field as fast as they could. Guerrillas were streaming in from everywhere, the older lads who had been training in the forest, the boys from guard duty or help in the fields, sprinting from a thousand different directions towards the main square, leaping over boulders, rifles slung on their backs, waving and tumbling in their haste to be there, where the news was.

The screen in the square had been a good one once, and even though it was old now, the picture was still as clear as ever under the dirt. When not in use it lived, rolled up, in the largest of the barns. However much those setting it up dusted it, the pictures were always seen through a garland of dried ferns.

It was plugged into a large fuel cell, recharged, like all their power cells, in secret from the government's power lines miles to the south. The scrambler was set by Dano the tech expert on the roof of the church. It was programmed to change its frequency every twenty minutes; the interruptions in the broadcasts were annoying but necessary if they didn't want their signal to be traced back. The original equipment, much embellished by Dano's improvements, had been registered under a web of aliases, but you couldn't be too careful.

They had never really used it much, even in the old days when they would sit round and discuss, earnestly, accounts of other planets' revolutions. A low power drain would never be traced in the cloud of line taps all the peasants put in, but heavy usage would have eventually showed up. Now it was kept for only one thing, so that you only had to hear the words 'we're on screen' to know exactly what they meant.

Terise hurried, still puffing from the incline, into the square behind Pedro and the boys. The space in front of the screen was already full of squatting men, laughing and jeering at each other while the talking head on the screen talked of a new restaurant in Airdrossa. She couldn't see Issa anywhere, but Ladyani was beside the screen, exchanging witticisms with the front row while preventing the crush from barging it over. He caught her eye as she entered and she thought, briefly, that he smiled.

Around the edges of the square, a few women leaned back against the walls. Terise spotted Elenore in a gaggle of her kitchen girls, but there were too many people in between for her to join her. She found her own place against the church door, just as the announcer finished praising the place to be seen and assumed a frown over his usual fixed grin.

'And now,' he pronounced in solemn tones, 'we return to our main story, the latest terrorist outrage at the famous Costas emporium in downtown Airdrossa. Our reporter Maria Morales is on the scene. Maria, is there any word yet on casualties?'

The picture shifted to a slim, pretty girl, whose yellow hair blew distractingly about her face as she talked.

'Thank you, Flavian,' she said. 'As everyone knows, the Costas emporium is the number one place for relaxation and enjoyment in Airdrossa, the place anyone who's anyone comes to spend their leisure hours. There must be thousands of images, all over the galaxy, from tourists who've come to see the famous stained-glass facade, supposedly two hundred years old. It was one of Airdrossa's glories. But today, this is what remains of the Costas.'

She stepped back and waved her hand. In the distance behind her right shoulder, something dark was smouldering. Something piled in the street, smoking, a gap in the street line where the eye, uselessly, searched for a familiar roof.

The camera focused again on Maria's face. 'The Costas,' she said, with portention, 'is gone.'

Someone cheered, the rest of the square picking it up until the noise drowned out the broadcast.

Another voice wailed in falsetto, 'The Costas is *gone*!'

'Shut up, you stupid fucks!' Ladyani yelled, 'I'm trying to listen to this.'

'…late this morning when a cargo carrier similar to this one pictured was left outside the Costas, which was packed with people enjoying the holiday. It is estimated that the carrier contained a large amount of hydrogen explosive, detonated by a crude timing device.'

Terise looked round for her trainee group. She imagined them listening to this in awe, realising suddenly that what they had seemed so unwilling to learn could have impressive uses after all.

'Police say they are anxious to interview two men seen leaving the area shortly before the explosion.'

A picture of the two flashed up on the scene, all unshaven chins and villainous hats. 'Hey, Marsana, love the hair!' 'Stevio, Stevio!' the crowd chanted.

'Casualties are unknown at this stage, but police say they could be as high as 300, making this the worse terrorist atrocity for four years in the capital, since the terrible loss of life in the North Station bombing.'

'Yeah! Kicked their ass!' someone shouted. The others laughed and cheered.

'And is there any word as yet as to who could have done this?'

'Not yet, Flavian, but all suspicions point, as always, to this being yet another incident in the murderous career of ViaVera.'

More cheers, and someone broke out into song. 'ViaVera, ViaVera, on the true road we will be marching. ViaVera, ViaVera, on the true road we will be free'. Above the bobbing heads, Ladyani punched the air in time. She couldn't hear the screen any more, only the song and the cheering, then someone rushed past her and caught her by the hands and it seemed as if the whole square was dancing, round and round, round and round, through the laughing, bouncing throng, and she was laughing too, breathless laughter in her throat that she couldn't quite get out, and with every spin she saw Ladyani, standing on the power cell with the light of the screen catching the red in his hair, and she thought needle-sharp each time she turned, *I'll have to go to Airdrossa again.*

Ever since the beginning, and more so since they had been driven back to the mountains after Mara's death, ViaVera had kept cells in all the major towns in Benan Ty. Mara had believed in visiting these, and in the old days Terise had been to Airdrossa, Biterra and Camino, as well as Chaireddan. Issa's style had been different. For many years, Terise had stayed closer to the base, while others went out to hide and die in their lonely cover. But four years ago, Issa had sent her to liaise with the different groups in Airdrossa.

'It's good for them to see someone from the inner circle sometimes,' she had said, 'it makes them feel wanted. And I need to know exactly what they are doing, and who else could I trust better than you?'

She'd had been several times since then, almost a regular visit, but as always, she didn't know how to suggest it. The idea had to come from Issa, not from her. On the day after the broadcast, she knelt beside the chest in Issa's room, folding the clothes Issa had dropped on the floor before her bath, trying to think of ways she could raise the subject.

Do you think the Airdrossa groups would like some personal congratulation? No, too pushy, too presuming. *Now the heat will be on in Airdrossa, they could do with some encouragement, don't you think?* No, counterproductive: if it was so dangerous, no one who knew as much as she did should go within a hundred miles of the place. *Don't you think...*

'You know, Terise, I've been thinking,' Issa said.

She was standing in front of the mirror, wrapped in a dark green towel.

'I think, after they've done so well, the boys in Airdrossa would probably appreciate a personal touch. A word of congratulation, encouragement, don't you think?'

Her eyes were wide and guileless. Terise searched her face, saw only interest there.

'I suppose so,' she faltered.

'Yes, I think so, too. You're always right about things like that. Now, you needn't worry about Ladyani, you know I'll take care of him for you.'

She turned away from the mirror. Terise stood up. Issa walked up to her and took her chin in her hand.

'You know I trust you more than anyone else, don't you? No one else can do this like you can. That's why I have to ask you, and hope you'll agree. I think it's time for you to go to Airdrossa again.'

She looked so young, her, 'You will go, won't you?' innocent.

'Yes, I'll go,' said Terise, and pressed her lips light as night wings on the cheek Issa presented to be kissed.

Part 4

Quila

1

After the ship, the bustle of the Thousand StarWay was almost overwhelming. Quila had been so proud of being untouched by it once, ambling through the crowds on her way from the Academy to her mother's house, insouciant. She couldn't do it now. Everything was just too bright, too noisy: sales pitches from every flickering shop front, entertainers dancing or playing in admiring circles, luggage carriers bleeping their proximity alarms, announcements of yet another boarding flight booming and clicking from the speaker system and voices, always voices. People arguing, people shouting, people dragging mountains of fraying luggage or striding confidently with none; every language of the galaxy merging, deafeningly, into din. The blue light bathing the walkway in front of her changed, abruptly, into green as she stepped into the grab of another shop, yellow searchlights dancing across it. Quila winced, rubbed her eyes.

'I've been away too long.'

'What was that?' Du'Fairosay, beside her, bent his head. 'I didn't catch that, what did you say?'

'Nothing much. Just that...'

He spread his hands apologetically.

'I still can't hear you.'

'I should come back more often!' she bawled. 'I used to think this was fun!'

'It is fun though, isn't it?'

They had found a bar out of the worst of the hubbub, with tiny high tables and delicately sculpted metal stools. A small screen embedded in the table top told them the progress of their onward flight. Still a standard hour to go. Quila stared at it, warming her hands on her cup of hot finla juice. It never ceased to fascinate her, ever since she was small, how you could go to so many far-flung destinations from the same place. Most of the flights were to other Chi!me worlds, of course, but there was the morning planet hopper to Gargarin with a stop on Iristade, there was the high speed shuttle to Terra and the slow picket to Darien. So many places you could go, so many times you could get up, walk away, run onto that ship to Ursa 9 or Herantive or Qiva Maior and never come back, so far away... So far away she didn't even hear Du'Fairosay start to speak.

'I'm sorry, what was that?'

His face was a study in subordinate shame.

'No, I'm sorry. You're tired, I shouldn't bother you. I'll be quiet.'

'It's all right. I was thinking, but one shouldn't think alone for too long.' She smiled, she hoped encouragingly. She had never had a deputy before. 'What was *your* thought? Tell me.'

'Nothing really,' he said, depreciative. 'I was just remarking that you were right, what you said before. This place, it is intense, but it's fun too. And we should come here more often. Every time I pass through here, just stepping off the ship and seeing all that colour, it's like coming home. Don't you think?'

'I don't know, I haven't really thought about it.' She looked at his hand, curled round his cup on the table top, so much darker than hers that was bleached by the Chi!me sun. 'Of course, I was born on Chi!me, so in a way I suppose it is, but, well, when you travel as much as I have, you don't really think about a home in that way.'

Her mother's house, so far away she could hardly remember what it looked like; the compound on Zargras, dim in its dome beneath the dust.

'Home is people, trust, doing the work that has to be done. Don't you think?'

He smiled at her, appreciative and dutiful rolled into one.

'Oh, absolutely,' he said. 'May I get you another drink?'

The trip from Zargras to Thousand StarWay, the space port for Chi!me, was a quick one: with no stops and priority at both jumping on and off points, it took less than a day. It wasn't the distance that took the time so much as status when it came to space travel. Civilian ships would often only stay in hyperspace for a couple of days; and the longest part of any journey was not the flight but the waiting for clearance to get back into normal space, the taxiing in to the space port, refuelling, shopping and snacks for the passengers then loading up and waiting again in the queue for the station point back into the dark.

Military ships, if they were sophisticated, could transfer themselves into hyperspace on their own whenever they wanted, but no civilian ship could muster the power. Civilian ships did not jump, they were thrown, and when you were thrown and before whom depended largely on who you were. The Zargras to Chi!me shuttle was one of the most important routes in the galaxy: nothing took longer than it should. The rest of the journey would be different.

The Benan line was a new route, as star services went. Before the civil war the only transport had flown from Terra itself and after that all civilian traffic had had to route through Gargarin. It was less than a cycle since the regular service had started running from Chi!me but, judging from the number of people gathering at the gate, it was already a popular one. Mostly Chi!me, Quila noticed, though there were a few here and there who looked Terran. She didn't know how to tell if they came from Benan or not.

She walked down the gangway to the ship, Du'Fairosay following behind her with the bags. They were supposed to follow you wherever you went, but every old travel hand knew that they tended to be wayward. Du'Fairosay had looped the handle of one of his bags around his wrist and was twitching it in the direction it was supposed to go with flicks of his hand. Quila glanced behind her and saw that he wasn't even watching it, he was looking out of the window at a large transport creeping into dock. His assurance was a good IntPro trait, to be sure, but an uncomfortable thing to have in a deputy. She would just have to get used to it.

At the bottom of the ramp, two of the ship's crew, a man and a younger woman resplendent in gold uniforms, were stationed to meet the passengers. Quila fumbled in her waist pouch for her terminal to confirm her identity, stifling the annoyance she always felt whenever she had to show it more than five times in quick succession. The woman took it one-handed, saying something over her shoulder to her colleague, then she looked at it and her demeanour changed.

'Ambassador Ar'Quila, welcome aboard the *Flower of Benan*,' she said. 'The Captain has asked me to show you to your cabin personally, with your travelling companion, of course.' Her tone was so respectful, she was almost bowing.

The cabin when they got there was on the upper deck, with a window in the ceiling so that she could look out on the stars. It was enormous, twice the size of anything Quila had ever travelled in before, and had, as the attendant pointed out, its own private bathing and meditation room attached.

'We hope you'll be very comfortable,' she said anxiously. 'We may not be as well-equipped as some of the larger lines, but we make every effort…'

'It's fine. Really, more than fine.'

She smiled in what she hoped was a reassuring manner and the attendant went on.

'The Captain looks forward to seeing you at dinner at his table. I hope you will be able to attend?'

Quila composed her face.

'Of course,' she managed, 'please tell the Captain I would be delighted,' quite as if she did this every day.

Du'Fairosay, she gathered, had a cabin on the deck below: not as luxurious as hers, of course, but still a long way above what his IntPro salary would have brought him on his own. She unpacked and sat on her bed, feeling the engines starting up, reverberating through the floor as the ship moved slowly away from its bay out into the inner orbit. The station was some way out from the space port: the speeds at which some ships would come through it meant it had to be, but the queue of ships waiting to leave stretched back so far that they had to wait in the hangar for clearance even to move into the line.

There was a good view from the cabin window, better than she had ever had before. Leaning back on her bed, she watched the train of ships moving slowly towards the gate, green lights and blue lights, yellow and red and orange against the twinkling void. After a little while she fell into a doze. When she woke the lights in the cabin were lower to indicate evening and there were only three ships in front of them, two in the queue and one, a freighter from its bulk, in the station itself.

She had only rarely had the opportunity to watch this, the entrance to hyperspace that underpinned her life, so necessary and common it was never remarked. The freighter hung motionless, as if nothing was going to happen, then suddenly green lights ran in a delicate pattern down the length of each of the rails. The space between them seemed to crackle, the freighter gave a great shudder, the air blurred right across her sight like blinking, and when it cleared the freighter was no longer there. The green lights pattered again on the steel and the next ship moved gently into position.

Quila watched the last two ships go through, but as soon her own had finally leaped, she found the button to slip the opaque film over the windows. It was chaos, hyperspace, no place, and though she knew there was nothing out there but particles she couldn't help the shiver of primitive dread it gave her, like when as a girl at the Academy she had lain awake at night and imagined voices calling her in the wailing of the wind. At least there was no sound in space. Quila changed into her smartest clothes, put on her smile, and went to find

Du'Fairosay in the bar.

The Captain went back to the bridge after dinner, leaving Du'Fairosay and Quila to their drinks on the terrace. Not a real terrace, of course, but the appearance of a temperate evening was impressively convincing, almost like Iristade. It was strange, how differently everyone treated her since she had returned from her mission there. Before Iristade, she had been just another IntPro official, not worthy of anyone's attention, but now...

Ambassador Ar'Quila, the Captain had called her, in every phrase he said. Sometimes it still took her a moment to realise that was her, but she was getting used to it. Getting to like it, too: after all, it was only her due. A night like this, with the silver wings of the insects fluttering amongst the flowers. Tables covered with the ruins of a feast, air thick with celebration, *And so we drink to you, Ar'Quila of the Chi!me...*

'This is a nice garden, isn't it?' Du'Fairosay said. 'They're quite new on the smaller ships.'

Quila agreed. 'It is nice. It reminds me a bit of Iristade, the place where I was last posted. And, I suppose, a lot of other places too. Is it anything like your home?'

'My home?' he looked surprised. 'Teyro, you mean? No, not at all. It's probably why I like it.' He smiled, without bitterness. Bitterness would not have been approved.

'What is it like, then?'

'Watery, very watery. There's lots of land, but there aren't any large land masses, there's just thousands and thousands of islands. The biggest of them is maybe two days' walk from end to end, and most of them are exactly the same as they have been for thousands and thousands of cycles, too. It rains all the time, and everything is black, or grey, or dark blue, the sea, the sky, the leaves on the plants, all of it. I didn't know what red was till I went to Chi!me.'

'It sounds interesting.'

He laughed.

'Not really, take it from me. When I came to Chi!me I thought I had died and sailed to the bottom of the sea, as they say on Teyro. I was never so pleased to leave anywhere, believe me.'

'So, you haven't been back?'

'I went to see my parents once after my first cycle of school on Chi!me and again when I got to the Academy. I can't go more often than that: there isn't a regular shuttle and the weather is so bad you can get stuck there, if you're unlucky.'

Quila smiled. 'Which you patently are not.'

'No,' he said, smiling back. 'Of course not.'

Du'Fairosay's father was a ship repairer and fisherman in a village called Senna, on Fingue. Fingue was the second largest island on the Heliostir archipelago, three clusters east of the capital. It was not the richest place on the planet, but neither was it the poorest: it was ordinary. Like his two older and three younger brothers, Du'Fairosay, whose name in those days had been simply Faro, had gone for basic religious tuition once a week with the priest of the small village temple.

The priest, Johasa, was neither wealthy nor especially well-educated, but he was the only person in the village to have studied in the capital and returned. From the first, he had recognised in young Faro something he had once seen in himself. The islands of Teyro had rich and largely oral poetry cultures, and Faro at two cycles could not only recite perfectly any one you cared to mention, but take the theme and begin to compose his own.

It was clear that Johasa had little to teach him by the time he was three, and, in another time, he would then have stopped attending the school and simply gone to sea with his brothers. But Teyro, poor as it was, was nominally part of the Chi!me dominion, and there were avenues open to Faro that there had never been before.

One day, visiting the temple in Kaiohiri, the largest town on their part of the island, Johasa met an old acquaintance from his own schooldays, who told him about the scholarship established with Chi!me funding for one child to attend the high school in the capital. Johasa put Faro's name forward that day. Faro had spent a cycle at the school and then won a place in the Academy out-world programme. A cycle-long intensive introduction to Chi!me education and culture, this was designed to bring the brightest young people of the outlying planets into the Chi!me system, to enter some form of government service or even IntPro itself. All of these were worthy ways to serve, they were taught, but it was IntPro which was the real prize.

Faro had fixed his eyes on IntPro from the moment he had stepped off the ship from Teyro. Hadn't he always been told that if he worked hard enough he could win and make them all proud? He graduated top of his class and entered the Academy itself in the following cycle. He had been IntPro for two, now, and although there always seemed to be too many calls on his pay for him to be able to send home as much as he would like, he knew his family were proud of him. Even though he never went back.

'Don't you miss them, though, your parents?' Quila asked. She hadn't seen her mother for almost as long, of course, but she had been brought up to expect such separations. If you came from a more restrictive culture, it had to be hard to adjust.

He tried to look unconcerned. 'It can't be helped.'

He remembered the sun on the water, the heat on his head as he sat cowering under his hat on the jetty, watching them put out to sea. His brothers bent over the ropes, their backs smooth with muscle, shouting commands to each other in the local sailing argot he hardly understood any more. His brothers in his father's boat, sailing out to fish with their father as their father had done with his, as they would do with their sons who were now only squalling bundles in their mothers' arms.

'Don't you want to come, Faro?'

On the first day at the Academy training they had given them all Chi!me names. They had made him Du'Fairosay; they had explained that you could never hope to fit into a culture if your name marked you out. His brothers with the sun behind them ranged along the side of the boat, bare-chested in the loose short trousers they wore all over the islands.

'Come on, Faro,' they'd called again, and he'd waved his hand to them and said no.

She looked impressed, he thought, as if he had fitted in, though she would be careful not to say so. She wouldn't want to sound patronising, when all the time she was thinking, *how well he's done for an out-worlder.* She was nice enough, but she wasn't any different from the rest.

He was smiling at her again, but he didn't say anything. Quila couldn't think of any more conversation. Instead, she gulped down the rest of her drink.

'Well,' she said, 'I'm tired and I'm sure you are too. Perhaps tomorrow we could meet and go through our briefings on Benan Ty? We want to know what we're dealing with.'

'Of course. I'll see you at breakfast, then?'

'Alright. At breakfast.' The expression on his face was perfectly pleasant, but she couldn't help sensing a chill from him. Probably he was tired.

'Good night,' she said. She could feel his eyes on her all the way she went, watching her walk away.

After almost seven standard days' journey, the *Flower of Benan* reached the hyperspace point that corresponded with the Benan station and settled down to wait for its clearance to land. This was not as lengthy a process as it would have been at one of the major centres. Thousand StarWay had recently expanded the numbers of its incoming berths to reduce hyperspace queuing, but at Gargarin, for example, waits of four or five days were not uncommon for civilian craft, even if your ship was Chi!me. Benan, however, had little space traffic, and after less than a day, the *Flower of Benan* took up position on the other side of the station, and was pulled through.

Quila, making last use of her luxurious cabin, watched through her porthole. Much though she disliked hyperspace travel, the step back into normal space was always a wrench. In hyperspace you were suspended, literally out of time, in a place where no usual concerns could touch you. It was what made it frightening, but on a ship like this, with every comfort ready on command, it was also attractive. To float in nothingness while people brought her things, hung on her every word and called her Ambassador, with no doing, no action, no work and no duty, nothing but nothing, the floating and the void…

'It's like being dead,' she'd said on the last night to Du'Fairosay, as they leant with their after-dinner drinks on the balcony rail over the garden. 'If you could watch while people praised your life, and all you had to do, all you could do, was listen. As if you were a dead god; you know, one of those primitive deities you find people still believing in, not having to do anything but sit back and be worshipped. It's not good for the character, of course, but I do rather enjoy it.'

She'd been foolish, she supposed, the drinks and the scent of the false flowers making her lower her guard. Ceronodis would have known what she meant; she would have laughed, accepting the thought for what it was, and they would have talked of other things. But Du'Fairosay was not Ceronodis.

'That would only be the case if it were something desirable,' he'd said stiffly. She hadn't noticed at the time that he hadn't even brought himself to say the word 'dead'. 'I'm afraid I can't agree.'

She hadn't spoken to him since, she'd been too busy packing to venture out that day.

'I must find him before we make landfall on Benan,' she told herself, 'I'll need him to keep the Benans happy while I talk to our Ambassador. I'd better check the information for that as well, I can't even remember his name.'

She leant over the edge of the bed to rummage in one of the bags half-filled on the floor. Above, the sky in the porthole flashed white and green. For a brief moment it was as if the whole ship were being turned inside out, a pulling sensation in all directions at once, then it ended and the porthole showed blackness studded with stars.

'Good morning,' a voice said from high on the cabin wall above her head, 'this is your Captain speaking. We have now crossed back into normal space outside the Benan system and will be docking in Benan spaceport in approximately two standard hours. Would all passengers for onward flights to the Terran system please make themselves known to the cabin crew to obtain their forward transfer clearances. Thank you.'

The speaker crackled and fell silent. Quila opened her terminal and flicked the screen to the information on Benan.

2

From Benan spaceport, Quila and Du'Fairosay transferred to a shuttle that would take them down onto the planet. It wasn't necessary for their journey, as the onward connection to Benan Ty would also leave from the spaceport, but it would have been a snub for the Chi!me Ambassador to pass so close to Benan and not stop. They might bow over her hand again and call her 'Ambassador'. They had to stop on Benan. It was only polite.

She met Du'Fairosay in the queue to disembark. Despite her worry that he would have held a grudge for her stupid remark the previous evening, he seemed his usual courteous self. If anything, he was even more deferential, as if he was sorry. He obviously was not going to mention it, however, and if he did not she was certainly not going to bring it up. Conciliation was silence, so she had always been taught. So she returned his greeting as if nothing had happened and they walked on to the shuttle in companionable quiet.

Benan hung red and heavy in the shuttle window, as if it were more solid than anything else. It had been settled by Terrans for mining, and it was still attached to Terra, was one of the few planets to cling to the trappings of the Empire even when the power enforcing it was gone. The settlements were almost all around the coasts of the two main continents, Quila had read, hardly anyone ventured into the interior. It was too hot there, too barren, although the indigenous people had lived all over the land and left their cities behind.

She had seen pictures of those, of spires of sculpted rock, wind-eroded inscriptions that no one living could read. An enigmatic place, she thought, guarding its primitive secrets. She shivered.

Du'Fairosay bent solicitously over her. 'Are you cold?'

She was IntPro, she was Ambassador Ar'Quila, who was not afraid.

'Yes,' she said. 'Would you ask them to turn the heating up?'

They landed just over an hour later at the main spaceport, just outside the capital San Fredo. As diplomats, Quila and Du'Fairosay did not have to wait to have their IDs checked or their bags examined. They were whisked through Greeting with hardly a pause, sweeping past lines of travellers grey with tiredness, too beaten down with waiting even to watch with resentment as they passed by. They stepped through the last silver gateway into the main body of the spaceport and there, leaning on the barrier as if he were not the most important person in the building, was the Chi!me Ambassador to Benan,

Pen'Eriten, waiting for them.

He was much older than she had expected. Quila stepped towards him with her hands held out for the ceremony of meeting, and all the while she was thinking, *I can't believe he's so old.* Ai'Amadi had told her he was a senior man, 'very experienced,' he had said. She had thought he had meant he was someone who would help her, she had not realised it was a euphemism. Why, he was older than her own mother, he must have been here on Benan for ten cycles at least.

They walked through the terminal to the pick-up point, where it seemed there was a problem. As they stepped through the tinted glass doors of the building, a young Benan female ran up to Pen'Eriten and started whispering urgently in his ear. It was too quiet and too rapid for Quila to make out; despite her emergency language study, her Terran was still rather rusty in real life. It would pick up in a couple of days, she knew, that was one of the things this side trip was all about.

'I'm sorry,' Pen'Eriten said, 'I don't know if you heard any of that, but we have a slight hitch with the transport. You see, when we were told that an Ambassador would be coming, we were just told an Ambassador, on their own, no one ever mentioned to us that you would be bringing an assistant. They laid on the best transport they had for you,' he gestured, 'but, as you see, it's a bit unfortunate.'

The car sat low and shining above the road, just large enough for two.

'They are looking for another one now for your assistant and the luggage, but if you would rather take the shuttle to the other airport, or wait here for one big enough for the whole party, of course we would completely...'

91

Quila considered. Outside the terminal building the sun was very strong; uppermost in her mind was the need to find some shade. Du'Fairosay could wait, she was in no mood to begin her visit by being difficult.

'Don't worry about it,' she said, 'let's go.'

Settled into the corner of the glide car, away from the bright Benan sun, she studied Pen'Eriten's face, looking for signs of failure. He was plump for a Chi!me, his belly pushing at the smooth cloth of his tunic like a starving child in an ancient report, and his hair grew in a plume all down his neck in a way that no one on Zargras had worn it for three cycles. It was warm in the car - the best design on Benan did not seem to include really efficient air cooling - but there was only a slight flush on his cheeks to show it.

As he sat he drummed the fingers of one hand on the side of the door, dadum, dadum, dadumdumdadum, over and over as if it meant something, but his expression as he gazed out of the window was cheerful enough. Dadum, dadum, dadumdum-dadum…dadum, dadum…he caught her eye and stopped it with his other hand.

'I'm sorry. My youngest daughter is learning the zither, and there are some tunes you just can't get out of your head once you hear them.'

Daughter? No one in Pen'Eriten's position was allowed to bring a child from her mother's house and, in any case, his records showed he was uncoupled. She stared at him, unable to think of anything to say. He returned her gaze, abashed.

'I haven't been on…um…Zargras for…a while. Obviously.'

He looked away, out of the other window. They were out of sight of the airport now, passing through wide plains of clay-coloured earth under an orange sky. Every so often, the roof of an agriculture dome flashed in the sunlight. The sides of the road were scattered with hoardings. 'Old Coke, for a taste of home'; 'London Fried Chicken'. They gave no clues to what they were.

To break the silence, she asked, 'what's a zither?'

It was the easier of the two obvious questions. She couldn't even begin with the other.

He brightened up immediately.

'Oh, it's an old Terran instrument, with strings. Very ancient, and very difficult as well. There's hardly any music written for it, and every time she breaks a string we have to send all the way to Terra for a new one, but it's the fashion. You know children, they always have to have what everyone else does. Do you have…' He caught her look in time. 'No,' he said, 'of course, you wouldn't have.'

She felt discomforted suddenly, as if there had been a transgression against the bonds between guest and host and she had been the one at fault. She wanted to make it right, to recapture his enthusiasm.

'I was very impressed with the new direct shuttle,' she offered. 'It was very quick, very smooth and the crew on the ship couldn't have been more welcoming. It must be a relief to you, after the journeys you used to have to make.'

'Chi!me to Gargarin, Gargarin to Terra then a hopper here. It wasn't so bad, really. I've always liked long journeys.'

'But the new route must open up so many more opportunities, mustn't it? It must be very exciting, thinking of how much closer it brings you, Benan, I mean, to Chi!me and the rest of the galaxy. You must be very proud.'

'Oh yes.' He stared out of the window. 'Very proud.'

'It was set up with UP money, is that right? For one cycle, then once it's established the government can take it over? You must be working hard to make sure they see advantages.'

She tried hard to show the excitement in her voice. It was exciting, this opening up of a whole system to the rest of the galaxy, especially after its only outlet for so long had been poor, dangerous, riven Terra. She supposed he must have lived with the thought for longer than she had done, for he didn't turn.

'Oh, I think they see what it means for them,' he said. 'Look, we're coming into the city.'

The fields on either side of the road gave way to lines of buildings. Solid and plainly built in brick the same colour as the earth, unlike the other cities she knew, they were all in the style of the host culture, with no leavening of Chi!me or even Gargarin construction that she could see. Just lines and lines of clay houses, with only the different colours of their shutters to distinguish them from each other, except that every so often one would have a flag pole sticking horizontally out over of the street and from it would be flying the Terran flag.

'Very colonial,' said Quila.

She meant it as a joke, but Pen'Eriten didn't smile. 'They are very attached to Terra, particularly since the Terran government hasn't collected taxes from them for the last fifty or so Terran years. As they say, patriotism is easy when it's free.'

'Patriotism?' Despite her study, sometimes the language could flaw her.

'Literally, attachment to or love of your planet, love beyond reason, belief that it is right whatever it does, simply because you come from where you come from. It's a Terran word. I don't think there's a Chi!me equivalent.'

'I should think not,' Quila laughed. 'It doesn't sound a very useful concept.'

He gave her a look she couldn't interpret. 'No. Well. It's the poorer classes, the working people who fly the flags, of course.'

'Are the others less unreasonable, then?'

'It's a good outlet for the mob's enthusiasms, but flag-flying is thought over-demonstrative for anybody else. The middle class has other ways of celebrating Terra, but mostly they're no less attached. There are small groups of what they call internation- alists, in the larger cities, but they don't amount to much. I'm afraid you won't find much support here for your…our side.'

He'd covered the slip but she still noticed it. She said, slightly huffily, 'every reasonable person is on the side of peace, surely?' He glanced at her as if surprised.

'Oh, yes,' he said. 'Well, people like peace in theory, but they're always suspicious of alien powers intervening, whatever their motives. You must have seen that?'

'Oh yes, I've seen that. The propaganda war is going to be just as important as any other part of my mission, I'm sure; it's not just getting the agreement, it's winning the hearts and minds over to our point of view. There won't ever be peace without it, and peace, let us remember, will be as good for Benan as it will be for Benan Ty in the extra investment it will bring to this system.'

'Oh, of course.'

Pen'Eriten peered out of the window. 'Actually, I think we are nearly at your hotel. We've arranged for you to have a brief audience with the President at six this evening, which should give you a few hours to rest from your journey before you need to leave for the palace.'

On cue, the transport juddered to a halt outside a four-storey building topped with an extravagantly carved pediment. Best Outwards, the sign proclaimed, enigmatically.

'Here we are,' said Pen'Eriten, clambering hastily out. 'You're all set for Benan standard time, I assume?'

'Of course. They told us on the shuttle.'

'Good, good. Well, here's your assistant now, so I'll leave you to get settled in and come back to collect you at five.'

The glide car was so low on the ground when it was stopped that any sort of manoeuvre was difficult. Quila slid out as gracefully as she could and, as soon as she was clear, Pen'Eriten took hold of the door flap and started to climb back in.

'I'll see you later, then?' she asked.

'Yes, see you later.' He got one leg over the seat then stopped as an afterthought hit him. 'Oh, by the way, welcome to Benan.'

He climbed into the transport and shut the door. The engine whirred back into life. It lifted to its cruising height and purred away.

3

It was very late by the time Quila returned from her audience with the President, but Du'Fairosay was waiting for her in the lobby. She had invited him to come with her, of course, she would never countenance any suggestion that her assistant was not good enough to meet any alien dignitary, but he had said he had things to do. It had been on the tip of her tongue to ask *what things?* but at the last moment she had thought better of it. She liked Du'Fairosay, she thought in time they could even be friends, but something told her that prying was not the way to win him. He was a private person. She could respect that.

So when she slipped round the front door of the hotel in her best IntPro wrap and leaned against it, there was a movement from among the chairs, and Du'Fairosay's voice in the shadowed lobby, asking 'How did it go?' She wasn't sure if it was welcoming or not.

'What, my interview with Mr President Robbio Gonsales, you mean? It was all of ten minutes and he didn't say a word either of us couldn't have heard on a broadcast. All that "our two peoples have a unique commitment to peace" rubbish when he knows I know Benan has just as bad a record as anywhere in the Terran empire. They're hardly an open society, after all, and just because they have this election show every ten years doesn't mean he speaks for his people. But he pretended and I pretended and a lovely evening was had by all. Stars above,' she exclaimed, 'you wouldn't think sitting and waiting would be so tiring, would you?'

He watched her as she threw herself into a chair.

'It's not the waiting, it's the acting you don't like. You'd like to be honest.'

'Yes,' she laughed. 'I want to get down to business, dispense with the diplomacy. Funny thing for a diplomat, isn't it?'

'But you don't give into it. You act if you have to, and you do what you must, because in the end you know what's right.'

'Of course. I couldn't do this at all if I didn't have that, something, to hold onto. Could you?'

She meant it as a rhetorical question, but he seemed to take it seriously, considering with his head on one side. It was strange the way his people looked sometimes, how he could look so much younger and yet at the same time so much older than her.

'No,' he said at last, 'You have to have something. But...' He stopped, shrugging off whatever he had been going to say. 'I'd better be getting to bed. I only stayed up to see how it went.'

'I'll see you tomorrow? You are coming, to the ruined city?'

'Yes, of course. I wouldn't miss it. I'll see you tomorrow.'

'Sleep well, then.' Her voice in her own ears still sounded unsure.

He disappeared into the dark of the stairs.

'This is the most ancient part of the city,' Pen'Eriten said, 'from that spire there all the way to that column in the distance. It's difficult to tell, of course, but some people think it's almost a thousand cycles old.'

Quila, squinting into the haze, drew in her breath politely. Her first school, at home on Chi!me, had celebrated its two-thousandth cycle while she was a pupil.

'Goodness,' she said, 'That is impressive.'

The native city was half a morning's journey into the interior from San Fredo. The car picked them up early from the hotel, Quila, Du'Fairosay, Pen'Eriten and a Presidential aide called Carlos Morales. From the coast, the route took them into the surrounding range of low hills, climbing up the beds of long-dead streams until the sea was far behind. Gradually, the ground levelled, the tangled scrub which leaned over both sides of the paths died away, and they emerged onto the plateau, the high table that was the major feature of the main Benan continent.

Only ferns grew here, battered by winds, crouching under

the open expanse of sky. Even inside the car it was oppressive, a vista so wide you could fall into it and be lost. Quila would have liked to pull down the blinds, so that she did not have to look at it, but that would not have been good behaviour when Pen'Eriten had gone to so much trouble to take her sightseeing. After a while, another range of higher mountains began to appear to the left and right of their course, signalling the end of the plateau. They came down into the valley at almost midday and there, spread on the valley floor between the plateau and the mountains, was the city.

They called it Tass, or Tassiren, from a carving of what looked like those letters in some Terran tongue. What its people had called it, no one would ever know. In its heyday it would have looked like a forest, a forest of slender, stone spires, carved and designed by the wind and by hands into twisted shapes so delicate the mind could not comprehend how they could hold their own weight. Many of them did not, the scattered stones over the ground bore witness to that, and it was not safe to go inside any of the spires any more. Sensible hosts would not even take their guests in amongst them, particularly on days like that day when the wind was blowing, and Pen'Eriten prudently kept Quila to the lookout points on the outskirts.

Like all old Benan cities it copied its environment, and distorted it. The shapes of the spires took their forms from the edges of the cliffs surrounding its valley, but echoed it back in such an exaggerated form that the juxtaposition of the natural and the made was alien in its strangeness. It had no centre, the city, no place for people to meet, no differentiation of different areas for government and residence. No shape to it, no form, no society, just those pillars in tortured red rock, crying their ancient complaint to the sky.

'They must have been a strange people, the Benans,' Quila said.

She and Pen'Eriten were walking slowly around some of the perimeter, carefully keeping in the shade of the cliff face now the sun was at its worst. Far behind them, Du'Fairosay and Morales huddled in the lee of the car, out of the wind. It was almost always windy at Tassiren. Quila would have wondered how they had stood it, but the guide Pen'Eriten had played on the way had explained that the climate had changed since the city was built and that once all this land would have been green and lush. Quila pushed her hair out of her face. It was difficult to imagine gentleness, here.

'Don't you think?'

'It's a strange place,' Pen'Eriten agreed. 'Nothing ever has only one meaning. Nothing is ever quite what it seems.'

Quila assented, sagely. Her feet in her open shoes were scuffed with red dust, like a supplicant's. 'Like Ty.'

'Exactly. What?'

'Like Ty, the word, Ty. Doesn't it mean both "slave" and "God", or something?'

'Oh, yes, sorry, for a moment I thought you meant something else. Yes, like Ty. Or like the Caduca, in fact.'

'You mean the Jeban god? I thought the Jeba weren't related to the old Benans?'

'They weren't, as far we know. They weren't space-faring.'

'Their cultures don't seem very similar.'

'No. No, you're right, they don't seem so.' He looked around, assessing their position with one hand over his eyes. 'We've come nearly halfway round now, shall we turn back?'

On the way back, the wind was in their faces. Sand swirled into their noses and mouths, whipping around as if it wanted to make columns of them, too. It was difficult to breathe, impossible to talk, hard enough to see when to raise your eyes was to lose them in a watering cloud of dust. After a while, they came to a place where a section of the cliff face jutted out into the valley, making a sheltered hollow out of the wind. They stopped in it gratefully, Quila leaning against the cliff wall while Pen'Eriten settled himself heavily on a rock facing her.

'So,' said Quila, 'is there anything you think I should particularly watch out for on Benan Ty? Anything you think I should know?' She was only asking for form's sake, but it was important that he should not feel it. The wind hurled itself, howling, at the cliff. She raised her voice. 'I'd really value your thoughts.'

If he could read her insincerity, he did not show it.

'Well, I don't know very much about the terrorists, but I'm sure anyone would tell you that the most important person on Ty at the moment is Desailly.'

'The head of the intelligence service? I've heard of him.'

'The CAS are more than just intelligence, they're the force that props up the government. Desailly is an ambitious man, many people think a dangerous man, and for a Terran politician he has honesty, of a sort. You won't get anywhere offering him private advantages. If you want him on your side, you'll have to give him something real.'

'Of course.' Quila was stung. 'I'm not here to bribe anyone. I have the authority to make whatever political settlement is necessary and that's what I intend to do. I'm a little surprised that you would think I would do otherwise.'

'I didn't mean any offence. I'm only telling you what other people will think you're about.'

'Of course, I'm sorry.' Her tone was still huffy. 'I'll just have to make sure I convince them. I know Desailly will be difficult, but I will get him on side in the end. I have to, this mission will have been for nothing if I can only come to agreement with one side. I have the authority to make him an offer he can't refuse and I will, if I need to. I'll do whatever I have to do.'

'And what would it be, that offer? Just out of curiosity.'

Quila shrugged. 'That I won't know until I meet him. But this is where you and I have such an advantage, isn't it? We're Chi!me.' Smiling. 'There's always something we have that everyone else wants.'

She peered around the side of the cliff face, into the wind.

'Well, I suppose we'd better be getting back. It would be tempting to make Fairo mount a search party for me, but I don't think he'd ever forgive me if he found I wasn't really in trouble. I just wish I'd thought to bring a sand mask.'

'I'm sorry, I forgot. People don't really use them out here, I think Benans are used to sand.'

She smiled, to show she didn't mind.

'I'm sure it's good for me to feel the pain of other cultures,' she said. She took a deep breath.

'Come on then.'

'Ar'Quila.'

She stopped, one hand on the rock. Pen'Eriten regarded her solemnly.

'Yes?'

'Why did they choose you for this mission?'

'I suppose because I have a background in Terran Studies.

I've worked in other cultures, of course, but it always helps to have a deep understanding of the culture you're helping. That and Iristade, of course.' A brief smirk, quickly suppressed. 'Why?'

'I was a Terran specialist too, once. I thought I knew it all, there was nothing about Terran cultures that could surprise me...'

'I don't think that...'

'And now I've been here longer than I lived on Chi!me and I have a Benan wife and Benan daughters and I'm still a stranger. They aren't my daughters, of course, not really, but I like to think they are. They think I've gone over, on Chi!me, I know. If you ask anyone, they'll tell you, I've forsaken my people. Some day, when they get around to it, I'll be recalled and this will all have meant nothing but a little disgrace. I thought I could have both, I could be both Chi!me and Benan, but it seems actually that I'm neither. It's a strange place to get to know. You make them your people but you still never really understand it, never really know when the ground beneath your feet is hollow.'

'I think...,' she began, although she didn't know what she thought at all, except that it was a sad illustration of why they were told not to get too attached to one posting, and she could hardly say that. His expression was earnest, as if he was trying to warn her of something, but she couldn't imagine what. She was hardly going to go native, after all. Even though he was so much older, she felt very much wiser than him.

He went on, 'And Benan Ty isn't Benan. There's more than one history, and unless you know them all you'll be lost. This is a great system for getting lost in, Ambassador.'

She didn't understand what he meant, not really. She smiled

because the image was suddenly funny, because in this strange place he had reminded her that she was Ambassador Ar'Quila, the victor of Iristade, and it made her happy. 'It's alright,' she said, 'you don't need to be concerned. I know the way.'

Du'Fairosay was already in the car when they finally staggered back, peering at the pictures on a screen foggy with afternoon light.

'Hello, Quila, had a nice walk?' he said. 'I just found something really interesting, listen to this. You know what they think Benan means, in the old tongue? It's one of those dual things, they think, those concepts that mean two different things, both opposite? Well, Benan, they think, is the dead end and the way through, as well, and it can mean both of them together, as well, like, the maze. Isn't that interesting?'

Part 5

Terise

1

Most of the songs she knew weren't safe this far south, but still, Terise liked to sing as she walked. The sun glowed on her bare arms, her jacket flapped against the backs of her legs, its arms tied around her waist. The packed earth of the path was springy under her boots, stuck here and there with clumps of thin ferns where no feet had fallen to discourage them. It was not well-used, this path, which was why she chose it.

ViaVera had a number of transports which, although in varying stages of decrepitude, were all serviceable enough. They still had the ship, the short-range spaceport shuttle acquired in Mara's day from a decommissioned fleet on an ex-Gargarin colony and housed in a shed behind the kitchen buildings in the camp. There were many ways that they could have got Terise to Airdrossa, but none that were safer than this, the simplest.

They had learned that elaborate covers were rarely worth the trouble; that the easiest stories to believe were always those closest to the truth. Terise was a peasant on a journey, so she travelled as peasants did in the highlands where the roads were bad, on foot. As to why she was travelling, what did that matter? No one cared what peasants did, or why.

It would have been even safer if she could have disguised herself as a Jeba, but they had found to their cost that that alien, alienating look was impossible to fake. But she was a peasant on a journey and she sang as she walked the old peasant songs of her childhood. 'One pietera, sitting on a tree, Nobody here but you and me,' sang Terise to the still countryside, 'Tell me pieté if you see, What is there in this world to be? Two pietera, sitting on the tree, Nobody here but we three. Tell me pietés, I beg thee, What is there in this world for me? Three pietera, sitting on a tree…'

She couldn't remember how it went after that and broke off into humming. Ladyani would know, she thought. She would have to remember to ask him. She made camp in a copse just off the path when it got dark and caught and cooked a cachou for her dinner. Sometimes she thought she liked these journeys most of all, these in-between times when everything was so simple. Her clothes on her back, the path at her feet, her knife at her belt to hunt her dinner. Walk, eat, sleep, with the sun on her head all day and her fire to warm her at night. Why would anyone, anywhere, need anything else?

Ladyani thought it was too dangerous. He always complained when she went to Airdrossa, wondering who would keep their hut tidy while she was gone and keep him warm at night. She always wanted to retort that she knew he wouldn't have a problem there, but that would never have been true. There was no other woman he wanted, she knew that. None that he could have. But this time he had seemed genuinely worried for her. She had been in their hut, by their bed, packing, and he had come in and gone up to her and put his arms around her waist, like he used to do years and years ago when they had first come to ViaVera.

She'd squirmed a little in protest, 'Lad? What's this for?'

'What? Can't a man hug his woman when he wants to?'

'Yes, but if you never do you have to expect her to find it surprising.' She wriggled round in his grasp so that she could face him. 'What is it?'

'Nothing.'

'Lad?'

'Nothing! Well, I…I just don't like you going, that's all.'

'Because there'll be no one to mend your shirts? I'm sure Elenore would do it if you asked her, or one of her girls. Or if it's the bed again, I don't think Elenore would help you there, but…'

'It's not safe!' He burst out over her teasing. 'You'll get your-self killed. I don't want you to go.'

His face was anguished and she felt a great wave of affection for him. She didn't want to go either, if that was how he felt. She wanted to say, *No, I won't go, I'll stay here and die with you*, just to see the gladness on his face when she did.

'You know I have to go,' she said. 'You know it's necessary.'

'It's always bloody necessary. You could get someone else to go. Stay, for my sake.'

'You know I…'

'Oh, as if you even care.'

He flung away from her, arms folded, his back radiating a scowl.

It's for your sake I'm going, she wanted to say. Instead, there was only one answer.

'Issa asked me,' she said.

There was a pause, then his shoulders drooped and he sighed.

'I know, I know. But you will be careful, won't you? You will come back?'

She had promised. 'I will come back.'

She slept that night rolled against the cold in her long shawl and, the next morning, continued on her road south. The path wound out from between the overgrowing hedgerows into open land, sloping down before her into the distance. It was too exposed and too far from a village for any cultivation, though away on her left a few sheep regarded her, chewing. On her right, outlined in yellow haze, a group of Jeba were crouched around something hoist on a pole. She couldn't see what it was and slowed her pace, curious. One of them, nearer to the road than the rest, gave a high, looping call like the wind screaming in the night, then they all broke and ran into the trees. They left the pole behind.

Terise knew better than to meddle in the affairs of the Jeba, but she was still intrigued. She stepped off the path and walked towards it until she was just near enough to see it was a skull. A sheep's skull, it looked like, with many-coloured streamers tied each side of its bony cheeks and in each eye socket an empty nut shell, hollow side out. It was a strange thing; the hollow nut eyes emptier somehow than the bare sockets would have been. There was something expectant about it also, something called and waiting to come. She would ask Ihanakan what it was, perhaps, when she got back. They were watching her from the trees; she could not see them but she had not fought for twenty years for nothing.

'I haven't touched it,' she said, out loud.

Silence. But were those leaves rustling a little too vigorously, when there was no wind? Trying to scare her, punish her for trespassing? She strode quickly but calmly back to the path. The muscles of her back prickled all the way down the slope.

The next morning, she came down into the foothills, where patches of scrubby crops grew between the hedges and the trees and ramshackle villages clung to the side of every valley like babies on their mothers' arms. She kept clear of the path. The villages were poor places for the most part, even poorer than the far-away village of her childhood.

They were usually accepting enough of ViaVera control - they certainly had no time for the government in Airdrossa - but Ladyani had warned her before she left there had been some trouble. It was the common phrase. What the police said on the screen broadcasts, what ViaVera said to each other, the hand on the shoulder and the bolt through the head, wiped over into nothing very extraordinary: some trouble. As it happened she had heard the story, but even if she hadn't she could have imagined the details. She knew what would have happened, well enough.

You know when the soldiers are due to come through. Sometimes you intercept transmissions, sometimes it's whispered by Ihanakan to Issa and handed out in the meeting like sweets. Sometimes the gossip from the villages tells you. There are a thousand different ways to get information, that isn't the predictable part. So, you know when they're coming, and you make sure you get there ahead of time.

You choose your spot carefully, a bend is good, with plenty of cover, never in open ground. You disperse your troop on either side of the road, hidden in the bushes, and set lookouts in the trees for the direction from which you're expecting them to come. Then you wait. When Ladyani is there, the troop industriously cleans its rifles and gets an early night. When he is not it is otherwise.

You have to keep quiet but that doesn't mean silence and the wood is soon alive with whispers and crouched figures slipping from one side of the road to the other, cadging a degya pellet to chew or a gulp from your flask. You always bring something stronger than water, for the waiting, and cards to play until it gets too dark. When you can't see to do anything else you sing, gossip about who's fucking who and sing again, until the low voices straggle away into sleep.

In the morning the soldiers come. You get the call from the lookout at first light and you shake the others awake with many whispered imprecations for their having slept so long. They complain, looking surly, at this moment the last thing they want to do is fight. But they take up their positions, dead silent now. When the whine of the transport motor is heard you feel your back straighten, your head coming up like the note for a charge. You're grinning, breathing through your open teeth, your hand clenched round your rifle so tight even though you know you must never clutch it. You catch someone's eye.

You'd think there'd be slogans, but when it comes to it, it never seems right. The act itself is slogan enough.

'Be ready,' you say, and all along the bushes they nod.

The transport comes past slowly, the roads are too bad for speed. You can mine the road if you want to, there are good

Terran mines that the vibrations of the floater will set off, but you have to plant them well in advance and you can never be sure that something else won't ride over them first. In any case, you don't want to blow up the transport; they have things in there you need.

You can't shoot through the front screen, because that's resistant to all but the most powerful Chi!me blasters that you don't have. You throw a charge in front of it, maybe not even hit the transport at all, but throw up enough dirt and rocks to make it stop. As soon as it stops you leap on it and pull open the hatch before the troops inside have time to react. There'll be four of them, perhaps five if you're unlucky. They'll put up a fight but they won't win, they're in the worst position and they know it.

You're laughing now, all of you, gasping laughter you don't have the breath to get out. You get the driver through the back of the head, still in his seat, brains and blood splashed all over the window. One of them makes a run for it the way they came. You leave him for the lookout, you can tell by the screams he doesn't get away. Two of them make a stand behind the hull of the transport; you shelter behind the trees and blast them until the taste of hydro burn is tangy on your tongue and the transport is nothing but smoke. When it clears, there aren't even bodies there, just things, pieces of things.

Their blasters are Espada crap so you leave them, but you take their charge packs and the comms equipment: this stuff you can use. You set fire to the transport, they can see the black smoke for miles. Then you run. There will always be someone injured; someone with a bolt cut on their arm, someone whose leg caught a chip when a door burst apart. You take them with you if you can, and if you have to leave them you kill them.

You never leave the living behind. You'll lose someone maybe every other time, one dead for eight of theirs. It's victory, it's what you do. It's the cause.

They'll find the bodies within a couple of hours and take them back to Chaireddan or Ultima or Biterra, wherever they came from. The next day or the day after that a larger troop will come back and raid the nearest villages, looking for you. You won't be there, you'll be back in the camp by then celebrating, but even though they know that they still come.

Sometimes when they find nothing they look significantly at the headman and say, 'this time you are lucky, but next time you may not be, so be careful'. Sometimes they beat the headman, sometimes they take him and the young men away with them, never to be seen again. Sometimes they line the headman up against a wall with all the other men of the village beside him and shoot them, rape the women and children and fire the village until there is nothing left. Sometimes this is what they do, and this too is victory.

There was a village on the lower slopes called Santa Clara, but not any more. Terise skirted around through the ragged gardens, not looking at the road, and continued quickly on her way.

2

Terise came down off the hills into San Crusada two mornings later. It was set to be a fine day. In the fields beside the path, insects hummed in the chari flowers, and birds sang in the hedge. The pink blooms were at their largest size now, just before the harvest, the heavy petals drooped down the stems as if tired. They were a pest once, the chari flowers, farmers had fought to keep them out of their fields, until someone in a laboratory somewhere on Terra had discovered that their pollen could be used as a drug. Now all the farmers in the highlands grew the chari flowers and the food crops were kept to the plots around the houses, just large enough to keep the people from starving when the chari prices were bad. Or that was the idea, anyway.

Above the waving heads, the bell tower of San Crusada's church rose into the sky, the sun glinting off the grey roof in the places where it had once been blue and gold. When they could, the villages in the north province would always paint their church roofs. It was a competition to them, to see whose church could be the most colourful, could dazzle even God. It was a matter of pride. They hated to see just grey, although to Terise, from the eastern province, it always seemed more like home. San Crusada's church was nothing special but the bell tower was a landmark of sorts, the boundary between the world of the hills and the guerrillas and the Jeba, and the civilised places, where she must take more care.

It was warm enough in the sun that she had not been wearing her shawl, but now she rummaged in her pack for a black cover-all, the traditional dress of women everywhere in the plains. She pulled it over her head, adjusting it so that only her face and a few wisps of fringe showed, and slipped her pack onto her shoulder beneath it, leaving only an anonymous hump in the folds. So she remembered her mother, bringing lunch and extra warm layers to her father and brothers on their boat, hidden beneath her cloak so that no one could see what they were and nothing could get inside. Terise wriggled her shoulders a few times for comfort, pulled the edge of the headscarf a little further down over her face and set off down into the village.

The village of San Crusada was isolated, but unlike the settlements further into the hills, it was not without access to the outside world. The village street was wide enough to admit a proper transport and turned, at the outskirts, into the highway which wound its way eventually all the way to Ultima. By the time Terise reached the main square, the sun had been up for almost three hours and a transport was waiting, the hover motor whining, outside the church.

There was no one inside it: the driver sat some distance away against the wall of the priest's house with his hat pulled down over his eyes. In the shade of the church porch waited two would-be passengers, an old woman and an adolescent girl. They looked tired, and the older woman's face lit up as she saw Terise approach.

'Thanks be!' she exclaimed. 'That son of a donkey flat refused to take us with only two, and we've been waiting since before sun-up to go. I remember the days when they would be glad to take you even if you were all on your own, eager to take you, they were. It's the same everywhere today, no one is willing to help anyone. Of course, I was younger and prettier then, perhaps that had something to do with it!'

She chuckled, with an effort that made her chins shake.

'Hey, driver! Forget your sleep, we have three passengers now and we wish to go!'

She didn't ask Terise where she was going; there was no need. In San Crusada, there was only one direction: away.

The driver slouched across the dirt and slid into his compartment. As soon as he was inside, the doors to the passenger section unlocked, although since this was not an automatic model Terise and the older woman had to haul them open themselves. The driver watched them with a blankness too bored for contempt. There was no point offering help to people like these; out here, if they accepted the services they certainly couldn't pay for them. Next year maybe he would go to Airdrossa, drive for the fine ladies who would tip more for a single journey than he could earn in a month.

They said bad things could happen in Airdrossa, that the CAS men were everywhere and people disappeared just like that for a wrong word or even a look, but even though it scared him the idea of the money was still alluring. He would fix the transport up, or maybe sell it and trade up for something a bit better suited to the capital. Maybe his brother-in-law would help him, he was always talking about going into business. There was always the other possibility of course, the hope from the mountains he held to himself but didn't quite believe in. He was a practical man.

He would go to Biterra for the rains, whatever his wife said. He had a cousin there, and there would be other women in Biterra, other women who might appreciate a man who was going places, who was not afraid. He would tell her that, perhaps, because he didn't really want to go without her and the children. They would all go, his cousin would help them and then, next year in Airdrossa, riches would be his. Next year, in Airdrossa…

The transport powered up with a rattle, making the tangle of rosary beads in the centre of the windscreen dance. There was a cheap crucifix swinging among them, and a piece of black wire, twisted into the outlines of a person. Terise noted it immediately, as she always did. They were never mass-produced, for obvious reasons, and it always amused her to see how many different characters the little bent effigies could have. This one was particularly lopsided, speckled with silver where the paint was wearing off the wire, but it had a jaunty, hopeful air. She gave it a brief salute with her fingers as she climbed past.

She took the backward-facing seat. The other two passengers settled in opposite, the woman a little older than her, dressed all in black with a lace headscarf over her hair and her sleeves falling back over the muscles in her forearms, and the girl sulky-seductive in a low white top and dark skirt pulled tight on her thighs. Her hair was loose in waves around her face, hiding her as a coverall would do one day, like a premonition of age.

The transport jolted forward and Terise clenched her jaw firmly against the nausea. It made her sick, riding backwards, but it made everyone sick, and as the last comer and single at that, she had no right to claim a better position. The older woman eyed her sympathetically.

'I find a touch of tarbis root helps if you're feeling poorly,' she offered. 'Here, have a bit, I've got plenty.'

Terise smiled wanly. 'Thanks.'

'I never travel without it, there's no air in these cars. If someone would turn the conditioning up,' she raised her voice so that the driver could hear her, but he didn't turn his head. 'They never listen. I'm Ma Fortuna, by the way, and this one,' she indicated the girl, who was staring out of the window as if by concentrating she could make them disappear, 'is Juanita'.

She gave the girl a prod, but she ignored her.

'Your daughter?'

'No!' Her tone was amused, almost scornful, as if she could hardly believe anyone could be so ignorant. 'My daughters are married now, off my hands these ten years. No, Juanita's my youngest sister's girl. My sister died three years ago, and with her husband run off to God knows where, who was going to look after Juanita if it wasn't me? God knows it's been hard enough, but I promised my sister and I've seen her right.

'She's getting married in a month, that's why we came out here. There's only my great aunt left in San Crusada now, every-one else has gone down to the city. I said when her brother's children left last year, Aunt Edita, you must let me take you home with me, but she's too old to change now. Her neigh-bours look out for her.

'Poor old soul, she doesn't have long left, but she does like to see the young ones before they get married. It's better than the wedding, she says, having the party come to you. Juanita likes her,' she went on, in defiance of all apparent evidence, 'they were chattering away like a couple of old hens from the moment we stepped through the door. All about the husband to be, of course. Aunt Edita never married, she was the religious type, but she does like to hear about other people's.'

'So what is Juanita's husband like?'

'Oh, he's a bad, heedless boy who'll break her heart, just like all the others. So what man doesn't? My husband was a clever man, a serious man, worked thirty years as overseer on the river docks, then one day a crate fell on him and that was that. My brothers left their wives to work in Airdrossa, first thing they

117

know, they're come home with some floozy half their age and don't want to know their own family any more. And then my Johnny, my eldest boy…'

She stopped, glanced towards the wire man in the driver's window as if to check it was still there.

'Well, let's just say he got into some bad company, and now I don't know where he is. I tell Juanita she should follow her great aunt's way, but she knows too much to listen to me. They all do, don't they, the young? They think they know better, they think they know it all. But you know what I mean, don't you? The men fight and the women wait, that's how it's always been. We wait for them to break our hearts.'

Terise made herself nod agreement.

'So, you're married, then?' Ma Fortuna asked.

She had her story pat for moments like this, worked out over years for the times when she had to account for herself, the times when someone, making conversation or trying to be friendly, asked her.

'My husband's the village mechanic,' she said.

'Oh, aye? Where would that be, then?'

Terise's tone was airy.

'Oh, it's only a small place, you wouldn't know it. Two days north of Camino it is, by the sea.'

Ma Fortuna nodded, digesting.

'I thought you weren't local,' she said. 'It's not like you've an accent, but there's something. So what brings you all the way out here? If you don't mind me asking.'

'Not at all,' Terise murmured. 'My husband's mother's sister married a man from Three Trees, up in the hills. She's dead now, long ago, but there's still family up there. I go every once in a while to see them, take them anything they need. My husband comes sometimes, of course, but mostly it's just me. For all it's his own, it's out of sight, out of mind with him, while he has his transports to see to and his blessed boat. You'd think she'd been my aunt, the way he carries on.'

Red hair with less grey in it, a smudge of grease on his cheek. 'What do you want to go traipsing all the way up there for when I need you here? You've no call to be sticking your nose in.'

Scowling at her belligerently, daring her to disagree. Standing by the corner of the workshop to watch her go, his eyes screwed up against the sun, innocent.

'Aye well, that's men for you, isn't it? My Pedro, he wouldn't have seen his mother once in thirty years if I hadn't arranged it. They see what's in their bellies and in their heads, and that's about the size of it.'

Ma Fortuna shook her head at the self-involvement of men.

'So, you have children?' she asked. Out of the corner of her eye, Terise saw the girl, Juanita, look up.

Two blond heads beside their father at the door, a girl with pigtails holding her little brother's hand. The boy would be Ladyie for his father and the girl would be Mara, although she would only have heard the name…

'No,' said Terise, 'No children. I had a daughter once, but…' She let her voice tail away. Juanita swung her hair back, suddenly, over her face. Ma Fortuna patted briefly on Terise's hand.

'Never mind, dearie,' she said, 'never mind.'

Ma Fortuna had the driver drop her and Juanita off at a crossroads just outside Ultima. Their village was some way off the road, but it was an easy enough walk and certainly not worth paying the high price they would be charged for the detour. Terise watched them heading off into the evening, Ma Fortuna striding ahead with the baggage while Juanita trailed sullenly behind.

The driver had wanted to wait for more passengers before going on to Ultima, but he had agreed easily enough when Terise had pointed out that he could be waiting all night and that she was not paying extra for his time. She could, she said, perfectly well walk from there, and then he would not be paid anything at all. So she rode into Ultima in solitary splendour and settled down for the night waiting for her onward connection to Chaireddan.

After a while, the wind got up and not even her shawl, dug out from the bottom of her bag, could protect her against the chill. Ultima was an uncomfortable place, a small town of mostly ramshackle buildings, huts so temporary they looked like little more than tents, spreading out from the lonely planes of the main square.

She supposed the architect had been thinking of vistas and wide-open spaces, but even the great church, its two matched west towers and delicate spire an imitation in miniature of Airdrossa cathedral, was dwarfed by the expanse of surrounding paving. The church stood at the east end, looking out over the steep drop to the river. Back from it stretched the expanse of grey paving, flat, featureless, a desert in stone, where there was nothing to break the wind or shelter you from the sky.

The transport point was by long custom at the west end, where the shadow of the Ministry building gave some sort of cover to those waiting, and where at least you had your back to the warm tumbled suburbs. Sometimes people set up tents against the Ministry wall, cooked their meals over the little halo stoves, vital in Ultima where the wind would blow any real flame out.

Everyone chatted to everyone else, asking where you were going, where you were from, trying to build a group large enough to commandeer a transport for their own direction. The camp was not allowed, of course; when they got to work in the mornings the Ministry staff would come out and tear down anything left behind, but every night, after they had gone home, it would come creeping back in a motley tide. There was a lesson in that somewhere, something she could tell Pedro for his class when she got back, but she was too tired to formulate it. Terise pulled her shawl further up around her ears and slept.

3

The transport came early the next morning. The route from Ultima to Chaireddan was a regular one. Since medical care, government, employment and shops for the province were all in Chaireddan, there were plenty of reasons for people to suffer the six-hour ride. It was why she came this way, the reliability, normality; the comforting anonymity of the transport full of bags and noise and identical, black-clad women. She did not permit herself to avoid it.

That she wanted to avoid it, even after twenty years, was foolish, she knew. Chaireddan had changed so much since that day, it was hardly recognisable as the same place. The missions in the old district had been pulled down, the Office of the Department of Northern Trade now dominated the hill-top where the Adicalan mission had once stood. The rest of the area was largely in ruins, shells of buildings turned into makeshift homes by some of Chaireddan's poorest and most recent residents.

The population was much larger than it had been, swelled to almost twice its size by immigration from the countryside around, even from towns like Ultima, where the people had found that there was also little money and no jobs. There had been no shanty towns in their day, no straggle of huts out along the Ultima road or thin, ragged children to watch the transports with listless eyes. It was hardly the place she remembered, and yet...

It was the same heat, like a lid on the sky. The same yellow haze in the narrow streets, the black flies and cooking smells in the middle of the day. The same snatches of laughter from behind shutters closed with age, the same clicks as the old men played the same complicated ball games in the dust. The same shuffling, secret women, their heads bowed, melting away. Terise got out of the transport with the others, narrowing her eyes in the late afternoon sun. She hated Chaireddan.

She found the group waiting for the Biterra transport easily enough; again, they were by far the largest group on the plaza. There was usually something around sundown, she gathered. The road to Biterra was one of the few in the area that was good enough for civilian craft to travel after dark. She settled down beside a family group, mother, grandfather and three small children round a halo stove. They were taking the girl to the clinic in Biterra, the mother said, for her heart. They had heard there was a clinic there that sometimes gave free treatment, if you waited long enough, and so...

'We'll find a nice doctor to make you well, won't we, Serilla?' The mother ruffled the girl's hair, smiling determinedly, while Serilla leaned in the curve of her arm and looked out with elderly eyes. Terise gave her a heba from her pack. The younger boy, Marco, climbed, laughing, over her lap.

It was about two hours later that she noticed the man. She couldn't have said what it was about him that made her look his way, over the head of the now-sleeping Marco. She hadn't planned to. She was used to waiting, she knew how to be inconspicuous. 'Take no interest in the people around you, and most of the time they will take no interest in you.' How often had she said that, over the years? 'If you catch someone's eye they will watch you, they will see what you do, and they will remember you when the CAS come knocking. Don't talk, don't look, and they won't look back.' But something made her turn her head and there, across perhaps a transport's length of space, was the man. Watching her.

He was young, younger than her, dark-haired and dark-eyed like almost everyone on Ty. His clothes were mismatched and as shabby as anything you would see on Chaireddan's streets, but something about him still said prosperity. The way he held his head, perhaps, the way he leaned with his hands in his pockets, not in defiance but from an unconscious assumption of ownership, the smoothness of his face that told of a life that had treated him well.

Whatever it was, it was not something she expected to see in a Chaireddan layabout, yet he was familiar too, somehow. Like they said in the villages, a person she should have known; would have known, on a different path. She looked away, pulled the edge of her headscarf more closely about her face as if the sun was in her eyes. He might not have been looking at her, his mind might have been miles away. He might have gone, started staring at someone else. She risked a quick look back. He was still watching her.

Terise pulled her headscarf even further down over her forehead and turned brightly to the family.

'I'm so hungry I could a skin a mule,' she remarked, loudly. Marco stirred sleepily and she shifted his weight to his mother. 'What do you say if I go off into town and find us all something to eat? There's plenty of time yet before the car gets here, isn't there? What would you like?'

Unused to such largesse, Marco sat up. 'Can I have a strawple slide? One of the pink ones? Can I? And a Coke and a Whizzer and a…' His older brother said nothing, watching Terise as if he didn't quite believe it. In a couple of years he would be sure that the stranger could not be trusted. She felt in her pocket, brought out an empty charge case that could have been there for months. 'Here,' she said. 'I found this on the path outside Ultima. You have it till I come back.' He was still holding it reverentially on his palm as she walked away.

She didn't look behind, she knew better than that, but halfway along the street, a small transport slid past her. It was one of the latest models, it must have belonged to a tourist, its roof and sides made up of square panels of one-way glass, set at angles to catch the light. As she waited for it to pass her, she could see the street at her back quite clearly. He was following her.

The market had packed up hours before, and the shops were closing. She picked up her pace, she could maybe allow herself to seem a little anxious now, as the women slipped round her on their way home with their shopping on their heads. Hurrying and trying not to show it, stepping with stiff legs and dread pounding in her chest, but she was going down the hill, not up, and at the end of this walk there was no one she knew.

There was one particular shop, she remembered, off a little square beside the church. Ceru and Cesna had gone there sometimes, even though they'd derided religion as loudly as the rest of them when anyone asked them. She didn't know why they'd chosen that church and not the cathedral, she hadn't been to church since she was seventeen. All she remembered was that she'd walked down sometimes to meet them and pick up a few things they needed in the shop there, the shop with the one interesting feature that she needed it for.

The name on the signboard above the open front was different now, but the customers still crowded round the fruit and vegetables set out on long benches as they had always done and picked over the dusty jars inside with expert eyes. She took her shawl out of her pack, shook it so that the bright colours would catch his attention, and knotted the corners together to make a bag.

She selected some hebas, hesitating over her choice to make sure she was getting the ripest and the best, then pushed her way inside. She made her way down the narrow aisle until all she could see of the entrance were snatches of sky between black heads. He wouldn't come in, she thought, that would be too obvious. He knew where she was, marked out by her distinctive shawl he could hardly miss her when she came out. He wouldn't know about the other way, the corridor behind the staff door and the steps down to the basement, nor that the basement of this shop connected to the basement of the building behind, a warehouse on a completely different street. He was doing his best to dress like Chaireddan, but he was a stranger and, much though she might hate it, she was not.

She tipped the hebas out onto a shelf and stuffed her shawl back into her pack, attracting a startled glance from a woman standing next to her.

'What are you doing? You can't leave them there.'

Terise looked at her thin, pointed face, her upper lip quivering in indignation.

'I changed my mind,' she said, her hand on the door. The woman's expression was so repressive she couldn't help laughing at it, the outrage of one who would never be free. She plucked one of the hebas from the shelf and pushed it into the woman's unresisting hand.

'Here, have one on the revolution.'

She didn't know how long the man waited for her outside the shop, if the woman had told him of the stranger who had dumped her purchases and run away. It didn't matter if she had. The only thing the man had to go on was that she had been waiting for a transport, and by the time the Biterra transport would have been pulling up on the plaza, Terise was out of Chaireddan and heading off the road south. After three days of cross-country walking, she reached a sizeable village where she could get a transport to Biterra, and she was sure that the man could not possibly have followed her.

She wasn't sure what to make of it. She couldn't take any chances, of course, she was right to make the detour, but she couldn't quite believe that he had been really tailing her. There were always traitors, she knew that. Always someone hungry enough, or scared enough, she'd caught her share in her time. But he hadn't had the look of an informer, too comfortable and well-fed for desperation despite his clothes.

CAS did try to infiltrate them, there had been Rudi, her friend for almost a year until they'd found out he was a spy. They'd killed him, of course, killed him as she'd watched and sent him back in pieces, afterwards, as a message. But he hadn't followed her, he hadn't staked her out at a transport stop, he'd joined them and lived with them for nine months. And he was after higher game than her, because when it came down to it, she was not very important. Why would anyone bother to follow her?

The man must have been simply playing some masculine game, she thought so even as she tramped through the brush. She was not important enough for the local police to follow, for a local informer to turn in. They would barely even get a reward. And if he was CAS, well, she had good reason to doubt that a tail on her would be worth their while. So she told herself. But she went the long way and spoke to no one in Biterra, just the same.

The journey from Biterra to Airdrossa was a slow one, mostly because the transport wove from village to village, setting down and picking up passengers at every one. This was the most fertile soil on Benan Ty, where the villages were closer together and more prosperous, although even here most of them showed a gaggle of derelict cottages, where families had abandoned the land and fled to the city. Those with the money to be in a hurry took the tube. Everyone else just had to endure it.

The transport picked up in Biterra at midnight, and it was getting dark again by the time they reached the wide road on the approach to Airdrossa. There were no trees at the side of the road now, just scrub and tangled ferns and the long-life boards with their bright images of other ways to live, if only you could buy them. On their left, a steady stream of private gliders swished past, setting the transport rocking in the slipstream.

Ahead of them were the lights of Airdrossa; a white haze on the sky, interspersed with the multicoloured pinpricks on the cathedral spire and the red-lit towers of the business district. It was a famous view, Airdrossa from the north, it was the backdrop for the news on the main three channels as if nowhere but Airdrossa existed. Every now and then the bank beside the road fell away and she caught a glimpse of huts, their walls of mud and rubbish and roofs of anything or nothing at all. In the dark she couldn't make out any people.

She left the transport at one of the suburban stops, a wide concrete plaza under yellow-tinged lights, desolate in the empty evening. A few others got out with her, an old woman from a village outside Biterra, a couple of young boys from the last village before the wide road, a mother with a family and a man on his own who she didn't remember getting on.

They dispersed quickly, without a glance at each other, so that by the time the transport had rounded the corner she was alone. She strapped her pack onto her shoulders, looked around her carefully. She knew the instructions off by heart by now, but she couldn't help repeating them to herself. 'The second road on the left from the square when you're facing the house with the pink shutters, then take the first right by the little church and right again.'

She walked quickly down the narrow street down the side of the church and emerged into a little square. It was dark, the buildings seemingly deserted, except for one small, dimly-lit restaurant. A bell above the door buzzed in a desultory fashion as she entered. There were six or seven tables in an empty room. She waited. Eventually a man came out of the back, wiping his hands on his shirt.

'You want a table?' He made it sound like a threat.

Terise gazed expressionless at his apron, at the flies circling beneath the light.

'No. Thank you. I'm looking for Mario.'

'Oh.' The man, losing interest, turned away. 'Mario! Someone here to see you. Ten minutes.'

The door swung to behind him, opened again almost immediately as Mario came through. He was younger than his boss and slimmer, his black hair pushed neatly back into a ponytail at the nape of his neck. Underneath his apron, his black shirt was worn but clean, and despite the heat, buttoned right up to the top. He stopped beside the filthy counter, radiating nothing but polite interest. Terise had never been a good actress, but she always tried.

'Hi Mario,' she said, with as much conviction as she could muster. 'Do you remember me? I'm a friend of your cousin's.'

'My cousin Katia?' His effort was as stilted as hers. She met his impassive eyes.

'Yes. Can we go outside?'

They stepped out into the little courtyard. As soon as the door was closed, he flung his arms around her.

'Terise! I'm so glad to see you. Did you have a good journey? Are you tired? Are you hungry? If you can wait half an hour I'll be finished my shift, so I can take you. You can wait in the church, if that's alright? It's so nice to see you!' He hugged her again. Terise pretended to choke. He let her go, stepped back to see if she was annoyed.

'I'm sorry, I was getting carried away, wasn't I? It's just so nice to see you! Are you alright?'

Terise pulled a face of mock resignation.

'I'm fine. Hello Marsana,' she said.

Part 6

Quila

1

The spaceport was some way outside the capital. Because of the noise, Du'Fairosay opined, and the fumes from the shuttle engines. The days before the silent models were a distant memory everywhere that Quila knew, but she accepted the explanation without comment. If anyone would know about poor transport and outdated equipment, it would, she supposed, be Fairo. The Chi!me Ambassador, Par'Lennan, had not been there to greet her at the spaceport, though the glider had been laid on with a driver. He was unavoidably detained, the driver had explained, evading her eyes. Clearly it was not the first time.

The spaceport was set in a circle of low hills, like landing in a salad dish. The trees leaned across both sides of the road, the sun dappling the surface with green light, and flowers grew multi-coloured on the verges beneath. She knew from her research that Drossa province was the most heavily popu-lated, but she wouldn't have guessed it from the spaceport road. There were no villages that she could see, only a few tumbles of broken stone walls and every so often a glider going the other way, as if it were a paradise, a sanctuary in soft green, untouched by working hands.

After about an hour they came out of the woods to see the edge of a wide plain, with Airdrossa sprawled across the horizon. It was low and black with a clump of towers at one side, hazy with distance, and the sky above it was tinged with dirty yellow. It was not an attractive sight, but it was clear that efforts had been made to make it so, from the pink-blossomed branches planted on either side of the road to the industrial areas carefully hidden away so that only a glimpse of flat corrugated roofs gave them away.

'Airdrossa is supposed to be beautiful.' Du'Fairosay was scornful. 'I'd hate to see the rest of the place.'

Quila had been thinking the same thing, but his tone stung, as if the poor, grubby city was something to her.

'Beauty is fitness, the right form for the right occasion,' she said tartly. 'Don't be so quick to your aesthetic judgements, unless you want others to make them against you. Study what the city is and how it does it, then you may be in a position to make criticisms of its beauty, not before.' She sounded in her own ears like her teachers, like his.

Airdrossa looked better from close quarters. When the famous towers were overhead and the suburbs and the smog lost to view, it was not without its charms. The glider pushed slowly through the crowded, narrow streets and Quila pressed her face to the window. This was the oldest quarter, a maze of narrow stone buildings. The shutters were all closed - against the sun? - and over them swung plaques of filigree metalwork, leaves, animals, the sky and the stars dancing on the painted wood. When the glider moved close in to let another past, she could see that the walls themselves were also carved with patterns of stylised leaves.

Even though it was the middle of the day, the streets were busy. There went a pair of young women, their hair teased into elaborate piles and set with feathers, pink and purple froth dancing round their knees as they walked. One of them had a small animal, crouching on her shoulder, that chattered and twined fingers in her hair. There were older women with black scarves over their heads, young men in grey shouting into communicators, other men with tattered layers and bundles in their arms.

There were old men chewing in doorways, watching the crowds go by, waiters wiping tables in the cafés with practised hands, balancing laden trays on their hips, crowds and crowds of Terrans, of every age and type she could imagine. And, every so often, a face that was not Terran at all. A smaller face in greenish grey, a pointed chin and large, blank eyes, taking the trays in the café, pushing a food cart, following a high-heeled lady with a larger animal on a lead. Standing in groups at a busy junction, pushed by a dark, raddled man to wash the drivers' windows while they stopped, for a price. Quila had studied Terrans, but she had never seen a Jeba before.

When the glider pulled up outside the hotel, the doormen were Terran but it was a Jeba who rushed out behind them to shepherd the suitcases up the magisterial steps. He (she supposed it was a he, although with the Jeba she didn't know how you told) wore the same red uniform as the other staff, even though on him the gold epaulettes on each shoulder practically overlapped. He looked temporary in it, she thought, as if at any moment he might disappear, leaving only his coat behind.

He gathered the suitcases outside the door, corralled them aside so that the passengers could walk in first. His head was bowed, a perfect impression of servility. She pressed ten UP credits into his hand as she passed, but he didn't say anything. He couldn't have seen that much money for a very long time, if at all, but she couldn't tell if his silence was reserve or really disinterest. For a moment she watched him as he turned back to the suitcases, wondering how he did it. Then Du'Fairosay called her and she dismissed him from her mind.

Par'Lennan had left a message at the front desk, to say that he would meet her the following evening. She spent her first day wandering through the streets, listening to the talk in the cafés, watching the old men gathered in the doorways, the young women in their sharp bright shoes, and the Jeba. They were everywhere once you started to look for them, but they were difficult to spot and to follow, as if the camouflage they had acquired for living in the deep forests worked equally well in the stony city. There were no statistics, as far as she knew, for the numbers of Jeba in Airdrossa or even on the planet. She tried an estimate, but had had to give up the count after only ten or so. She could not even be sure that her ten were ten, and not five or fifteen. They were so difficult to see and they did all look the same.

She returned to the hotel with the dusk, tripping lightly up the stone steps with a friendly nod to the doorman, making sure she got to the door before he did so that she could open it herself. The lights in the lobby were very bright after the dimness of the streets; Par'Lennan, waiting to greet her, was little more than a dark shape.

The first thing that she noticed about Par'Lennan was that he managed to look nonchalant and comfortable in even the most unpromising surroundings. The second thing, as her eyes adjusted, was that he was young, a bright star in his first real posting, who had been on the planet for less than six of their months.

'But it's a great place, I feel like I've been here forever. You must let me show you around.'

His hair was cut into a fluffy point in a style she had seen on the young civil academy men in Zargras, the ones who were good enough and lucky enough to be sent to work with IntPro. He had their suit, too, with the shiny collars pinched into points so long they reached half way down the front, and their way of pushing all his hair back from his forehead and holding it there on the top of his head when he wanted to look charming.

'That would be nice. But I thought we could sit down, have something to eat perhaps, talk over developments?'

'Well, we could, but…'

He waved a slender hand, pushed it through his hair. His skin was the seashell shade found on Chi!me itself, delicate as a flower.

'I suppose we could go and sit down in there, but, uf….' Up went the hand to the hair, back went the dark fluff, 'You won't see anything of the real Ty in there. In there are only diplomats and has-beens. You don't want to meet them. Come with me, I'll take you to some place *real*.'

His grin was broad and friendly, two lines of white, regular teeth.

'Alright,' she said, wondering if she would regret it, 'maybe for a little while.'

The real place was a bar of shadowed corners in a street just off the main square. What it was called Quila never knew; the lettering on the signboard was too weathered for her to read. Par'Lennan, who had walked a little ahead of her all the way from the hotel, stepped ahead to open the door, then stood back ceremoniously to let her through first.

She paused just inside the door, unsure in the sudden gloom of where to go. Par'Lennan let the door slam behind him.

'Try that table there,' he pointed. 'Really we should stand at the bar, but I'm sure you'd prefer to sit down.' He made it sound like a fault, as if she was irredeemably staid, and she was tempted to march up to the bar just to show him. But they did have to have some discussion about the planet, and she couldn't imagine talking with the barman listening in. Keeping her sleeves away from the sticky patches on the table she settled herself into the seat he'd indicated and waited for him to return with the drinks.

'I love this place, it's so full of all the worst types of life,' Par'Lennan announced as he set the glasses on the table. 'Smugglers, gamblers, drunks…policemen, they're all here. See that man over in the far corner, the one with the hat? Gangster, if you want anyone dead he's the one to see, for a price. Mostly workers who make everyone else refuse to work, you know the Terran term? Union organisers? But anyone you like, really, your wife or your husband, your father or your business partner, as long as you can pay.

'The scarred man at the games table, his businesses pay no taxes except the protection to the police. Last year his wife died with her lover in their glider and now his new wife is younger than his eldest daughter. The policeman's by the bar, the one with the largest glass, and the man with him you don't ask where the money for his drinks comes from, not if you want to leave by the door and not in pieces. There's probably a CAS man in here as well, but I can't see anyone I know tonight.

'The man by the door, the one with his face in his terminal, is a writer for one of the news casts, he came here to investigate and clear up the seamy side of Airdrossa, but they've got him now and he only says what they want him to say. That's what it's like here, it takes you in and you never come out the same. Not just this bar, the whole planet. You think I've brought you somewhere unusual, but it's not true. It's all like this, all of it, all just dirty and chaotic and dangerous. It gets you and it never lets you go. It's fantastic. Don't you think?'

Quila took a sip of her drink. It was oddly sweet, with an oily aftertaste that sat on her tongue after she swallowed. She set it down and edged the glass away.

'I don't know,' she said. 'It's not quite like anywhere I've been before. Sometimes it seems so familiar, I think I'll have the hang of it within a day, then the next minute I'm up against something so strange I could live a thousand lifetimes and never get to understand this place. You don't find that?'

Par'Lennan laughed. 'But that's the charm, that difference, that edge of strangeness that means you're never quite sure. The difference between Airdrossa, which let's face it could be anywhere in the Terran empire with no problem at all, and the villages that are just in another age. If you didn't know better, you'd think they were the indigenous people, that they'd never flown here from the stars. It's amazing to think that we can be sitting here and two days' ride away are people who are still obsessed with that ridiculous Terran sky god cult…'

'Christianity?' Her tone was dry, but he was unperturbed.

'That's it. I forgot you were the big Terran expert. And that's just the Terrans, the Oneness only knows what the Jeba get up too. Now there's a strange people, with all this Caduca stuff and all. It's all over the place at the moment, you must have seen the signs?'

'The signs?'

'The little hollow men? You must have noticed them, they're everywhere.'

The outline of a man painted on a wall, a twisted piece of metal hanging from a waiter's belt…

'Yes,' she said, 'I just didn't know that that was what they were. It's not just the Jeba, then?'

'It's a Jeban idea, but the villages are in it too, somehow. It's like a god figure. I don't understand it, no one does. I don't think they understand it themselves and isn't that just the most amazing thing? It's astounding.' He pushed his fringe back with one hand, again, and smiled. 'Isn't this just the most fantastic planet?'

She said, conservatively, 'I'll have to see a little more of it before I make my mind up on that.' She pushed her glass further across the table. 'So, what should I know before I meet the President?'

Par'Lennan pulled a face. It was unlikely, he explained, that she would meet the President at all.

'No one sees him, I mean no one. For days at a time.'

'You mean he doesn't do audiences?'

'No, I mean no one sees him. Not his staff, not the house journalists, no one. Even his relatives are turned away. The last hot season, it went on for so long, people began saying he was dead.'

'But he wasn't.'

'No, not that time. They rolled him out quickly enough once that rumour started going round. But then it was weeks before anyone saw him again.'

'So what do people think is going on? Does he just not like seeing people? Is he being ousted?'

He shrugged. 'They say he's ill, he's got that old multiplying cell disease that all these Terrans still seem to get.'

'But we've taught them how to cure that, haven't we? You said this has been going on since the last hot season?'

'Longer, it was just before I was sent out that he had his first withdrawal. Yes, it's usually curable for Terrans, but there's still a few cases where nothing can be done, so maybe he's one of those. Or maybe it's something else he has. Either way, they say he's dying and that makes things very interesting for us.'

'Does it? Why?'

'Because his successor will be the man who's effectively his deputy now. Desailly.'

He shot her a significant look, waiting for her to confess her ignorance so that he could be worldly-wise.

'Oh yes,' she said, 'I've heard of him, I discussed him on Benan. They told me he was a dangerous man, but I don't see why. Surely, if his ideas are so ridiculous, he won't win the election and he won't even become President.'

Par'Lennan laughed, shortly.

'Oh, he'll be President, you don't need to worry about that. As for danger, well, I suppose that's a matter of opinion, but he's certainly a complication. You'll see when you meet him, he's no friend to Chi!me.'

'I don't expect him to be, or any of them, until we've proved ourselves their friends. The President has always been willing to talk to us. He's not been an enemy to us.'

'Well, that's as maybe, but Desailly is different. You know the Terran saying, "keep your friends close and your enemies closer"? Here they have a different version, "keep your enemies in the grave."'

His tone bordered on the portentous and Quila had to suppress a snort. She narrowed a sceptical eye.

'Thanks for the advice.'

'Fine. Well, I'm sure you know what you're doing. You've been briefed, I'm sure.' He looked away from her at the dimly-lit room, his face suddenly as sulky as a child's. 'I'm just telling you. You should be careful.'

The Airdrossa night was stickily hot, and her room was muggy with it. Quila threw her wrap on the bed and flung open the window. The city stretched away beneath her, the orange street lighting and the dark roofs, the whine of the transports on the road outside and the distant clamour of a siren. The flashes and bangs cutting the sky over the city, pattering, fizzing sounds like blaster fire. On one of the shuttered houses below a door opened and music drifted tinnily out into the air. Voices called something that didn't sound like the Terran she'd learnt, foot-steps rang on the pavement. Someone laughed, further off, glass smashed and someone screamed.

Away on the horizon was a darker line that could be hills, or cloud. She leant her arms on the cill. Even this, the best hotel, looked shabby from a distance, but now studying it closely she could see that what she had taken for pockmarks were actually carvings, whorls and waves cut into the stone all the way up the walls. It must have taken so many days of skilled labour, have cost so much in time and money and effort to execute and she thought suddenly how secretive it was, how strange in a place whose Terran poverty, hopelessness and violence were all too achingly familiar.

A breeze blew the window gently back against her arms. A flying insect blundered past her head, seeking the light. She winced as it crackled in the light killer, she always disliked those things. Perhaps she had better shut the window. It felt so immense suddenly, the knowledge that beyond that line were miles upon miles of fields and trees and people, all alien to her, and that was odd, because as planets went Benan Ty was absurdly small.

The settlers and the Jeba lived on only one of the three main continents, and the smaller islands were similarly uninhabited more than a day's sail out from the mainland. The others were too barren, their topsoil too shallow, to grow enough to feed a population; even the mining operations were almost entirely automatic. There was no dark heart, no void at the centre of the maze to be lost in. She knew that. She knew that. Determinedly, sensibly, Quila closed the window and went to bed.

2

Petrus Desailly yawned, suppressing the urge to put his head down on the desk and sleep. He had never really accustomed himself to going without a siesta after lunch, even after all these years. He had a reputation for it, like that irreverent little cartoon he'd seen on one of the news channels, himself tucked up in the parliament chamber with a large white nightcap drooping over his face. It had been a good drawing, remarkably like. He had thought of requesting a copy, but they would most likely prefer to offer him one, the next time the editor needed a favour. They said it was because he was provincial, he knew, the Airdrossa elite who had always been suspicious of him. He heard it in their voices when they thought he was out of earshot, in odd snatches of recorded conversation, 'Of course, in *Chaireddan*,' the downward intonation, as if it was the back of beyond. It bothered his wife.

Oddly enough, when he was in Chaireddan he had never wanted to sleep the afternoon away, not since he was a small child at school, fighting and kicking at the white-swathed nuns who glided, clucking, round his bed and tried to cage him. Yet here in Airdrossa, where it was not done, every afternoon, all he wanted was to lie down and shut his eyes. At least his meeting with the Chi!me woman had not been difficult. She was quite a good-looking woman in her way, if you could get used to the blue, and younger than he had expected. It had been interesting. Once, long ago, he might even have identified the slight pang he felt for her as pity.

Par'Lennan had set them up an office in the Chi!me embassy, a white, gracious house with an air of hard times. Du'Fairosay hung a blue crystal from the ceiling, the light clashing with the green-dappled sun that shone through the trees outside. After the first day he spent most of his time there, working on their ViaVera contacts while Par'Lennan liaised with the government. There had been a UP team on Ty for months, Quila understood, though it was not clear if the government did. Du'Fairosay did not like to be asked about this work, the few enquiries she made were met with evasions and silence. It was best not to pry too closely. It was not unusual, she told herself, for the members of a team to have different orders, different information. Repetition was waste, after all.

Du'Fairosay and Par'Lennan reported to her, dutifully, every day. 'We're making good progress.' 'It's going very well.' Beyond that there was little she could do. She occupied herself walking the streets of Airdrossa, breathing their air; taking the place in through her skin. The cathedral, its spire towering above the flapping scaffolding and the pink-lit sign of the club against its walls. The crumbling elegance of the main streets, wide opulence of unrealised hopes. The swooping stone between peeling shutters, carven trees and hills of a Terra left far behind.

A house in a turning off the shopping street had a great tree etched into the whole of its side wall, with advertising screens fitted to every fruit. They changed every minute or so if someone was passing; Quila liked to stand there and watch as Aztec trainers gave way to Peron shirts, to DeBeers gliders and back, the tree fruiting a confusion of berries. She wondered sometimes what they were, and if people bought them. She supposed they must.

She never tried to hide who she was when she went out walking. She could have covered her head and been more anonymous - older, poorer women in Airdrossa did so, after all - but she was never prepared to. She didn't believe in concealment, felt that people had the right to know that the Ambassador, the special envoy, was passing by. Not that anyone seemed very interested.

They were not outwardly friendly, the Airdrossans. Like Terrans everywhere, they were reserved and inclined to be suspicious of new situations. The service in the shops was polite but expressionless. It was only sometimes, turning away, that she thought she caught a raised eyebrow, the ghost of a smile. Once there was a muttered comment, but her Terran was not quite like Ty Terran and she couldn't make it out. There was only one time she was afraid, but after that she had bodyguards.

She had been sitting in one of her favourite cafés, near the hotel, making her midday meal last longer. She had her terminal and some links to study, but she wasn't really paying attention to them. The café was on one of the busier streets and the temptation simply to watch people go by was too great. It took her a while to realise that the people had gradually become all men, mostly middle-aged, swarthy men in clothes even she could recognise as shabby, all going the same way. They walked with purpose, in silence, not like people going home. One of the Jeban staff was clearing the table next to hers.

'Excuse me,' she said, leaning over, 'but do you know what's happening? Where are all those men going?'

The Jeba stopped, a glass hung from each spindly finger, and looked at her. Under its scrutiny she could feel her cheeks purpling. 'It iss demonstration.' Its tone was measured, an air behind it she couldn't catch.

'A demonstration of what?'

It spread its glass-decked hands. 'Yess.' It turned back to the table.

'Well,' Quila addressed its back, 'thank you anyway.' She

would have to go and see, after that.

She followed the last of the men to a plaza by one of the bridges. A platform was set up under the riverside trees as if for someone to speak, although no one was on it. In front of it, the men milled around, shouting. Some of them had placards, but the slogan was too idiomatic and the lettering too wayward for her to be able to make them out. Something about hitting, she thought, about work and hitting, but she could not be sure. It all seemed rather desultory, like a ritual no one was interested in performing. She was about to leave when the police arrived.

She saw the heads turn first, a rolling movement on the edge of the crowd, swinging to watch the carriers push into the plaza. The placards hoisted higher; someone leapt onto the platform and started shouting something into the magnifier. The police climbed out of the carriers, formed up in lines in front of them. They each had a shield which they locked together to make an armoured line, covering their fronts and their heads, their black uniforms a menancing blur behind. She realised that these had to be the paramilitaries, the CAS.

They shuffled forward, slowly, as the first missiles bounced on the top of the shields. The man on the platform screamed a slogan and the crowd picked it up, roaring. The CAS started beating on the insides of their shields, in time with the chanting so that for a moment it was as if both sides were making music together, coming together to dance. Another rock landed on the shields and, for no reason Quila could see, one of the CAS men pushed his blaster through the shield wall and fired.

In the front a man fell. There was a silence like an intake of breath, then the crowd broke and ran. Quila, on the edge of the group, found herself in the front as they sprinted for the side streets, rushing to put enough distance between them and the demonstration so that they could become ordinary citizens again. For her, it was easier; she told Du'Fairosay afterwards that she had never been in any danger. She did not tell him about the man they shot, about the dark patches on the earth when she went back that evening, but he still didn't believe her.

The next morning when she came down from her room, she found the bodyguards waiting for her. They stood motionless on the floor of the lobby; if she hadn't known they were Terran, she would have sworn that they didn't even blink. Two of them, hulking mountains of Terran muscle, dressed in army fatigues so tight they might have been poured into them. She walked round them slowly.

'Very nice,' she said like a general on parade. 'Very...military. Very good.'

Du'Fairosay was waiting behind them, a satisfied smile on his face. She hissed, so as not to offend them, 'This is your doing? What in the stars are you thinking of? I don't need, I won't have, minders!'

'You need protection. After yesterday you can't deny that. I'm sorry if you don't like it, but it is necessary.'

He didn't sound very sorry, in fact, he didn't sound sorry at all.

'Necessary? Are you suggesting that I can't judge what's necessary?' She was indignant. The cheek of it! 'I think you forget yourself. You will send these...bruisers away and next time you feel it necessary to so exceed your orders, you will remember...'

'My orders are to take all necessary measures to ensure the success of this mission and this is one of them.'

'I fail to see ...'

'Of course you do!' His tone was as exasperated as hers. 'You want to walk among the people. I know. I know, believe me, Ar'Quila, I know exactly why you don't want to take these measures. But this is not Zargras, nor Iristade; on these Terran worlds your worth is judged by how far away from the people you can afford to keep yourself. When you walk alone through the streets you harm your standing, not help it, and you put yourself in danger. I won't let you do that.'

His expression was intent. She was touched, even in the midst of her rage, by his concern for her.

'It's something I have to work to change, something we all have to change, I know that. But we won't do that hiding behind muscle. You must see that.'

'All I see is that changing a culture is a long, slow process and now is not the time. There are people here, many people, who would like nothing better than to see you dead and the peace process extinguished. ViaVera, the government, every organisation has their renegade factions, the people who think their leaders are wrong to compromise, wrong to talk and try to end the killing. There are always people who don't want the peace. Don't you know how much danger you are in? Don't you know that there are people who want to kill you? You have to be careful, you have to be suspicious. If you have not been trained to be these things then you have to learn.'

'And take the bodyguards?'

Although he didn't move, it seemed as though he stepped back. His expression was relieved.

'And take the bodyguards,' he agreed. 'They're here, after all. You might as well accept them as not. You know we have the budget for it.'

She realised she hadn't even considered the money, only her visceral distaste for hierarchy and show. It was natural, she supposed. The Chi!me were not a material people.

'Oh well,' she said, 'If we have the budget for it, I suppose I'd better make the best of it. I promise I will take them with me whenever I stir outside the hotel. Does that satisfy you?' She smiled, to show she did not hold his concern against him.

'It's a start,' he said.

She found she couldn't enjoy her trips out with the bodyguards in place. She stayed in the hotel, waiting for Du'Fairosay and Par'Lennan to report to her on progress with the guerrillas. She decided that she would not call them terrorists, despite the appellation given to them by the Benan Ty press. It was judgmental, it was not respectful, and it was a fundamental of peace that all sides deserved respect.

'I don't know what to think of them, though,' she said, 'only that I can see them but I can't imagine them at all.'

It was the afternoon of the second day after the demonstration and she was recording a message to send to Ceronodis. Ty was remote enough to make real-time communication more difficult than it was between, say, Zargras and Chi!me, and she found she liked the excuse to talk and not be interrupted. She was sure that whatever Ceronodis would say would be helpful, insightful, and she was, oddly, equally sure that she was disinclined to hear it.

'I think we all have a fixed image of what a guerrilla would be like, sneaking through the ferns with the war marks on their cheeks and a knife in their teeth, a gloating shadow on a wall as a building blows. I know they do things like that, why else am I here, but I have to think them just as *kusay* as anyone in Airdrossa, or how could I do any good?'

Kusay was a Chi!me term, developed when they had first gone to the stars. It meant a person, Chi!me, human, Gargarin; someone who had lived up to the minimum standards for their species and was therefore allowed to be included in it. By claiming it for ViaVera, she felt enlightened.

'They must eat, and sleep, and talk and laugh and receive communications from Chi!me peace envoys and talk about them, too... I know they do all these things, but I can't imagine them doing them, and I don't know what I do when I actually meet them. It's quite a challenge, I hadn't realised, and that's all to the good, of course. It's just that I've had a sheltered upbringing, I've never met a murderer before.'

It was odd when she thought of their work, her little message of peace going out at the same time to palace and forest, through the most and least official channels there could be, but she did not think of it much. It was for Par'Lennan and Du'Fairosay to do, not for her. It was her place to leave them to it.

The next day, Par'Lennan told her she finally had an audience with Desailly, and she was realist enough to recognise that if she was going to get to the President, it was only going to be through him.

'I'll go, because I have to go,' she told Par'Lennan, sitting in his office, 'but I do not like this system of government. Once we have peace again, this is another one of the things that will have to change.'

Par'Lennan leant back, tipping his chair so that the front legs left the floor. The headrest hit the wall in the centre of the long black smudge of his habit. He smirked at her.

'Whatever,' he said. 'Just don't tell that to Desailly.'

'Of course I wouldn't.'

'Although, come to think of it, I expect you already have.'

He gestured at the ceiling with a knowing finger and sauntered back upstairs to where he and Du'Fairosay were working. She wanted to be angry with him, but she could not. He had told her the embassy would be bugged, just as the hotel was. It was not his fault she had forgotten.

Waiting in the presidential anteroom for the attendant to usher her in, she realised she didn't know at all what she expected Desailly to be like. In her head she ran through everything she had learnt about him; it didn't help. He was from a humble background, a childrens' report Du'Fairosay had found for her had been heartrending about his poor widowed mother, scrimping and saving so that her only son could get an education and better himself.

He had had three sisters and they had scrimped and saved so well he had made it all the way to the university, the top level of schooling available on Ty. After he had finished, he had come home to Chaireddan and joined the police force, in which his natural talent had been recognised so quickly that he swiftly moved up the ranks. Either that, or they were short of recruits; Quila wondered if most bright, ambitious young Chaireddan men didn't stay as far away as possible once they had escaped. He had been chief of police before he was thirty, the youngest they had ever had, and his poor old mother had been proud of him. And then he had killed Mara Karne.

He had become a star overnight. Invited to Airdrossa to receive a medal from the President, he had not been able to move without all the broadcasting stations surrounding him, showing the watching parts of the world what their hero was doing every moment of his day. The only place they had not gone was the President's private suite, and no one ever knew what had been said there.

They only knew that the President had come out onto the balcony with Desailly at his shoulder and had introduced to the people the new head of the CAS. He had held Desailly's hand up in his own to acknowledge the cheers; Quila had seen the pictures. Many of Airdrossa's political class had died over the next few years, but Desailly had survived and flourished with the CAS behind him, until now it seemed all his enemies were contained or dead.

He had a name as a private man: he was never one for parties and had remained with the Chaireddan wife he had married straight out of university and who was too shy to say a word when she appeared with him at functions. It was said about him as if it was a wondrous thing, a man still married, as if it showed something in him they would otherwise have thought was lacking. He had a name for ruthlessness, also.

The bench where they had told her to sit was a Terran antique, and uncomfortable. Quila wriggled, trying to spread her weight from one numb buttock to the other. She had met ruthless men before, men whose private lives were exemplary, men who tried to put their opponents at a disadvantage through judicious use of hard seats. She had dealt with them all, on Zargras, on Iristade, and it had never bothered her. She was IntPro, it was what she did.

He would be genial on the surface, polite and smooth, he would chat to her, try to make her like him, because that was how men like him always treated females like her, and she would smile and nod and keep her distance, as she had been taught. She knew all this, she had done so many times, yet the picture in her head was flimsy as insect wings, like ViaVera in their mountains or the people behind the closed shutters of Airdrossa, and behind it she could see nothing at all.

A door opened a little way down the corridor and a man stepped out. The light was shining in through the window beyond him, so that all she could see was his shape, silhouetted against it. She raised her head, trying not to screw up her eyes.

'Ambassador Ar'Quila?' the man said. 'I'm Petrus Desailly. Won't you come in?'

He was better dressed than she expected. Many of the men in Airdrossa were sporting copies of Chilme dress, overjackets with round collars and fastenings down one side, made up in such cheap, dull materials it made her wince to think of wearing them. Desailly's was higher quality than that, but cut in a strange, symmetrical style with diagonal lapels folding back on either side of his chest that she guessed would be Terran. The jacket was plain, but on each lapel he wore a small badge. On the left it was the lion of Benan in the traditional green and gold, on the right an arrangement of stars she didn't recognise in the red, white and blue she knew to be Terran. As she walked past him into the office he saw her looking.

'You're wondering about my badges?' He smiled. 'I never take them off. The right, here, is for thinking, action, politics, if you will. The left, that's for emotion. Where the heart is.'

He was a Benanist, of course. Everyone said so.

He was a small man, hardly taller than her, his face a white stain under the dark brown of his unruly hair. The overwhelming impression she had was of seriousness, a concentration in that unremarkable face and the watchful eyes. You wouldn't notice him in a crowd and that would be, in the end, all the worse for you. She shook his hand when he offered it. It was cool, clean, not too firm, and with half her mind she thought, inappropriately, *this is the hand that held the blaster, this is the finger that fired.*

'Please, sit down.' He gestured to an armchair beside the window. She sat.

She talked like all her kind. He had met enough of them, over the last years, to recognise the type. She was pretty, he decided, half-listening, with her indigo hair all piled up on her head and her blue skin under her robe so delicate that a movement could shatter it. It was a time of great opportunities for Benan Ty, she was saying, they could go out there and take their place in the galaxy.

'All those resources can be yours. We've learnt to grow past the stage where any other race is seen as a rival. The galaxy is limitless. There is no space to defend, no borders, no protected trade. There is only us and all the other races, doing business and helping our people to grow, expand, be all they can be. Ty can be a part of that. We will help you, we will give you everything you need and a thousand other things you don't even know yet that you want.

'We can bring you the galaxy, we can open up the galaxy to you. Trade, growth, UP membership, even. I know Ty shares representation with Benan, but wouldn't you like your own voice? Your own chance to participate in the democracy of planets? We can help you help your people, if you'll let us and, in turn, you can help us, because I'm sure we have much that we can learn from you, trade with you, as well, once we get to know you better.'

She leaned forward as she spoke, belief shining out of her like a beacon. If he heard the spaces between her words, it was clear she didn't.

'Ty has been independent for longer than you've been alive. Why do you come to us now? What is so special now?' It was a difficult question, designing to trip her. She smiled a little, not disturbed, and he liked her better for it.

'You mean, is this about Terra? Of course in a way it's about Terra. "When Terra sneezes, all the colonies catch a freeze", isn't that the saying? So of course, now that there's a government again on Terra we're trying to help rebuild in a way we just couldn't before. We know you've been though instability in this part of the galaxy for many years and we want to help you get over that. And I do think this is a crucial time. You were a Terran colony once, and you can choose to remain one, in spirit if not in fact. Or you can choose to open yourselves up to other possibilities. It's your choice.'

'But if we don't 'open ourselves up', we'd have to deal with ViaVera on our own, isn't that so?'

Touchingly, she was outraged.

'Not at all!' she exclaimed. 'I'm here on behalf of my government to offer you a continuing dialogue, if you want it, about how the Chi!me can help you, but that's completely up to you. On behalf of UP and my government, I'm also here to help you make peace with ViaVera and that doesn't depend on anything else you choose. I don't expect you to make a choice now, it's not like one sweet or another, I know! I throw it out as a possibility, a dialogue for the future, if you like. For now, what we need to consider is the peace.'

'Ah yes,' he said. He stretched his legs out in front of him, pushed his fringe out of his eyes. 'The peace.'

'And for that, I will need to speak to the President.'

'The President is unavailable.' It was his stock answer, so well-used it was automatic. 'I am his representative, I can speak for him.'

'I know that. Nevertheless, my instructions are that I must speak with the President himself concerning whatever we might agree here, and I cannot bring anything to a conclusion until I have done so. When will he be available? I can come back any time that would suit.'

She had put it so firmly there was no refusal short of rudeness, and it probably wasn't worth that. He said, conservatively, 'I'll see what I can arrange.'

'Good,' she replied. 'Now, what we need to do is open up a dialogue with ViaVera, see if you can negotiate a settlement with them. So the best way to do that is to set up a meeting. I've got my people working on contacting them, and if you can have your people talk to mine about arrangements, I think we may be able to move forward to talks pretty soon. I think...'

He cut in. 'They won't talk.'

'You don't think so? I disagree, our preliminary contacts have been most hopeful. I think they will.'

She looked so smug, sitting there, so foolish and so sure. It made him angry.

'They won't talk,' he repeated. His voice was thick in his own ears, rough like a day of shouting at his troops. 'They won't talk because they have nothing to talk about. You think they can negotiate, that they have something they want? They don't

155

know what they want, they kill and they kill and that's all they are. It's all they ever were.'

Her eyes had widened. He swallowed, moderating his tone. 'They've never shown any interest in coming to talks before and you won't get them to come now. They won't talk.' He leaned back in his chair, deliberating lightening his tone even while the irritation throbbed inside. 'I'd bet on it, if my wife let me gamble.'

She smiled at that. 'Even if you don't gamble, will you let me prove you wrong?'

'You can try.'

'And if I do, will you come?'

'And if I come, what then? What guarantee do I have that when you've gone back to the stars they won't just turn their backs and start killing again? How do I know they'll abide by anything they agree? I need surety if I'm to sell anything like this to my people, and I don't see it.'

'I can give you surety, UP power is your surety.'

He suppressed the urge to snort, allowed himself to look politely sceptical instead. 'Ambassador, I don't think ViaVera care very much for UP power.'

'They will if it's armed and pointed at them. UP isn't just an abstraction, you know. We make sure it has teeth. They'll know that, because we'll make sure they know that. You'll find they respect that more than you think.'

Her expression, as far as he could tell on a Chi!me face, was quizzical. He knew what she wasn't asking him, what the whole purpose of her visit was to establish. *Are you with us, or not? Do you support us, will you make trouble for us, do we have to deal with you? Are you with us?* The same question, every time.

With every previous envoy, with that idiot of an Ambassador he had avoided an answer, but she was the figurehead, the one sent with the official question he had pretended had not been asked until now. He had always known that some day he would have to decide which way he would jump.

He nodded as if considering, giving himself time. He didn't like the Chi!me. He didn't trust the Chi!me, he wished they were a galaxy away. They had been once, and that had been better, but now they were here, and it might be the work of his days to keep them at arm's length. But since they were here, and since they wanted to appear helpful, did he have to rebuff it? He had been circling the question for months, and still he came back to the same reply. Could it do so much harm, to take their bait and deal with the hook when he found it?

Back in Chaireddan when he was a little boy, some of his ever-changing uncles had taken him fishing. Sometimes the fish avoided the bait and went hungry. Sometimes it took the bait and died. And sometimes, just sometimes, it took the bait and got hauled out and at the last moment twisted from the hook and leapt back into the water, with food and freedom and all. It depended, really, on what the fish were prepared to risk, on the quality of the bait and the ruthlessness of the fisherman reeling them in. On what effort, ultimately, the fishermen were prepared to expend to catch them.

She was looking at him with her head on one side, in that birdlike way all the Chi!me had. He had an odd sense of lightness below him, like the highest rock above the diving pool, himself perched on one leg while all around was sky.

'But if you're wrong,' he said, 'if they won't make peace, if we can't come to an agreement that they will keep and end their violence, what will you do then? Will you leave us to it, will you abandon us? Or will you do what my people really need, and help us wipe them out?'

He watched her narrowly as she struggled with it. She wanted the peaceful solution, both sides dancing cheek to cheek. The sun was shining all around him and if he looked down he would fall. But he would not look down. He could hear the words in his head, stretching out before him like a bridge. If he just held himself still enough, if he didn't hesitate.

'Will you?' he repeated.

She swallowed. 'I think we can talk our way to a solution, you know that, and I won't give up on that while there is still any way we can make it work. But if they really won't talk, if they really won't see that their only way forward from here is to accept a compromise that suits everybody…if they really are so blind…' Her gaze slipped over his shoulder, as if watching an image on the wall that only she could see. She took a deep breath. 'Then, yes. Ultimately, all legitimate governments have the right to deal with criminals and violence by any means necessary and the Chi!me will never fail to support law and justice. So, I suppose, yes.'

'So…?'

Her tone was bleak.

'If there are truly no other options to stop the killing, UP will kill them for you. You have my word on that.'

He had reached the other side, the ground was under his feet, and in another moment the image was gone as if it had never been. After a few pleasantries, she was almost ready to leave. 'I'll be in touch about a Presidential audience,' she said, getting to her feet. 'I really do need to see him, even if it's not for long.'

'I'll see what I can do. And if there's anything else I can do, anything I can tell you…?'

She started to shake her head, then held up her hand.

'Actually, there is something. It's just curiosity, but I've been hearing about it since Benan and no one seems to be able to give me any details. You can tell me about the Caduca.'

'The Caduca?' He relaxed, chatting. 'I don't know much, I don't think anybody does. It's some Jeba idea originally, I think, some mystic leader who comes once a generation if you really deserve them, or something like that. The name "Caduca" is old Terran, though, something to do with a snake symbol, an old, dead snake, something like that.'

'It sounds pretty harmless?' she ventured.

'Maybe it sounds it, but it's got the peasants going round the villages with snakeskins round their shoulders, singing nonsense they don't even know the meaning of and blathering on about the leader, the one who will save them all at the end of the world, or some such rubbish. ViaVera say that they have it, do you know that? Whatever that means, the peasants believe them. You didn't believe me, when I said they wouldn't talk, but there's your answer for you. In their eyes, they're not just murderers; it's religion, and you can't argue with that. You can't have dialogue with the divinely-inspired; you can't reason with someone who thinks they're sent to blow up buildings by the nearest thing they've ever seen to God.'

He took a breath.

'So that's all I know about the Caduca, and if you ever meet the snakeskin God out in the forest, I'd be grateful if you'd introduce me, as I'd like a few words with it.' He smiled. 'Dialogue, you see? I'm learning your ways already.'

'It's always good to learn new things, but they don't always supersede the old ones. Thank you for telling me about the Caduca. I always try to hear as many sides of a thing as possible and it was very interesting.' She was half-smiling now, her face shining with surety. 'But I still think you're wrong,' she said.

She went soon after that, with many polite promises to return. He asked her, as he had planned, to save a dance with him at the formal ball that evening and she had agreed politely enough. He couldn't tell if she relished the prospect or not.

He watched her go across the courtyard with her bodyguards. She had covered her blue skin with a cloak like the local women wore, but she was still instantly recognisable. She stepped through the gate past the guard post and out into the street. She should have come in a transport, he would have to mention it, it wasn't safe for her to walk the streets as she did.

If she was a daughter of his…but she was too old to be anyone's daughter, too old to be his, and sometime he would have to work out what it was about the Chi!me that allowed them to do so much and see so little that they remained like children; powerful, sophisticated children but still children, inside. The guards closed the gate behind her. He shrugged, he would think about it another time, when he had leisure. He tapped his terminal screen, sending the messages that had come in during the meeting to his secretary to deal with. Then he opened another door and went to see the President.

3

Quila strolled away from the Presidential palace, her body-guards obediently at her heels. She knew the moment she had stepped outside the room that it had gone well. She would not allow the creeping disquiet the aftermath of any occasion brought to obscure it. It had gone well, she had done well. She had talked Desailly into agreeing to talk to ViaVera if she could get them to the table, and that was all she had had to do. Admittedly, he did not think ViaVera would ever agree to talks, but that was her problem, not his. She would see the President and confirm it, and then when the meeting was arranged, Desailly would not be able to withdraw.

She would have done it, when even Du'Fairosay who was supposed to be her assistant might have doubted that it could be done. She saw it in his eyes sometimes when he looked at her, she thought, a kind of condescending sadness like an adult watching a child that does not know it's sick. She would have showed him, she would have showed all of them. She would have to get her message off to Ceronodis tonight; she would be so proud.

It was too hot for walking. She realised that, deep in thought, she had slowed her pace to barely a crawl. The road from the palace was usually a busy one, particularly here where it turned into the main shopping street, but although most of the shops were open there were hardly any Ty people about. They must be staying inside, away from the heat. Sensible of them. Her hood was sticking to the back of her head, she could feel her hair, heavy with sweat, clinging in runnels all down her neck.

Where the sun caught the material it was so warm it felt like it was melting and although there was nothing in front of her face she could hardly breathe. There was a limit to anyone's endurance and she didn't care if she did get stared at.

'Bother Fairo and his rules,' she exclaimed, and pulled the cloak off.

It was easier going without it, but the heat was still so intense she found herself disinclined to walk much faster. It didn't matter, she wasn't in a hurry. The other times she had been down this street, there had been so many people she had barely been able to see anything. It was pleasant to stroll down the centre and survey the shop windows; the things on display were some of the most valuable clues to the culture, after all. It was mostly local produce, she thought, though she did see some heavy-duty clothes with a Gargarin cut. There were fewer Chi!me clothes, which did not surprise her. That would change.

One of her bodyguards, Beres? Peres?, turned to survey the street behind her, tripping slightly on the uneven roadway as he did so. It was the third time in as many minutes, and she couldn't help noticing that his finger was curled on the trigger of his blaster.

'Is anything the matter?' she asked.

'No. Keep walking.' His tone was brusque, stressed. He turned round again, rather obvious, she thought, if there was anyone behind them. He was supposed to be a professional.

'Is there someone following us?'

'There's no problem. Just keep going.' The other one, Micail, glanced back now as well, but only for a second. 'Can you walk any faster?' he asked.

Quila turned to the window of the nearest shop, on the

corner with a narrow side street, and stopped dead. It was a jeweller, the display a collection of bright green stones set in silver. She couldn't tell how it was supposed to be worn, she hadn't seen enough ladies with jewellery in Airdrossa.

She kept her voice low, but as steely as possible.

'If there is someone following me, I would be obliged if you would tell me,' she said. 'Now, let's try again. Is there anyone behind us?'

Micail nodded.

'Following us?'

Another nod, both of them this time.

'Where are they now?'

'Back at the window of the vegetable shop, Ambassador.'

'Waiting for us?'

'Yes, Ambassador.'

'Good. So, this is what we'll do…'

'Um…Ambassador?' That was Beres, braver than his colleague. 'If we could keep moving, we should soon be back into the hotel district and once we're there…'

'We'll be in a place with wider streets, more vegetation and even fewer people. An ideal spot, in fact, for them to jump us. So we won't be going that way.' Her soles were light on the pavement, muscles tense and ready. She smiled at their worried faces. 'In fact, all you have to do is follow me.'

Without another word, she plunged down the side street, and ran.

For the first few steps it was a mistake. Her feet ached from the hard road, her breath pounded in her ears. Her cloak, folded over her arm, began stickily to slip and her legs ached from the unaccustomed exercise. It was foolish, ridiculous; she would be caught, shamed. Then, and she did not know how, she felt her stride lengthen, her feet trip airily over the stones. She let the cloak drop.

She remembered this. At school on Chi!me Two, she and Ceronodis sprinting together from the pursuing team, ducking through the alleyways as fast as they could go, hiding behind bushes with their hands over each other's mouths to stop the giggles. Later, on Zargras as a young trainee, when the boy supposed to ambush her had let the muzzle of his dummy blaster stick out a little beyond his cover, she had grabbed and seized it without breaking stride, whirled it round and tapped him on the head before racing away. She remembered she was good at this.

She supposed she was in some danger, but she couldn't really feel concerned. Not when she could run so fleet and true, not when she had two bodyguards puffing stentorously behind her. She wasn't sure there was really anything to be running from, but that didn't really matter. She remembered how this had always made her happy. Arms pumping, hair flying free, Quila sailed round the next corner into another alley and slowed. At the end, nearer than she had expected, the blank wall of a building blocked the way, but she thought there was probably a passage out around the rear, to the left. It was as good a place as any to pause. She dropped her pace to a walk.

'Are they still behind us?' she puffed. 'Did you see?'

No reply. She realised suddenly that she couldn't hear anything. No rustle of protective clothing, no breathing but her own. She swung round to the empty street and, as she did so, something whined past her ear. She felt a small, sharp cut like fire on the side of her head and when she put her hand up to it, it was wet. She brought her hand back so she could see what the wetness was, stared at the indigo stickiness webbing her fingers.

Everything seemed to be happening very slowly. She had been standing there, staring at her hand, forever, yet she could feel herself still gasping at the first pain. She heard the words 'I've been shot,' and she didn't know if she had said them. Shot. It was so strange, she could hardly understand it. Shot. It was so strange.

There was a sound behind her, and without knowing she meant to, she dropped forward and down and dived for the only cover, a stack of metal crates halfway along the right-hand wall. Something whirred down the alley and crashed into the wall of the house opposite the other end in a shower of splinters. Blaster bolts, part of Quila's mind registered. Good ones. She raised her head gingerly so that she could peer over the top of the crate. Another bolt whistled past her, too high to be any danger.

They were on the roof at the end of the alley. It was a good position for covering the entrance, just as if they had known she was coming. But maybe not so good for covering her escape. She slipped down again into the shelter of the crates. It was a stroke of luck, their being here, and she was suitably grateful to them. There must be a café or a bar nearby that dumped them there. Some of them had been there a long time, their metallic surface scratched and pitted as if with messages; a rough sketch that almost looked like a human, outlined in white, strokes and angles in lines like a doodler's impression of writing. It seemed a little futile, whatever they meant, for who was going to see it there?

She pulled her attention back to the problem at hand, and considered. There was a passage off to the left at the end of the alley, she was sure, leading around the back of the building and away. The shooters were on top of that building, so their view of the end of the alley would be limited at best. If she crept very fast along the wall to the end, they would not be able to aim at her, and she could be away round the corner before they had been able to get into place. It was all about knowing the angles; she remembered saying that to By'Remse, the class champion, one day after she'd beaten him at chase, and he was so angry she had thought for a moment he wanted to hit her. The situation then had almost been similar; the blocked alley, the field of fire. She had won then and she would win now, however bad the situation might seem; she knew it. She was Ar'Quila and she could do it.

She was sure they would be watching, so there wasn't much point in peeking out.

'Oh, stars protect me,' she muttered. Her hands clenched once on the side of the nearest crate. She shut her eyes and launched herself blind down the wall to the end of the alley. The whirr of the bolts started almost at once. She kept her eyes closed, wincing at every explosion as if she did not know yet whether she had been hit. She could almost feel it ripping through her breastbone, severing her head, running her limbs with fire in her imagination as she ran. Ears ringing, she cannoned into the wall and quickly felt along it to the passage out. Mercifully, this was covered.

She sprinted along it for a short way, ever conscious that the assassins would know exactly where she was going, that they would be waiting for her when the roof ran out. She panted round the corners. Maybe she could get out before they made it there? She knew she was fooling herself, could not quite believe that there would be an escape at the end of it, when she saw the door. The broken door leading into an overgrown garden, hung around with trees so that no one looking down into it could see anything but green. Bounded by a low wall, with the gardens of other houses stretching away beyond it.

'Thank the Oneness,' Quila breathed with a devotion she only felt in crises, and dived through.

Du'Fairosay pulled the hotel door open just as she was reaching for the handle. He stopped so abruptly she thought he would fall over and stared at her.

'Quila.' It was hardly more than a breath. His eyes closed.

'Fairo…' she began.

His lids snapped back. After the first shock of seeing her, he had remembered to be furious. Her words died on her tongue. He held the door open for her and, meekly, she went in.

She wasn't used to rebukes, but in a way she couldn't blame him. Du'Fairosay must have had almost as great a shock as she did, when the bodyguards had returned without her.

'You ran away from your bodyguards! Someone was chasing you, and you ran away from them! That was…that was…'

'Irresponsible.' He didn't dare to say it, but she could. 'I know. I know, I'm sorry. I thought they were right behind me, then they weren't. I'm sorry.'

All the way back to the hotel through the gardens, she had been storing up rage against the bodyguards who had deserted her and Du'Fairosay who had made her rely on them in the first place. But somehow on the doorstep of the hotel, after that one brief moment of gladness, he had made it all her fault, and she was suddenly so tired she had let him. It was the best way to get through it, anyway. Take responsibility and be better, wasn't that the idea?

'I'm sorry,' she said again.

Du'Fairosay smiled thinly. 'You don't have to apologise to me.'

His anger was concern for her, of course, and she appreciated that he cared. If it seemed extreme, strained, she shouldn't wonder at it. She supposed he would be censured if she died. Off-worlders were always particularly sensitive about that. She realised suddenly how tired she was, how much she longed to lie down and rest before she had to dress for the dance.

'It's alright, Fairo,' she said. 'It was only a little danger and I'm trained to handle that. Anyway, didn't you warn me to take the bodyguards with me? You did your job. After all, if I escaped, I owe it all to you.'

He stared at her with a strange look, as if she had spoken the words in some forbidden language she didn't understand. His lips were pursed so tight he could hardly get the words out.

'I have things to do,' he said, then turned on his heel and strode away.

Part 7

Terise

1

'Why are you putting that on that side?' Terise asked, conversationally.

The man at the table didn't reply.

'Because if you bend it back that far, it will only…'

The man at the table picked up the blaster. The strut holding the barrel flew across the room and buried itself in the door.

'…ping off again,' she finished. 'Told you. Of course, if you'd put it on the other side…'

Stevan gritted his teeth. 'Will you fuck off and stop blocking my light?'

Terise leaned back against the window, drew her other leg up onto the cill.

'Suit yourself,' she shrugged. 'I was only trying to help.'

She said it in faintly injured tones, though she knew she was being annoying. It wasn't that she didn't like Stevan, she was just nervous, about…well, the truth was they were all on edge. Since the Costas bombing, and the arrival of the Chi!me Ambassador, security had been so tight they had not dared any operations and the combination of tension and boredom was never good for inter-group relations.

That Stevan was even trying to repair the blaster at all was not a healthy sign. Although it was their only Chi!me weapon Marsana had said it had been ancient before Kelya had dropped it and then fallen on it in a shoot-out almost two years before. Like Kelya, it was beyond saving, but unlike her it was valuable and difficult to replace, so they had not thrown it away. Stevan used it, Terise thought, when he wanted to work himself up into a temper, picking away at it for hours until he was on the beginning of the path to the killing rage that would overcome caution. Ladyani had often done the same.

'You're still doing it wrong,' she remarked now. 'Do you want me to show you?'

'Bloody hell, Terise, shut the fuck up!' Stevan tossed the blaster into the corner. 'I'm going to see if Marsana wants a drink.'

The door slammed behind him.

It was just over a week since Terise had arrived in Airdrossa. Marsana had walked her round to the house after the end of his shift, flung back the door crying, 'Look who's here!' He had hardly had to announce it; forewarned of her arrival, she learnt later that the young men had been waiting at the windows for the past hour to see her. They had clustered round her, Vlad and Paulo, Big Agnos and Philip, eager in their adolescent enthusiasm just to be near someone who had been there, with the Caduca.

'Issa says she is proud of you,' she'd said, and she'd seen their eyes widen, slightly, at the fact that she could use the first name. 'Issa says that when you come to the mountains, every one of you will be given a seat of honour for what you have done here in Airdrossa. She sends me to say, she is honoured herself, to be served by you.'

'Tell her she's welcome!' Paulo had shouted, overcome, and they'd all laughed at that. She'd laughed with them, joining their laughter deliberately so they'd like her, and all the while knowing that before they could come to the mountains they'd most likely be dead. They had a saying that the old had weak stomachs.

It was damp on the window cill and her legs were cramping. Stiffly, she pulled herself down and walked to the table. She might as well try her hand at the blaster, she thought. She had an hour before she had to go and really, until then, she had nothing better to do. Stevan always let it infuriate him, raging against something he couldn't control, couldn't defeat, but she always found it rather calming. She liked trying to mend the unmendable. No pressure.

The barrel was a network of scars where it had been welded together, pushed so far out of the shape that the casing would not hold it. She rubbed it diligently with a sanding cloth and screwed half the strut back on. Like that it at least looked like a weapon, they could use it for show, maybe, if they had nothing else. They would have to be desperate… She shook her head to clear the unwelcome thought and, as if she had called, the door opened and Maria, Stevan's woman, poked her head round.

'Hi Terise. Is Stevan not up here? I thought I'd get him a little supper, he hasn't eaten all day.'

'He went out drinking with Marsana.'

'Oh.' Her face fell, and she pulled it, unconvincingly, into a smile. She shrugged, trying to look unconcerned. 'I'll see him later, then.' It seemed to Terise that she'd seen that same smile a thousand times, from the inside. The smile you smiled when you knew in your heart they weren't coming back, and that even if you were wrong this time and the one after that, one day you would be right. She wondered if she should say something to her, offer her some wise words from her unexpected years of experience, but the very fact that she had noticed might shame her. You weren't supposed to be afraid. In any case, she had no answers she could share.

'I'm getting bored up here, fiddling with this junk,' she said instead, lightly. 'I'll just get a drink from the kitchen and then I have to go out.'

Maria, Terise had gathered, had been Stevan's woman for a little over a year, and in the time she had lived with the Airdrossa cell had taken over almost all the work in the house. Marsana, by virtue of his restaurant job, could cook, and had been responsible for this when they were all bachelors, but now maintained that he was too tired after spending all evening at it to do the same all day.

It could not be an easy task, being housekeeper to the seven of them. The house the cell occupied was an old one, in a crumbling district a mile from the centre of the town. It had been converted into flats some time before, but the owner had been able to let none of them, and it had been almost derelict when a ViaVera sympathiser had bought it and allowed the group to use it. He was a businessman, quite successful with a chain of shops, but he had been with them since the early days with Mara. Terise had heard that he had once been a student of Mara's father, but she didn't know if that was true.

The group had rigged up a temporary power supply for the lowest floor from cells hidden in the basement, but they were squatters and squatters were not entitled to buy water. The only fresh water was from a makeshift pump in the tiny central courtyard and it was a long haul to the top, third floor. Downstairs they left all the flat doors open; it was upstairs you went with your own lamp if you wanted to be alone. It all needed occasional cleaning, and Terise, when she watched Maria, thought it was a shame that there was no one else to help her. There was another woman in the group, but no one could ask Anjeta to do anything.

Terise expected her to be in the kitchen when she entered, but her usual chair was empty. Anjeta would spend hours there, plaiting the ends of the rug and singing *The True Road* under her breath while the others pretended not to see her. You would think they hated her, if you didn't know. She watched Maria pass the chair on her way out to the courtyard to draw the water, watched her pluck a strand from the rug and stuff it furtively down the front of her dress. It wasn't easy, living with the dead.

It was a month now since Anjeta had volunteered to die in the cause, and so far, the group had been keeping such a low profile that she had had no opportunity to carry out her wish. Anyone else would have backed out by now, no one would have blamed her if she had decided to volunteer again at a better time, but Anjeta had not. At first they would have tried to treat her normally, even with the extra jollity and backslapping she had seen so many times in camp before a big mission. But there was no big mission, and in the meantime, what could she do? She could not work. How could they ask a martyr to clean a rifle, still less the stove? So she wandered around the house as if she were already a ghost while the others avoided her eyes and picked up small items she had touched as relics when she had passed by.

They were in awe of her and they were jealous of her, for whom the central secret question of their days would soon have an answer, and Terise thought they should throw caution to the winds and find as soon as they could her way to die. *I'll talk to Marsana,* she decided, and immediately felt better, as if she had contributed something. At least she had done some good. She walked to the courtyard door. Maria was swinging on the pump handle.

'Agnos was supposed to have fixed the motor for this, but it never bloody works,' she puffed. 'Can you have a look?'

'Sorry, I'm no hand with motors. I'll mention it to Agnos, but it'll have to be tomorrow. I've got to go out now. Don't worry about supper for me, I won't be back till later.'

Any of the others would just have accepted it, but Maria had been with them only just a year and after all, she was only Stevan's woman.

'Where are you going?' she asked.

Terise shot her a quelling look, harder than she deserved. 'Issa's business,' she replied, shortly. 'If I think you need to know it, I'll let you know.'

Maria dropped her head to the pump handle. Terise stalked out. It was dusty in the courtyard and her mouth felt gritty, the taste of it clinging to her tongue all the way up the street like shame.

She walked into the central district, and while her feet trod the familiar path she tried not to notice where she was going. Think about Anjeta, that was the trick. What could she blow up? There were shuttered shops all around her, merchandise winking at her through the security grilles as their owners finished their late-afternoon meals. They would be opening soon, another half an hour and the street would be bustling again with shoppers. She had seen them so many times, the great ladies of Airdrossa with silver and pearls in their hair, the self-satisfied husbands with their wallets making a bulge in their perfectly-cut suits. Sometimes even Chi!me suits.

They were an obvious target, but they weren't, when it came down to it, a very impressive one. Bomb a shop, kill a few assistants with children to feed, what difference did it make? They were the scum, those people, only the scum that the waves left behind on the sand, ephemeral. Not the important people, the people who really mattered, forever beyond their reach.

Terise turned the corner away from shops and into a wide street of tall, white buildings. This was the government area now, the houses that had been built as homes for merchants become offices for ministers and obscure, secretive agencies. They were quiet as well at this time of day, although behind the closed slats she supposed there must be work going on. None of them were marked. She had no idea what they held; what crimes perpetrated in fire and blood were dreamed up here in the quiet of the rich men's street among the rustle of the trees and the dust under her feet on the pavement.

A transport whined softly past, making her jump. It stopped a little way up the pavement and a small crowd of men came out from one of the buildings to stand around it. Terise slowed her pace, not wanting to draw attention to herself. Another man got out of the front and walked, stiff with self-importance, round to the pavement side. He swung open the passenger door. There was a pause, then a rustle went through the watching men and a woman the colour of the sky stepped out into the street. Terise stopped.

The woman was wearing what Terise supposed must be evening dress, incongruous in the late afternoon sunlight, a cloak of some swirling silver stuff falling from her shoulders like stars. Her hair was piled up on her head and studded with so many points of light it too seemed to glimmer. She held up her long skirt with both hands to step from the transport, hands the perfect, translucent blue of winter mornings.

A man in formal Army uniform leaned forward to receive her, flanked by two from the President's special guards. He took her hand to steady her as she straightened. She lifted her head, the coils of silver catching the sun, and looked straight over the guards, looked straight down the empty street to Terise in the shadow of a doorway, and smiled. It was a momentary smile, a single, tiny flash before it was bent in full force on the general escorting her, but it was there. She was too far away, she couldn't have seen her, but it was there.

Terise pushed herself further into the doorway until they had all gone in. The blue people, Issa called them. She had never seen them, but she knew who this must have been: the Chi!me Ambassador, in the flesh. She had no idea what she was doing there, some sort of official function, she supposed ambassadors spent their lives at them. It wasn't important, she didn't know why she felt it, it was only an irritating delay that she had to wait here until they had gone in before she walked on up the street. There was nothing for Anjeta here, nothing except a story for Maria about clothes, that was all. She pushed herself back out into the street. It was unimportant, she told herself, nothing. She'd looked younger than she would have expected, rich, but honest, somehow. Clear, as if the sky colour of her skin went all the way through.

Around the corner was an anonymous wooden door, the number 11 nailed above it in a red just bright enough to show through the dirt. Terise stood on the opposite pavement and looked at it. Every time she did this, every time she told herself she could walk away. What could they do to her, after all, that they would not already do? She didn't have to be here, she didn't have to. She could turn around, go back to the house, not have to pretend nothing had happened because nothing had. Go back to the camp, see Elenore, see Issa, carry on with the round of her life until one day the lads went out on a mission and Ladyani didn't come back… Terise set her teeth and marched across the road.

Beside the door was an intercom, the labels beside the buttons so faded as to be unreadable. She pressed the third one from the top.

'Yes?' An educated voice crackled out of the speaker. She could not tell if she had heard it before. She took a deep breath and spoke the code phrase into the speaker.

'I've got an appointment with the General,' she said.

2

The receptionist was a young man in CAS uniform.

'So, you're for the General, are you?' he sneered. 'Name?'

The half-second of panic that she'd forgotten the name she used was the same, every time, but she never had.

'Silla.'

'Silla...right...' He ran his finger slowly down his list. 'Silla...'

Where he bent his head, Terise could see the red line on his neck where his collar chafed him. He had shaved that morning but not well, and in amongst the stubble and the dried blood nicks were the remnants of adolescent acne.

'Ah, there you are,' he said. 'Room 212, second floor. Up the stairs, turn right. You understand? Second floor.' He held up his hand to demonstrate. 'Two, one, two.'

His pronunciation was as clear as an elocution prize, his expression disdainful. She knew what he saw, this child in an ill-fitting suit whose family probably spent more money in a week than hers had done in a lifetime. Another peasant woman from the back of beyond, short and squat in her dusty black, greying and wrinkled. The sort of woman who might once have cleaned for his mother, though she would be one step down from a Jeba now. The sort of woman who might only speak dialect, so that he had to shout at her in his percussive Airdrossa accent. She wished for a moment she could put him right, see the fear and revulsion and sneaking curiosity on his face when she told him who she was and what she'd done. He wouldn't despise her then.

'Two, one, two,' she repeated, haltingly. '*Gracias.*' She ducked her head to him respectfully and shuffled to the stairs.

There was another man seated at a little desk outside the door. He gestured her to a seat opposite him. She sat waiting for half an hour, fidgeting on the hard wooden bench and trying hard not to be as discomforted as they intended her to be. They always played games, she knew that. The man peered at his screen, scratching something busily with a stylus. The sun slid slowly down the window, dust motes danced in the beams as they slanted across the floor.

It was never very clean, this building, the abode of men who had more important things to do, although once, leaving, she had seen the Jeba team who were employed to sweep up. You could see the little Jeba marks if you knew where to look, tiny scratches in the window frames or on the skirting boards. Ihanakan had told her once how the whole world was a book to the Jeba, waiting to be written and read. There was one of their marks on the wall just below the top of the bench, she noticed, an oval open at one end with a reed above it. Ihanakan had not said what they meant.

The man glanced at the time display. He tucked his stylus into its holder, very slowly, clicked the windows on the screen closed one after the other. He looked at the time again, counting under his breath. '58, 59, 60. Right.' He shoved his back chair. 'Come this way.'

He pushed the door open and stood holding the top of it so that she had to duck under his arm to go through. It was dark. She took a couple of steps forward, bent over, and as she straightened up, she heard the door slam behind her. A light flicked on, dazzling. Through the sudden glare, she made out the face of another man at another desk.

'Hello Silla,' he said. 'Have a seat.'

'Captain Rosares.' She reached out to pull the chair towards her, but a movement in the back of the room made her stop. As never before there was second man there, older than Rosares, grey-haired with the too-large look of men who are used to a uniform. It was suddenly very cold. 'Who's that?'

'A colleague. Why don't you sit down?'

She let herself be aggrieved, voluble, anything to hide the still pricking of fear.

'No way. I'm not talking with him here. I'm not saying anything. I talk to you, that's the deal, I only talk to you. You want to play silly games, fine, but I'm not staying here if he does.' She could hear her voice shaking and she couldn't stop it. 'Get him out of here.'

Rosares was unruffled. 'I think he'll be staying. Why don't you sit down, Silla? You don't really have much of a choice, do you?'

She could walk out. She could just leave, go back. They might follow her, they might not, but she could shake them whatever they did. She could leave and never come back… She pulled out the chair and sat down.

She always forgot how handsome he was. She remembered the first time she'd come, how taken aback she'd been by his clear blue eyes, his light, smooth skin and jet black hair. She didn't know what she'd been expecting, probably nothing but a faceless shadow on the other side of the table, and she'd sat there and marvelled at his smooth Terran suit and his expensive smile and the sheer urbaneness of it all.

'You know who I am?' she'd asked.

'I know you're from ViaVera. Give me one good reason why I shouldn't have you shot right now.'

'Because you wouldn't know why I've come. I'm not just ViaVera, I know the inner circle. I see the boss, I talk to her every day. I've got a proposition for you. Are you interested? I'll give you everything you want to know, everything you've ever dreamed of knowing, and in return…'

'We'll protect you. Of course we will. You're no good to us

dead.'

'No, that's not enough. I want immunity for Ladyani as well.'

A startled pause, then he'd laughed.

'Ladyani? You must be joking.'

I want him out of ViaVera, free, and safe and alive. Give me that and I'll give you everything, everyone all tied up like a Christmas present with a bow on top.'

'Including the boss?'

She'd swallowed, she still remembered how ridiculously hard it had been to say. 'Even the boss,' she'd managed. 'Just give me him.'

That had been four years ago. Even though she had been thinking about it ever since Issa had told her to go to Airdrossa, she hadn't quite been able to believe it. But he had agreed and for four years she had been his source on ViaVera. She tried to give him as little information as possible, and what effect it had had on ViaVera she did not know. She tried not to wonder.

'So, Silla,' said Rosares. 'What's new?'

She shrugged. 'Not much.'

'How long have you been in Airdrossa?'

'Don't you know?'

'Strange as it may seem, Silla, we don't spend all our time following you around. How long?'

'A few days. A week, maybe.'

'And you have nothing to tell me.'

'We've been pretty quiet.'

'You weren't quiet at the Costas.'

'That was last month. And I'm sure you know who did it without having to ask me.'

He smiled at that. 'True. I don't want to know about the Costas. Let your little group plant their big bombs, I'm not interested in them. Tell me about the Chi!me.'

She'd been shocked, the first time she'd realised the CAS weren't trying to stop the bombings. She'd even queried it once, at the end of a session when Rosares had been in an expansive mood. He'd leaned back in his chair, laughed at her.

'Why should we stop you?' he'd asked. 'Before you started your little campaign, we weren't allowed to even search someone's house unless a judge gave us permission. More budget, no restrictions, bigger army... where's the downside? I don't know who you think you're hurting, but it's not us.'

'Or Desailly?' she'd added, but he hadn't answered that. It was all the game, all the game to them and even though she cared more than they ever would, somehow she was playing too.

'The Chi!me? Big empire, lots of money, blue skin, that kind of thing?'

'Very funny. We know they've made contact with you. We need to know what you're going to do about them. What have they offered you?'

'I don't know. I don't know much about them at all. The boss said...'

'The Caduca.' That was the other man. Terise shot him a glare.

'Yes, the Caduca. The boss said the Chi!me had made contact and we were going to talk to them, see what we could get, but that's all, I don't know anything else. Really.'

The older man snorted.

'Oh come on, Silla, do you expect us to believe that? You're close to the inner circle, that's what you've been telling us. Of course you know something.'

'Tell us what you want from the Chi!me,' said Rosares. 'What do you expect to get from them? What can *they* do for *you*?'

She heard the scorn in his tone for the Chi!me and ViaVera both. She should have been used to it, but somehow this time it made her bristle. She said, unwisely, 'The Chi!me are the most powerful race in the galaxy, what can't they do? They'll do anything we want.'

The older man moved so fast she barely saw him. She felt his hand slap on her face, so hard it knocked her over, and she was on the floor with her leg singing in pain where she'd landed.

'What the fuck…?' she managed to gasp before he hauled her up by her hair. 'Fuck…' He threw her back onto her chair. She held one hand to her throbbing cheek and looked in astonishment at Rosares.

'What the fuck was that for?'

He had never laid a hand on her before, not once in the years she had been coming to him. She expected him to look embarrassed, contrite, apologise for his colleague. At least pretend he needed her goodwill.

'If you don't like it, don't be impertinent,' he said coolly. 'Now, I'll ask you again, what does ViaVera expect to get from the Chi!me?'

'I don't know.'

Rosares signalled with his eyes and the older man moved towards her.

'No, I really don't know,' she repeated hastily. 'I'm not fucking with you, I don't know.'

She felt his eyes meet his colleague's, over her head, and

braced herself for another blow. He seemed to consider it for a moment, then visibly dismissed it, moved on to the more mundane subjects of guerrilla movements that she always covered with him. And even there, there was not much to tell.

'Alright,' he said at last. 'You'd better leave Airdrossa as soon as you can, get back to the camp and wait for instructions. The usual channels.' They used code words in news broadcasts to tell her to come in, although they knew she could not respond quickly. It always had to seem like Issa's idea.

Terise got up. Her cheek was still stinging where the other man had hit her and her leg ached. 'I'll look forward to it,' she said with an edge of sarcasm. Rosares smirked.

'You'd better,' he said. 'From now on, you're going to have to actually do some work.'

'Work? What have I been doing all this time, plaiting my hair?'

His tone was suddenly rough, as if he wanted to scare her.

'You've been fucking with us, that's what you've been doing. You think you can string us along, give us a couple of little titbits when you feel like it and that's it? If you think that's enough, you're going to find out your mistake. You're ours, you belong to us, and you're going to do exactly as we say when we say, or you won't even live to regret it.'

He wasn't managing it. Terise sneered.

'Oh, so you'll have me killed? Try another one, I've heard it.'

'If your friends at ViaVera knew what you've been telling us, we wouldn't have to. You know what they do to traitors, don't you, Silla? You and your nice little friends? We'll do it, don't think we won't. We'll make sure they know everything, *Terise*.'

She gaped at him.

184

'Now get out.'

The other man grabbed her elbow, started pushing her towards the door. For a moment she was too stunned to react. They knew who she was. She had never told them, she had kept that to herself, so that they wouldn't know, but they did know, they knew her name. What else did they know? Rosares must have known all along, but if he knew all along, why reveal it now? She felt a hand gathering material at the back of her neck, ready to throw her out. She clutched hold of the door jamb and twisted herself round.

'What about Ladyani?'

Rosares looked at her stony-faced. 'What about him?'

'If something's going to happen… I mean, if you're… you promised me I could get him out.' She heard her voice rising desperately. 'You promised me immunity for him.'

'I may have done.'

'You may have done! You promised! Are you going to keep it?'

He smiled. 'Maybe, maybe not. You'll just have to do as you're told and hope, won't you?'

'You promised, you fucker, you promised!'

She tried to lunge at him but the man holding her was too strong. He pushed her head back against the wall and kicked her hard in the stomach. She doubled over, retching. Dimly through the pain she heard Rosares.

'You think you have bargaining power here? You think you can get anything you want from us? We're all you've got, don't you understand that? You have no choice, nowhere to go. Do what we say and be grateful and you might not die, *Terise*.'

The other man pushed her out into the corridor and slammed

the door. She sat on the floor of the corridor, feeling sick, while the young man on the door watched her with incurious disdain. He didn't offer to help. After a few deep breaths she managed to get up, collected the ends of her coverall around her and limped away.

3

Terise left the CAS building without even looking where she was going. It was almost dark now, the streetlights making the leaves on the trees shine like gold. It had never been easy, of course it had never been easy. She had never wanted to do it; didn't she feel torn in two every time she came here to betray the group that had been her life for twenty years? Didn't it hurt every time, just like the first? She had done it for Ladyani, for herself when she realised she couldn't wake every morning and wonder if it was the day he died. It was a hard choice but it was enough, if it was for him.

But if it was for nothing, if she was just to betray and betray, simply because by doing so she could be free to betray some more... But what else could she do? She couldn't let them tell Issa and Ladyani, she couldn't. She was trapped and Ladyani was dead and she couldn't see any way out. 'We're all you've got,' Rosares had said, and it was true. She had nothing but them, nothing but them and nothing to bargain with, alone between the sides that were only CAS and ViaVera, on and on and on.

She tripped on an uneven patch of paving, put her hand on the wall of the building beside her to steady herself. She was going back the way she came, she realised, passing the place where she had seen the blue woman, the Chi!me Ambassador, getting out of her transport. Terise had seen aliens before, although not very many, but they had never seemed as other-worldly as the Chi!me woman, as far removed from all of it. She had walked as if her feet were too clean to touch the ground. Which was odd, since she was here to get embroiled in the middle of it, with the peace treaty she was supposed to be making. With the peace treaty...

'What can *they* do for *you*?' Rosares had asked, and his contempt had been distributed evenly between them, the guer-rillas from the hills and the blue people from beyond the stars. She'd told him they could do anything and he'd knocked her down, because it was true. The Chi!me were more powerful than the CAS, more powerful than Desailly, they could do whatever they wanted. While Rosares skulked in his office they were out there, ruling the galaxy, and now one of them was in this street, dancing in a dress that shone like the stars. Terise hitched the hood of her cloak further over her hair and shuf-fled forward, rounding her shoulders. Suddenly, desperately, she had a plan.

Juan Desales was bored and his feet hurt. He'd been on duty all day, had been supposed to be off at dusk except that half the evening squad were sick. He didn't even get the overtime. The Captain said they all had to pull together for the sake of the unit, but when it was all for some stupid function, it was difficult not to mind. He'd had plans tonight, as well. He'd squinted at the party when it first started, but had soon lost interest and sloped back to his post by the back door. Some of the women weren't bad, he supposed, but they were all the same, just rich fucks with too much power and money, wearing posh clothes.

His girl Alana hadn't had a new dress in three years. The last time he'd taken her dancing, she'd told him she'd had her mother send her grandmother's old tablecloth for her to make her costume. If he could get promoted he could get her something; he'd like to now but privates didn't earn much. If he could get to sergeant he could marry her, but the Captain said there wasn't much chance of that. 'You'd better hope she's patient, boy,' he'd say when his boots weren't clean or it had been just too long since he last shaved. Bastard.

A noise in the alley in front of him made him jump. He sprang to attention, trying not to wince at his sore soles in case it was the Captain.

'Who goes there?'

A figure stepped out from the shadow of the wall and shuffled towards him. As it came into the light, he relaxed. It was only a woman, too old to be interesting, flapping along in the black coverall his mother and sister wore when they went outside the house. He put his blaster back down and leant against the wall.

'Hello young man,' the woman said, 'long night?'

Juan grimaced. 'Long enough.'

'Tough, isn't it? Here, have this for energy.' She rummaged in the depths of her cloak and brought out a shiny heba. 'I was bringing it for my Carlos, but he'll never miss it. He never eats the fruit, he thinks I don't notice. Boys, eh? But then you're not so much more than a boy yourself. Your mother coming down with something for you later, is she?' Juan shrugged non-committally, unwilling to admit to anything so embarrassing but aware that she probably was.

'You should be grateful to your mother, she's only trying to look after her son, just like all of us. My Carlos is a waiter in there tonight, and I know he's not supposed to have a break, but I don't like to think of him going all night without anything to eat, not when he's working so hard. He's only fourteen. So I'll just slip in and give him a spot of dinner and I'll be out of your way.'

She smiled at him winningly, but it wasn't really necessary. He sympathised with the absent Carlos, but it didn't occur to him to try to stop her. He was there to keep strangers out, he knew that well enough, but she wasn't a stranger. A woman like his mother, like his sister and Alana would be one day, how could he not know her? He spent his life being bossed by voices like hers, he could no more be rude to her than he could fly.

'Sure,' he mumbled, and shuffled up to the door, to hold it open for her as she went through.

Once inside, Terise slipped through the kitchen as quickly as she dared, muttering something about her boy Carlos to anyone who seemed likely to show any interest in her. The dinner was mostly over, and the kitchen was a whirl of washing-up steam and noise. Waiters rushed to and fro, shifting half-finished platters from one vertiginous pile to the next while their superiors yelled at them, the shouts periodically drowned out by clatter as they tottered to the floor. No one looked twice at Terise. The kitchen led out into a wide hallway, at the other end of which a set of double doors led into the ballroom.

With the kitchen door swung shut behind her it was very

189

quiet, the only sound the music filtering through the gap between the doors. Through the middle of the doors she could get a blur of colour, but it was far too exposed a position to stay for long enough to make anything out. From the side she could see a little more round the hinge, but there was no cover and if anyone came out of the ballroom she would be discovered immediately. It was one thing to be bringing dinner to Carlos, however illicit, quite another to be spying on the Chi!me Ambassador.

She pressed her eye to the crack. It was no good, the field of vision was not wide enough for anything more than an impression of light and movement as the dancers swung past. But she could see that all along one wall were tall windows opening out onto a darkened terrace. There would be bushes on the terrace, there were curtains at the windows, places to hide. Relieved, she hurried back down the corridor.

A door past the kitchen entrance led out into the gardens, and it was unguarded. She installed herself comfortably behind a bush about halfway along the ballroom wall. It wasn't long before she spotted her; with her blue skin, she was difficult to miss. She was quite a good dancer for an alien, she'd obviously learnt all the steps beforehand. The tune was an Airdrossa version of an old country dance. At the familiar melody, Terise could almost wish she was dancing too, spinning and swaying like the Ambassador in the arms of a slight, dark-haired man in grey. It took her a minute to realise it was Desailly, and then she felt sick again.

Desailly spun the Chi!me woman around and caught her, deftly, as she swung back into his arms.

'This one doesn't give much time for conversation, does it?' he said as she turned away for the next spin.

'Maybe it's deliberate.'

'Planning, you mean? Not by me. I only want to ask you...' The dancers split into two lines, then the partners stepped into the middle to come back together '...how you're getting on with ViaVera really. Are they co-operating at all? You can tell me.'

She smiled sharply at him. 'What makes you think that?'

'It's unofficial, I promise. I just want to know.'

Into the lines again, round the next couple and back together.

'You do know. It's going very...' Turn, step, turn back '... nicely, thank you. The meeting is almost arranged.'

'And that's all you're going to say?'

Swing out, swing back, turn and step away.

'If you think I'd say anything to you, even if it was true, you must think me very stupid, Petrus Desailly,' she said.

They spun away from the lines, him holding her hand. She really was quite pretty, especially in the balldress, and she danced well. He smiled at her in his turn.

'On the contrary, I don't think you're stupid at all.'

Du'Fairosay had studied hard to master all the Ty dances, and he was uneasily aware that the effort showed. Quila was making a much better fist of it, he thought, spinning forward and back with Desailly, flirting with him as if she had been doing it all her life. He thought Chi!me women weren't supposed to know what flirting was. His partner, the minister for culture, wriggled in his arms. 'So, how are you enjoying our great city of Airdrossa?' she asked. She slipped forward, turned and spun under his lifted arm.

'Fine. Thank you.' Quila was further up the line than them, he could only just see the edge of her dress. It was a Terran fashion, the dress, but it suited her.

'You have visited our famous art galleries? People from all over Benan come to see Ty art in Airdrossa.'

Turn, step, spin, step, together and apart again.

'No. Sorry. I don't have much time. I'd like to.'

He watched Quila, swirling in a cloud of white light. The minister, stepping around him, followed his gaze. Her voice was sharp.

'You are bodyguard as well as assistant? Or you are just very devoted to your mistress? I think that's nice.'

Momentarily, he was disconcerted. Eventually he said, stiffly, 'it's my job,' but he had mistimed it, and by the time he had got the words out she was already spinning away.

Par'Lennan liked dancing, if only it could be with pretty women. There were some lookers here tonight, a couple of them previous conquests. He winked at them knowingly as he twirled past. He didn't think much of his present partner. He knew he had to do these things but Desailly's wife! She was so small he could see the white parting in her hair where it was beginning to thin, and she never had a word to say for herself in public. He had to dance with her, but that didn't mean he had to talk to her. At least she was easy to spin. She winced a little when he trod on her foot, but she should have been paying attention. They were all too elaborate, these Airdrossa dances, what counted was the verve. One, two, step, or blast it, was it the other way? Maybe, if this didn't finish too late, he would pop down to that little bar on Quarter Street, see some real action. He was entitled, after all, to some fun.

Quila danced the next dance with General Morales. It was a slow one, suitable to his age. He didn't approve of talking to terrorists, he told her. In his day you knew what to do with them, you just shot them and none of this messing around. She'd understand when she was older, it was the only language they'd understand. Shooting was too good for 'em.

Quila nodded in the right places, using the Terran gesture, but she could tell he wasn't really talking to her. Over his shoulder she could see Desailly dancing with his wife, Par'Lennan with a giggly blonde and Du'Fairosay with the wife of the general. He was better at it than Par'Lennan, better than her. It occurred to her briefly to feel guilty about how little she had practised, but she put it aside. She could step where she had to go as well as anyone there, and that was all that mattered. It was difficult not to feel that style was not paramount, but really, how you did it meant nothing at all in the end.

'Don't you agree, my dear?' the General bellowed at her. She smiled and nodded, dipped and smiled as the music spun her on.

It was past midnight when they finally left. Terise had taken up her position at the front door an hour before; she was so cold she could hardly move by the time she heard them coming down the steps towards their transport. The Ambassador said something in what she supposed was their language. It sounded light, teasing. The man, her aide, replied stolidly and the Ambassador laughed. She came down the bottom step and stood there, waiting, and Terise came out of the shadows and into the light.

The aide whipped out a blaster and tried to pull the Ambassador down. She shook him off, cried out something that sounded like, '*Ni'cha!*', high like a bird call, and went on in Terran. 'It's alright. What do you want?'

She was younger than her, the Ambassador. Up close her skin looked like eggshells, with lighter lines on her hands and forearms, silver tracery set in flesh.

'I want to talk to you. I need your help.' It rang false in her own ears, ridiculous.

The aide sneered. His Terran was more precise than the Ambassador's but less fluent. 'Why should you think the Ambassador would help you? What do you want, anyway?'

Terise licked her dry lips.

'I'm from ViaVera.'

The Ambassador's eyes were suddenly very wide.

'Tell me what you want.'

Terise looked around at the empty street.

'Not here. Is there somewhere we can go?'

The Ambassador glanced at the aide. 'No!' he burst out. 'You can't take her back there! Are you mad?'

The Ambassador looked uncomfortable. 'Fairo,' she said reprovingly, and went on in Chi!me so that Terise couldn't understand. Whatever the argument was, she seemed to win it.

'Come on,' she said.

Terise and the Ambassador got into the transport and the man called Fairo shut the door.

Part 8

Quila

They took the ViaVera woman straight up to Quila's room and left her there waiting while they went back outside to the street.

'This is insane,' Du'Fairosay said. 'Have you any idea…'

'Obviously not,' Quila snapped back. 'Your objection is noted, Fairo, will you leave it now? I need to know if you can block the bugs in that room.'

He considered. 'For how long?'

'A couple of hours, no more.'

'Yes, I can scramble them, it's not a problem. I've got the kit set up in my room, so I know it works. Terran bugging isn't very sophisticated.'

'Good,' she said, then the meaning of the rest of his sentence hit home to her. 'Why did you fix the stuff in your room? You wouldn't say anything in there worth hearing, surely?'

He shrugged.

'I like to sleep in private.'

Quila couldn't think of a suitable response. 'Oh,' she said. 'We'd better go back up.'

When she came back into the room the ViaVera woman was sitting exactly where they'd left her, hunched on the end of the bed with her black cloak pulled back from her head. They watched each other in wary silence until Du'Fairosay came in behind them with his terminal in his hand. He counted down silently with the other; 3...2...1

'All right, it's clear.'

The ViaVera woman smiled. 'That's a good trick,' she said.

Du'Fairosay looked startled. 'Your good opinion is noted,' he said stiffly, then smiled briefly back.

'So,' said Quila, cutting across them. 'You said you wanted my help? How can I help you?'

The ViaVera woman looked at the floor, struggling. Then she collected herself, took a breath and said, with only the faintest quiver, 'By saving someone's life.'

'That's a laudable objective, but I need to know more than that. Who is the someone, another guerrilla?'

The woman smiled slightly at the word and Quila was fleetingly proud at having remembered to say it.

'Yes, another guerrilla. My...my man. I need to get him out, I need to get him away from it all, he'll die if he doesn't. I can get him away, but he's wanted, he's got a price on his head whole cities would envy. I need immunity for him, and believe me when I say I will do anything for you if you'll help me.'

'I don't know what you could do...'

'I could give you information. You want to know what ViaVera are thinking? I'm part of the inner circle, I can tell you. I can tell you things you didn't dream you wanted to know, you'll never have a source as close to the boss as me. But I need your guarantee, that you'll help him.'

Her words were rapid, tripping over themselves, desperate. Quila felt for her. She said gently,

'It's true information is always valuable, but you must

understand, I can't just protect anyone I choose. I have to give accounts of my actions, justify myself to my superiors. Do you understand? I can't just agree without knowing anything about him, or about you. My name is Quila, I don't even know yours.'

The woman bit her lip. She was older than her, Quila thought, though by how much she couldn't tell, and her face was criss-crossed with lines carved by the sun and the wind. Above her sun-tanned cheeks her eyes were unexpectedly olive; a clear green like a pool so that she saw for a sudden moment what she would have looked like as a child.

'My name is Terise,' she said.

Behind her right shoulder, Du'Fairosay made a noise, quickly silenced. The woman, Terise, stared at him.

'You knew I was here? Have you…?' Her eyes widened. 'Was it *you* who were following me?'

Out of the corner of her eye, Quila could sense Du'Fairosay start to answer. Over whatever he was going to reply, she said decisively, 'no, of course not. We would never do anything like that.'

Terise nodded, Quila didn't know her well enough to tell if she looked convinced.

'And your man is…?'

'Ladyani.' She smiled. 'I'm sure you've heard of him.'

Du'Fairosay said 'One of ViaVera's leaders. He has a reputation for being both mad and dangerous.'

Terise glared at him, but she didn't comment. 'He and I joined ViaVera together when we were young,' she said.

A long time ago, that must have been, Quila thought. If she had that past with anyone, she would want to save them too. She watched the woman sitting on her bed. It was so strange, actually having a terrorist, one of the feared ViaVera, here in her room, picking at the fringe of her cloak. She probably shouldn't ask, but she couldn't resist.

'Why did you join?'

Terise shrugged.

'When I heard what they did to our place, our people, I didn't have a choice. Do you want to know the story? Ladyani and I came from the same village. It was just a little place by the sea north of Camino: on a clear day you could see right across the bay to Trentama. My father was a fisherman and his father was the mechanic, and he used to sit behind me in the priest's classroom and flick things at my hair. He didn't care about learning, Ladyani, all he wanted was to get back in his father's workshop, get on with the job. They had this big pit in the middle of the floor, you know? There weren't a boat in the village that hadn't been over that one time or another, with Ladyani and his father stood underneath.

'The children didn't stay in school for very long, usually by the time you were ten or eleven you'd be working and there just wouldn't be time. But, I don't know, I always liked it. The priest used to give me extra lessons, after the others had gone, and my father wouldn't take a girl on the boat, so I just carried on. When I was fourteen, the priest wrote to some friend of his in Biterra, and the friend told him about this scholarship that poor kids could go for. It was once a year, and there was one scholarship, can you imagine, one, for everyone in the whole of Ty who couldn't afford to pay, but if you got it, you went to college in the city and everything was paid, even your food. You've heard of things like that? I can tell your friend has.'

Quila looked round, but Du'Fairosay's face was expressionless, betraying nothing.

'They take one poor kid a year and make out it evens the scales, it makes it all alright that that one kid has the chance to fit in and be ashamed of where they came from all their life.'

Du'Fairosay opened his mouth as if to say something, but turned away to the window instead.

'Well, so,' Terise went on, 'I didn't think that then. I suppose I thought it was exciting, like everyone does, a chance to get out of the village. And it was an excuse to go on studying and it was better than getting married. My parents didn't mind, so I tried for it when I was sixteen, and I got it.'

Quila smiled. 'Out of everyone in Benan Ty? That was impressive.'

Terise shrugged again. 'It was a long time ago. Everyone was really worried for me. It was strange, they'd all been so pleased when I was taking the exam, and then when I'd won they were all, 'Oh, be careful, we wish you weren't going, we'll pray for you.' They'd have done better to keep their prayers for themselves. I'd had a thing with Ladyani that summer, nothing serious, but I gave him the address of the place I was staying, just in case he wanted to write. I went off to college in Camino two days before my seventeenth birthday and I didn't think I'd see him again.'

'How did you like the college?'

'It was alright, I suppose. It wasn't what I thought it would be like, I remember I could just feel myself being remade, every day. I suppose if I'd stayed there I'd be a good little civil servant now, wondering what to do about the ViaVera problem. But instead, when I'd been there about two months, Ladyani came and found me. He'd walked all the way from the sea to Camino

199

with no map and no money and nothing but the clothes he stood up in. He woke me up by banging on my window at four in the morning. I let him in, sat him down and he told me…'

She stopped.

'What?'

'That everyone was dead.'

'Everyone?'

'Everyone. The whole village. The men, the women, the children, the animals, even the boats smashed on the beaches and left to burn. It's what they do.'

'But…why? What was the point?'

'It was punishment, you see. They'd killed a CAS man. Oh, not deliberately, not like that, they hadn't even known who he was. Ladyani said a stranger had come ashore in a little boat for the night, and got in an argument with Big Tel in the cantina about some stupid game the men had been playing that afternoon. The way Ladyani told it, he threw his drink over Tel, Tel hit him and he knocked his head on the edge of the bar and went down stone dead. It was when they were going through his pockets that they found his ID.

'Ladyani said Tel got up with it in his hand and went straight off to turn himself in. He didn't say a word, didn't even stop to say goodbye to his wife. They hung him on a hook outside the police station in Saibre and he took three days dying, but that wasn't enough. CAS men are worth more than other people, you see; one death doesn't quite cut it.

'Ladyani was in the pit when they came, underneath my father's boat. They searched through all the buildings, dragging people out, but they didn't find him. He had to stand there for two hours and listen to it, listen to them shooting and killing, raping the women, chasing the children down so they could cut them in pieces… I'd like to say I can't imagine what it was like, but I can. They were everyone he knew in the world.'

She looked across at Du'Fairosay, in his place by the window. 'If he is mad, or dangerous, he has cause.

'He climbed out while they were finishing and ran away before they fired the workshop. He said the last thing he saw from the hilltop were all the boats tied up along the shoreline, burning so bright it looked like the sand was reflecting the sun. I don't know why he came to me. He said he remembered where I was and he thought I should know. In the morning when he said he was going to find ViaVera and join them, I said I'd come and join them too. We walked our shoes to ribbons getting to them and when we limped in, the first thing Mara said was…'

'Mara? You knew Mara Karne?' A young woman with an ancient weapon, black hair falling round her shoulders like a curtain. Was that another woman in the group behind her? She would never see the image again to check.

'Of course I knew her. I was her friend. I was there when she died. When I said I was part of the inner circle, I wasn't lying to you. Anything you want to know, I can tell you.'

'I believe you. But the thing is, I don't need information.'

'Don't you? Are you sure?'

'Yes, quite sure. I know what you're thinking, but I'm not here to spy on you or outwit you. I'm here to make peace between ViaVera and the government – what I need is honesty, far more than clandestine information. I need you to talk to each other, and that's where you can help.' She leaned forward. 'You say you're part of the inner circle? Do you influence what they do? What your leader does?'

'Does anyone? Well, I suppose so. Yes. It's not easy but, yes, I have as much influence as anyone.'

'Then that's what you can do. You get ViaVera to the talks table with the government and whatever happens at the talks, I'll get you and Ladyani immunity. You'll be able to get him out whenever you want, no one will stop you, you have my word.'

'You'd do all that, just for the talks? You don't want to know anything?'

'That's right.'

'Are you a fool or a saint, do you think?'

Quila laughed.

'We don't have saints on Chi!me, but maybe here I can be both. We'll see what happens to the talks. But I mean what I say. You get your people to the talks table and you'll have everything you want, I promise. And now you'd better let Du'Fairosay take you outside, before someone comes to find out what's wrong with the transmitter.' She stood up. 'It was nice to meet you, Terise.' To her surprise, she found she meant it.

'How do I contact you?'

'You mean all that secret codes over the networks stuff? You don't. I'll see you at the talks, remember?'

'Yeah. I'll look forward to it.' She took Quila's hand and gripped it, quite hard, for a second before releasing. 'Thank you. And it was nice to meet you too.'

Part 9

Terise

As she reached the last village the rain started. It had been cold enough for her shawl since Ultima, there was nothing she could do except pull the folds closer round her face and plod on. The chari flowers had all been harvested now, leaving only brown stalks where the blooms had been. They would be drying in the barns below, waiting for shipping to Ultima or Chaireddan for half the price it took to grow them. There were no growers to be seen today, no farmers tilling their fields or Jeba on the higher slopes, nothing but the clouds lowering over the shoulder of the hill and the grey scarves of rain.

The wind swooped through the trees like the sea at high tide, tossing handfuls of brown leaves onto her shoulders as she climbed the ridge. The trees grew more closely at the top, away from the fields, crowding around the road that was suddenly just a path through the trunks, the beginning of the great forest that stretched from here through the mountains to the northern sea. She was back in ViaVera territory now, and as if to welcome her the rain began to fall with renewed persistence through the leaves. Despite the cover, the path was already muddy and treacherous. Terise suppressed a sigh and struggled on.

It was just beginning to get dark when she passed the two

trees leaning together and turned left for the last long push up the hill to the camp. Of the two young men on guard at the gate, she could almost remember the name of one of them, while the other was somehow familiar but she couldn't recall having met him before. From their attitudes it was clear they knew her, though she went through the password as a matter of form and they answered as they should. It was always a good idea to teach the young ones good practice, she had learned that. She thought as they opened the gate that they looked at her oddly, but with the rain and the gloom it was difficult to say. She raised her hand in thanks and passed through.

The first thing she noticed was the quiet. Like any small town, the camp was usually a bustling place, guerrillas coming and going on a hundred different tasks, laughing and shouting and arguing as they did so. Now that it was evening, the young ones should be coming back from the practice field with the training weapons on their shoulders, the women preparing the dinner and calling to them. But all there was, was the sound of the rain. Terise wiped the water from her face and went on up into the centre.

Most the huts were closed and shuttered, the thin plumes of smoke from their chimneys the only indication that they were not deserted. She walked past an open door and inside saw several men, talking in low voices. They broke off as she came into view but said nothing, just watched her pass with expressions it was too dark to read. She was sure she would have known them, but none of them called out. She picked up her pace. When they'd come back from Santos it had been a hot, hot day like the whole world was burning, but when Mara died it had been like this.

They'd landed in the dark to the north of the camp and come the rest of the way on foot. There'd been a cold wind from the east and it had been raining then as well, hard sharp drops with a presage of winter in them, stinging where they fell. She had walked in behind Ladyani and everyone had stood at the doors of the huts and watched them, just watched them without any sound at all, because there were no words for what they had to say. Like now; because she knew what had to have happened now.

A woman stepped out of a hut ahead of her, carrying a basket. She peered through the murk.

'Elenore?'

Elenore stopped dead.

'Terise.'

She was too far away for Terise to hear her clearly, but neither of them seemed able to come closer.

'You're back, then.'

'Yes. What's happened?' She could hardly make herself form the words. 'It's Ladyani, isn't it?'

'What? I can't hear you.'

She shouted above the noise of the rain, exorcising.

'Ladyani's dead.'

'What? No, of course not.' There was still this absurd distance between them, the news that Terise didn't know.

'Then what? Is it Issa? Is she alright?'

'Yes, she's fine. You mean you don't know?'

Terise screeched in frustration.

'Know what?'

'The Airdrossa group. They tried to blow up a ministry and it went wrong. Stevan's dead, Marsana's caught, they're rounding

205

up supporters all through the city now. The whole network's gone. You mean you didn't know?'

She thought of Marsana as she had last seen him, walking away from the transport stop with his waiter's uniform gleaming from its wash. She thought of Stevan playing with the broken blaster, of Maria, waiting for this. Had the survivors come running back to the house, had they rushed in, calling? Had they told her gently, or over their shoulders as they packed up the weapons, no time for more? Or had the first thing she'd known about it been when the CAS kicked down the door?

She could see them now, in a room in the ministry building like the ones she'd known, telling her how it had been. Did they expect her to cry? She'd had the tears waiting so many years they'd dried behind her lids. For a moment, she was standing at the top of the stairs in the Airdrossa house, looking down the well to the ground floor and the CAS men running in. Then she blinked and the rain fell into her eyes, ran down her face, uncaring. At least she wasn't waiting any more.

'I didn't know. I've been three weeks on the road, I didn't even know they were planning anything.' *I didn't mean a ministry, I meant a shop or something, a soft target, they knew that, surely. And I meant Anjeta should be alone*. She could justify herself, but it was safer to deny any knowledge at all. 'They knew security was tight, they should never have tried...' She let herself tail off. 'I had no idea.'

Elenore put the basket down on the mud and ran up to her.

'I knew it wouldn't be your fault,' she said as she embraced her. 'But I'm so glad you're alright, I was worried.' She pulled back a little. 'And you're soaked. Come and get dried off, and you can tell me all about Airdrossa.'

'I'd better go and find Issa first, tell her I'm back.'

'She never thought...'

'No, I'm sure. But I should still see her. I'll come by after dinner, maybe, if you want.'

Elenore dropped her hands. 'Of course. I'll see you later.'

She gave Terise a final pat on the back and watched as she went on up the path to the palace.

Marsana had come to the transport stop with her on his way to his shift. He'd stood on the edge of the pavement, rocking his heels back and forward in the gutter as the transports buzzed past, looking dutiful and faintly bored.

'You don't have to wait with me, you know. Really, it might be ages yet. You might as well go.'

'I don't mind,' he'd said. 'After you've come all that way it's the least I can do.'

'I would have thought you'd've had enough of me by now.'

'Not at all! We might not always be the easiest bunch to get on with, but you're always welcome. I mean, anyone would be, but I'm always glad it's you.'

She'd looked away, embarrassed.

'I've been thinking about what you said about Anjeta,' he went on. 'I think you're right, it has to be soon, I don't think they can take much more of it. If we have to be extra careful then we'll be extra careful.'

'I'm glad to hear it.' It was far too public a place for a discussion. Someone pushed past her, and she felt a light touch on her bag. She grabbed it, whirling round, but there was no one there, only a small group of Jeba, walking away.

Marsana stepped back onto the pavement.

'There's your transport,' he said. He put his arms around her. She rested her head for a moment against the clean, uncomplicated, detergent smell of his jacket, then pushed herself away.

'See you again, Terise,' he said.

'What a nice young man,' the woman next to her had remarked as they stowed their bags above their seats. 'Your son?'

The shutters on all the palace windows were closed against the rain. The door was also shut, but under the porch, sheltered by the overhanging roof, was Ihanakan. As she came up he made no movement at first, then, as if remembering a custom foreign to him, he raised one hand and waved. Terise waved back, feeling absurdly happy to see him.

'She iss waiting for you,' he said as she reached him. 'I will take your pack while you go in.'

She shrugged the bag from her shoulder and let it fall to the ground between them.

'I'm sure she can wait a little longer. How are you?'

Ihanakan had knelt to pick the bag up, his long fingers stroking the top back into place. For a moment it seemed as if he was taking something small and white from it, but that was surely only the way the light flickered in the dusk. He looked down at his hand for a moment, considering.

'I am...good. Very good.'

'And everyone at home, in your village, they are well?' She remembered the slopes on the way down from the camp, the Jeba and the skull on the pole. 'I saw some of your people on my way to Ultima, with a sheep's head on a pole, I wondered what they were doing?'

'They are all well, thank you.' He paused, as if he would

rather ignore the question entirely, then went on. 'It iss inter-essting that you have seen what you have seen. It iss a calling ritual that my people do sometimess.'

'Sometimes?'

'At timess like these. Issa iss waiting for you.' He clearly did not want to answer more questions about it. As was often the case with Jeban religion, it was not for outsiders to know.

'Oh, one of those rituals, was it? Never mind, I can take a hint.' She straightened up, smiling. 'It's good to see you again, Ihanakan. I'll talk to you later.'

He made a clicking noise with his tongue, something she had learned was an acknowledgement, then translated. 'Yess.'

Terise shut the palace door behind her and peered into the dim interior. There was a light on the first-floor landing, but nothing below. 'Issa?' she called. 'Issa?'

She heard footsteps, then Issa's head appeared at the head of the stairs, looking over the banisters into the hall.

'Terise! You're back! You had a good trip, come up and tell me all about it.'

'A good trip? Are you sure about that? You have heard the news from Airdrossa?'

'Oh yes, well,' she waived a dismissive arm, 'It's to be expected. Now come up, I'm getting a crick in my neck talking to you down there.'

'So,' Issa went on as Terise seated herself on the cushions in her room, 'you're feeling guilty about Stevan and the others, are you?'

'No, not really. I didn't tell them to attack a ministry, it's their own fault for being reckless, something I warned them about more than once. I know it's not my fault, but still… I told Marsana they needed to do something with Anjeta, if I hadn't been there, they'd still…'

'Who's Anjeta?'

'The suicide…' She remembered Issa's preferred term. 'The dedicated one. I don't know if she was one of the others who were killed, I hope she was. It had been weeks since she'd dedicated herself and they hadn't had a chance to do anything and she was still there, in the house, making them all edgy. They had to do something with her, I know, but…'

'But you feel guilty because they did.' Issa regarded her with interest, head on one side. 'You should have guessed what they were going to do, and stopped them.'

'Something like that.' Terise tried to smile, but it came out more like a sigh. 'So, not a very successful trip. Maybe,' she added, feeling the sudden freedom that she could, 'you should send someone else next time.'

'No, Terise. No.' Issa leaned forward, holding her gaze. 'You did exactly what you should have done, exactly what I wanted you to. I couldn't send anyone else to do what you do. Your trips to Airdrossa were so important for all of us.' A smile lurked for a moment at the corners of her mouth and was gone again as she went on, seriously, 'You can be sure, you were where I needed you to be, and I'm pleased, very pleased with you.'

Terise didn't know what to say. 'Thank you,' she faltered.

'Though you're right, it's all different now, I don't know if you'll need to go again.'

'Now the group's on the run? But there'll be another, won't there? We can't lose Airdrossa.'

'What? Oh,' Issa said vaguely, 'no, of course not. We'll have to see. Now, it's nearly dinnertime and I haven't been to the hall since you went away. Will you do my hair for me?'

Terise finished braiding Issa's hair with just enough time to slip back to her own hut and change before dinner. She hadn't asked Issa where Ladyani was, somehow she never liked talking to Issa about Ladyani, although she was sure that she, out of everyone, would have had the answer. She would probably see him at dinner and she wanted to look nice for him, get out of her road-splashed clothes and into something a little more enticing. She hurried up the path to the door.

The power was out again in their part of the camp and there was just a single candle burning, so dim she hadn't seen until she opened the door that there was any light at all. The rough walls were covered with flickering shadows, the bed, the chest in one corner where they kept their clothes, and Ladyani, standing in the centre of the room with a blaster over one shoulder. Terise stopped. It was suddenly difficult to breathe.

'Lad,' she said.

'I heard you were back.'

'Yes.' She tried a smile. 'Here I am.'

His face cracked into a grin. 'I'm so glad you're back.'

Terise let go of the door. 'Oh Lad,' she said as his arms went round her and the blaster fell to the floor, 'so am I.'

They were late for dinner. They walked into the hall together as the top table was being served. Terise's hair was tangled all down her back and the shirt she had travelled in was missing a button where Ladyani had not been able to undo it quickly enough. There were whistles and laughter as they made their way up to their places, but Ladyani had her hand and he was smiling at her, laughing at her as she blushed like the girl he'd brought there years before. He kept his hand on her knee all through the meal and she could feel the warmth spreading through her. He filled her cup up for her and she drank it, an incongruous happiness jumping inside her, like hope.

Part 10

Quila

The Montcada gardens were famous. The hotel lobby was full of them, screens listing their attractions in the wet season and the dry, pictures cast onto the walls behind reception showing the flowers in full, lurid bloom. She found them very different from the night gardens of Iristade; from moth wings, silver against the memory of cheers. Even though it was nearly the end of the season it was still very hot in Airdrossa. She and Du'Fairosay strolled along the fountain path, the jets forming a watery arch over their heads. She could hear the faint hiss of the mechanism as they passed each one, and the cries of children playing on the distant lawns. The sun bounced, iridescent, off the droplets on her arms.

'You must tell Par'Lennan how pleased I am with his work,' she said after a while, 'in case I don't get a chance to. And yours of course, setting up this meeting. Everyone on this world said ViaVera would never agree, after all, and you've both proved them wrong. You should be proud of yourselves.'

She looked sideways at Du'Fairosay, but his face betrayed little emotion. If anything, he seemed slightly uncomfortable at the praise.

'We only try to serve,' he said.

'Well, of course, but that doesn't mean I can't recognise

when you serve well, and you have.' She wanted to tell him he should not defray deserved congratulation out of bashfulness, but it occurred to her suddenly that she was always lecturing Du'Fairosay.

'I expect Par'Lennan told you I've finally got an interview with the President arranged? I have to wait three weeks, if you can believe it, but I'm looking forward to seeing what he's like. For all that Desailly has all the power, he's still the President, after all. It will be interesting to find what's actually in the hollow centre. Do you want to come? I'm sure I can arrange it if you do.' Du'Fairosay spread his hands no. 'Ah well, I suppose you have enough to be getting on with.'

They reached the end of the fountains and started back the other way.

'I wonder how much Terise did to get this agreement,' Quila mused.

Du'Fairosay turned his head towards her. 'Terise?'

'You know, the ViaVera woman. She said she would try to get them to come to the meeting, and now they are. I just wonder if she had anything to do with it.'

'If she was who she said she was, I'm sure she would have moved the sea and the stars to get you what you wanted,' he said. 'For what she was promised, anyone would.'

It sounded sour to her. She shot him a narrow look. In the month since her meeting with Terise, they had somehow not found the time to discuss it. At the depth of his rancour, she wondered suddenly if she had been avoiding it.

'Do you think I shouldn't have done it, then? I should have sent her away?'

He averted his gaze, pinch-lipped.

'No. You were correct.'

'Come on, Fairo. Be honest with me, at least. Clearly you don't think I was correct, or you wouldn't have spoken in the way that you did. Do you think I should have had nothing to do with her? But then who knows what the consequences would have been? She promised that she would help us get our meeting, and we have it. We don't know how much that was her doing, but we can't deny we've got what we want. I don't think there are any guarantees that we would have done otherwise.'

'No, I know.'

'Then, what?'

He was silent for a moment.

'I just think it's a high price to pay, that's all. I don't think it's one UP, or Chi!me, can afford.'

'A price? You mean her man? The amnesty?'

'I've read about that man Ladyani. Do you know what he's done? He's been the head of ViaVera operations for more than twenty years, he's a mass murderer. If the Chi!me let him go, if we seem to condone those actions, we will never win. The Chi!me have to be seen to be just, we can't seem not to know about the people he's killed. We can't turn a blind eye, not when the universe is watching us. We have to be seen to do justice. You remember the train to Santos? The way those people died? They say they stood round and laughed, have you heard that? That's what they say of him.'

'I didn't know you knew so much about him. You should have said something.'

'Would you have wanted to hear?'

The fountains pattered on the ground around them. She couldn't think of a reply to that.

After a while, he added, stiffly, 'I'm sorry if I have been disrespectful.'

'No, Fairo, it's alright.' She sighed. Some things should not be said, some things should be simply understood; the gap between intention and action, possible and desirable, promise and result. She had not wanted to have to explain this, but she could see it was necessary if she was to keep his trust. Trust was so important between them; she owed him an explanation.

'You're not wrong, to say what you've said. You're right, some crimes can't be forgiven, can't be wiped out however much we might want to. And no crimes can be wiped out because it is expedient to do so.'

Terise would be back at ViaVera now, with the man Ladyani. She couldn't picture her there. It was very possible that she would never see her again, never know if she tried to help them, or have any chance to try to keep the promise she made. It still felt strange.

'Sometimes you have to undertake one thing and mean another,' she heard herself go on. 'I had to agree to her request to help Ladyani, because if I hadn't, she would not have helped us. And I did mean, I do mean to help him, in a way. If we take him, we will not terminate him out of hand, we will not torture him and put him on show in the way I am sure Desailly would love to do. I would see he got a fair trial and a fair ending. I think in the circumstances that is all she could reasonably expect from us, whatever was said. If it wasn't made exactly clear, well, sometimes these things have to be done. It's not ideal, it's distasteful, even, but it's what we have to do to bring peace to these people.'

She looked out through the scarves of water, over the park.

Nearby a few young couples were scattered over the grass; beyond them, a group of children played a shrieking game with sticks and a brightly-coloured ball.

'I remember once when I was very young, maybe only two cycles, my class at school were taken on a trip to one of the outer worlds. You maybe came too old for them, but we always had trips when we were little, it's how we learnt. I don't remember the name of the world. I think we only went to part of it, one continent, maybe. It was a mass of plants, I remember that, leaves so thick you had to hack your way through to follow paths that people had cleared only the day before, that was how fast they grew. It was an incredibly fertile place, but it wasn't any use. No one could live there, it was so dense it might as well have been a desert. We camped there overnight, and on the second day we carried on slashing our way through the plants to the edge of the sea where we were being picked up.

'It was about midday when we came to a sort of clearing, not really clear, but easier, somewhere where the plants didn't press quite so close around you, where you could look about without the leaves getting in your face. I remember there were all these bumps, hummocks really, and I asked my teacher what they were. They were ruins of homes, he said. They were the houses of the people who had lived there off the land when it was farmland, not jungle, and prospered there for a long time. Then a war came, and bad men came, and they were being killed and couldn't keep their farms any longer, and the jungle came creeping back and took it all so that no one could live there. A whole continent, lost, because the law was lost.'

One of the children fell over, screaming. The others picked it up.

217

'That's what we're doing, you and I, that's what we're defending. All the people who need to know that they are safe in their homes and their fields, who need to know there is a system of justice, of law and order. A gardener that can keep the weeds from the beds and make it bloom in beautiful harmony as it should again. It's not the most heroic calling, maybe, it's not one for which we ever receive much thanks, but that's not the point. As they used to say when I was first training at IntPro, if you're here for the honour and glory, you shouldn't be here. Gardeners are never the aristocrats, never the rich or the well-respected, but they are necessary, the most necessary sometimes of all. We are the gardeners. It's all we are, and all we should hope to be.'

His face was unreadable. 'Don't you ever think you should leave them to their own gardens? Sav - Serve yourself and leave them to find their own way? It would be easier.'

'Well, of course it would, but we aren't here because things are easy. We had the luck, the tremendous good luck to be Chi!me, and we have to use that luck to help other people who were born into much worse situations than we. If it means we have to be humble, then we have to remember whom we serve, and what it is we are set to achieve. And if it means that we have to dissemble to get where we need to be then so be it, because men like Ladyani are a blight that cannot be allowed to go free, no matter how useful their women may be to us.' Her throat felt oddly thick. She swallowed. 'However much we may like their women, however much we may sympathise.'

The sun beat down through the arcs of water, shining in her eyes. She stopped at the edge of the path and let the droplets run down her back.

'It has to be about the law,' she said. 'In the end, there's nothing else.'

The jets hissed in the air around her. Du'Fairosay looked at her with an expression she couldn't interpret.

'We'd better be getting back to the embassy,' he said, neutrally. 'We told Par'Lennan we wouldn't be long, he'll be wondering where we are.'

Part 11

Terise

Beyond the heba grove, the land sloped steeply down to the river. It was narrow and fast-flowing, full of stones. The kitchen girls called it The Rushing One. They would take water sometimes from it when the dry season was at its height, but otherwise they used it seldom. The fish were small and spiny, all bones among shreds of translucent flesh, not worth the trouble of catching. But it was a place to go.

Terise picked her way carefully through the ferns on the bank. It was three weeks, almost four, since she had returned from Airdrossa. The torpor of a hot afternoon, the grubby, fugitive heat of the wet season lay over the camp like a blanket, men lounging under the trees or in the hut doorways, hats hiding their eyes; the women nowhere to be seen. It was difficult to work in this weather, she told herself, but she knew it wasn't the only reason.

Ever since she'd come back it had been different. In the past, a setback like the loss of Marsana's group would have been a spur for renewed action, something burning inside them all calling for vengeance. But now there was nothing being planned, no new initiatives even thought of. The odd escapee from Airdrossa came in and was made welcome, but the questioning sounded desultory to her ears. None of it really mattered any more, it seemed, the old tale was over. They were all just lying in the shade, waiting.

She'd been in the palace, in the little room beside the council chamber, sorting through some clothes of Issa's. Issa was always hard on her clothes, they seldom survived long enough for her to tire of them. She'd been working out which could be mended and which only given away when she heard them come in. Ladyani and Issa.

She couldn't hear what they said, only the clear tones of Issa's laugh and the low rumble from Ladyani, the way he sounded from deep in his throat when he was pleased. They went on up the stairs to Issa's chamber and closed the door. He had seemed happier recently than he had for a long time, calmer. She'd looked in his eyes sometimes and almost been sure it was the other Ladyani, the one only she remembered, looking back. There was no way he could know, but she wondered if somehow he sensed there might at last be a way out.

It had taken her two weeks to broach the subject of the Chi!me meeting with Issa. She'd tried to think of a way of bringing it up naturally, but there was never an opportunity. In the end, she had asked her straight.

'I heard in Airdrossa there's some talk of a meeting between us and Desailly. There's some Chi!me Ambassador who's arranging it. Are you going to go?'

She'd struggled to keep her voice casual. Issa had regarded her with kindly disdain, as if from a great height. 'You think we should be talking, then, do you, Terise? I daresay it can be arranged.'

Ladyani had been having a lot of meetings with Issa, up in her room. He was her commander, her righthand man, it was natural that they would have things to discuss that could not be aired in front of the others. It was necessary. She had lived with military discipline since she was seventeen years old, she understood these things. She knew it was necessary. Terise had slammed Issa's clothes back into the trunk and gone out.

There was a shadow under the trees by the water's edge. At first she couldn't make out what it was, but as she drew closer it resolved itself into Ihanakan, sitting on the bank with a rough fishing rod in his hand. She made no special effort to be quiet, but perhaps she still had the knack of moving silently. At any event, it was only when her shadow fell across his back that he looked up, unconcerned.

'Afternoon,' she said. 'Do you mind if I join you?'

'The river iss for all, I think.' He waved his hand briefly over the bank. 'Ssit.'

She slipped off her shoes and, dropping to the edge of the ferns, dangled her toes in the water.

'So, have you caught anything?' She said it with a smile, teasing; his rod looked so primitive it would have been difficult to catch anything in a fishpond, let alone the Rusher. Ihanakan lifted up the basket beside him so that she could see the handful of tiny, tentacled creatures nestling in the bottom.

'Lovely,' she said, pulling a face. 'You're not really going to eat them, are you?'

'To my people, these are, how do you ssay…delicacy. It iss a great day when there are *siekehana*.'

'Really? Fair enough, I suppose. It depends what you're used to. In my village, because it was by the sea, we always had huge fish, as big as the kitchen table. My mother used to smoke them, we could never get through them before they went off, else. I haven't had a good fish for years, I've almost forgotten what they taste like. Maybe I should try your, what was it, sikihana.'

'Among my people, we also ssay, he who will not eat anything there iss to eat iss doomed to be alwayss hungry,' Ihanakan remarked.

'I bet your mother used to say that to you when you wouldn't finish your wriggly things.'

He gave a little snort, the nearest the Jeba ever got to a laugh.

'It iss ssomething to be told to children, yess. I remember you ssay before your father wass fisherman. My people also ssay to children how once, long ago, we too used to ssail the sseass in boats and bring back the huge fish, the fish ass big ass two men, and we would feast for a week when the shipss came in. We tell them while they eat *siekehana*, take their minds off it, yess?' He snorted again, softly.

She didn't ask why they had stopped sailing; she didn't have to. That would have been when the settlers came from Benan, people like her family, and took the land and sea together from them. For something to say, she commented, 'I didn't think you were still here. I thought you would have gone back to your village by now. Or have you gone and come back?'

She looked sideways at the Jeban, sitting still on the bank beside her with the fishing rod held loosely between his long hands.

'My kinsmen think ass you ssay,' he said at length. 'They think I have been long enough with the *frickadele* this sseason and I should come back. But I do not go. I am in the correct place, here. I sstay ass long ass I need.'

She said, teasingly, 'For the fishing?' and he answered her as if it was a serious question.

'For, ass you ssay, the fishing. But alsso for the *kabila*.'

From her talks with Ihanakan over the years, Terise had learnt a number of Jeban words, not least the derogative *frickadele*, 'people who are not us'. But she had never heard this one.

'Kabeela?'

'It iss…' he hesitated. 'It iss…the time before.'

'Before? Before what?'

'That iss what you do not know. It iss… when a day iss like any other day and the people go about all the thingss they would normally do, and yet there iss a feeling on the wind like there iss ssomething that will happen, and then in the evening one person startss the, how you ssay, holy dance, and ass you follow you look back on the day and you ssee, like footprintss on the earth, all the sstepss of the people in the day were in the shape of dance; then that time, that day before the dance, that iss *kabila*. *Kabila* iss when you do not know what you are waiting for, but you move ass you must do, be in the place you must take.'

She thought of the guerrillas stretched out asleep in their doorways, inertia hanging between the huts like fog. Once, when she was a child, her father's boat had nearly been wrecked. She remembered how her mother had thrown a shawl over her head and gone out into the storm with the other women to watch for him, and how when the door opened at last she'd crept out of bed to listen while he'd told his story.

He said they'd seen the storm gathering a long time before it hit, the black clouds massing out to sea while they were still in bright sunshine, but the tide had been too strong for them to power away from it. For an hour all they could do was sit and watch it crawl up the sky towards them, not knowing if they would ever come out. Her mother had made him a hot spirit drink to warm him and had not asked him how he had felt, waiting. He had not been the kind of man who would have answered.

'Well,' she said, trying to sound relaxed, 'I suppose it's a long time since we had a dance, we've been too busy, I suppose, and have forgotten how. You'll have to show us some Jeban dances, if we have one.'

He turned to look at her, his eyes wide and opaque and very alien.

'There iss alwayss a dance,' he said.

Terise climbed carefully through the fading light back up the hill to the orchard. She had sat for a long time with Ihanakan, watching as he caught the tiny, spiny things that lived in the river, not speaking. You often didn't talk much with Ihanakan. You could tell him things and he would seem to listen, but always, when you felt you were getting closest to him there would be that barrier, that moment of strangeness when you would see not Ihanakan but a Jeban, who was not your kind and whom you would never really understand.

'Alright, so explain it to me, this kabeela,' she'd said. 'How do you know where you have to be? How do you know you need to be here?'

'I know. I am certain. It iss not a thing for explaining, it iss knowledge merely.'

'So what do you do while you wait?'

'Make ready. Arrange your affairss. Listen to the wind.' He'd paused, then held up his rod. His face was as solemn as it ever was.

'And fish,' he'd said.

Part 12

Du'Fairosay

Mario Agana, personal assistant to Petrus Desailly, looked at the clock on the bottom of his terminal screen and noted with a sigh that it was already twenty to eleven. He glared at the flashing reminders and the reminders, not cowed, gazed back unperturbed. 'Maybe he'll be late,' he thought, hopefully. He knew he wouldn't be.

Agana had worked for Desailly for a little less than a year, about the time it took for people to stop saying how impressive it was he had got the job and start to watch to see what he would do next. Not that there was any doubt about that, of course. He had it all planned out. He often said he couldn't remember a time when he hadn't wanted to be in politics, and it was almost true.

When he was very small, he'd wanted to be a gardener, following old Nūno through the damp green fronds of his grandfather's garden in Santana like an acolyte, but he'd soon grown out of that. Politics was in his blood, handed down like the name from his grandfather, who'd been Santana's mayor for twenty years, and a long-dead ancestor who once, back on Terra, had been a president. The ancestor's picture had hung on the wall in the dining room, the features disappeared into black mould, and little Mario had replaced them in his mind with his own. He knew what he wanted.

He'd known what he wanted when he was sent away to school in Airdrossa, known it with such certainty he had hardly even cried. He'd known it when he'd got into Santa Maria college, the best on the planet, and when he'd graduated sixth in his year and persuaded his mother to fund him making tea for no pay in the agriculture office, to learn. And when he and his best friend Damien had gone for the same job in Desailly's private office, he'd heard himself mention in crisp clear tones to his interview panel how Damien had a problem with drink and a loose tongue with prostitutes and he'd known it then, as well.

He hadn't seen Damien for years, he was probably still there, making the tea. You had to choose your friends for the job you wanted, not the job you had. It wasn't very moral, maybe, but everyone knew that morals didn't really come into it. He hadn't been back to Santana either, his mother guilt-tripped him about her advancing age every time he made his duty call. Since it had been Sept Karne's home town, it didn't do to remind people of the connection.

Sometimes, waking to a clear Airdrossa sky, his bones would remember warm wet air lying on skin like a flannel, pink flowers pushing through the slats across the window and insects calling to each other through the garden, but that was all. His secretaries complained that he kept his office too hot when it was raining, but he had excised the south-western sibilance from his voice at school long ago. Now he spoke in the dry tones of the professional everywhere on the continent, shaded at important moments like everyone else's with Desailly's Chaireddan twang.

The communicator on his desk buzzed and he flicked it on.

'Yes?'

'Mr Agana,' his current secretary, Adéla, announced. 'He's here.'

Ten minutes early. 'I could really do without this, this morning,' he said, resigned, and she giggled. 'Shall I tell him to walk round the corner and back?'

'Tempting…but no, better not. Show him up, gorgeous.'

'Charmer.' She giggled again. 'Anything for you.'

He sat scratching the side of his hand, until he noticed and slapped his other hand down flat on the desk. It was absurd to be nervous, excited. He had seen aliens before, plenty of them, he had seen the Chi!me Ambassador and the special envoy more times than he could count. It didn't do to be at a disadvantage, the alien would have met plenty of Terrans, after all. The alien had probably been meeting Terrans all his life, and if he, Mario, had never actually met a Chi!me in his turn, he didn't have to show it. There was a knock at the door and Adéla swayed in. She held the door open with her hips and let the alien walk past her. 'Du'Fairosay,' she said with a show of indifference. 'I'm just going to get him a drink.'

'No, thank you. I don't want anything.'

It spoke Terran perfectly, a little high-pitched, but otherwise with hardly a trace of accent, cool and clipped. *Typical*, Agana thought. 'Thank you, Adéla,' he said. She tossed her head and let the door bang at her departure.

The alien sat down and looked at him. The blue skin was disconcerting but only that; only slightly different, like paint that someone might put on for a party. The eyes were worse, dark and closed so that you couldn't tell what it was thinking, or if there was anyone behind there to think at all.

'Agana, right?' it said. 'Du'Fairosay. Pleased to meet you.'

It held out a hand, as it did it every day. Agana took it. It felt light and slightly dry, like his own.

'Shall we get on? We've got a lot to get through.'

The tone was efficient, with an energy driving behind the words that was immediately, reflexively familiar.

'Sure,' Agana said.

'I understand you have the location of the meeting confirmed?'

'Yes, that's right. My secretary has recorded the directions for you, no doubt you'll want to check them yourself…'

'Of course, but if in the meantime you had a map?'

'You're sitting at it.' Agana permitted himself a slight smirk. That would give the alien something to think about. They might not be Chi!me, but they were not exactly Jeba, either. He passed his hand lightly over the surface of the desk and the contours of Benan Ty sprung faintly glittering into 3D life under his palm. The alien gazed at it. Agana could almost believe he looked impressed.

'As you know,' he went on, gesturing with one finger, 'the meeting place is here, at a place called Cairn Fields. See it? In the south of North Province, east of Chaireddan but south of Ultima. I know it's as far south as ViaVera would agree to come, but it's not too bad from our point of view. You'll note it's directly north of Biterra, and there's a good road running almost all the way. It will make travelling much easier. It's a good choice.'

'We do our research. I assume you've started the checks of the field?'

'I've had people crawling all over that field and the village for the past two weeks. I promise you, by the time of the meeting there won't be a gnat on a fern that I won't know the business of.' Du'Fairosay smiled. Agana added, 'Seriously, I can personally guarantee that there are no booby traps in that field. It's clean.'

'Good. The Ambassador will be pleased to hear it. Now, about transport…'

'Well, the heavy stuff, the tents, tables, equipment and so on, that can all be taken up ahead of time. Like I said, we've got a crew up there now round the clock, so there's no problem with setting things up early. That way, the dignitaries can travel light and have an easier trip.'

'About how long will it take?'

'To get to Cairn? Well, it's not as quick as if we'd been able to use aircraft, but of course we had to agree a no-fly zone with ViaVera, so that's out. But, as I said, there's a good road from Biterra almost all the way, and there'll be a tube laid on to Biterra, so it shouldn't be more than the best part of a day. We thought the Ambassador would travel up with the Presidential party on the day before the meeting, if that is acceptable? The tents are very comfortable, and they'll want to be rested. Of course, if she wants to make other arrangements I can…'

'No, that's fine. The Ambassador will be delighted to accompany them.'

'And of course there will be the usual press corps with the party. As far as I know there are no journalists embedded with ViaVera, but you never know. I would suggest that the ceremonial handshake for the screen is at the end, not at the beginning of the meeting though, we really don't know how amenable ViaVera are going to be to anything.'

'I agree. But I'm not sure about the presence of reporters.

I've seen your press and I have to say, I am not impressed. It won't do anyone any good if they dress up the whole meeting, or denigrate it just to feed the people's appetites for scandal.' His voice took on a faintly lofty air. 'At UP, we would issue our own report to the broadcasters, we would never let them compose it.'

Agana allowed himself a smirk. 'Ah, but you misunderstand the relationship of the government and the press. It's true we can't issue our own statements, we have to allow them to say what they want to say, but you can be assured that all the reporters who travel with us will want to show and say exactly what we would want them to show and say, no more and no less, entirely of their own volition. It's a little thing we call influence. You should try it.'

'Thanks, I think I'll leave it to the experts.' Du'Fairosay smiled drily. 'But, if you can confirm that there will be no negative coverage I'll accept the reporters have to come along. I suppose your people have to hear about it somehow.'

'Exactly, and we have nothing to hide except whatever we want to hide, which they will do for us automatically. Neat, huh?

'Now, about security. We've agreed that there will only be ten personnel per side in the meeting itself, and they will not be armed. As you know, the security is to be provided by neutral guards hired for the occasion, and I understand that your envoy's office is dealing with that side of things?' Du'Fairosay waved his hand in assent.

'Now, our intelligence is that there is unlikely to be a problem in the meeting itself, since both sides will be disarmed and both will have their most important people there, although we will have the security guards keep a cordon around the field just to be sure. We think any problem will come either before or after. Obviously the security of the party travelling will be handled by the President's guards, but I assume that the Ambassador will also want a squad of personal guards, both for the journey and the meeting? I can arrange for six of our best – '

'No.'

'I'm sorry?'

'The Ambassador will not require a Ty bodyguard. We will arrange our own security.'

Agana stared at Du'Fairosay in puzzlement. 'Well, you can, of course,' he began, 'but wouldn't it be better…'

'I have had experience of Ty security, when I hired Ty bodyguards for the Ambassador and she was nearly killed when they ran away under fire. In the streets of Airdrossa, in broad daylight, while she was returning from seeing Desailly! I do not intend to repeat the mistake. The Ambassador's security will be provided by Chi!me guards.'

'Well, of course, that incident was most regrettable and those responsible have been disciplined…' He was mumbling. He pulled himself up, took a breath. 'But you have the right to arrange any security you choose, of course. That will be no problem. If you let me know how many guards the Ambassador will be bringing, I will arrange the seating on the train accordingly and let you have the passes.'

Du'Fairosay looked gracious. 'Thank you. Now, about armaments, I understand there might be a problem?'

Agana rolled his eyes. 'You could say that,' he said, rueful. 'The idiots down at Espada, they've had the order for the new carriers for months and they leave it till now to tell us they won't be ready. Programming problems, they say. They didn't even have the courtesy to let us know, I had to call them for the delivery date before I found out. It's not a problem, of course, we have plenty of older stock we can use, but we did want everything to be the best.'

'So in fact the answer might be not to use Espada at all?' It was said straightfaced, but the intent was clear. Agana permitted himself a short laugh.

'Against Espada I cannot possibly comment,' he said. 'But if you have a suggestion, I'd be glad to hear it.'

'I think,' Du'Fairosay said slowly, 'that you will find yourselves more than adequately equipped with Chi!me carriers in time for the meeting, and blasters too. Call it a little gift in recognition of friendship.'

'Really? That's marvellous, I mean, it would really...does the President know?'

'I haven't told Mr Desailly yet. I thought I would leave that to you. Credit where credit is deserved, after all, I know that doesn't come too often.'

'And that's the truth.' Agana looked at his watch. 'It's nearly lunchtime. Shall I call Adéla for something to eat?'

'Won't she be busy?'

'You've obviously never had your own secretary. You, my friend, are important. She's probably listening right outside. Watch. Adéla!' he called, raising his voice. On cue, the door swung immediately open.

They looked at each other, suppressing laughter, across the table. The lights from the map danced over their faces, brown and blue, casting the skin into shadow so that from where Adéla stood in the doorway, they looked exactly alike.

Part 13

Terise

Terise stood in the doorway of the palace and surveyed the crowd. It was a clear day but windy; even in the sheltered square their blue and green scarves flapped and twisted on each gust. They looked like seabirds, she thought, swooping over cliffs, the swift lines of movement and the stillness beneath. The stillness of every member of ViaVera in the base camp, listening to Issa.

She could always hold them when she needed to, even when she was a tiny child. She must look like little more than that now, so thin and small in her habitual green, hardly human; their strength in weakness, their Caduca. Ladyani had taught her the words but she was the one who could speak them, who could take his plans and make them holy. She had always been able to do that.

'Comrades,' she said. The others used 'brothers and sisters', but it was understood that Issa never would. 'I've asked you to come here to listen to me because I have to tell you something very important, something that will change everything. Some of you will have heard that we have been in contact with the blue people, the Chi!me. Their envoy is here on Ty to set up a meeting between us and the government, to help us settle our differences.' The sneer in her voice was clear and a rumble of laughter spread around the square. Every eye was fixed on her. In the shadow of the church porch, Terise caught a glimpse of Ihanakan, apparently as intent as the rest. 'To make peace. Well, we can show them what we think of their peace.'

She'd told the council they could not lose. That had been over a week ago, when the waiting ended, and even though they had debated it several times since, no one had been able to come up with any convincing arguments against it. Marius had been suspicious, Roberto and Sario cautious, Wolf detached as he always took care to be until the decision had been made. That was to be expected and Ladyani had had all the answers for them. But Terise, watching from her usual corner, had seen the excitement glimmering under the harsh experience in their faces.

It had been so long since they had done something really big, so long since they had had more than the occasional success-ful bombing to set against the years of attrition and gradual, grinding defeat. Airdrossa was the last of them. It had not had to be, but it was. They had sat in the camp and known, every one of them, every day, that the old way was over. They had lain, listless, outside their huts, wandered down to the river because they had not known what they could do next. They had waited for Issa to show them and now she had. How could they reject it? What would they have to replace it with? They had worked for so many years and had grown too old for long-term solutions.

'The Chi!me say they're here to bring peace,' cried Issa to the crowd, 'but that's a lie. They've lied to Desailly, and like a fool he's bought it. They've lied to everyone, but they can't lie to me. Do you know why they're here? They want this bit of space for themselves, to serve them. When Desailly gets to be President he'll sell us to Terra and they don't want that. They want to get rid of Desailly and they think we're the ones to do it. So we're going to go to the meeting, but we'll let our blasters do the talking. Through the Chi!me we've got a big new shipment, better stuff than we've ever had before, and we're going to use it. They've given us the opportunity by setting up this meeting and they've promised us that they'll stand off while we do what we have to do. And what do we have to do?'

'The Chi!me want Desailly gone, that's the bottom line,' Ladyani had said. 'They don't care how it's done, but they can't do it themselves. They're the big UP guys, after all, they might rule the galaxy, but they have some sort of reputation, if only to their people back home. It's how they work, they never go in straight if they can go in crooked, always through someone else. There's loads of worlds they've done it on, you can look it up. They want to use us and we should let ourselves be used.

'So what if they have their own agenda? So do we! They want Desailly gone, we want Desailly gone, our interests as far as that are the same. We get rid of him for them, they'll show their gratitude and when the Chi!me are grateful, they really are grateful. They need someone to run this place for them, and who better than us? This is big, this is our chance. No more skulking in the highlands, waiting for our time to come, this is it. Make no mistake, if we do this right, come next year we won't be fighting the government, we will be the government.'

'Under the Chi!me,' Marius had objected.

'Yes, under the Chi!me. They're not exactly going to let us loose, are they? Not immediately, anyway. But there are ways, governments have ways of getting what they want. Don't we know it? If we accept the Chi!me for now, we can deal with them later. Pretend to be compliant now, and then we can shock them when we show just how strong we are, when it's too late for them. Brothers, we have to be canny here. This is high politics, this is where we want to be. They are the Chi!me, yes. They are very powerful, very rich. But we, we are ViaVera.' His eyes had been shining. 'We are the true road, we know the way. Once we have what we want from them, we can defeat them, because we have passion and that's the one thing they lack.'

'What do we have to do?' Issa repeated to the square. 'We have to kill Desailly. That's all we have to do and then the Chi!me will help us get everything we've ever wanted. It's there, all that we've fought and died for, right in front of us and all we have to do is take it.'

She held it for a beat, assessing.

'You know, I've been thinking ever since the Chi!me first came to us, what would Mara have done? She'd want us to get the scumbag that killed her, no doubt about that, but also she would want us to win this way. She always reached out to people, however different they were from us, she always said that even the most unlikely people have a use. Well, the Chi!me are the most unlikely people and they have a use. For the sake of everything Mara died for, we should let them think they can make use of us. I say we go for it, I say we take their weapons and we go to their meeting and we kill Desailly and we take back our country.' Pause, beat. She raised her arms, holding them out as if she could embrace them all. 'What do you say?'

The cheer, predictably, was deafening.

Issa smiled. 'Good,' she said when it had at last died down. 'We leave in the morning. You'll get your instructions tonight and no one is to leave camp until we're ready to go.'

We can't lose, Terise thought behind her. *The Chi!me will back us. I won't need the pardon now. No more spying. I wonder if this is what she meant, when she told me to get them to the meeting? I've kept my word, she might keep hers. It doesn't matter, we'll be in Airdrossa by Christmas, I won't have to get him out.* There was something strangely desolate in the idea, but she brushed it aside. *I won't have to get him out, it will all be alright,* she told herself. *I won't have to do any more deals, I can be whole again. It will be alright.*

She knew that Issa wanted her with her; the packing was already half done. She watched as the guerrillas clattered out in clumps, their excited chatter rising from the square like birdsong. Ihanakan detached himself from the wall of the church and slipped up to Issa. Terise couldn't hear most of what they said, only his last few words. 'My people are in place and we will bring you word, honoured lady.' He turned to go and, raising his head, caught Terise's eye where she leant against the door frame. He did not acknowledge her, merely looked for a long moment before moving away. He looked taller than usual and his skin shone bright green as if there were a lamp lit inside it. She supposed that even Ihanakan was excited too.

They left the next morning in the rain. The main party comprised Issa, Terise, Ladyani and ten of his most experienced squad as a guard. Fifty others, under the command of Wolf and Marius, were to travel down with them as far as the edge of the hills and would then be led to the meeting place via secret ways by Ihanakan and his people.

They could not prepare the ground beforehand, Issa had said, as it was certain that the government would check it. The security at the meeting would be tight, that was the agreement, and no weapons on either side would be allowed in. But the Chi!me had arranged the security and they would keep the government forces back while allowing the fifty-man squad of ViaVera to get in. With their Chi!me weapons, and the element of surprise, it should be enough. The Chi!me-hired guards would be looking the other way.

As they rounded the bend in the track, Terise looked back. The camp was still and huddled under wisps of cloud. If everything went well, she might not see it again. Roberto and Sario would be ordered to break it up and bring the rest of the guerrillas south. For a while there would be the huts as a reminder of their presence, but then the villagers would take the materials they wanted and the forest would eat them and there would be nothing to show they had ever been there at all. It felt almost as if she would miss it. She sighed, and Ladyani swung round to investigate.

'What?'

'Oh, nothing much. I was just thinking, in a few years you wouldn't even know the camp existed.'

He considered this. 'I don't know. There's a few babies in the villages might give you a clue.'

She pulled a face at him. 'Well, I suppose there is always that.'

He slapped her encouragingly on the upper arm and length-ened his stride to catch up with Issa, out in front with one of the Jeba who had come in that morning. Behind the party, the camp faded into the cloaking rain.

Part 14

Quila

In the presidential palace, above the second staircase, was a ceiling which was nearly two hundred years old. Quila's guide, a young guard with a single officer's stripe on his sleeve, took care to point it out. It had been in the first palace, back when the colony had been founded, and had been the only part of the upper level to survive when the building was stormed by the army thirty years later. They had built the new palace up around it, and here it still was.

They stopped halfway up the steps to admire it. It was Neo Neo Classical, the guide said, a very important Terran style at the height of the Empire. It showed a middle-aged Terran woman, dressed rather inadequately in pale coloured draperies, seated on a cloud against a lowering sky. In one hand she held an ear of a withered yellow plant, her other was stretched out in front of her.

She was, the guide said, an ancient Terran goddess of fertility. She was reaching out across the plaster for her daughter, trapped by eating fruit given her by the King of the Underworld. The daughter had once been on the other side of the stairs. Some people thought that at the top of the next flight a third painting had shown them reunited, but that was all gone. The goddess's pink features were contorted in anguish, her plump arm lifting over the swirled paint sky into nothing. Quila asked, 'Did she get her daughter back, in the story?' but it was not the current religion and the guide did not know.

Almost because of the absence of anything to worry about, she was nervous about this interview with the President. It was, of course, strictly a formality, all the arrangements had been made weeks ago with Desailly and his people and in two days she would be leaving for the summit meeting. She had been given to understand that the President did not permit long visits, she would probably be in and out in little more than the time it would take to greet him. He was an old man and all she had to do was tolerate him for a little while.

This wing of the palace was full of mid-afternoon torpor, dozing in its courtyard in the sun. No hurrying footsteps echoed in the marble corridors, no terminals whirred in the shuttered offices on either side. Unlike the previous occasions when she had been to see Desailly in the other wing, she and the guide could have been the only people in the place. Quila twitched the shoulders of her best jacket straight and followed the guide up the stairs.

He had them put his chair in the centre of the room. They had not intended to, they had had a desk put in the corner for him to sit behind. It was better that the Ambassador did not see the hover chair, they said, but he had no truck with that. Juan Gutierrez had been and done a great many things in his life and he had never apologised for any of them. 'Whether I can walk or not, I am still the President,' he had shouted, and they had murmured back to him, soothingly, 'yes, yes, you are still the President.'

Petrus had ordered them to humour him, like he did. He used to hate that. 'Don't humour me, damn it!' he would yell, and Petrus would laugh and show his honest face behind his politician's facade. But he was so tired now, so tired, it was too difficult to fight it any more. He was sinking into pillows and soft, soothing voices, struggling for the last time, drowning.

They had put him into his best coat, the military uniform with the general's insignia and the medals of his youth drawn up in ranks across his chest. That one was for the revolt in Terra Nueve, that one the space battle with the pirates on the other side of Benan. The one on the end was for keeping order in Kayro, the year the rains failed. The bottom line was honorific, medals he had given himself, mostly, to commemorate this or that. He could hardly remember what. They had been necessary to impress people, to make a statement. He supposed the Chi!me Ambassador would be as impressed as anyone else.

The sun fell, slanting, across the room from the wide windows. He watched the dust motes dancing across the beams. In a little while it would be dazzling, but he was stranded in the centre of the floor where there was nothing within reach to draw the curtains. He could call, of course. 'If you had sat at the desk, you would have had the remote,' they would say, as if to a small child, chiding. He sat still.

There were footsteps outside in the corridor, a whispered confabulation. They thought he was deaf because he was old. The door opened to admit a corporal in the uniform of the Presidential guards. He advanced just far enough into the room to be heard and clicked his heels together precisely. An exemplary young man, who should be promoted. He couldn't remember his name.

'Sir, may I present Ar'Quila, Ambassador of the United Planets, sir.' He bowed.

Juan Gutierrez waved a hand. 'Thank you.'

The corporal, still slightly bent from his bow, shuffled out of the line of the door. The Ambassador started the long walk into the room.

It gave him a chance to study her. They were strange people, these Chi!me. Not so much the skin colour, he'd been around in his time and he'd seen far too many things to be fazed by blue skin, but their thinness. He'd always liked a woman with a bit of meat on her bones; these Chi!me were so slender they looked as if a gust of wind would topple them. Yet they were the ones with the wealth and the power, these tiny creatures that looked like Jeba. He had always thought, watching them, that the blue people were some slave race, impersonating the rulers of the universe. He smiled at the thought of it, of springing up from his chair and shouting, 'I've unmasked you, I've got the joke, will the real Chi!me please come out!'

The Ambassador returned the smile. She stopped a few feet away from him. The corporal hurried up behind her with a seat.

'Mr President,' she said. She held her hands out in front of her, palm up, then bent her head and sat. 'I trust you are well?'

'As well as I ever am.'

'In that case, I am even more grateful to you for granting this interview. I did feel it was very important that I come to you in person before the meeting with ViaVera. Of course, all the details have been worked out with Mr Desailly and his office, but I do think your blessing, as President, in such an important matter is vital. I am sure you agree.'

She had a very smooth voice, the Ambassador, lilting in and out without leaving a trace.

'ViaVera, eh? Bunch of murderous gangsters, the lot of them. Petrus is too soft on them. Always has some plan. Should all be shot, that's what I say. Never mind the messing around, should all be shot.'

'I gather there are many who feel that way. I remember your General…Morales, is it, saying something very similar to me not many weeks ago. But shooting, as I am sure you know, only leaves the bereaved to shoot and be shot in their turn. We have another way. That's why these talks are so important. If we can open up a dialogue between you and ViaVera, we may be able to end this without violence. Find out what the real problems are and address them. I am sure they are just as anxious as you for this all to end.'

She was a talker, all right, a politician. He'd never been a politician, never trusted words like he trusted a blaster. She talked and talked like she was enchanted with them, like they could change the world outside just by being said. He remembered people like that.

'I remember the first time I ever heard Sept Karne speak,' he said. He had the vague impression that he had interrupted her, but that didn't matter. 'In Keltan, it was, the year the rains failed in Kayro. Must be, ooh, thirty years ago now, more. He was just a professor then, no one special. They'd asked him to come and speak at one of the big price demonstrations. I'll never forget it. There was a whole line of other people waiting their turn and he went on. It was an hour, hour and half and these people with all their little speeches prepared were standing there, hanging on every word.' He chuckled. 'Some of them must have been so mad inside, but they had to keep on looking keen or the crowd would have throttled them else. They couldn't have held them like he could, though. Never been no one could hold a crowd like Sept Karne.'

'I've never heard any of his speeches,' the Ambassador said. 'I've only ever heard his daughter.'

'Mara? Ah, yes, well, Mara was a different thing altogether. Sept Karne, he was all for reform. Make it fairer, make the system work better, whinge along with the whingers, that was his line. He could tell you for hours everything that was wrong with everything. He always knew every detail, how much you had to pay for a doctor in Ultima, price of chari flowers. He was a professor, you know? Details were what he did. Now, Mara, she never wanted to reform anything. Smash it up and throw it away, that was more her thing.' His cracked voice lifted, high and mocking. 'The glorious revolution of the people!' He burst into a paroxism of coughing.

When it had subsided, he remarked, 'I saw her once, you know. We let them out, her and her mother, to bury him. Her mother was all tears and screaming, you know how women do. Always was a silly woman, Harana. Pregnant, too, right out to here, looked like she was going to drop it right in the grave. Mara was only a girl then, sixteen maybe, but she didn't cry, not her. She didn't touch her mother either, she just stood there, and I thought, *that's a hard little bitch.*' In a voice tinged with admiration, he added, 'And I was right. Reform wasn't enough for her, not after what happened to her daddy. Her and the other one, but her I never saw...' He stopped as another bout of coughing shook him.

'Well,' said the Ambassador, 'I hope that will convince you, if nothing else, that it's worth giving peace a try. Isn't it time to talk?'

She was persistent, he would give her that. 'Oh, you can talk all you want,' he laughed, 'if they'll listen! I'll give you my blessing, if that's what you want, if that's what Petrus sent you for. You can go and have your talks, my dear, go and have as many talks as you like. If you can make them listen!'

'I'll make them listen.'

She got up and stood there looking down at him. There was something stern in her expression, something cold and unbending on the small, thin face.

'I don't apologise,' he said, suddenly. 'I'm not ashamed.'

'I know. You kill each other and kill each other and after all of it you're not ashamed and neither are they. And we are not ashamed of making you talk to each other and finding out how similar your interests really are. Thank you for your time, Mr President.'

She turned and walked to the door, her heels clicking sharply on the tiles. The sun from the windows licked the brow of his cap. He fumbled in his lap for the button which would bring them running to take him to bed.

The same guard took her back through the silent halls to where Par'Lennan's staff would pick her up with the transport. Even she, unwilling as she was to hide behind an entourage, had seen that she could not walk to her presidential audience on her own. The drawback, of course, was that it did mean more waiting around. The guard, apologetic, had offered her a seat and a drink, but she preferred to wait outside. The desolate air was less pronounced on the ground floor, where at least half of the rooms off the corridor seemed to be in use, but it was still not somewhere she wanted to linger.

She stared across the broad expanse of the courtyard, shielding her eyes from the sun. A tall, slight figure rounded the corner of the building, heading for the top gate. Silhouetted against the sinking light, he was still unmistakeable.

'Fairo!' she called. 'Over here.'

He was walking quite fast towards the gate and she was sure he paused. She saw his foot suspended for a moment off the ground, saw his head turn. Then, stiff-shouldered, he went on.

'Fairo!' she shouted again. She could not believe that he was trying to ignore her, but she could not quite keep the amused surprise from her tone. 'Where are you going? Come here!'

She started to run after him. He turned his head, peered as if making sure who she was, then waved. She stopped running and let him walk up.

'I can't believe you didn't hear me,' she said. 'I thought I was going to have to chase you all across town. What are you doing here? I didn't think you had a meeting today?'

'Oh, Agana wanted to go through a few things, last minute details. You know.'

'Any problems?'

'No, it's fine. Agana's very capable.'

'Good. Then you can relax, and come back with me in Par'Lennan's marvellous transport. No,' she chided as he started to protest, 'no arguing. You've been working just as hard as anyone else on this, you deserve a bit of luxury. Come on.'

He seemed perfectly composed, but his face she thought was a little pale. He had been working too hard. She slipped a proprietorial arm through his.

'You know, I think I feel more optimistic now than I have done at any time before,' she said. 'I mean it. I mean, I've always believed in our mission, but now I really feel like we're part of something much bigger here. Like my meeting today... he's a dreadful old man, the President, all hunched up in his crimes like one of those armoured insects that live in sand holes. He's what this place used to be, he's the past. Desailly might have his faults, but he's not like that. He believes in dialogue, in politics, if you like. They've gone from people who could only communicate through killing to people who are prepared to talk to each other. That's such progress. And if they can get there without us, well, what can they achieve with us to help them along?'

The transport had arrived and stood before them with its side open for them to climb in. She let go of Du'Fairosay's arm, lifted her face to the sky. As if addressing an invisible crowd, she beamed at the courtyard and said, 'We're going to do it. I really, really believe we are going to do it.'

Du'Fairosay had waited until she'd left their office in the transport before he'd followed her to the palace. It wasn't that it was a problem, of course. He had any number of reasons he could give for going out, but he didn't want to see her. He hadn't planned to have to do this. All the arrangements had been made at a distance, after the initial meeting, and she had done that herself. But there was no avoiding the summons.

'By the way,' Agana had said, 'the boss wants a word before you leave. Tomorrow, if possible.'

He hadn't asked for what. 'Alright, I'll stop by.'

He knew he was going to have to sell it all over again, but he could do that. Desailly was a cautious man making a rash move, it was not surprising that he would have to coax him. He could do it. After all, he had always known at base that he could not stay at arm's length forever. He had always known himself to be the one outside the circle, the one who had to work eight times harder than anyone else just to get a fraction of what they claimed by right. They who knew nothing about anything, who travelled the galaxy bringing their ignorance like a blessing.

He knew. He knew how to bear the stares of the people in the streets when you were the only one with the dark blue skin of an off-worlder. How to go to bed in a strange place and sleep sound. How to make yourself into somebody else and never go home again. They had taught him, perhaps because they could not learn it themselves and they needed someone like him; someone they despised, to do the jobs they preferred to overlook.

There were birds screaming over the river when he crossed the bridge to the palace. Their harsh calls sounded like the flying creatures on the shore outside his father's house on Teyro, wings beating the surface of the water, throwing up great plumes of spray that caught the light and threw it back, refracted, over the boat. Skeemas, they were called, for the noise they made. His brothers and he had spent long hours learning to imitate them. They'd killed them for their grey and blue fur, which his mother used to cure and sew into coats for sale in the market, but their flesh was so tough and greasy they would only eat it if they were desperate.

They had eaten enough skeema stew in his childhood, when

the catch was small or the winds too strong to put out or simply when the taxes were too high and the fish prices too low. His brothers went out with their father, working, but though he was never a fisherman he was the one who had seen to it that they never had to resort to skeema again.

He could see them now, small from the distance, standing as if in an image projected on to the palm of his hand, his father and his brothers in the boat he had paid for, his mother and sisters in their new dresses next to the house with its new turf roof and painted beams. Behind them, half hidden by the shadows of the eaves, was a smaller boy, with a shock of hair flattened down from brushing and a gap where his front tooth had been.

It had fallen out the week before they came to take him away, he remembered his mother worrying that it would be a reason for them to change their minds. The family did not know he was there, one lost child among all the others they had lost. He didn't mind, it was not as if they would recognise him now. One of the first things he had learned was not to miss them, to keep them closed off in their image from everything else he had become. To keep himself there with them, cleaned and done up in his best clothes for the city people to take.

He looked up and saw that he was almost at the palace gates. Gently, with infinite care, in his mind he shut the projection away.

'I get the impression,' Desailly said, 'that you're the one to talk to. I could discuss this with Special Envoy Ar'Quila, but I don't think I would get anywhere. I could discuss it with Par'Lennan, but to be frank, he's an idiot and I think he would only have to ask you, later, what to do. So I come back to you. Do tell me if I'm wrong.'

Du'Fairosay smiled. 'It depends what you want to say.'

'What do I want to say? What *do* I want to say?'

Desailly got up and paced to the long windows overlooking the courtyard.

'I want to say that I am starting a war here that I cannot finish. I am taking on an enemy that I have spent my life fighting and know I cannot beat. I am enveloping this planet in a tide of blood so deep that none of us will live to see it turn and I need to know that you will keep your promises. I need to have it from you, yourself, in person. I need to be sure that the Chi!me will stand aside and let us deal with the ViaVera leadership at the meeting and I need your assurance that you will still be there afterwards, to deal with the reckoning, because reckoning there will be.'

'Maybe not,' Du'Fairosay offered. 'Maybe the fight will go out of them when their Caduca is killed and they will disperse to their homes. Maybe there will not be anything left to do.'

'That's bollocks and you know it. They don't have homes, if they had anything to return to they wouldn't be there. We'll have to fight them until every last one of them is dead and there are many. If you don't have the stomach for it, tell me now, because if you tell me later you will have the blood of a great many innocent people on your hands. I need to know you are with me on this, because if there is even the slightest doubt…'

Du'Fairosay cut in. 'There is no doubt. We have said what we will do and we will keep our word. We were sent here to assess the situation and this we have done. We have concluded what needs to be concluded about this. You know we cannot take sides openly, you know we have to be seen to be open-handed, to want only dialogue. That is the UP way, and as we walk the galaxy it is UP's reputation that we must maintain.' He smiled at Desailly.

'But only fools and children believe that everything can be resolved by pleading. UP is all about helping people find their own answers, but sometimes a little force is necessary before those answers can come into view. As agreed, you may bring an additional force to the talks. The security will not stop you. It will allow you to wipe ViaVera's leadership out. And when you have done that, we will do everything we can to clean the stain of ViaVera from the face of this planet, because ultimately, as the Ambassador has said, we cannot tolerate violence. We are about law and order and we will help you uphold it. Does that satisfy you? I cannot do anything else to prove it.'

Desailly took a long breath. 'Yeeesss. Yes, I suppose I will have to be satisfied with that.' He turned towards Du'Fairosay, dark against the sunlit window. 'What will your Ambassador make of this, do you think? Does she even know?'

'The Ambassador is committed to the cause of peace,' Du'Fairosay replied, austerely, 'far too committed to allow that commitment to be occluded by inconvenient facts. Ambassador Ar'Quila understands as we all do that the first good is obedience. She will do what it is necessary to do; that and no more.'

He could not see Desailly's expression, any more than he could read the tone in his voice. 'Poor Ar'Quila,' Desailly said.

Then he'd stepped outside and he'd met her, as she was leaving her meeting with the President.

'Fairo! Fairo!' she'd called. *'Where are you going?'*

'You deserve a bit of luxury.'

Her hand slipped through the curve of his arm, her body breathing against his side.

'They've gone from people who could only communicate through killing to people who are prepared to talk to each other.'

Her voice was light and happy, sure of success. He couldn't think of any way to stop her.

'We're going to do it. I really, really believe we are going to do it.'

The appalling words went on and on, the whole way back in the transport to the hotel. She didn't reach for him again, but all the while the imprint of her fingers lay on his skin beneath his shirt; her touch so clean it burned.

Part 15

The Summit

Jaime Delterro rested his booted heels on the dashboard of the brand-new carrier and wished he was in the second group. Mostly, this was because he was stuck with Fuggle as the carrier captain and ever since that business with Fuggle's sister last year, relations between them had been a little strained. It wasn't even as if he had done anything to the sister, she had come onto him. It was completely unfair that whenever he was in Fuggle's group it was him who had to change the lubricant and get a face full of muck, or fill in the potholes when they disrupted the sensors too much for the carrier to go on. It wasn't that he was afraid of hard work, not at all, but he had the uncomfortable feeling that Fuggle would love to get him killed.

He sighed, crossed his legs the other way, and earned a glare from Mikey, the driver.

'Oy, don't fuckin' sleep. You're s'posed to be the fuckin' lookout.'

Jaime sighed again and addressed himself to the green gloom on either side of the road.

'D'you think it ever stops raining? I hate the fucking mountains.'

When he was given the assignment, the captain had stressed what an honour it was. He had been chosen to be part of the honour guard because he was one of the best, because his shoes shone brightest and his jacket cleanest and he was one of the toughest fighters in his unit. But it was all very well being honoured if he couldn't tell anyone about it.

'Just guarding some diplomatic thing,' he'd told his mother when he'd gone home on his half day's leave. The barracks were only two streets from the house, he'd said in his interview that he'd grown up with the army in his ears. 'It's nothing special.'

'Ha!' his grandmother had snorted from her seat by the heating element, 'talking shops!'

'Mother,' his mother had admonished. She'd rubbed his arm sympathetically. 'They'll recognise you in time, you just have to keep trying. Keep doing your best and it will come, don't worry.'

She'd said that because she was worried, he could tell. She'd given up so much to get him into that school, she'd always said so, especially after his father died. Joining Desailly's guard was a chance to make something of himself, but only if they noticed him. She hadn't scrimped and saved for him to remain a private forever.

'Yes, Ma,' he'd said. 'I know, Ma.'

She would have been proud that he was in the lead carrier, if he had been allowed to tell her. Desailly's state car was directly behind him, followed by the Chi!me Ambassador and her surrounding Chi!me security. He'd seen them for the first time at Biterra when they'd left the shuttle. They were thin, and supercilious, but he would give a week's pay for a day with one of their blasters. The one he had now was pretty good, better than that Espada crap, but it was nothing to the latest models. They were something else. He'd seen the Ambassador as well, standing on the platform at Biterra while everyone bustled around her, like it was nothing to do with her at all.

'Do not, I repeat, do not discuss the orders with the Ambassador or any of the Chi!me party, do you understand me? If they ask you a direct question, all you know is you are a guard for the President and your orders are to protect him. Anything else you think you know, you do not say. Am I making myself clear?' Fuggle, eyeballing him as usual. He hadn't asked why they couldn't talk about the mission to the Chi!me, you weren't supposed to wonder about your orders. Probably, he thought, they wanted to deny everything, in case it all went wrong. They were like that, the blue people. Tricky.

It was probably a mistake to have Mikey as the lead driver. Snail's arse, they called him, because even snails could overtake him. He supposed they had to go careful with the new kit, pretend to be a ceremonial procession, but it was boring. Old Tagger, now, or Pedro, they would have been halfway to Ultima before Mikey had got them out of Biterra, but they were in the second group, half a day behind.

It was getting dark already, here in the mountain country where the clouds sat down on the hillsides like they were tired and you could never see the sun for the rain. They would have to get the camp set up when they arrived and he knew what that would be like, blundering around in the wet gloom and bashing into each other. Getting a dressing-down from fucking Fuggle for 'showing their calibre as guardsmen.'

The second group would stay in the village they'd passed a little while before, sleep dry in the villagers' huts and be entertained by the villagers' daughters. He'd spotted a couple of likely ones as they'd glided through, he'd bet they'd've been up for it, if he'd been in the second group. He never had any luck.

They'd spent the night in Place of the Trees, a day's march away, and when they started out on the last morning, Acacio made sure he was behind Ladyani. There was no one who could move like Ladyani; who could be quite so swift and yet so stealthy. On long marches, when he could, Acacio liked to study him, place his feet in his footsteps as if that way he could learn it. Of course, he had not had so long to practise.

It was five years since he had come, a sixteen-year-old revolutionary, to ViaVera; a little over three since he had been admitted to Ladyani's squad. He'd known he had done well at his training, but he had still been astounded. 'I can't believe it,' he'd said. 'I'm never that lucky.' Ladyani had grinned at him. 'What are you, a girl? "I can't believe it"? You sound like a village tart with a ring on her finger. You're not lucky, you're good. Believe it.' He'd followed Ladyani then to the battle with the soldiers down on the Ultima road, when they'd taken out six carriers, and to countless others since. He'd taken tribute from the villages, dispensed justice, pretended he didn't know how many people he'd killed.

He knew the rhythm of their expeditions; the silent departure from the early morning camp, the stern concentration to start with until it came back to them so well that they could do it without thinking about it. While they were still in the hills they would sing, quietly, as they marched, swap dirty stories up and down the line. Ladyani's were always the filthiest. When they got near to their destination they would always quieten down again and if it was as much from nerves as caution they would never admit it.

This march was different, and only partly because *la dona* was with them. Since his arrival he had encountered her only at a distance, addressing the crowd in the square or toying with her food at the top table. Seeing her marching beside Ladyani's woman, chatting lightly to Ladyani or one of the Jeba was certainly peculiar, but it wasn't entirely it. Was it just because of *la dona* that Ladyani was laughing, calling a joke back up to the lads at the end of the line? Was it only her presence that made the path seem less muddy, the hills less steep, even the soaking rain less wet?

Acacio didn't know much about politics. He knew they were going to a meeting with the government but on the details he was sketchy. He only knew that the blue people had given them a way to win and that they were being carried to the meeting place on the great cloud of their success. He couldn't predict what was going to happen. He couldn't imagine the meeting, or how the Chi!me could have lined up so many powerful enemies to die, but it didn't matter. They were together, they were legion. They were ViaVera, the great armed snake slithering out of the mountains, and there was no yesterday and no tomorrow, only the endless present and their victory.

Jaime woke to find Mikey shaking him. He thought for one confused moment that it was morning already, but then the fact that it was still dark penetrated the fog of sleep.

'What the fuck...?'

'Come and have a look. They're here.'

The cairn field was a large, flat expanse of stubby ferns, bounded on all sides by scrub and on the north-west by a thin band of trees. The road from the south ran along its eastern edge on its way between Cairn Fields village and Place of the Trees. The gate was in the south-east corner. The government party had pitched their tents at the south end; one for Desailly and his personal bodyguards and another for the guards. The journalists had set up next to them and spent most of the evening muttering identical reports back to their stations while pretending to be the only ones there.

The Chi!me had their own tent in the middle of the field where the pavilion was to be set up for the meeting. Jaime had watched them earlier drawing the exclusion lines across north and south, marking where the guards were not supposed to cross. They had taken a lot of trouble over it, considering, but that was the Chi!me for you. As he had predicted, erecting the tents was chaotic, irritating and damp. He had been relieved when it was finally all done and he could wrap himself in his bedding and sleep.

He unstuck the side of the bed and crawled out. Mikey had gone back to the tent flap. Tereno and Saik were up as well, standing silently by the entrance.

'What is it?' He didn't know why he whispered.

'Can't you see the lights?' Tereno muttered back. 'It's them, they're here.'

Jaime peered. Over the darkened field the rain was still falling, but at the far end, he could make out a line of sparks, moving from left to right across his vision. There was no noise, no voices, nothing but the hiss of the rain as they crept into the field, moving so lightly it could all have been illusion, as if there were no real people over there at all.

'It's them,' Tereno repeated.

Jaime fixed his eyes on the bobbing lights. When he was a

child, his grandmother used to tell him stories about spirits when his mother was working late. There was one about the lantern ghosts, who would appear to lonely travellers as lights flickering in the darkest night and would lead them off the road to their deaths. The lights gathered themselves into a circle and his palm ached for the comforting feel of his blaster. They seemed sinister, beyond his ability to express.

'Creepy,' he said.

In the morning, the Chi!me security guards put the pavilion up. Strictly speaking they were UP troops, brought in for the occasion by Du'Fairosay, but since they were all Chi!me, Quila was sure no one would appreciate the distinction. She had tried to chat to them in the tube to Biterra, but they had not been very forthcoming. She supposed they were right to keep in their place, she had only been making conversation out of nerves.

The pavilion was dyed deep purple, with a rich peaked canopy and open sides, for transparency. The light underneath the canopy clashed oddly with her skin. It had been so difficult to find a colour which was not claimed already by one side or the other and she had read that for Terrans, purple meant prosperity. It was only lucky that it was no longer raining; she was not sure the dye would not run. She looked round for Du'Fairosay to share the joke with, but his expression was so forbidding she decided against it. He was right, it was time to be serious.

Over on the south side of the field, the flap of Desailly's tent was pushed open. There was a faint confusion of movement inside, then Desailly stepped out. He was wearing a white uniform in a style she didn't recognise, with red trimmings on the shoulders. He walked, slow and measured, with his guards to the exclusion line, then crossed it with his aide Agana and two bodyguards.

From the other side came ViaVera, in procession. In front was a thick set man with a tuft of red-grey hair and a blue bandana, leading their two bodyguards. Beside him was Terise, looking more relaxed than she had in Airdrossa, and on her other side a small, thin girl in a green dress. A thin girl with dark hair and Mara's face.

She couldn't ask the question, she couldn't let it put her off. The UP guards escorted both parties to their seats. They all seemed calm, she thought, and that was a good sign. She even thought, though she could not be sure, that between the thin girl and Desailly there was a momentary bow. She would be happier if she knew who she was. Du'Fairosay sat, still unsmiling, behind her, she could feel his gaze boring into her back. It was time. Ambassador Ar'Quila of the Chi!me, United Planets envoy to Benan Ty, got to her feet and with a deep breath, did what she had been sent to do.

'I would like to welcome you all on this historic day. This is a day that will be remembered long after we are gone, the day when the old hatreds were put aside, the old differences bridged and a new future was built together, working in co-operation for the good of all. I am proud to be here, proud to have a part in the making of history. I am sure you are too, and I would like to thank you from the bottom of my heart for the work and the trust that you have given so far to this peace process.

'I know that you have all had difficulties with your own sides, convincing them that it was worth doing. All I can say to you is that that work *was* worthwhile and it will bring great benefits, to both sides. I won't pretend it will be easy. I know there are issues between you which cannot be resolved in a moment. But I truly believe that everything, however difficult, can be resolved by honest and open negotiation between people of goodwill. And that is what we have here today.

'Now, I am sure before we get down to details both sides would like to make a short statement of what they hope to gain from these talks. I would ask you to listen to each other without interruption, you will have plenty of chances to respond and to question. I think also we will stay seated, it gives a more informal atmosphere. Mr Desailly, on behalf of the President, perhaps you would like to go first?'

She sat down, smiling. Desailly had been staring down at the table as if he hadn't heard anything she said, but as she stopped he got slowly to his feet.

Jaime Delterro, at the south side barrier, saw the Ambassador put out a hand as if to try to stop him, then drop her arm as if she realised there was nothing she could politely do.

On the other side of the table, the thin girl stood up. She moved around the table to face him.

Desailly reached into his coat and pulled out a blaster.

The Ambassador shouted something. Acacio, at the north barrier, could not hear what it was. She gestured at the Chi!me guards, but they did not move. Ladyani's woman made a half-movement out of her seat towards Issa, stopped before she had even straightened.

It was all absolutely still, a graven tableau with only the breeze blowing Issa's dress to show they were not all frozen into stone. Somewhere off in the trees, birds were singing, loud in the sudden quiet.

'I have waited for this for so long,' Desailly said to Issa in caressing tones, 'that I find I no longer care what the consequences may be. Whatever comes, I want you to know it will have been worth it.'

Issa looked up at him, her head cocked to one side. Behind her shoulder, at the edge of the field, a flicker of movement spread among the scrub. She smiled.

'Both of us, Mr Policeman? Not this time.'

Desailly's gaze slipped beyond her. Down the field, men were running through the security line, towards the pavilion. There was an abrupt pink blossom. Agana shouted out, 'Sir! Get down!' and Desailly sprawled beneath him on the ground as the first blaster bolt whistled over them.

Terise pushed the table over. Ladyani, leaping forward over it, grabbed Issa and pulled her back through the legs. Acacio joined the attack group as they charged through the barrier. Behind the shelter of the table, Ladyani and Terise were screaming at them. 'Give me a weapon, give me a weapon!' Desailly was still on the ground, wriggling back into the shelter of his table with his aide shielding him from further blasts.

Someone in the press handed Acacio another blaster and he threw it into Ladyani's outstretched hands. 'Alright! Now, you bastard…' He poked his head over the edge of the table and dropped back abruptly as a blast from the other side of the field whistled past his ear. Desailly disappeared into cover.

'We've got CAS coming in!' Terise shouted to him. Acacio

reached the pavilion.

'The bastards,' Ladyani gave a breathless laugh 'don't they know it's only us who can cheat?'

A blast took Acacio straight in the chest and he collapsed over the table leg.

Terise shouted again. 'Lad, we need to find some cover, they're coming in!'

'I see them. Alright, get back! Get back! Issa…'

He grabbed her shoulder.

'Not this time,' she repeated. 'Alright, let's go.'

'Sir,' Agana yelled, 'we need to get back to our lines, we're too exposed here. I'll cover you.'

'I can still get them,' Desailly shouted back.

'Yes sir, but not today. Come on!'

'I can't. Just one shot, that's all I need, just one shot…'

'Sir, come on! Please!'

'Just…'

Jaime, running up the field with the second group, saw the next president and his aide apparently wrestling. He saw the ViaVera fighters moving, saw one of them stop to take aim. He didn't think about it, in the end there was not time. He flung himself across their line of fire.

'Alright, come on,' Desailly said. Agana stooped over the trooper who had taken the bolt. 'Are you…'

'Sorry, Ma,' the trooper whispered. His eyes fixed.

Agana grabbed his blaster. 'Yes sir,' he said.

Quila hardly realised when she began screaming. Weaponless, she stood still at the middle of the line of tables, while the others were overturned and bolts sailed past her nose. Du'Fairosay and the guards were nowhere to be seen, she could only hope they had gone for reinforcements. She was all alone in madness and all she could do was shout as loud as she could, 'stop, please, please stop!'

Nobody listened. On each side the fighting continued, both sides killing and dying right in front of her. A guerrilla fell at her feet, blood streaming from a hole in his chest; a presidential guard flung himself in front of another bolt, landed with half his head blown away. Every thud of every body was one more judgement on her failure, one more statement that she had not done what she had been entrusted to do. Everyone would be so disappointed in her. She had to make them stop. It didn't matter what happened to her if she couldn't. But they couldn't hear her! She had to be higher. Desperately, she hauled herself onto the central table.

'Stop it,' she cried. 'Stop it right now, I mean it! Stop it!' A bolt, she never knew from which side, winged by, ruffling her hair, and struck one of the struts holding the cover of the pavilion. She watched, unable to prevent it, as she was enveloped in a falling tide of purple cloth.

She was surrounded by dark seas, drowning in dye. She fought her way up through the folds, pushing and tearing at the oceans of fabric until they at last gave way to light. Everyone else seemed to have escaped the pavilion; she was alone in her calyx of purple, in the middle of a field covered with knots of fighters. For all her experience she had never seen a battle before, she had no idea how she could work out who was winning. And it should not be happening at all. She pulled herself to her feet. She didn't know what she could do, how she could make them listen, but she had to try.

Terise, from the position hastily constructed from the wreckage of the north barrier, shot her third guard and looked round for Ladyani. 'Lad, we should retreat. Marius's boys are fucking exposed and we're getting nothing this way.'

Ladyani's grinning face was covered in other people's blood. He considered, watching the clump that was Marius's group firing from a patch of scrub to the east of the pavilion.

'Desailly's back behind their lines. Alright, I agree. You tell Marius to get back to the trees; I'll take Issa.'

'Done.' They had had no communicators on them; it would have looked suspicious. Bent double against stray bolts, Terise set off over the field.

Quila, struggling out of the tent, drew breath to shout and saw Terise sprinting towards her.

'Terise!' she called. 'You have to stop them. You have to tell them!'

At last, at last something would go right. Du'Fairosay had disapproved of her talking to Terise, but now she was proved correct. Terise would do it, she would stop the fighting and it would all be alright, even now at the last. 'Terise...'

Terise frowned. Quila thought she looked puzzled, and then a little annoyed. She raised her blaster.

'Oh no, no, not you as well! Terise, please – '

The blaster flowered towards her. She froze, braced for it and the bolt flew past her shoulder.

'What...?'

Something hit her, hard, in the small of her back. She saw

Terise start to run, all askew as if on a broken screen. She couldn't read her expression. She tried to ask her again to stop them, but the words wouldn't come. She watched Terise looking down at her as she fell, turning, backwards into the dark.

Part 16

Quila and Terise

The house on the corner was pale yellow again. She knew faintly that there was a time when it had not been, when she had come back from somewhere – from school? – and it had changed, but now it was yellow and familiar again. The whole street was laid out before her, the set of the buildings and the lines of the roofs exactly as she remembered them from the upper window of her mother's house. She tried to concentrate on them, but it was no good, they slipped away. She found herself in the street outside. Rain was falling from a heavy sky, drops bouncing on the stone beneath her feet. She stuck out her foot to catch them. Her sandals were white with red bows and she thought, *I remember these.* Her mother lifted her up to the door of a transport, Stelfia moved over to let her sit by the window. The transport started up and she pressed her nose against the glass.

The rain was falling so hard the street was like a great lake. At first the transport still skimmed over the surface, but as the flood got deeper, it rose closer and closer until they were pushing through the water, waves of grey rain, crowned in spray, pluming out on either side. They turned the corner past the yellow house into the square. That too was covered in water, water so deep it was halfway up the doorways of the houses.

Strings of lights were hung between the buildings and people in transports were floating along the lanes, laughing and calling into the windows as the lights danced their own reflected pattern beneath. She gazed out of the window, enraptured. She was just over a cycle old and it was the first time she had seen the great rain. It was so familiar yet so different, she had never known that the places she knew could change, could not be trusted.

She heard her own voice and she knew this was what she had said then so long ago, only the voice was hers now, adult. 'It's so pretty, so pretty. Why isn't it always like this?'

Another voice, not her mother or Stelfia, not in the transport at all but in her head. 'Ah, but it is. You wade through the water and pretend it isn't here, but it doesn't stop your feet getting wet.'

'My shoes...' Her sandals were covered in mud, caked and bedraggled in water and filth. If only she could find something to clean them, something to cover them up so that no one would know. If she could...

'Does she know?' something whispered, insinuating, into her ear. 'Does she know?'

She could hear the answer, but she couldn't understand it. The square and the transport disappeared and she was standing all alone somewhere in darkness. She repeated the words over and over to herself as if she should be able to make them make sense, but it felt as if they were slipping through her fingers and the harder she tried the more they escaped from her.

'I ikatane issanteke kaedukele,' hissed a third voice. It seemed much closer than the other two, low like a secret.

She whipped round to find it.

'Oh no,' sniggered someone. 'Not your back.'

There was a bright light and a pain that ran right over her. Then nothing.

Terise looked down to where the Ambassador lay crumpled on the ferns. The noise of the fighting seemed suddenly distant, quiet enough for her to hear the tick of her blaster as it cooled at her side. She should leave her there, she knew. If she was not already dead she was dying; what good was a dead Chi!me to her? There was no point in burdening herself with her, no point at all. As if one meeting was enough to make them comrades, it was stupid, sentimental. But you never left your wounded behind. It was the first lesson you learned. Terise slung her blaster back over her shoulder and hoisted the Ambassador into her arms.

The Chi!me were lighter built than Terrans, but she was still enough of a burden that it was difficult to run. Terise waddled towards the trees as fast as she could. Over on her right she saw Marius and his group sprinting for the cover. Something warm dribbled over her hands, webbing them over with sticky tendrils, attaching her to her burden as if the alien was growing into her flesh.

A little way into the wood she caught up with the others, waiting in a small clearing. Faces were averted; she couldn't tell who was missing. Ladyani was standing on a fallen tree.

'Terise, where the fuck have you been? I told you to get Marius and get out. Are you the last?'

'As far as I could see. Sorry. I got held up.'

He raised an eyebrow.

'So I see. You've found a pet?' That earned a weary snigger

271

from the others.

'Yeah.' She kept her tone light, matching his. 'One Chi!me Ambassador, slightly soiled. No one else seemed to want her and I thought she might be useful.' A breathless minute, while he considered the unconscious Ambassador. His eyes narrowed. 'Could be, might be, probably won't be…' Abruptly losing interest, he concluded. 'If you want her you can keep her. Just keep her out of the way. Alright, brothers, enough of the fucking mothers' meeting. Let's go.'

There was no time to rig up a litter until they camped. A couple of the lads went off into the trees to find some branches for her and Nico even offered to help her carry it tomorrow. She didn't know that it would be needed. The wound in the Ambassador's back just wouldn't stop bleeding; every time she thought she'd got it she'd take the pad cautiously away and there it would be, another trail of thick purple like a snake leaving its skin. There seemed no reason why it would ever stop, slithering out until all that was left was husk. She kept on dabbing it away and the Ambassador moaned and moved and looked round at her with blank, frightened eyes.

After a while, the Jeban scouts reported that no one was following them and Ladyani cleared them to dig the heating cubes into firepits. By evening, there were five firepoints dotted over the clearing, a circle of guerrillas crouched around each. No one said much. Terise sat off to one side, nearest the fire where Marius was hunkered down with some of his group, but far enough away that it would not disturb them if the Ambassador died. Through the heated air she watched Ladyani against the far trees. The Jebans had also done some hunting so there was dinner, if sparse. When they finished, Darsin, Marius' second, tried a song, but no one joined in and *The True Road* petered out after one reedy verse.

Marius threw his bones into the stones round the edge of the heating cube. 'Well,' he said, quietly enough that it wouldn't carry, 'that was a fuck-up and no mistake. Shall we talk about whose fault it was?'

Darsin exchanged glances with Itani across the fire.

'Well, come on,' Marius persisted. 'What, we all just pretend like it was just one of those things, these things happen? For fuck's sake, we could all have been killed. Some of us were.'

'Yeah man, but it was the fucking Chi!me's fault, wasn't it?' That was Itani, always the peacemaker. 'What are we supposed to do?'

'Was it, though?'

'Wasn't it?'

'Who was it was dealing with the fucking Chi!me in the first place? Who was it told us, what was it, 'we can't lose, we'll be in Airdrossa by Christmas?' Who was it gave us the idea that this stupid-arse scheme was the answer to all our prayers, then let us walk right into it? Christ on the cross, and you think it's the Chi!me's fault? We were sitting up and begging for it, and you know it!'

His voice raised. On the other side of the clearing, Ladyani lifted his head.

'Shut up man, keep it down!' Darsin whispered urgently. 'This isn't the time, alright? Let's talk about this when we get back, not now. Do you want the whole fucking government to hear you?'

'I don't fucking well care who hears me, it's about time we had some debate around here,' Marius proclaimed, more quietly. 'You wait, I'm gonna tell that son of bitch exactly what…'

'Yeah man, whatever you say, only keep it down, alright? Chebo, can you hand me that flask? Have another drink, man, you look like you need it.'

Marius subsided, muttering. From over the heads of the cadre, Ladyani considered him.

She was lying down. Quila realised she had been aware of this for a while. She was lying on her side on something soft and scratchy; something that sent little prickles of itchiness all up her arm and leg. Her head was propped up by something harder, less yielding; her neck felt fixed enough that she could tell it would hurt to move it. She had the sense that it was not the only thing that might hurt, a great white nothing beneath her thoughts where her back should be, but for the moment she was safe, asleep. As long as she was asleep, she did not have to know, did not have to feel, she could stay asleep forever and she was so tired… She forced her eyes open.

Beside the bed was maybe a little more than her arm's length of brown floor. On her left, at the head, was a small wooden table holding a cup and a couple of vials. There was nothing else save the wall.

She lay and looked at the wall. It was brown like the floor and as her eyes accustomed to the dimness it was clear that it was wood. A wall made of wooden planks, fixed together rather inexpertly so that all along its length there were chinks and spots of gold where the light outside crept in.

She couldn't see clearly without moving her head, but it seemed more than likely that the floor was wooden, too. She sniffed and the air in her nose was musty, like rain allowed in to dry slowly. Cautiously, she lifted one hand from the covers and gasped at the sudden pain, worse than she could have imagined, that tore through her. There was a movement behind and someone came round the foot of the bed to her side.

It was a Jeba, a Jeba not as she had seen them before, wearing the uniform of some hotel and herding cases, but dressed in a medley of browns and greens that seemed to melt into the walls. It regarded her impassively. It came to her that she had to think of something to say.

'Pleased to meet you,' she croaked in a voice rusty from disuse. 'I'm not in Airdrossa, am I?'

'No.' The Jeba pushed a beaker towards her. 'You drink.'

'Thank you.' The water was strange-tasting but welcome. She gulped it down and handed the beaker back.

'I'm Ar'Quila, I'm sure you know,' she said over it. His face remained expressionless, she couldn't tell if he did know or not. What did she know? She remembered a girl who was and was not Mara, a purple sea in a green field and shouting, crying… 'What's your name?'

'They call me Ihanakan.'

'And this place?'

'To my people, it iss Iska kamele, you would ssay the place of the sstony river…'

'The place of the…'

'…You would alsso ssay, the place of the camp of ViaVera.'

'ViaVera!' Blaster fire, blossoming like flowers. Not this time. 'How did I…?' Unwisely, she tried to sit up and sank back onto the prickly bed, gasping. 'What am doing here? What happened? I can't remember anything. Please tell me what happened!'

The Jeba looked for a moment as if he was going to refuse, then it passed and only the faint air of apology remained.

'I wass not there, you understand. I wass with the fighterss on their journey but I wass not there at the cairn field. It wass not proper, I think, for uss to be part of ssomething between them. Sso I waited at the place agreed and after the fighting wass over I ssaw Terisse come in carrying you.'

'Terise! So she… she captured me? Is that what happened?'

'She ssaid you were shot. She brought you back.'

'Shot…yes, I remember…something…' The blow in her back, Terise's face as she slipped away into nothingness. The conviction burst in upon her and she said, excitedly, 'She saved me. The government must have thought I was already dead, they would have left me. She saved me, she didn't have to do it, she had every reason to leave me there but she saved me. Why did she do that?'

Ihanakan's face was even more expressionless than before, his tone stiff.

'I do not know. It iss not for me to ssay.'

'No. No, I understand, of course not. It is not for you to say…' Her voice sounded very far away suddenly, the room echoing as if someone had raised the roof and made it a dome. 'I think I feel a little…'

'You should eat ssomething. I will go and ssee.'

She tried to protest, keep him there, 'No, I'm fine. I want to ask you…' but she couldn't make her voice obey her. The Jeba slipped silently round the bed and disappeared.

She lay still in the dimness of the room, watching the light between the slats making up the wall. There was a faint pattering noise, as if it was raining; in her mind's eye she saw the drops bouncing, kicking up red earth where they landed all round the hut. She imagined bare feet splashing through them, soles covered in a thin sticky coating of mud that however hard you brushed would always leave a stain. Feet, unhurried, reaching the door.

A patch of light appeared briefly on the wall while it was open, then it was dark again. The feet moved slowly around the bed; there was a shuffle and clunk as something heavy was placed on the table beside her head. She thought perversely of pretending to be still unconscious, but that was cowardly, wrong. She opened her eyes.

'Hello, Terise.'

Terise's face seemed thinner than she remembered it, her hair scraped untidily back behind her ears with a strip of purple cloth. Her hands, brown and sinewy, carried on arranging the tray.

'Hello yourself. Did Ihanakan fill you in?'

'He told me a bit. Not much.'

'That's Ihanakan. But really there's not much to tell.'

'He said you got me out.'

'Yeah. Well,' she shrugged, 'I was feeling generous. I brought you something to eat. I don't suppose it's what you're used to, but you could do with something solid. You've been on nothing but slops since we got back.'

Quila obediently accepted a spoon and dug it into the bowl Terise held out to her. It was some sort of stew, earthy but not unpleasant.

'How long have I been here?'

'About a week.'

Quila choked, sprayed her second mouthful over the bed. 'A week!'

'A shot in the back's not an easy thing to live with. We thought you were going to die.'

'And I'm grateful I didn't, but...' She stopped, reeling. 'Does anyone even know I'm here?'

Terise looked at her obliquely. 'Eat your food,' she said. 'It'll get cold.'

She came back every day or so after that. They kept clear of recent history, restricting their conversation to their homes, families and friends. Terise told her more about the village by the sea and Quila rejoined with the little rain festival on Chi!me, from the years before she went away. They only once strayed into politics, when Quila, following a train of thought, remembered a question unasked.

'I was wondering about your leader?'

'Issa?' She'd wondered as she'd said it if she'd blundered, but Terise seemed relaxed enough. 'What about her?'

'When I saw her, I couldn't help noticing... I mean, how she looks, she... she looks so like Mara. It's uncanny, when she came into the pavilion, it could have been her. Is she... did Mara have a daughter?'

'Mara?' Terise snorted. 'She didn't have time for men, let alone babies. She never sat still for two minutes together, never stopped to look at what she could have had just by stretching out her hand. Everybody loved her and she didn't love anyone... well, not like that, anyway. I've never thought Issa was anything like her.'

'Really? To me she's so like she could be her. I used to have images of Mara when I was at school and Issa could have stepped out of them.'

'And we don't have any pictures at all.'

'Well,' Quila said rapidly, 'you see Issa every day. That sort of resemblance is easier to spot when you don't know people well. I'm sure it's not really that pronounced, it's been years since I've seen my images.'

'She's smaller, of course. We thought when she was young that she was going to be tall, but it never quite happened. Mara was taller than me.'

'Well, that sort of thing you can't tell from a picture. But she is related?'

'Oh, yes. She's the little sister.'

'Really? I didn't know... oh, yes, I do remember Desailly mentioned a sister. She was born after their father died, is that right?'

'That's it.' Terise leaned back, reclined on one arm across the end of the bed. 'Two weeks into Sept Karne's death and a month early, my mother said. My mother liked Sept Karne, she said he was a real man.'

'What happened to her afterwards?'

'Well, she went into house arrest with Mara and their mother and when Mara bust out, she stayed there. I suppose Mara thought she'd be safer there than in the mountains. You wouldn't really go carting your baby sister around when you go off to start a war.'

'But she got her in the end.'

'Yes.' Terise sighed. 'This was before my time, so I don't know everything about it. As I've heard it, their mother killed herself in house arrest when Issa was five. Mara thought Issa might not be safe there, that without their mother they might kill her. They spent so much money on keeping them in that prison and what good was a little girl to them? Children die so easily. So they went in and got her.'

Running feet over the boom of blasters, air thick with dust from the new holes in the walls. Someone grabbing her, holding her, sobbing breath repeating 'don't worry, you're safe, you're safe' in a tone that didn't know it at all. Harsh light in her eyes, the gate that was always closed lying on its side on the lawn, more running, jolting, stopping. A stranger with long black hair. 'It's me, Issa. It's me.' Quila shook her head to send the image away, setting her vision spinning instead with the unaccustomed movement.

'Ow. I must remember not to do that. Does she remember it?'

'She says not.'

'And she's been here ever since?'

'Ever since. Twenty-five years; it's strange to think she's older now than Mara ever got to be. I suppose we're all used to thinking of her as a kid. Do you want anything more to eat?' She held out the bowl, full this time with a rather unfortunate green stew. Quila pulled a polite face.

'No, I couldn't. Terise?'

'Yes?'

'Talking of rescues. I seem to remember the first time I came round I said Ihanakan told me you rescued me. I don't think I said that I'm grateful, or even remembered to thank you.'

'You don't…'

'I am grateful. I do thank you. And I haven't forgotten my promise. I won't be so stupid as to mention it in anyone else's

280

hearing. I just want you to know that when I said I would get you both out, I meant it, and once I get back to my people I will do it. I promise.' She had to mean it now. Terise never had to know what she had planned to do.

Terise regarded her steadily. 'I don't doubt it and, for what it's worth, thank you.' She got up. 'I have things to do. I expect Ihanakan will look in on you later. He's being very attentive for him, you should be flattered, he doesn't usually pay any attention to the wounded.'

'I'm doubly honoured then.' She paused. Terise opened the door. A patch of grey light streamed damp over the threshold like the curtain in a Terran play, like the end of intermission. Outside, someone whistled, discordantly, as they tramped past. She asked, suddenly, 'Did you see what happened? When I was shot, I mean? Did you see?'

Her face, silhouetted against the light, was blank. 'No. I didn't see anything,' said Terise. She let the door bang shut behind her. Quila lay on her side as her footsteps splashed away.

Part 17

The Invasion

The kaleidoscope explosion resolved itself as it always did into the familiar green, orange and blue of the TyCorp logo. Underneath the graphic, the anchorman stared commandingly into the camera.

'Hello and welcome to TyCorp News today, bringing you a planetary view of the stories that matter to you. Our top stories this hour: as concern grows for the health of the President, we have an exclusive interview with his last doctor. Two dead in Biterra as the handbag killer strikes again. Flooding in Kayro, will Airdrossa be next? And Sybil Andronite talks to Benito Toro about life and love after fame. That's all coming up in the next hour, so stay tuned.

'But first,' his face turned even graver, 'in the aftermath of the failed peace talks with terrorist group ViaVera, concern is growing for the safety of the Chi!me UP Ambassador Ar'Quila. Our political correspondent Maria Morales is outside the Chi!me embassy here in Airdrossa and sends us this special report. Maria, what can you tell us?'

The screen cut to a young woman in an evening street, her spiky yellow hair framed against her white umbrella.

'Well, Flavian, tonight hard questions are being asked about the whereabouts of UP Ambassador Ar'Quila, who has been missing since ViaVera's cowardly attack on the peace talks over a week ago.'

Rain, glinting in the arclight, drifted in front of her face. Amid the trees lining the street behind her, the top storey of the Chi!me embassy peered over its shuttered gates, a point of orange in the tossing dark.

'I understand the Chi!me Ambassador is there now, is that right?'

'Yes, Flavian, that's right. The Chi!me Ambassador, Par'Lennan, has been in the embassy since early this morning and has been having, we're told, a high-level meeting and consultation with the Chi!me government.'

'Do we know what they were discussing?'

'Not as such, no, but sources close to the Ambassador say he is very concerned about Ambassador Ar'Quila's safety.'

Flavian pulled his gravest face. 'So, do you get a sense of how the Chi!me might want to resolve this? Are they likely, do you think, to join in with the investigation? After all, with their resources they could make a big difference to the chances of success.'

'That's right, Flavian. The Chi!me, of course, are one of the wealthiest powers in the galaxy, although some experts believe that Terra's recent economic growth spurt might change that very soon. But the question with the Chi!me is always how they choose to use their power. The feeling here tonight is that there's unlikely to be any joint effort any time soon.' A gust threw a handful of raindrops against the camera lens, blew her umbrella askew. She blinked, recovering herself.

'We've been trying to interview Ambassador Par'Lennan,' she raised her voice over the wind in the leaves, 'but so far neither he nor any of his staff has been available to talk to us. A short while ago, however, he made this statement to the press.'

She stood aside with the air of a showman ushering on her next act. The screen flickered and over the luminous half-dark behind her the Ambassador appeared. He was wearing a stiff white jacket with blue and green fringes all the way down the edge, dazzlingly bright against the pendent black sky.

'This is a prepared statement on behalf of United Planets,' he said. He held the terminal in one hand while his other ran up his forehead and through his hair, pinning it there for a moment so that it stood up like a crest.

'United Planets is inexpressibly concerned about the disappearance of Ambassador Ar'Quila following the collapse of peace talks with the terrorist group ViaVera. The Ambassador came to Benan Ty on behalf of United Planets to make peace between the government and the terrorists. She worked closely with the government on the arrangement of the talks and all other matters to do with security. We accept that the breakdown of the talks was unforeseen, and no one regrets their failure more than the United Planets organisation.

'However, even in failure it is incumbent on the government to provide for the security of all those participating in the talks. We note that there were no significant casualties on the government side and that troops appear to have been deployed, with success, to enable the principals to escape. We make no accusations at this time, it would not be right. We merely state that Ambassador Ar'Quila, as the duly appointed representative of United Planets, was entitled to the highest possible level of protection and that if it becomes apparent that it was not received in this instance we will be holding the Benan Ty government responsible at the highest level. We trust that every measure is being taken to recover Ambassador Ar'Quila unharmed but assure the government that United Planets will do everything necessary to protect the safety of all their representatives, whatever the circumstances.'

The Ambassador lowered the terminal. A clamour erupted from the unseen press corps. 'Ambassador, do you mean you think Ar'Quila is dead?' 'Ambassador, do you think UP was wrong to talk to terrorists?' 'Ambassador…' 'Ambassador…'

The picture darkened suddenly and Maria Morales' face appeared over Par'Lennan's.

'Well, Flavian, that was the position of UP earlier tonight and only time will tell if Ar'Quila is recovered safe and well.'

'They seem to be taking a bullish line, Maria?' asked the anchor.

'They do, and in fact UP insiders have told us that this is the most aggressive response they have seen from them in a long time.'

'Has there been any response from the President to the Ambassador's statement?'

Maria pulled a serious face.

'Not yet,' she said, 'but sources close to the President say that he is following the current situation closely and will be making a statement soon.' Her expression became pious. 'In the meantime, we must all be strong and resolute in the face of any external threat.'

Flavian, in the studio, looked the camera in the eye. 'Amen to that.'

Agana sent records of all the reports to him, but after the

first couple of days, Desailly had stopped watching them. He justified it to himself by saying that Agana would tell him if there was anything he needed to know, and it was true that the broadcasters were well-trained enough to say only what he needed them to say, without him even having to tell them what it was. It was delegation, in the current crisis he was too busy to worry about such details, he told himself, knowing that wasn't the reason at all.

The recording of the latest special report sat untouched on his terminal. He leaned his head against the office window. Far below, beyond the perimeter wall, the lights of transports crossed and re-crossed, threading the city like sparkling yarn. The people didn't support him to be supine, to allow the Chi!me to take them without a fight. He would have to make a statement soon, he could sense the phrases bubbling under the surface of his thoughts. Agana was working on the rumours already.

He was not finished yet. If the Chi!me thought they could have Ty without a fight they would soon realise the depth of their mistake. He hadn't failed, this wasn't failure, if it was easy to escape them, they would not have half the galaxy for their own. There was nothing for him to apologise for. He had an uneasy flash of himself under a purple canopy while a girl laughed at him. 'Both of us, Mr Policeman?' He should have left it to his marksmen, maybe it was undignified, reckless of him. Then again, in the end what difference had it made? Just a little embarrassment, an odd snippet to add to the legend. It did no harm for people to fear him.

The glass was cold against his forehead, speckled with condensation below from his breath. As a child he had loved to write on the windows, had drawn out whole cities on freezing nights, great edifices that would disappear by morning. He raised a forefinger and drew a line down the misted pane. It started to bleed straightaway at the edges; he remembered it would do that if it wasn't really cold enough. He looked round for something to wipe his hand, thinking of the golden time when nothing had mattered any more than this; when his world was pared down to one finger on a trigger and no duty, no decisions at all.

The bulletin the next night mentioned that Desailly was expected to speak to the nation and the night after that, he did so. The news reports next day in Airdrossa were full of it, blaring the highlights in their largest letters, just legible in passing as they were scrolled past on the way to the sport. 'Desailly defiant: CAS chief lambasts critics in robust speech.' 'Desailly to Chi!me: We will not be blamed.' 'Shut UP! Desailly tells it like it is to interplanetary whingers!' In the articles themselves, the extracts were set within decorative borders as if to incite readers to keep and cast up.

'We utterly refute any suggestion that we are not doing our utmost to search for Ambassador Ar'Quila. We are not and have never been complacent at the disappearance of any sentient being and we will not lie down under the heinous accusation that we have less regard for life than the Chi!me. We may be poorer than the Chi!me, we may be of less renown in the galaxy, but we are as civilised as they, with just as much knowledge of how to behave decently. We will continue to look for Ar'Quila and we will continue to pray that our efforts will be successful…

'…We have no reason to suppose that she is not well and safe and will soon be returned to us. But if she is not, we have this to say. We received Ambassador Ar'Quila with courtesy, because of all things what we desire most of all is peace, both on our planet and with our neighbours. We listened to her proposals and we were prepared to co-operate with her plan for peace talks, although we warned her then that our experience of ViaVera made it unlikely that such talks would succeed. Unfortunately, we were proved all too right. But though we received Ar'Quila as we did, let us make one thing very clear.

'We did not invite her here. Her mission was from UP, not of our choosing. We do our utmost to protect our guests, but when those guests force themselves upon us unasked, and insist on being taken into the most dangerous circumstances, we cannot be held responsible. We hope that the Ambassador will soon be found and returned to her people, but if not, we accept no liability for her fate. Her actions were not ours, but her own. So must the consequences be.'

For a few days, there was silence from UP. The crisis was even replaced in the top billing slots by rumours that a new doctor had been summoned to the Presidential palace. Then, an announcement came direct from Chi!me One that Ambassador Ar'Quila was dead.

There were very few details at first. As Maria Morales told the camera solemnly from her usual spot outside the Chi!me embassy, the story was so hazy it was difficult to give credence to it at all. 'It's significant that this comes from Chi!me One and not from the UP office on Zargras,' she opined, her expression at knowing the difference ever so slightly smug. 'This means the

Chi!me are going it alone on this one and they may be facing an embarrassing climbdown when more details are released. For the moment, we can only wait and hope. Back to you, Flavian.'

UP's statement, following hard on the Chi!me's, was that nothing could be done until there was more proof. For a couple of days, it looked as if it was not going to be forthcoming. The story had even slipped again from the top spot in the newscasts when the witness account came out. It was late in the evening when it was first shown. They said later that everyone who was at home had gone to bed, so its first audience were the young men in the bars.

The witness was a youngish man, pale under black stubble, in the eclectic mix of quasi-military uniforms favoured by private soldiers everywhere on Ty. He was sitting on a bench against a white wall, staring straight ahead, expressionless. A voice spoke, twittering, out of sight and the translation appeared at the bottom of the screen. 'Please proceed.'

The man swallowed. His face was jowly but somehow liquid, as if he had once been much fatter than he was now. He spoke.

'I was one of the guards hired for Ambassador Ar'Quila while she was on Benan Ty,' he said. 'I worked for her in Airdrossa and then I was one of the ones chosen to go with her to the talks. I wasn't in the pavilion that day with the leaders, it was decided that we weren't necessary, but I saw what happened. When the shooting started, she was standing up, trying to stop it. I saw security guards protecting Desailly and others from the government, I saw ViaVera protecting their own, but no one was protecting her.

'I saw ViaVera shoot her, and I saw that we let it happen. I hid until the fighting ended and afterwards I saw ViaVera dragging her body away. I heard them saying they were going to bury her somewhere the mountains, where no one would ever find her. After they'd gone, I ran away. I admit it, I was scared by what I'd seen, too scared to stay in case I was stopped from saying what I knew. I managed to make contact with the Chi!me and they came for me.'

He paused, gathering himself for the peroration. All over the capital the bars were silent. The clientele, forgetting their drinks, stood gathered around the screens.

'I am Ty born and raised. I love my world. But Ambassador Ar'Quila was coming to do good, to end the suffering, and we let her die because we didn't care enough to protect her. I think we should be ashamed of that. I think those responsible will have to pay for that.'

A murmur of comment ran through the city streets. Far away, the man lowered his head. 'That's all. I've finished,' he muttered.

The birdsong voices closed in.

Par'Lennan stood on the embassy roof and thought, not for the first time, that it was a shame he had to leave behind his hat. He had only bought it a few weeks ago from a stall in the main market. Its wide, straw brim was quite unlike anything he could get on Chi!me and when pulled down, shaded his face with an air of mystery he relished. Like the men you saw sometimes in the streets late at night, folded bundles of cloth topped by a huge hat that hid their features completely. He knew of course that they were just drunk, but it always seemed to him that they were watching, seeing without being seen, superior. But it was far too large to fit into his case and he could hardly carry it in his hand; he had to maintain some dignity, after all. Fortunately, the Ty spirits were easier to transport.

At least it wasn't raining. He moved away from the rest of the embassy staff, dotted about the roof with their baggage around them, and squinted at the horizon. Against the pink-dyed clouds he could just make out a black dot that could be the flyer, although it was a little too far away to be sure. He had originally planned to drive everyone out to the spaceport, but after last night it hadn't been safe. At least half the windows had been smashed and the gates were still smouldering where they'd tried to burn them down. The additional police presence seemed to have prevented any recurrence so far, but Par'Lennan could hear the shouting and was not entirely sure the police would not, given the chance, turn round and join the rioters. As well to be hanged for a something than a something else, wasn't there a Terran expression? He couldn't remember how it went, his Terran was always shaky. Quila would have known.

It was the flyer, finally, he could see it clearly now. He stiffened his back. He might be evacuating, but he needn't look as if he was afraid. In a few minutes he would be on board and then he would never see any of this again. He had no illusions about that. Whatever happened in the current crisis, for his next posting he would be lucky to be in charge of dome cleaning on Zargras.

It was nothing to do with him, it was not his failure, but it still felt wrong to be leaving without them. Even though he hadn't liked Quila very much, even though Du'Fairosay had been superior and withdrawn and he'd always worried he'd been secretly laughing at him, they should have been here. Quila angrily refusing to leave and Du'Fairosay patiently persuading her up the ramp with the hot look in his eyes that glinted, *one day*, and then, like imagination, disappeared. He didn't suppose he'd ever really know what had happened.

The flyer loomed overhead, flattening his hair with slip-stream. A curved gangway swung out from its side. The crew at the top of it locked the bolts in place and gestured at them impatiently. Par'Lennan waved the staff forward. Everything else notwithstanding, he was shunned if he wasn't going to go last. Over the edge of the roof he caught a glimpse of upturned faces, as the crowd at the gates watched. They had stopped shouting, he realised, and despite the racket of the flyer it seemed oddly quiet. The administrative grades first, then the guards and the technical staff, trying to look insouciant as if they were airlifted to safety everyday. Everyone was in now, except him.

The bottle in his jacket pocket pressed, comfortingly, against his side. Par'Lennan, Chi!me Ambassador to Benan Ty, gestured for his case to follow him and mounted the ramp. The onlookers below saw him pause at the top, as if for something left behind, then they saw him shrug and disappear into the ship. The crew shut the doors behind him, hurrying. The flyer wheeled round the empty roof, then streaked away.

They announced it in the middle of the afternoon. On TyCorp channel 1, Our Street was halfway through and Rosala was just about to reveal to Jaime that it was his brother who was the father of her baby. Cristiana Charisma, the actress, excelled at scenes like these, she had made her reputation on them. 'Oh Jaime,' she breathed, unshed tears glistening in her eyes, 'I've wanted so much to tell you, but I didn't dare. Oh, you won't be angry with me, will you Jaime? It was only a mistake, I didn't mean it, you know I only love you. It meant nothing to me, surely I must be able to put it behind me? He's not yours, but you know he thinks he's your son.'

Jaime's rather small eyes narrowed further. He opened his mouth to demand the name of her seducer, but the announcement interrupted him, replacing the soundtrack with the news while the picture carried on running beneath it.

'We interrupt this programme to bring you tragic news,' poor, cuckolded Jaime seemed to pronounce. 'At one fifteen this afternoon, our beloved President suffered a myocardial infarction. His doctors were summoned and for two hours they worked to save his life, but they were unsuccessful. It is my sad duty to inform you that the President died thirty minutes ago, at three thirty this afternoon. Mr Desailly has asked you all to remain calm and return to your homes as quickly as possible, where you should stay tuned for further announcements. For your protection, a curfew has been announced from seven tonight in all the major cities. Thank you.'

Rosala turned to Jaime scornfully, as the soundtrack was abruptly restored. 'You are unbelievable,' she said.

In the streets of Airdrossa, the church bells started to toll.

Part 18

Quila and Terise

By Quila's counting, she had been sure for eighteen days that she was not going to die. She could tell the wound on her back was healing from constant itching that turned into pain whenever she tried to touch it. She could not yet stand, but she could sit upright for a little at a time and, with care and time, even turn over. She was proud of these markers of her recovery; it showed fortitude, she thought, to have made such progress in circumstances such as this. It was only a pity that there was no one to be impressed.

She had not seen Terise for twelve days, not since their conversation about Mara. Her food was brought occasionally by the Jeba Ihanakan and more often by a girl with a sullen expression and an overflowing top. She had not learnt her name: the girl was so monosyllabic Quila wondered if she even understood her painstaking Terran. She didn't know why Terise had not come back, she supposed she was not very high on her list of concerns. It was understandable, she knew what it was to be busy, not to have time for the things you would wish. She understood, but the hurt, sharp as an itch, was still there. She missed the company, that was the thing. She thought Terise… well, she had thought she would be more interested in her than that.

It was very dim in the hut. She thought it was probably late in the afternoon, though from the light it could have been earlier or later. The rain pattered steadily on the ground, interspersed with occasional rushing like wind in the trees. Far off, someone shouted something, there was a rattle of blaster fire, then laughter. It was about time for a meal, she thought, and as if she'd called them, she heard footsteps on the other side of the wall. A light tread, too delicate for the girl.

She pulled herself as far up as she could in the bed and watched as the door opened to admit Ihanakan with a tray. He set it down on the table by her bed and retreated back out of her sight. There was a faint scrabble as he sat down on the floor by the door. He would stay for hours sometimes. He didn't usually say anything; she supposed it was the custom of his people. She respected it, of course she did, but she suddenly felt the need for more comfort than silence.

'Ihanakan?'

There was a pause, then his answer as if from very far away. 'Yesss?'

'Talk to me. Tell me about, I don't know, the world outside this hut. I haven't been out for so long I could almost forget it exists. Tell me the news.'

'The newsss…' He let out a long, sighing breath. She tried to twist over to look at him, but sank back, wincing.

'I'm sorry, I can't stay facing that way. I'm still listening.'

'Yess.' Another pause, so long this time she wondered if he had slipped out without her hearing. She stared at the wall. His voice came finally, disembodied, whispering over the dark behind her.

'They ssay that in Airdrossa the Pressident hass died. They

ssay he hass been buried with the bodiess of all the dead Pressidentss, in the great cathedral in Airdrossa. The newss ssays that ten thoussand people wept for him.'

The hyperbole gave her the strength to be cynical.

'I don't believe that.'

'Nor do they. They ssay Dessailly will be Pressident now.'

'Desailly?' She would have thought once that the failure of the talks would have spoiled his chances, but somehow, she was still not surprised. She had learned that she could not avoid the worst outcome just through wishing. She couldn't reveal her feelings to Ihanakan; in any case, it felt so far away. She said only, 'So he gets what he wanted, after all. What else?'

'Your people have gone.'

He said it so baldly for a moment she could not grasp his meaning.

'Gone? How do you mean, gone? Has something happened to Chi!me? But no, that couldn't be, you mean, gone from here? Gone from the north province? Gone from Airdrossa?' He didn't make a sound. 'Gone from the planet?' Silence in the hut, in the dark. Someone singing splashed past the outside wall. She couldn't make out the words. 'That's it, isn't it?' she said. 'They've gone from the planet. They've withdrawn their embassy from Benan Ty. Is that what they announced?'

'There wass no announcement. But the diplomat and the sstaff from the embassy were flown out before the Pressident died.'

'They didn't do a press conference? No last words at the spaceport?'

He elaborated, unwillingly. 'They did not go to the sspaceport. The crowd in Airdrossa wass againsst them, they had ssurrounded the embassy and were beating on the gatess. The flyer landed on the roof.'

She laughed. 'From the roof! I'm sure Par'Lennan loved that, anyway. I always thought he was one for dramatic events. Was Fairo – Du'Fairosay, my assistant, was he there?'

'I do not know.'

'I suppose he must have been, if the whole embassy went.' Her thoughts were racing. 'If they all went, it means they've broken off diplomatic relations. But you only do that if you have the strongest, the most unassailable reason. You do everything you can to avoid it, because to break off relations only really means war...' She ground to a halt. 'Why,' she asked slowly, 'did they break off relations?'

'I don't...'

'And don't tell me you don't know.'

'You inssisst that you know thiss?' he asked. There was a strange note in his voice, not annoyance at her interruption at all. 'You are ssure?'

'Tell me!'

'I will tell you.' He stopped, as if preparing for some great announcement. 'They ssay they know that you are dead,' he said.

There was a silence. 'Maybe I am dead', Quila thought, 'maybe I died all along and here I am just pretending. After all, how do I know I'm alive? I only have my word for it.'

'They think I'm dead?' *Fairo, Ceronodis, Ai'Amadi think I'm dead?*

'They ssay Dessailly and the government are ressponssible, becausse they did not protect you.'

'And Desailly says...?'

'That he did not assk you to come.'

'Oh, stars above. That's it then. I suppose I wouldn't have expected anything less from him.' She pulled exasperatedly at the edge of the blanket, unpicking the fraying end with nervy fingers.

'They do know that they can stop this any time they like, don't they? ViaVera, I mean. All they have to do is let me tell my people I'm alive. Stars above, they could hold me for ransom if they wanted, I'm sure IntPro would pay for me. But if they just told someone I'm not dead they could stop this. They do know that, don't they?'

Ihanakan said nothing.

'But they won't, will they? Because Desailly is their enemy and they don't care who gets killed along the way as long as in the end he is defeated. They don't care if UP does it for them, as long as someone does. They don't care how many people die, just as long as that one man is one of them. After all, death is what they do.'

It was a lonely thought. She knew Terise was ViaVera and she knew what ViaVera was. But she'd met her and talked to her and until now she hadn't realised that innocent lives were merely something that got in the way.

'She is a terrorist,' she said, tasting it sour on her tongue. 'Is that why she hasn't come to see me?'

'She would have to tell you that hersself,' Ihanakan said. There was a rustle as he got to his feet. She knew he would go now, and suddenly, out of all the unendurable things, that seemed the most unendurable of all.

'Oh, Ihanakan, don't be offended. Don't go, please. I haven't had anyone to talk to for days. We don't have to talk about current events if you don't want to. Tell me more about your people. I know so little about you. Please?'

There was a horrible pause, then she heard another soft scrabble as he slid back down to the floor.

'I will sstay,' he pronounced. 'I will tell you what I can. What would you like to know?'

She considered. It was difficult to be interested, to drag her mind away from her present problems, but she was trained to gather any information that came her way on other cultures. She might be a prisoner, a hostage suspended between death and life, but she was still IntPro and she still had her job to do. She pulled herself up again, twisting round in defiance of the pain until she could see him. You always carried out interviews face to face. It was what you did.

'Well,' she said, 'I just want to understand your people.' Her voice in her own ears sounded different, like a classroom back on Zargras. 'I've heard so much about the Caduca, for example, it's fascinating but it seems so strange to me. Everyone I've asked has told me something, but it's so confusing. I've seen the signs in Airdrossa, the little wire men? I know it's some kind of leader and that ViaVera say it's Issa, but someone told me the name also means emptiness, something thrown away. Is Issa the Caduca? And if she is, what does that mean? What does that mean for your people, when the Caduca is someone from outside?'

'You wish to know about the Caduca? Why do you wish it?' His voice was as uninflected as always, but there was something in it nevertheless that made her feel she had trespassed.

'I'm sorry,' she said rapidly. 'I didn't mean to offend you, I don't mean to ask anything which is forbidden. I was just interested, that's all, I didn't mean to pry.' She remembered a phrase. 'I do not ask for anything which it is not licit for me to know.'

'No. No, it iss allowed. There are no ssecretss about the Caduca, it iss just the thing that everyone knowss but no one sspeakss. Issa, ass you ssay, wass ssisster to Mara and she iss leader of ViaVera in her place. In the villagess, there iss great belief in the Caduca ass a hero who will come and ssave them, like their Chrisst come again, you know? It iss a Terran thing, I think.'

'Yes, I have heard of it. But I always thought it was a sky god cult. How does that fit with the Caduca? I thought the name meant a worn-out skin?'

'I do not know. In our tongue, thiss iss not itss meaning.' If he had been given to gestures, she thought Ihanakan would have shrugged. 'Terisse ssaid once, their Christ wass god wearing a body, and when the body died he casst it off and left it behind ass a ssign.'

'Really? I hadn't read that about it. I know he died and went back to the world of the gods, but I didn't pick up on the importance of his human body. That's very interesting, I wonder if it's a Benan Ty variant. I'll have to remember to look up if there's anything similar on Benan, when I...' *get back*. The words hung, unforgiving, unsaid, in the air between them. 'So,' she went on, as if while she spoke she could maintain the pretence of going home, 'Issa is the Caduca and the Christ both?'

'In the villagess, this iss what she ssays.'

'And the people believe it?'

He snorted softly. 'Perhapss. Ssometimess.'

'And what about your people? Is Issa the Caduca to you, too?'

He didn't reply for so long she thought she had offended him after all.

'Ihanakan?'

'The Caduca for my people iss a different thing,' he said at last. His tone was firmer now, as if he had made a decision. 'Every year on the appointed day we dance the dance of the Caduca, in every village all at the ssame time, and each village tryss ass it can to be better, bolder, more than all the otherss. Each one wishess to have more honour, you undersstand?'

'You compete through the ritual.'

'I do not know "ritual", but yess. It iss competition. But this iss not Caduca. It iss acting Caduca, but it iss not Caduca. It iss ass if you looked into a clear sstream and tried to catch your reflection. It iss, and iss not. You understand? It iss not Caduca. It iss a picture only. For you cannot make Caduca, you cannot be Caduca jusst by sseeming. The Caduca iss what you are yourself. It iss inside you.'

'So the Caduca is just a person?'

'A person and nothing.'

'Nothing?'

'Yess. If you are Caduca, you do not lead, do not sspeak, do not tell how thingss should be done. You are empty. You will come to the village that iss mosst worthy, and if they are worthy, they will ssee you and will keep you all your dayss in honour. And you will be nothing.'

Quila spread her hands doubtfully. 'It seems a strange kind of leader. I'm used to the idea that leaders have to have some quality in them that means they can lead.'

'Yess,' Ihanakan said. 'But of all the thingss that musst be behind you, what better than nothing?'

She would digest that later, she thought. She couldn't cope with it now.

301

'I'm still not clear on how you get a Caduca,' she said. 'The ritual every year, that doesn't make a difference?'

'The dance, it iss a way of being worthy, that iss all. I can... that iss, anyone can wear the sseeming of Caduca but it iss jusst a sshadow, a reminder that it can be. We ssay, it keepss the place open for the Caduca when it comess, sso that the people do not forget and it knowss there iss a place prepared for it. For it will not come when you are not ready, we ssay.'

'You have to be worthy for it to come. I can see that. But when does it come? Is it something that happens once every few years, or when a star is in a particular place, or what?'

'No one can tell. No one can ssay when the Caduca will come, or where. The village that hass a Caduca has great honour, great sstanding among all the other villagess. The people of that village can walk higher, as the Terranss ssay, they will be lisstened to because they have their backs sset against the Caduca. But no one can ssay when it will come. There are dancess that can be done, thingss that we do to call the Caduca, but they do not alwayss work, you undersstand? There has been no Caduca for my people ssince the Terranss came.'

'Really? But that's a long time, isn't it? How have you managed all this time without it? Surely the destruction of your religion...'

'Iss not desstroyed!' He had not raised his voice, but she could hear the passion.

'I'm sorry, I didn't mean...'

'The coming of the Caduca iss a very great thing. It iss a time of marvelss, of great change and great deedss. We wait and we call for it. We know it hass not been the time, but we wait for our time, we wait as we musst, all through the night for the dawn. We are patient.'

'I can see you need to be.' She raised herself up on one elbow, trying to reach the tray. 'I wish I had something with me to record all this. Back home I've always studied religions, I would love to have a proper record of your Caduca. It doesn't sound like anything else I've come across, the whole Terran sky god thing is much more the type I've come to expect. Do you think you could pass me the water? I can't quite get my arm up that far.'

He unfolded himself from his squat by the door and padded over to her bedside. She took the cup from his hand.

'Thank you.' The water was warm and had a mouldy tang, but she was getting used to it. 'Were you here when Mara was alive?' she asked, over the rim.

If he was surprised at the change of subject, he did not show it.

'Yess.'

'I just wondered how she fit in with all this. Was she a possible Caduca too?'

He snorted again. 'Mara wass a good person. She fought for everyone, for the Terranss, for uss. We followed her because we loved her. She wass not god.'

'Interesting.' She reached out to put the cup back on the tray. 'You will come again, won't you, Ihanakan? This has been so fascinating, I would love to discuss all this with you more. You don't mind?'

She couldn't stretch her arm far enough. Gently, he prised the cup from her hand and set it down. 'I will come,' he said, 'and tell you what you need to know.'

Part 19

The Invasion

For three days after the President died, the people took to the streets. Despite the curfew, the police could do nothing to stop them. From somewhere, no one asked where, they had got placards, white with red lettering, saying 'President Desailly' on one side and 'The people have spoken' on the other. They wound quietly through the oldest part of the capital, from the high buildings looking like nothing so much as an illustration from a Terran history, blood smeared on snow.

After the second demonstration, Desailly, modestly, suggested the senate should convene an emergency session to decide how to deal with the problem. The crowds were hotheads, he said, and he had no desire for anything other than the proper procedure. But when the people were roused, you never knew what they would do. He would hate for it to become violent... The senators took the hint. After a night of deliberations half drowned out by the crowds outside, they declared that the election had taken place by popular acclaim and named Desailly President. Desailly appeared to the crowds on the balcony of the Presidential palace, waving while in practised harmony they sang his name.

On the second day of the new presidency, the state news company picked up a report from a Benan outlet that the

Chi!me had called a special session of UP to debate 'the Benan Ty problem.' They didn't explain what the problem was, seemingly even for Benan it had suddenly become a given. They did, however, show the speech the Chi!me First Representative made for the press.

It was repeated so often that many people in the cities could quote it verbatim. In every bar, in every home, over and over, the case against Benan Ty. The people to whom it was addressed were Chi!me and its dependants, Gargarin and the remnants of their Empire, a few Terrans on the edges, not daring to speak up. It wasn't said where it was, presumably Zargras where UP was based, or Chi!me itself. There were no windows, no scenery, nothing to place it, just a plain mauve screen behind him that could have been anywhere at all.

The Chi!me First Representative, Flavian Singolo explained on TyCorp's rolling news, was the leader of the Chi!me Council and the nearest thing those egalitarian people had to a President. Dir'Kennan, his name was. He was tall for a Chi!me, thick around the shoulders so that his tunic hung inelegantly, bulked under his arms and tight around the neck. He had come up, so Flavian reported, through the Office of Interplanetary Protocols as so many of the leaders they affected not to have had done before him. He spoke not like a politician, not like Desailly, but as if he meant what he said. Even through the translator on his shoulder, it was as if every word was only spoken because it was necessary, manifestly true.

'Ar'Quila went to Benan Ty in friendship,' he said, and in the bars of Airdrossa it seemed as if all over the galaxy people were agreeing that this was so. 'She went to bring peace between the government and the rebel guerrillas who have been fighting each other for the best part of eight cycles. Her thanks for this were no support, no help, no security and an avoidable, shameful death.

'She went to help the people of Benan Ty. She went to save their lives and in the end, they killed her for it. I am sure you have seen the footage of her mother, dealing with the news that her daughter, her only child, will not be coming home. You will have seen the pictures of the Dome One on Zargras hung with black for the woman who was very much a central part of that community and will never walk there again. I don't need to tell any of you how much value we place on one life and how precious it is, not only to those who had the privilege of knowing Ar'Quila while she was alive, but to all of us.'

His voice shook slightly on the last word. He glanced down, took a moment to swallow before he went on.

'But these are private griefs. They are not for UP to worry about. What is for UP very much to worry about is that Ar'Quila was on Ty not as a representative of the Chi!me but as an Ambassador for UP. When he killed her, Desailly was doing his best to kill UP too, because of what UP stands for. UP is for the rule of law, for order and security and that's what he hates. We have to show small-time thugs like Desailly that we can stand up to them, that we will not permit our galaxy to be ruled by their whims.' Even before the translation you could hear the scorn in his tone, grated on the edge of his teeth. Their *whims*.

'We will not allow violence and tyranny against any of our representatives and we will not allow the people of Benan Ty to suffer under this oppression any longer. Desailly is a danger to all of us and he is a danger to the people he is supposed to rule. That is why we have called UP to meet and that is why our motion calls for the most stringent measures against him. Of course, we require an immediate, complete apology for the murder of Ar'Quila, both to UP and to us. But we need more than that, we cannot allow Desailly to go unchecked. We have a responsibility and we must face up to it.'

His hand, lying on the side of the lectern, clenched into a fist.

'We are asking UP to require Ty to pay reparations of fifty million Chi!me din'arii. We demand the surrender of Desailly for immediate criminal trial at UP for his part in Ar'Quila's murder and his many other crimes. And we require the stationing of a permanent UP force on the planet to enforce and maintain a ceasefire between the government and the rebels.

'These measures will ensure the safety and stability of that whole region of space. They will make sure that Ar'Quila did not die in vain and they will free the people of Benan Ty from the tyranny they have suffered under for too long. If Ty will not agree to these conditions, or breaches them in any way, we are asking that the most serious consequences should immediately follow. We think that these measures are a fitting memorial to Ar'Quila, who worked so tirelessly in the cause of peace and more than that, a fitting future for the people of Ty. We very much hope that the members of UP will vote for them.'

He stopped. The screen was immediately obscured by blurred journalistic arms; the Benan station was obviously rather far back in the crowd.

'What happens if they don't?' someone shouted out.

Dir'Kennan's face was hidden, but he sounded unruffled.

'We hope for their sakes that they do the right thing. We

don't want, we have never wanted, to have to resort to extreme measures. But we will do what we have to do. Their fate is in their hands.'

Desailly sat in the President's – no, *his* – best transport outside the cathedral, waiting to be blessed. The inauguration wasn't often done any more. Old Juan had never bothered with ceremonies, he could almost see him pulling a blaster on the Bishop and telling him it was by that, and not the Church's approval, that he ruled, alright? Sept Karne had disapproved of ceremonies too, although for different reasons, and had been equally disdainful of God. He had walked the streets of Airdrossa on his own for the whole day after his election, shaking hands with everyone he met. 'The people will be my bodyguards and if they are not sufficient, I deserve none,' he was supposed to have said when his aides protested. He was never going to be a long-lived man, Sept Karne.

Felipe Silvio before him had had some strange secular ritual in the main square; it had rained and hardly anyone had come. Before that he didn't know, he had been a child, not caring. Maybe no one had done it properly since Benan had given them Carlo Morales to be their first President after the civil war a hundred years ago. He remembered being taught at school how shocking it was that the Benan leader had handed the Archbishop the holy oil to anoint Morales with, and how it had always seemed fitting to him, like coming home.

He had always thought it would be important to hold the ceremony, both as a symbol of a new start after the long years of Juan's illness and as a sign for everyone who might have doubted it that there was no link at all between Desailly, Juan

Gutierrez's faithful servant, and Desailly the President. He had had it planned down to the last detail for months, Agana's pert little secretary had had to stand on a chair in her heels to get the archive cubes down from the high shelf when he had stopped by last week to look over the arrangements.

The words were the same words used in that first ceremony a hundred years ago, when the Archbishop had blessed Morales and declared him President by the grace of God and the will of the people and Benan had looked on from beside the altar, approving. Tradition said that the Archbishop, who was a tough old fighter who had routed looters out of the cathedral in the civil wars swinging his crozier like a mace, had said to Morales after he'd poured the oil: 'My son, I will pray that you may be worthy of the great trust that has been given you. May you have the strength to lead our people into the dark places where they must walk.' He had always liked that, it had the combination of doom and philosophy of which good ceremonies were made. It seemed remarkably prophetic now.

A few spots danced on the windscreen and the chauffeur wiped them away. The cathedral bell began, slowly, to toll. The leader of his guard for the day opened the side of the transport for him and he stepped out. The rain was just beginning, nothing more than a mizzle hanging in the air, misting the shoulders of the guards' dress coats. The west front of the cathedral was still covered in scaffolding from the fire five years ago, the famous coloured window flicking in and out of sight as the tarpaulin rattled in the breeze. From the other side of the building he could hear, muffled with distance, the singing of the crowds. His organisation, at least, was better than Silvio's, he said to himself, and snorted with laughter at the thought.

The nearest guard turned to him, concerned.

'Sir? Is there a problem?'

He considered explaining, but the blank incomprehension was all too easy to imagine.

'Nothing,' he said. 'Never mind.'

'Continuing our extended coverage of President Desailly's inauguration here exclusively on TyCorp news extra, this is Flavian Singolo at the newsdesk. As the President leaves the cathedral for a well-earned rest before tonight's celebrations at the Presidential palace, over on News 2 we have a special retrospective on the President's life and career so far. If you've ever wondered what makes Petrus Desailly tick, this is for you. That's coming right up on News 2, but here on News 1, at the slighter later time because of the extended inauguration coverage, here is the evening news.

'First up this hour, more news from Zargras as the special UP session, convened by the Chi!me last week to discuss the death of UP Ambassador Ar'Quila at the hands of ViaVera, gets underway. We have exclusive footage from our sister station on Benan of the proceedings, including interviews with the various ambassadors who will be voting. But first, Maria Morales brings us this special report on the workings of the United Planets. Maria.'

Maria, her hair swept back so that it made a crest round her face, stood poised against a backdrop of Zargras, as seen from space.

'Thanks, Flavian,' she said. 'Tonight, all eyes are fixed as never before on UP while we wait for the result of the vote on the Chi!me's appeal. Are the members of UP going to see

310

sense, or are they going to agree to this unreasonable thirst for misplaced revenge over the death of the envoy? To know, we have to understand where UP comes from. What it does, what it represents, and who it serves.

'This,' she gestured at the screen behind her, 'is Zargras, home of the United Planets organisation since it was set up in the wake of the Chi!me/Gargarin war to promote understanding and dialogue between the different forces in the galaxy. Originally an unpopulated planet, the Chi!me have quickly made Zargras their own. Not only UP and its enforcement and special operations arm the Office of Interplanetary Protocols but many major Chi!me businesses are based there. In Dome One, it is only the fact that you are in a dome, they say, that tells you that you are not on Chi!me itself. In the same way, there has always been the suspicion that the Chi!me have undue influence over UP.

'When UP was founded, there were only five members: the Chi!me, the Gargarin, Zhairgen, Terra and Orrorin, which at that time had newly seceded from the Gargarin and indeed, was renowned for its consistent opposition to Gargarin motions for the first hundred years or so of UP's existence. Now it has grown to over two hundred members, covering huge sections of space, but the way those two hundred members are allocated has not always been fair. I spoke to Dr Ersine of Benan, an expert in the UP constitutional history.'

'Of course, as UP grew, so did the problems.' Dr Ersine, grey-haired with an improbably pointed beard, leaned back in his chair and steepled his hands. 'Inequalities such as the fact that Herantive, in the Chi!me sphere of influence, has its own representative whereas Ty with a much larger population shares representation with Benan were bound to create disagreements, especially when the advantage always seemed to go the same way. UP has also failed to move with the times, so that Darien, which is hardly more than a smugglers' lair, still has a representative while much of the former Terran empire does not. UP has been allowed to become monolithic and unresponsive and any independent observer would conclude that that is just how its most powerful member wishes it to be.'

The picture of Zargras reappeared and Maria went on.

'In fact, the Chi!me now count around one third of all the UP members as their direct dependants, including once-proud systems like Zhairgen, one of the founder members, and have often been able to swing the votes of many more. In fact, many observers feel the hope of a correct vote hangs on only a very few worlds.'

A younger man appeared, captioned as 'Dr Benite, political scientist, Carthia.'

'When we talk about UP deciding, what we have to remember is that effectively, it has already decided. Most of the so-called independent worlds are now so dominated by the Chi!me, or afraid of repercussions, that they will vote how they are told regardless of the issue. But interestingly, under the UP constitution, a simple majority is not enough. A resolution has to be passed by seventy five percent of the members, and those voting for it have to include at least three out of the five original groupings.

'Now, it is very probable that the Chi!me will get their seventy five percent, although many of the independent worlds will be reluctant to vote with them. But, out of the five founder members, only Zhairgen can be relied on to vote with the

Chi!me. Leaders from Terran worlds will find it very difficult to justify to their own people voting for action against Ty, and, remember, Terra's membership is still suspended, so we are talking about the colonial democracies, like Ty is, who are accountable to their people.

'Orrorin, after its flirtation with the Chi!me, now votes consistently with the Gargarin, so if we assume that the Terrans will vote no, to get their three out of five votes, the Chi!me need the Gargarin. It really comes down to how the Gargarin will jump. Do they have the will to vote against the Chi!me? They are opposed to Chi!me expansion, that's certain, but can they stomach another trade war with their economy in such a weak state? This is what we will find out.'

The backdrop changed to a view of a street in a Gargarin city, thronged with people.

'With so many cheap flights to Gargarin worlds,' Maria went on, 'many Terrans and Terran colonists have got to know Gargarin culture: their food, their music, the teeming life of the narrow streets which are such a feature of their major cities. Holidays on Gargarin are popular because of their very exoticism, because it is a culture so different from ours. So what does make the Gargarin tick?'

Dr Ersine again. 'The Gargarin are consciously a mysterious people. It's their way of relating to the outside world. You only have to remember their obsession with mazes to realise that. We've all had the experience of being lost in a Gargarin city, because they are designed precisely to disorientate the visitor. What began as a defence mechanism against invaders has continued as a way of defending their culture against those who they might see as attacking it.

'What you have to remember about the Gargarin is that they lost the war. They are a proud people and they do not take losing lightly. For them, the UP mission has been a difficult, an uncharacteristic thing to engage in. They might have their problems economically – they are dependent on Chi!me trade in sectors which have been hit by the galactic downturn – but we know that the economy is never crucial in these sorts of situations. They know that this vote comes down to them and the question in everyone's mind is whether they will be able to resist the chance to defeat the Chi!me. It may be too close to call, but in my opinion, everything we have learned about the Gargarin says no.'

Terrenkomo Barcharin, the new head of the Gargarin delegation at UP, squinted at the thronging cameras barring his way into the chamber.

'Ambassador Barcharin,' someone shouted, 'is it true that you knew Ambassador Ar'Quila?'

His heavy face betrayed no expression. 'Yes, I knew her. We were together on Iristade, where she made a peace no less lasting and historic than the peace on Benan Ty.'

'How did you feel when you heard she was dead?'

'She was someone who worked very hard for the cause of peace. I know that there were many people who wanted her dead, but I was not one of them. I regret her death and though I do not have much hope of it, I would be glad if one day, those responsible would be brought to justice.'

'You don't feel, then, that UP can do anything to bring her killers to justice?' the voice, sensing a story, was suddenly avid. 'Does that mean you will be voting against the resolution today?'

Terrenkomo's snout lifted.

'We are a simple people, my people,' he said. 'We do as we must do, our great days are done. Who are we to stand against those who know how best to right the wrongs of the universe, when we do not do these things any more?'

'So you're voting yes?'

Terrenkomo held up a steadying hand.

'As to how we will vote, I am sorry, but you will have to wait until we have voted. I know you have your story, but you will have to be patient, yes? But, we are not an unreasonable people. I will tell you one thing.' He did not move, but there was a sense, in the brief hush, of leaning forward confidentially, of the imparting of secrets.

'We have become accustomed, perhaps us more than most, to compromise and disillusion,' the Gargarin Ambassador said. 'But on the day Ambassador Ar'Quila's killers are brought forward to be judged, there will truly be a new beginning for peace and justice in the galaxy, even if none of us are there to see it.'

There was a short silence. Then,

'But, Ambassador…!'

'Ambassador, do you mean…?'

'Ambassador, are you saying…?'

He held up his hand again, pointed teeth appearing at the side of his long mouth.

'No more, no more questions. Now, if you will excuse me.'

The picture, wobbling, showed his bodyguards pushing through the throng, his bulk stepping into the chamber. There was a brief impression of light, of red and green hangings, then the doors slammed back and there was only dark.

It was the Benan Ambassador who brought Desailly the news. He had his people glued to the broadcasts, of course, but news reporting was restricted from Zargras. There would always be some delay. Claudius Dixon had been a consistent supporter of Desailly's; in his five years on Ty he had almost become a friend. When he was shown in to the Presidential office he hadn't really needed to speak at all, what he had to tell had been clear enough on his face.

'I've just heard from our people on Zargras,' he said. 'It's yes.'

Desailly nodded.

'I'm sorry, Petrus. We did what we could, we tried to tell them...'

'I know, I heard the speech yesterday. What was it, 'this misbegotten drive for empire, unknown since the days before we discovered the stars and justice, that masquerades under the banner of freedom...'? It was a good speech. Your guy couldn't have done any more.'

'It was those blasted Gargarin. We really thought we had a chance to turn them, but in the end...' Claudius shook his head. 'I thought they had more guts.'

'They might have guts, but there's not much you can do when your balls are on the block. The Gargarin are bought and paid for, we know they had no choice but to vote with the Chi!me. It would have been suicide for them to do anything else, they might be sympathetic, but they don't love us that much.'

'But still, there must have been something we could have...'

'I know you did what you could,' Desailly said. 'I wasn't expecting anything else. I know well enough that nothing anyone could do would change it.'

He got up, strolled to the end of the room where the window looked out over the forecourt. Claudius watched him.

'What are you going to do now? Negotiate?'

Desailly didn't turn. 'What would you expect me to do?'

'Can you surrender? Submit to a trial? You know how difficult it would be to pin anything on you.'

A guardsman crossed the courtyard, whistling. Somewhere out beyond the gate, a transport squealed with an outburst of hooting.

'I am not the stuff of which martyrs are made,' Desailly said to the glass, 'nor have I ever believed that a long death in prison was the purpose of my days. We may be outnumbered, outgunned, outplanned, but we are going to fight. It has never been said that the people of Ty lacked for courage.'

'Bravo.' Claudius clapped, half-ironic. 'That's exactly what I thought you'd say. You know I'll have to pull my people out?'

Desailly turned to face him. 'I'd be disappointed if you didn't have the transport already loaded. Leaving in half an hour?'

'Three quarters.' Desailly raised a questioning eyebrow. 'I don't like to run up gangways. At my age, it's bad for the digestion.' He paused. 'Petrus. You know I hate to leave like this. Ever since I arrived here, you've been… well, I wish it could be different, that's all. But, then,' he went on with forced jollity, 'When you've driven the Chi!me all the way back to Zargras, I'll come back, we'll have drinks at the embassy, what do you say?'

Desailly curled his lip. 'I say have a safe journey, and give my regards to Sophie.'

Claudius's bodyguard, at the door, saw the two men shake hands, dark heads almost meeting as they bowed. Then his boss came striding out with his head down. He went swiftly down the stairs, much faster than usual so that the bodyguard had to hurry to keep up, and on the turn, he stumbled, as if for some reason he couldn't quite see.

'By now you will have heard the news from Zargras,' Desailly's face, grainy with size, looked blindly out over the main square from the hastily-erected screen. All over Airdrossa, all over the planet, every screen in every bar was tuned to the same channel, an audience crowded around each. The words, at different pitches, echoed off the shuttered windows; soared choral over closed and tumbled roofs.

'You will know what the Chi!me have demanded. They have demanded that we pay them fifty million din'arii, that we allow them here, in our land, in a permanent presence, that you give your leader up for their "justice". These are their demands, but they have demanded still more. They have demanded our heart, our soul. They have demanded that we give up our pride to them, that we become an enslaved people like so many others have done and bow down. I have eight days to give them an answer. It is generous of them, but I do not need eight days to know your answer. I do not need eight hours, or eight minutes. I know that you say, as I say, no. We are Ty, we bow down for no one. We say, no. Whatever comes, we say no.'

'I am here today to express my thanks to our fellow members of United Planets,' Dir'Kennan said to the press conference. The Benan camera, at the back as usual, bobbed over the assembled heads to get a clear picture. 'In any great enterprise, it is doubly important that we go forward together, and I am proud to say that the yes vote for our resolution on Benan Ty was carried with the largest single majority for any vote at UP in the last ten cycles. I came here to ask the community of planets if we had the courage to deal with a rogue in our midst, to free a people suffering and broken from years of tyranny and I am glad, and proud, that the answer was yes. That however hard it may be, whatever we will have to do, we say yes.'

'They talk as if they want peace,' Desailly went on 'but they have only ever wanted war. They roam the galaxy looking for likely victims and we are their latest prize. They think they will capture us, that they will be able to tame us and make us dance to their tune. Well, we have to show them that they are wrong. That we are not their easy conquests that they have had before. That we are the sticking-place, the place that brings them down.'

Dir'Kennan shifted position behind the lectern. 'We have given Desailly eight of their days to respond, but to be frank, we do not expect him to do so. Desailly is a desperate man by now. He has never recognised the rule of law and he cares so little for his own people that he would even use them as living shields if it would buy him a little more time. We have never wanted a war, but we are prepared, if Desailly forces us, to remove him by force. You appreciate I can't give you confidential details of troop movements, but we are ready.'

'They are coming and we are ready for them. We have been preparing for this ever since the Ambassador went missing, because we know what they are like. And we need not be afraid of them. All they have is armaments, whereas we have the heart and spirit of a people fighting for their homes, who will not be beaten. Make no mistake, they will have no mercy on us. Soldier or civilian alike, we can expect nothing from them. So we must fight them from the moment that they land until the last Chi!me corpse is lifted off into space. If we cannot fight them openly then we will fight them secretly. We will follow them, surround them, every man, woman and child will be a warrior, until every step they take on our Ty soil will be bought and paid for in their blue blood.'

'We will of course make every effort to minimise civilian casualties, using surgical strikes to take out key military installations while leaving the hospitals, schools and homes untouched. We are coming for Desailly, not for the people of Benan Ty. They were not responsible for the murder of Ambassador Ar'Quila. They have suffered enough, we have no quarrel with them. But I give them this message: 'Rise up! Overthrow Desailly, put a democratic government in charge. We are not your enemies, we only want to help you. And you can help yourselves. You can break with the past and make a better future for yourselves.'

'They are not only coming for me, but for all of you. I will lead you, but it is for you to fight. We will stand together and together we will fight the Chi!me as no one has ever fought the Chi!me before. We will make history together, and they will say our names in free Ty with awe for a thousand years.'

'We do not want a fight, we would always prefer to settle a conflict with peaceful means. But we have right on our side, and justice.'

'It is our right to resist every attack on our planet, every attempt to take our land. We know that our cause is just.'

'We are coming, not for conquest, but to free the people of Benan Ty. And we resolve now not to shrink, not to yield, until they are free.'

'We are fighting together for our freedom, and we will not stop, will not give in until we are free.'

'Until we have won.'

'Until we have won.'

Part 20

Quila and Terise

'No way!' Marius, shouting. Behind the half-open door, Terise identified his voice without effort. 'There is no way we can sit here and do nothing! You're fucking mad if you think we're gonna waste this!'

'Not only think, but will.' Ladyani's tone was firm. 'I've told you what we're doing, all you have to do is go out and tell the others. Go out and spread the word, that's what you're good at, isn't it?'

A scrape, a wooden crash. Marius again, closer.

'What the fuck d'you mean by that?'

Terise dug her clenched fingers into her palm. *Come on, we don't want a fight now, not now. Back down, what does it matter, back down, back down.*

'What I say. I hear you're a great conversationalist recently, I've heard a lot about what you've been saying. You can say what you like, gossip all day with the other old women for all I care. But not about this and not in this place. This is not a debate.'

'You fucking arrogant bastard! You think...'

'Oh God, Lad,' Terise whispered. She knew the fight was coming now. She knew well enough what he thought.

'You think you can shut me up?' Marius yelled to Ladyani. 'You think you can proclaim whatever fucking stupid thing you want and suddenly it's law? You fucking arrogant bastard, what gives you the right?'

'You think you can play your little games, canvass all your little supporters, go round the camp bad-mouthing me? What gives me the right? What gives *you* the right?'

'Why shouldn't I? I've a right to my opinion.' Pugnacious as always. Terise could imagine him, squat and powerful on the middle of the floor, fists clenched, words with the cadence of a child's taunt suddenly, incongruously in his mouth. 'Who fucking died and made you king?'

Over a rustle of skirts, Issa answered.

'That would be Mara, my sister. I'm sure you remember.'

There was a small silence.

'You ask what gives me the right?' Ladyani went on. 'She does. She does and our destiny does. We are ViaVera, we are the true path and we are on the true path. I can lead us to our destiny, I can see where we are going. I have the right. I also,' a shuffle, a snick as something clicked into place, 'have a blaster pointing at your head. Any questions?'

In Terise's mind's eye, her wishful-thinking eye, Marius was abased, on his knees by now. He didn't sound it.

'Well, what gives you the right to come armed to council meetings springs to mind. So that's your answer, is it? You tell us you know what you're doing and we all just have to fall in line?'

Ladyani was almost laughing at him, joyous. 'We have our destiny to fulfil, we have the Caduca to follow, we have…'

Marius shouted. 'See, that's it, that's fucking it, right there. I am so fucking sick of all this fucking mysticism! Why does everything have to be so weird with you? Why is it all so damn…*alien*? We're fighting a fucking war, this is not the work

323

of the fucking Lord here. That Caduca shit might be good enough for the peasants but it's not tactics, it's not a fucking plan.'

'That Caduca shit?' Issa, unheard.

'We start thinking that and we're all dead. It didn't used to be like this, man. You were always a fucking crazy bastard, but you used to talk to us. You know this invasion is the biggest thing to happen to Ty for a generation. You know that. You bloody well know that. How can you possibly think the right thing to do is for us to sit up here on our fucking arses in the forest and watch?

'There's gonna be resistance, there's gonna be new groups, we need to be in on that. Recruits, money, ammo, even, think of the Chi!me weapons we could get! I don't give a fuck about the Chi!me but we can't ignore what's gonna happen. If we do, there's nothing left for us. I don't know what the fuck you mean by the true road any more, but I'm pretty sure that ain't it.'

Pushing her face into the corner of the door Terise could just make out the faces. Marius had his back to her, she could see only his thinning hair. Ladyani, she could tell was off to the left, because everyone was looking that way. Wolf, directly opposite, rocking his chair on its back legs; Sario next to him; Roberto at the corner where she could only see his profile. Variously bored, uncomfortable and resigned, as if they would rather be somewhere else, as if it were nothing to do with them. As if this were not the question the whole camp was debating, even her.

They'd known almost immediately that the Chi!me were coming, it was clear from the broadcasts from the first, whatever the announcers said. Everywhere she'd gone in the camp there had been somebody arguing about what they should do; she even saw Ihanakan a few times earnestly debating something with a crowd of Jeba. As if they knew, as if any of them could guess the Chi!me's intentions. It was Issa who had dealt with them, Issa and presumably Ladyani, though he had never said. Out of all the camp it was only those two and Terise herself who had even spoken to one. Elenore had summed it up: 'The Chi!me will come to kill us, the Chi!me will help us, the Chi!me will crown us with rubies and make us lords of the world, I've heard them all and I don't know how to pick. They're all just as unlikely as each other.'

'We gotta get down there, join in.'

The voices debating, everywhere you turned.

'Fight for the fucking government?'

    'Not for the government, fuckwit. Who wants to fight for them? I'm talking about fighting for us. I know what Ladyani says and he's bloody wrong. If we want to get anything out of this, we've got to be in this.'

On the steps, in the doorways of the huts, leaning beneath the eaves out of the rain. Arguing.

'I tell you, this is the best thing that could ever have happened to us. Never mind about that meeting shit, that's all in the past. I'm talking alliance, I'm talking the Chi!me coming to us. We come out and help them, they'll be falling over themselves to give us this province.'

'The Chi!me might be coming for Airdrossa but where d'you think they're gonna go afterwards? You think they're gonna leave us here, you think they're gonna welcome us? We gotta fight them, we gotta fight them with whatever and whoever we can, else they'll be coming for us.'

'We can't get involved. If the Chi!me come for the government, what's that to us? Let them kill each other, we're alright here. Ladyani and *la dona* are right. It doesn't mean anything to us.'

'All I know,' Elenore had said, 'is that we aren't people who've ever let others do our fighting for us. We've never waited before while our fate was decided far away by our lords and masters. If we had been, we wouldn't be here; we none of us would have come to ViaVera and we would never have done the things we've done. We don't sit at home; we act, we change things. I don't see any reason why we should stop doing that. And I think whatever the Chi!me think of us, they're still coming here to conquer and rule. Hating the government doesn't mean we have to love the worse bully that kills it, it just means we have two enemies to fight.'

There were lines under her eyes and streaks in her hair, and on her thin, brown wrist the veins stood out where she'd pushed back her sleeve.

'So, will you go?' Terise had asked her, wanted to plead and not daring to. 'If Issa says not, I mean? Would you really leave?'

Elenore had carried on staring at her hands.

'I'd like to say I would. I'd like to say I'd pick up my old rifle, leave the bread to burn and be out of here. I know I should. After all, if I'd stayed at home, I'd be cleaning up my father's old hunter right about now, sending my mother up on the roof to look for sharp slates to throw. Why should I do less? That's what they're doing down there. Whatever we do or don't do, whatever bloody Desailly says, they'll fight. They won't fight for him, but they'll fight for themselves, just because when the soldiers march into your street and kick down your door that's what you do.

'And I would like to join them, I really would. Can't you feel how good it would be to have something worth dying for again, go back to when everything was simple and just fight? We used to be so innocent, do you remember? So pure and righteous then, before everything. It's tempting, so tempting. I could just go, I can feel it, so close I can almost touch it.'

'Elenore…'

'But you can't stand forever with such a weight on your back, you can't keep your eyes on the prize when all you do is bake bread in the dark.' She'd smiled then, with no joy in it. 'So no, don't worry. I won't be going anywhere.'

'And you know all about it, of course. Everything there is to know about where we're going and what we should do and they'll all follow you. Of course.' Ladyani, richly sarcastic.

'Not all. Some of them will, if I ask them to.' It seemed to Terise that Marius didn't want to go where his words were taking him. She clenched her fists harder. In a more moderate tone, he added, 'I won't ask them if I don't have to. You know whatever we do we should do it together. I don't want to split…'

Ladyani didn't share his unwillingness. 'Split! You should be so lucky! Who do you think you are? You think you're the leader now, you think you're the Caduca? You think anything you do can make a difference to us? You're a fucking idiot. And I'm still holding the blaster. What makes you think you can even get out of this room?'

Terise heard a footstep, she couldn't tell whether it was forward or back.

'I don't get you, man,' Marius said. 'You know I'm right, you have to. Alright, it's a risk, I know it's a risk, but you're the fucking mad one. You don't care, you've never cared how many of us get killed when it's one of your schemes. You know the lads say you're only still alive because you're best friends with Death; you know that because you tell them the fucking story. You'll take us all the way to Ultima for that fucking stupid meeting but you won't take us to Airdrossa to fight. I don't wanna fight you, I sure as Hell don't wanna leave, I wanna stay and convince you we have to go together. What can I say?' His voice became scornful. 'And you can stop posturing with that blaster. You know you're not gonna use it.'

'No. *Wrong.*' Terise put her hands over her ears against the blast. Over the din, through the smoke she heard the others shouting, then Marius again, wavering with shock. 'You shot me! You fucking shot me! You fucking maniac, what d'you do that for?' She couldn't tell where he was hit. At least the volume of his shouts suggested it wasn't serious.

There was a click as Ladyani put the blaster back in its holster. 'I was tired of talking.'

'That's it. That's it, I'm leaving. I'm fucking well out of here and I'm taking with me anyone who'll come. Fuck you. We're going to Airdrossa and we're gonna to fight. Who's with me? Robbo, Sario? Wolf, you coming?'

If there was a reply, Terise never heard it.

'Alright then, never mind. Fuck the lot of you. There'll be plenty of us without you.'

The room was still filled with smoke. Try as she might, Terise could barely see Marius. She thought he moved towards the door, then stopped again.

'Anyone else wants to join us, they'll be welcome. But you, *brother*, not you. If I see you again, I'll kill you.' The door opened, wreaths curling out to the grey sky. In the distance, someone was calling, feet were running towards them. Marius stepped through. He said something, but she couldn't make it out. Nico and Jaiyro burst in.

'What happened? Is everyone alright? We heard a blast! And Marius, his ear...'

They exclaimed to the room at large and it was Issa who answered.

'Nothing's happened,' she said, in a voice so serene it could have been true. 'Everything's fine.'

Terise slipped out the back way as the council broke up so that she didn't have to talk to them. People had left before, of course, people had disappeared or died or just slipped away, lost in a hundred different ways. But not Marius, Marius who had been there since before she arrived, who had been there when Mara died. Marius was a fixture, ageless as stone, and she was sure that Ladyani and Issa would be snide about him. As she closed the back door, she noticed Ihanakan, coming towards her on the path from the kitchen.

'I hear you had an interessting meeting,' he said.

'You heard already? Yes, there've been better, you could say that.'

He stood against the wall of the palace, regarding her steadily.

'I don't know, Ihanakan. I don't know how many will go with him. His friends, I suppose, Pedro and Darsin and those lads, Chebo maybe, but I don't know how many others. It's not as if we've been brimming with recruits, this could really weaken us. And what if they're right and the Chi!me come for us next? What if half us of stomp off to get killed in Airdrossa and they come for the rest of us when we're too weak to even fight them? I can't say Marius was wrong, exactly, but this is the worst thing that could have happened, it really is.'

'You have ssaid thiss to Ladyani?'

'No. I know what he'd say. "We don't need them, it's just throwing out the fish guts," or something like that. He'd say that and I know he'd have a point, but...' She sighed. 'I can't help feeling it's just choosing the company you die in. And I know you'll tell me that's very important too.'

'Of coursse.'

'What about your people? What are you going to do?'

'What we musst. We do not know yet what we will be assked to do, but we are ready.'

She smiled, a little sourly. 'Nice to know that someone is. Have you come from Qui - the Chi!me woman? How is she doing?'

'She iss well. She iss much better. There iss pain, I think, but less and she can eat a little, now. I think in time she will be sstrong again.'

'That's good.'

He caught her eye and held it.

'She misses you. She wisshess to talk to you.'

Terise looked away. 'I don't see why. You've been doing such a good job nursing her...'

'Nursing iss not for the body only. She iss not a fool. She knows there iss ssomething she doess not know. She needss to know it.'

'So I have to tell her, is that what you're saying? I know you're right, I know, but I just...' She glanced back at him, shaking her head. 'I can't think how to do it. What would I say? I can't just come out with it. And then what? I've almost killed her once already, I don't want to do that again.'

Ihanakan's look was not unsympathetic, but it was clear that he was not going to relent.

'She needss to know and there iss no one elsse who can tell her. You musst.'

'I know. I'm just railing against the inevitable, as always. I'll go and see her.'

She grimaced, caught his eye, unforgiving.

'Alright, alright,' she said. 'I promise.'

Part 21

The Invasion

The rain stopped, the clouds cleared, and they saw the smoke rising. Three columns of black against the dull afternoon sky; two close together, leaning in to each other so that their tops, wisping, merged and palled, and one a little left. It was shorter than the others, like a child beside its parents. 'That's the station,' someone said, knowledgably. No one contradicted. It was what you knew about Nuerio, that it was the home of almond chocolates, purple roses and an ornate station canopy designed by Vittorio Nocte himself.

A small place, an insignificant place, somewhere seen for an hour's diversion from the spaceport, a picture of curling steel and some nutty sweets in a ribboned bag. The ribbons from the best shop were always purple, like the rose. Now fifty miles away the sculpted girders were melting, purple dye running in the gutters as steel fell like rain. The smoke stood sculpted against the skyline, elegant as if it was meant to be there, as if it had always been there. All over Airdrossa, people stopped and watched it, while beyond their sight Nuerio burned.

Cico Donato viewed the smoke for a while from the front door, but he didn't like to be away from his desk for too long. Not that there was much he should be doing; normal monitoring and counter-terrorism seemed to have been shut down for weeks and no one was coming in. He'd spent most of the last few days staring at the scratches in the opposite wall, concentrating so that, without moving, they looked just like a face. Sometimes it was a sympathetic face, sometimes leonine, noble. Other times it was just plain scornful; he would find himself trying not to catch its eye.

That was the trouble with not having enough work. It wasn't the largest CAS office at the best of times, really only Captain Rosares's team whoever else might be supposed to be based here. Nevertheless, he was responsible for security in the building and he had to do it properly. He rubbed his finger round the collar of his shirt. Almost a year he'd had this job and by the end of every afternoon it was still chafing on his spots.

By now there were hardly any of the staff in either. First it was the Jeban cleaning team who hadn't showed up, then two days ago they'd heard the Chi!me had landed and Captain Rosares hadn't been in since. After that, the numbers had just got fewer and fewer. He supposed they had other orders, important work to do to defend the capital. He tried not to be envious. His job was important too.

Paulo said they'd all run off. All the top brass had high-tailed it off to Keltan, he said, to Santos Nuevos or Aiga off the north-west cost, anywhere far enough and obscure enough to get away from the Chi!me. 'Unlike you, Cicero,' he'd said, using Cico's full name because he knew he hated it, 'they're no fools. They know what the Chi!me'd do to them if they caught them. They know the score. Transport waiting at the door, that's what you get if you're the likes of them.'

Paulo hadn't come back from lunch. He asked, quite friendly

for him, if Cico wanted to come with him, but he'd refused. Paulo was always looking out for himself. You couldn't do that if you were a soldier. You had to keep your post, you had to wait to be told to leave it. Anything else... well, go down that road and it was the end of the world. Cico had never seen a Chi!me and he wasn't afraid of them. He clung determinedly to his post as the smoke rose over the horizon and the face in the wall opposite laughed at him.

Old Mrs Delterro hadn't left the house since she'd told her Jaime was dead. Nadia had tried to persuade her to take some air, but there was nothing like her mother-in-law for stubborn. Juanita stuck to her chair by the heating element, putting down desiccated roots, keening. 'Paolo, Jaime,' she cried, 'Paolo, Jaime,' over and over again. Nadia wanted to shout at her that they were her husband, her son too, but she didn't. She was the one who'd wanted him to be a soldier.

It would be difficult without the wages he'd sent home. She'd been doing extra hours when she could at the factory, ekeing out the last month's pay packet they'd sent her with his things. Juanita had wanted to tear it up, send it back to them, but she hadn't let her. She'd taken the money from Paolo's boss when he'd been killed by the crane, marched down to the docking yard to get his rights with the child clutching at her skirts. She'd worked, she'd borrowed, she'd begged from the neighbours when she'd had to, when she'd needed to. Juanita thought she should be prouder, but then Juanita was a village woman. She didn't understand that you could be too poor for pride.

She'd burned his things. His ident chip, his uniform, his cards with naked ladies that she'd have burnt anyway if she'd caught him with them, his picture of a girl she didn't recognise, standing on a bridge. She'd burned them all in the yard at the back of the house, all the things with the cloth around them that they'd tied with such care. They'd been so pleased with themselves for doing it, so correct, as if instructed in a manual somewhere. She'd swept the ashes into a corner, underneath the rake. Every day, when she passed them on her way to work, she tasted them on her tongue.

It was halfway through her second shift that it happened. They couldn't see the smoke from the packing room, the windows were too high up and too encrusted with years of dirt. They heard the cries of the yard men outside, the calls of the office girls on their afternoon tea break, and someone near the door had risked the overseer's wrath and peeped out. 'Bloody hell,' her voice was shaking, 'they're coming!' There'd been panic then, women turning over tables, falling over each other in their rush to get out. Borne along by the throng, Nadia wasn't afraid. How could you be afraid when the worst had already happened? But she thought, before she could stop herself, with a fierce, vindictive pleasure, 'She can't stay in that chair now. At least now the Chi!me'll make her move.'

Agana told her at lunchtime to go home.

'Look, Adéla,' he'd said, when she'd protested. 'The Chi!me've taken the spaceport, they'll be in Nuerio by now. That's less than fifty miles away. You should go home. Do… whatever it is you do. Anyway,' he'd finished, brutally, 'you're no use here. Do you think I'm going to be sending much correspondence?'

He was right, she knew he was right. He smiled at her.

'Take care of yourself.'

He was so good-looking when he smiled, dark like all Santana boys, even the bruise on his cheek only made him look raffish. It was so sweet how sometimes you could hear the Santana in his voice, she and Mari the receptionist had often giggled over it, sighing, behind his back. She smiled back.

'Oh, and by the way, clear your desk before you go.'

She stamped down the street, carrying her box in front of her. She knew it, she knew it was too good to last. Not that she particularly liked working, but it paid for her clothes and anyway, you had to work. It was a good job as jobs went, Mari was fun, the pay was good and in government service you got benefits. She'd even got paid one time when she was ill for a week and you didn't expect that working for some company.

Sure, if she didn't work she could stay in bed all day, but when she couldn't afford to go out at night, what was the point in that? He hadn't paid her either, the tight bastard. Probably thought the whole invasion was just a good chance to save some budget, get another secretary in a month or two on a lower wage, bargain. There were some great silver shoes in a shop round the corner as well, she'd been planning to get them payday. Bastard.

The box was making her arms ache. She stopped on the corner and set it down, massaging her wrists against each other. She'd had a hundred left this morning till payday, less her bus fare this morning and the zine for her terminal. That left nearly ninety-five, and who knew how long that would have to last? Who knew what the Chi!me would do?

Ninety-five, and the shoes were seventy. Seventy and ten to get in at the club round the back of the cathedral, it was sure to be open, even at the end of the world they'd be welcoming the demons in. Ten for drinks and five for the way home, if nothing else turned up. She'd have nothing left then, no money, no job, even if she didn't have to pay rent, she still had to pay her parents housekeeping. She couldn't just blow it, it was so irresponsible...

'Stuff it,' said Adéla aloud. 'It's the end of the world.' She hefted her box again and made for the shop, stepping smartly as if the silver shoes were already glittering on her feet.

Juan Desales was digging in south-west of the city when he saw the smoke. It wasn't going well. The soil was so wet after all the rain it was more like wringing than digging; for every spadeful he slung over his shoulder, another glob of sticky mud would slither back. The Captain prowled along the top of the shallow ditch that was all they had managed, complaining. Juan and his colleagues bent and swore and bent again. When the columns appeared against the horizon, the Captain went off quickly to call someone and work immediately stopped. They leant on the ends of their spades. Juan stood a little way apart from the others, letting their talk ebb round him, half listening.

'I don't think they have a fucking clue what they're doing,' said Iro. He was older than the others, well into his thirties, and burly with it. He'd been a docker before he'd joined up, no one could match him for tattoos. 'I mean, digging? What do they think the fucking Chi!me are, space sheep? They're the rulers of the fucking galaxy and they're gonna stop for a trench.'

'We should put a sign up,' Raffi suggested. 'Stop. Please go away.'

'Yeah. "Go away now or we'll slap you." You should tell the Capt, he'd go for that.'

There was a general snigger. Iro pulled out his leaf pouch and took a pinch. 'Bloody officers. They're not the ones who're going to be here, are they? No, not them, safe and warm in headquarters they'll be, train to Santos - ha, we wish, train to Santos - needed for the war effort, don't you know. And there's not one of those fucking arseholes knows what he's doing. Say what you like about that bastard Desailly, and I could say quite a bit, at least he knows how to fucking well fight. Some of these arseholes couldn't find their rear end with a revolver, as my granny used to say.'

'Yeah,' Raffi chimed in. 'Desailly's alright, but the rest of them? Bastards the lot of them. Don't give a shit what happens to us. They've only got us out here in case anyone asks why they're not defending the city. Like it's gonna make any difference.' He flung his spade into the mud. 'We might as well be digging our own fucking graves.'

Iro perused the horizon.

'Big fires,' he said, with apparent inconsequence, nodding at the columns. 'What d'you reckon, spaceport?'

'That was this morning. Gotta be, what is it, Nuerio, isn't it? That town?'

'It's what, forty miles, fifty? And half a day for the ten miles from there to the spaceport...' He nodded to himself, satisfied. 'We're alright. They won't be here before tonight.'

Mario, the newest recruit, piped up. 'You mean we could des...?' He yelped as Raffi leaned over and slapped him on the head.

'How you doing there, Juan?' he asked, over Mario's squawk. 'You're quiet. Enjoying yourself? Fancy a midnight stroll tonight? Nice healthy long walk, long way away from here?'

Juan didn't look at him, didn't look away from the smoke.

'Alana went to Nuerio two days ago,' he said.

'Shit, man. That's your girlfriend, right? What the fuck she go there for?'

'Her family's there. She had to go, help her mum. She thought they'd go past. I mean, what's to take in Nuerio? There's not even any troops. She thought she'd be safer than here.'

'Shit. I'm sorry.'

'OK, lads,' Iro said. 'Break over, get your backs into it. Let's get this fucker dug.'

They bent to their work industriously, so low over the dark earth that it was as if they were avoiding the sky; averting their eyes from the horizon as if her body was laid out along it for them to see.

The call came in to Desailly's office as the Chi!me were landing at the spaceport, just as their jammers were starting to win. The Gargarin anti-jamming system was supposed to last for weeks, but it was becoming clear that a day or so was all it was going to manage. It wasn't particularly important. It had been expensive, but now that the Chi!me were in the system, who were they going to contact?

'Sir, I have President Gonsales for you,' said the secretary, sounding young and unsure. 'It's a very bad line. I'll try and boost the signal, but it's not been responding.'

'That's alright. I'm not going to be long. Put him through.' There was a click as she obeyed, then a crackling, open silence.

'Robbio?'

'Petrus, that you?'

'It is. If this is a courtesy call, it's a bit late. I already know they're here.'

The Benan President sighed. Desailly could feel the exasperation but was in no mood to relieve it.

'So, thanks for the warning, Robbio…'

'Look, I wanted to warn you, alright? I couldn't very well do that with the damn Chi!me standing over me, now could I? Be realistic, Petrus.'

'I am. I see you are too, since you're letting them use your space as their base for their attack. So much for the "misbegotten drive for empire."'

On the other end of the line, Gonsales huffed. 'You know I had no choice in that. I was calling you to tell you how sorry I am that I had to do that. We're UP members and we need to stay UP members, you know well enough that we need that protection. We can't afford not to help the Chi!me when they ask for it, it was hard enough to justify going out on a limb for you in the debate. We can get away with that, maybe, as long as it's not too often, but refuse use of the airspace? They'd just take it, you know that.'

'So you take the brave, the principled option of grovelling before them and giving them everything they want? The people of Benan must be very proud.'

'The people of Benan are happy not to be bombed.'

'Well, as long as the people of Benan are happy…'

Gonsales bridled at the tone. 'Look, I'm not overjoyed about the Chi!me in this system, either. You're not the only one with problems here. But I've at least got the sense not to antagonise them any more than I have to. For God's sake, Petrus, you know Benan supports you, we always have. You know that I personally would like nothing better than to see you ruling on Ty for the next thirty years. But you can't go round as if no world exists but yours. Why in God's name didn't you look after that damned Ambassador? All you had to do for all our sakes was make sure one woman didn't get killed. Even on Ty I wouldn't have thought that would be that hard.'

For a moment, Desailly was annoyed, but he was really too tired to sustain it. He laughed.

'You would have thought so, wouldn't you? I'm sorry if I've given you any trouble, Robbio.'

'Well, you know I didn't mean…'

'No, I know.'

'I am sorry we have to go along with this. You know that if there is anything we can do, safely, we will.'

'I know.' The crackling on the line was suddenly louder. 'Listen, I think this Gargarin rubbish is packing up once and for all. I'd better go. Take care of yourself, Robbio. Thanks for the call.'

'Petrus, you know if things were different, I'd love to have you here, but…' The rest of the sentence was drowned in static.

'Don't worry,' Desailly said as he put down the communicator. 'I know when I'm not wanted.'

The Chi!me were in control of what was left of the spaceport by mid-morning. There was no word on the troops stationed there to guard it. Desailly sat at the head of the table, looking down it at the faces of his generals. General Morales, the head of the army, General Casale of the air force, Berio his deputy, now head of the CAS, and Adriano of the Airdrossa police, all gazing back at him with varying degrees of concealed apprehension. Agana watched from a seat by the door.

341

'So, gentlemen,' Desailly began. 'As you know, the spaceport has fallen and, barring the usual police forces in Nuerio and a couple of other towns, there are no forces between them and the capital. I am sure that the people of those towns will fight bravely, but realistically we have to expect the Chi!me here sometime tomorrow morning. I take it all your troops are in place. General Morales?'

Morales cleared his throat. 'Three battalions are digging in around the south-west perimeter,' he reported, 'and we have another two in reserve in the city itself, ready to go where needed. As you know, without the spaceport it's difficult for the air force to support us, but we have all the air cover we can muster in place and ready to go. Casale, you'll confirm?'

Casale, a white-faced man with long, thin fingers, was drumming his nails on the table. He nodded agreement. 'We're as ready as we can be, sir.'

'Good. Adriano, how about the police? They're deployed to back up the army and keep order, yes? Get people to the shelters and prevent panic?'

'Yes sir. They know what to do.'

'Excellent. And, Berio, I'm sure your men are all prepared. So, it sounds like we've got everything in position. We're as ready as we can be.' He stared down at them. 'You know the forces the Chi!me have. You know their weapons are far superior to ours, that even though they don't have the numbers they can make up for it in technology we can never afford. Coupled with that they have the advantage of free use of the air. With all respect to you, Casale, you'd be the first to admit that your forces are limited without it. And what do we have?'

'The soldiers are loyal and resolute, sir,' Morales said stoutly.

'They'll fight till their last drop of blood. The Chi!me will have to fight for every inch of ground. They won't have the stomach for it.'

'So we hold them here, outside the city, and in the end they will withdraw? Is that what you're saying? Do we think we can do that?'

The truth, he saw, was on all their faces, the words that could never be admitted. They had not got where they were by truth-telling, not when the lie was required, demanded, needed, for the sake of their careers, their advancement, their not being dragged out and shot. They were where they were because they were the ones who did not tell the truth, who said nothing that was not what he wanted to hear. And so they could not admit what they knew, not even now.

'Yes, sir,' Morales answered. The others joined in, a craven echo. 'Yes sir. No doubt about it, sir.'

After they had gone, Agana asked him if he should get a shuttle ready. 'I'm shutting down my office from this lunch-time,' he said, 'I'll get the files wiped before I go. Do you want me to do the same thing here? Before you go?' In the outer office, in front of his secretary, he asked this. Desailly was so incensed that he knocked him down. He knew, even as Agana sat crumpled on the floor with one hand on his face, that he would arrange it anyway.

Alana hadn't told any of her family that she was coming, in case they told her to stay away. 'My place is with them,' she'd said over and over to Juan. 'I have to help my mother, she can't do without me.' What she really meant was that she couldn't bear to be away from them, not knowing. She didn't want to give them the chance to overrule her. Her mother shrieked and dropped a pot when she opened the front door; her father bounded up and slapped her on the back.

'You are a bad girl to come,' he said, hugging her. 'We thought you said you would stay in Airdrossa.'

Her small brother Sascha buried his face in her thighs and said nothing at all.

After dinner, when Sascha was in bed, her uncles Samy and Michele came over. She helped her mother serve the dinner and, after they'd eaten, came back out to sit with them. Her father clucked his tongue at her Airdrossa manners. 'Leave the girl alone, Pedro,' Samy chided. 'It's what the young women do nowadays, sitting with the men. Don't be so old-fashioned.'

'He's a married man,' Michele said slyly, 'so he wouldn't know.'

Samy laughed. 'Speaking of married men, I saw cousin Joshua on the corner, out of uniform, this afternoon.'

'Out of uniform? From what Mina says, he doesn't even take it off to sleep. You think that's all of them, then?'

'I wouldn't know. But you couldn't find a keener cop than Joshua. If he's deserting, you've got to wonder what the rest of them are doing.'

'I wonder what they know,' her father said.

There was a thoughtful pause.

'Father, do you really think the Chi!me will attack here?' Alana asked. 'I mean,' she went on as her father and uncles turned to look at her, 'I know they'll have to take the spaceport, but why would they bother with us? The talk in Airdrossa is all that they'll go straight there. After all, once they've taken the capital they won't have to bother with anything else. That's what they say, anyway.'

Her father nodded, looking dubious. 'Well, they may be right. Let's hope so. There's certainly nothing here they want.'

'Nothing,' Michele added to his empty glass, 'except a distressing shortage of drink.'

Alana got up. 'Here, Uncle Michele, would you like some more wine? Some people have even said that the Chi!me might not be such a bad thing.' She lowered her voice, but after what they had just been saying about the police, she wasn't really concerned any more that anyone was listening. 'If they really did get rid of… you know, certain people, might that be a good thing? If there isn't much fighting, if they can take Airdrossa without anyone getting killed, might it be so bad?'

'If they chopped Desailly, it'd be better than not bad,' Michele proclaimed, too loudly. Her father signed to Alana to put the bottle away.

'Yeah, Mica, tell the whole town, why don't you?' Samy chided. 'Still, I don't know that you're wrong. What would you pay to see him strung up? I know I'd pay quite a bit.'

Her father said, 'of course, it depends on who we'd have in his place.'

'But Papa, that's the point. We might get to choose. We might get elections, you remember how that guy on that channel who got disappeared last year always used to talk about that? The Chi!me might think that was the best way of, I don't know, keeping us quiet or something.

'I mean, they say they're coming to help us, they have to look like they meant it, surely? You must have seen those reports about the vote in UP, all those systems that supported them because they said they were going to help us against… well,

345

what Uncle Michele said. They have to have something to say to them, something to show them, or they're going to turn round to them and say, hey, you haven't done what you said you were going to do, we're going to make you. I mean, that has to be how it works, doesn't it? Don't you think?'

Her father smiled at her. 'What have they been teaching you in Airdrossa, girl? They've made a politician out of you! I don't know if you're right, but I do know they won't want a fight where they can help it. As long as we don't provoke them, they'll go straight on to Airdrossa, leave us alone. It's only people like that Joshua who have to worry and serve them right. Mina should have got shot of him long ago, everyone says so.'

'Well,' said Alana, smiling back, 'maybe now she will.'

The assault on the spaceport began that morning, just before it was light. Alana struggled up out of sleep to a banging so loud and continuous that the house throbbed around her, each wall vibrating its own strained sound. She leapt out of bed and ran to Sascha's room. Like her he had woken up and was sitting bolt upright in bed, tears running down his face. Over the bombing she could hardly hear him crying. She knelt down beside him and put her hands over his ears.

The bombardment went on until mid-morning, when it faded into a stutter of distant blaster fire. 'They've taken the spaceport,' her father said. 'Praise God,' said her mother. 'Maybe now they'll leave us be.' Her father went out to get news. Alana got Sascha up, washed his face and jollied him till he was smiling again. He wanted to play outside, of course. There was little room in the house; he always did.

She went out with him. It was a cloudy day, not cold, and with no wind at all. She sat on a block outside the front door and watched Sascha run the circles of his private game in the dusty street. It was very quiet. No calls, no voices, no transports; she could have believed that the whole town had fled but them, although she didn't think they could have done. Where would any of them go? Sascha ran round and round in circles, each one a little smaller than the last. It was pleasant here, really, pleasant for a change from the usual clamour, nothing but Sascha's small footsteps and a fly droning overhead. It was loud, for a fly. Getting louder.

Alana looked up. Away to the south-east, four black shapes stretched wing to wing across the pale sky. Droning. She got to her feet. 'Sascha, darling,' she called without looking at him, without taking her eyes off them. 'Have you had enough of your mazy game? I think we should go in.' He puckered his mouth to object and in the same moment, somewhere in the town a church bell started to ring. 'That's it,' she cried. 'Come on!' She grabbed his hand and pulled him towards the house. Her mother flung the door open as she reached it.

'Mama, they're coming! They're coming, we have to run, we have to get out of here!'

'Run?' her mother's face was bewildered. 'Where can we run to? How do we know where they're going to go? I'm not ready, I haven't dressed, there's your father...' She wrung her hands in panic.

'I don't know! Out, away, it doesn't matter, we can't stay here!' The droning was louder now, an oscillating buzz with a high whine over it, so high you couldn't quite be sure it was outside your head at all. Very loud, very near. 'Mama, come on!'

It was a little noise, at first. Just a little whistle amongst the droning of the engines, a descending scale. She didn't know

347

what it was, it was almost pretty. Just like fingers, running down a piano, to the end. The explosion was so loud it could only be felt, not heard. The house shook until she thought it would come down, just fold up around them and have done with it. Crashing from the bedroom as the wardrobe smashed like so much kindling, plates in the kitchen flying about, smoke everywhere and dust and the incredible booming through the floor, the walls, running all though her body like blood.

She thought she'd screamed, but she didn't know. She didn't know how she'd ended up on the floor over Sascha, how her mother had fallen beside her. It went on just longer than she thought she could bear. When she found she could breathe again she scrambled up, pulling Sascha up beside her. He was covered in dust, crying in little gasps as if he couldn't remember how to do it, but he didn't seem to be hurt. 'Don't cry, you're alright,' she said to him. Her mother hadn't moved.

'Mama?'

Her mother turned her head towards the sound. There was dust caked all over her face, her eye swollen shut with it.

'I'm…fine.' She sounded dazed. 'I just need a minute…' Someone in one of the other houses was shouting, high-pitched. Alana couldn't make out the words.

'I really think we should go now. We have to go!'

'I…' She trailed off, weakly. 'You go.'

'No!'

'Yes. Hurry up. Take Sascha. I'll follow in a minute.'

'But, Mama…'

'Alana, I won't tell you again!'

She couldn't have lifted her, she couldn't make her come if she wouldn't and she had to get Sascha out. Unwillingly, Alana

348

obeyed.

Outside, the street was wreathed in black smoke. She stumbled along it. All around she could hear screams, cries, snatches of speech she couldn't understand. In places the road was wet underfoot. After the first time, she didn't look down to see. She held Sascha against her shoulder, hiding his face. He was past crying now, stiff and obedient as a doll. A little way along it there was Mardi's orchard. It wasn't very big and it wasn't outside the town, but it was open and away from buildings. She felt very strongly that they should keep away from buildings. A crowd was breaking down the gates; Mardi could be heard inside the house, screaming. She handed Sascha to one of the women and went back to get her mother.

She was almost at the house when the bomb hit the street. Music, as if she was in it, part of it. Coming down... She saw it hit, saw it fall through Mr Sabato's roof three doors up, but she couldn't make her eyes understand what they'd seen. A thing, a small black thing, falling fast like dots on the eye, into the house as if it wasn't there. It fell, she heard it fall, but then there was... not silence, not exactly. A gasp, an inhalation like the last breath before drowning. For a moment, she never knew how long, she hung there, breathless, then the air came back, in fire.

Alana came to in the porch of Neruda's house across the street. Neruda had worked at the hospital, he'd earned good money and had been proud of his house. The porch had blue ceramic tiles on the ceiling, spattered now with blood or soot. It seemed a shame. Her shirt and skirt were torn away from her left side, her left arm matted in black blood so that she didn't dare to touch it. Her hair smelled odd, burnt, her face raw as if she'd been too long in the sun. She didn't dare touch it either. Her leg was cut but not as bad as her arm; she found, wincing, that she could stand. She staggered out of the shelter of the porch, into the middle of the street.

There were no houses now. No walls higher than knee height, no homes but piles of smoking rubble. Even Neruda's, she saw when she turned round, was gone, the porch standing freakishly to give entrance to a house that didn't exist. On the other side and four piles up, that was her house. That one. It was dark, so dark she could hardly make it out, dark as if it were evening, almost night, but surely that couldn't be? Not when her mother was there, somewhere under that pile, waiting for her to save her. Somewhere under there. She could hardly move, let alone dig, but she had to, she had to. There was a shivering noise from down the street. Painfully, she turned. She turned and saw the Chi!me.

A transport, blue-grey and shining in the darkness as if it had its own light. Gliding over the rubble, not even around it, not even having to stop and clear it out of the way. A turret open in the front and a thin, blue Chi!me in a helmet looking out of it, at her. It came quite close before it stopped, close enough for her to see him clearly, her liberator. Her mouth, caked with charred dust, was dry.

'Please help me,' she managed. 'My mother…'

The Chi!me cocked his head, regarding her curiously. Considering if she was a soldier, if she was resisting, maybe only what she'd said. But she didn't speak Chi!me; she hadn't known there was a need. 'Please,' she said again. He made a chirping noise, raising his blaster. He seemed to take his time about it, or maybe it was she who had hit her head, for she realised that she wasn't really surprised long before he shot her.

All day business had been terrible. It wasn't that there were no people about; that would have been an understandable thing and he could have stowed the transport in the boss's garage and gone home to his wife. No, there were plenty of customers, they just weren't where they should be.

No queues at the lunch stands, but a crowd all hailing him in mid-afternoon. Groups of girls, teetering on stack heels, demanding to be taken to a club at just past five, but no workers hurrying home. No passengers off the tubes and no one on the main street at midnight too drunk to remember their way. He flailed around the city, feeling always that he was in the wrong place, switching the orange sign on the transport to flash as if that on its own would summon up a client. He had to take three hundred or the boss would dock his pay. He was still paying off the transport as it was.

He hadn't wanted to be a driver, but it was clear very quickly when he arrived in Airdrossa that there was nothing else he could do that would earn. What did he know? How to grow the chari flowers that no one wanted to buy, how to sing the songs round the hearth at night that no one wanted to hear, the best way round the back of the mountain that no one trod any more.

His passengers didn't understand his small horde of Ty Terran. His daughters rolled their eyes at his dialect, complaining in their sharp Airdrossa accents. 'Oh, *Dad*.' They'd translated the broadcasts for him unasked, as if the war excited them. He'd pretended to listen to please them, but he hadn't really taken it in. Desailly, Chi!me, either way he'd still have three hundred to make and the transport to pay off and the rent due come Sunday. All politicians were liars, skilled liars who made it their art. Even if you remembered that you could still get sucked in, believing that terrorists or Kayros were your enemies when it was them all along. The only way to defend yourself was not to listen to any of them.

He didn't stop for the smoke like everyone else, didn't even give it more than a glance. You had to keep your eyes on where you were going, no one wanted to pay for bad driving. Gawping wouldn't pay the rent, it was nothing to do with him. He took the transport back to the garage, last back as always. The others muttered about him behind his back. Though he didn't understand what they were saying, he could guess. He took his time over locking up, double-checking the bolts on the shutters when he knew the first time they were secure.

The streets were deserted, growing yellow with the stillness of early morning. He couldn't even hear any birds. He turned eastwards into his own street. There were no clouds today, the sky a perfect blue like over the hills back home. The sun, just rising, threw black spots in front of his eyes. He blinked to clear them and when he looked again, there they were; the warships of the Chi!me, wing to wing across the horizon, coming like distant mountains up out of the dawn.

Part 22

Quila and Terise

They watched the fall of Airdrossa from as close as cameras could get. There was a pirate station over in Kayro that seemed to be able to evade the jammers. It showed any footage it could get hold of, scraps beamed in from outside the city, inside the city, wherever anyone was prepared to risk their neck to record. To say, this was what it was, no matter the cost.

The guerrillas spread groundsheets over the square where it was muddy from the rain. They kept the screens on all the time now, whether anyone could trace the power drain or not. Dano said there was no one left to find them, but casting off the secrecy felt as if it had been futile all along, like a worn-out coat that had never fitted even when it was new.

Issa watched seldom, she said she didn't need the screen to see, but Ladyani hardly left it. When she wasn't bringing him food, Terise sat next to him, leaning on his shoulder with his arm round her, his fingers tangling in her hair. They didn't talk much, no one did. Even when the government buildings exploded there was hardly a cheer, as if all those who would have made it louder were gone.

Once, a jerky grey fuzz appeared round the corner of a demol-ished building, light streaming from it to a Chi!me carrier. The recorder ducked before the blasts reached their target, but you could tell from the way the picture shook they found it. 'Bet that's Marius,' someone said and there was a general laugh. 'Good old Marius,' the way you spoke of comrades from the other side of death.

It was Ihanakan who told Quila when they landed; Terise still hadn't been near her. He'd put the tray down on the little table by the bed and announced it. 'You sshould know that your people are here', he'd said. She'd misunderstood him at first, thinking he meant more than he did.

'Here? *Here* here?' Looking round wildly, as if they would appear from the shadows, while he clicked his tongue at her, reproving.

'On Ty. They have landed at the sspaceport. They will be in Airdrossa tomorrow.' He turned as if to go.

'Wait, Ihanakan, there must be more than that! How many are there? What did the screen say?'

'I did not ssee the sscreen. But they are here and tomorrow, they will be there. I do not know how many there are.' A strange look hovered around his eyes, like bitterness. 'I do not think it matterss. But,' relenting, 'if I hear anything more I will tell you. They are your people, after all.'

Her people. It repeated, like wind in dry leaves, long after he had gone. Her people, coming to avenge her, because they did not know she was only bored and not in need of avenging. She was better now, so much better she could even take a few paces across the hut that seemed more and more like a prison. If they knew she was here they would rescue her. They would make a deal with ViaVera, come for her in a silver ship, take her home. She remembered bright soft floors in many colours, the

354

sun glinting off gleaming wings against the struts of a shining dome. The juxtaposition of the mud floor, the split wood walls and the rain outside made it seem that anything other than dirt and wind and weather was just fantasy.

Footsteps splashed through the puddles along the wall, two female voices chatting in the dialect she didn't understand. Far off, someone shouted, too distant to make out. They would have finished with the spaceport by now. They would have taken it today, carefully; just a little bombing, to soften up the troops, making sure not to damage too many of the buildings because they would need those, later. Then in with the carriers.

Sluicing out, the military called it, like a cleaner sweeping the house after a flood, as if they had nothing deadlier than clean water. They would have cleared up the corpses after them, put the fires out before they went on. She wondered how many ships they had. She couldn't guess, she had always been the worst in the tactics classes. She had never been interested in wars, only in the politics to help you avoid them. What was the adage? 'In war there are no victors, for to resort to war you have already failed.'

They would be on their way to Airdrossa, of course. They would be very neat when they got there, of course. The civilians would be in shelters, wouldn't they, and they would not bomb any civilian targets. Their targeting systems could pick out a single building, a single transport and lock on to it exactly. They could pick off Desailly and his hangers-on and leave everything else unharmed. They said, only half joking, that they could pick out even your thoughts. They did not make war on civilians and they were good at what they did. No errors, no doubts, just soldiers defeated and in the cold, clean dawn, the people emerging to their new city. Cheering, of course.

She knew all the arguments, but somehow for the first time they seemed less than convincing, when it was streets she knew, people she'd met. Would they all get to shelters? Was every bomb infallible? Could they really find only the soldiers so accurately when even Desailly's palace had guards and secret police and secretaries, cleaners and cooks?

It's no good, I can't let them do it. I have to tell them I'm here. I have to tell them now. Footsteps came back again past the door. One set this time, quicker through the rain. Quila took a deep breath, opened her mouth and screamed.

Terise was half asleep against Ladyani's shoulder when Maria shook her.

'Oh, get off!' she growled then, opening her eyes, 'Oh, sorry Maria.' She changed to dialect. 'What is it?'

'I'm very sorry to wake you, but, it's the prisoner. I was walking past to the well and I heard her screaming.'

'Screaming? Is she all right, has she had a…' she wanted to say 'relapse' but didn't know the word. 'Is she ill again?'

'She says she needs to speak to you, now.'

'Now? Did she say what about?'

Maria shook her head. 'She said she'd start screaming again if you didn't come,' she added, dubiously. 'Should I…?'

Terise patted Ladyani on the back, got to her feet.

'No, it's alright. I'm coming.'

'You should let that Chi!me bitch starve,' Ladyani muttered, but he let her go.

It was almost completely black inside the hut, Quila only a figure hunched on the bed. 'I'm sorry,' Terise said. 'I didn't

356

realise how dark it was. I should have brought a proper light. I'll go and get one.'

Quila's answer was low, reined in like a transport down a hill. 'We don't need to see to hear.'

'Fair enough.' She shut the door behind her, stood leaning against it. 'Maria said you wanted to speak to me.'

'Yes.' The words came but the shape on the bed didn't move. 'Ihanakan told me that my people have landed at the spaceport.'

'Past that, by now. We've been watching the news on screen all day. They've taken the port and a town called Nuerio and they're headed for Airdrossa.' She went on, harsher than she meant, 'What did you want, congratulations? Nuerio's just rubble, they don't know how many people've been killed. Did you want me to thank you?'

'I want you to help me stop it.' Her control broke, her arms reached out, it was recognisably Quila now. 'Do you think I wanted *this*? Do you think this is what I came for? Stars above, this is everything I came here to avoid! And I can't just sit by and watch.'

'Like us, you mean?'

'I'm not judging you. I can't tell you what to do, I wouldn't presume. It's not my business whether you fight or not. But this isn't your fight and it is mine. I am responsible. They're fighting because of me. My people are only here because they think that I'm dead, that Desailly got me killed. If it wasn't for that, the peace talks could still be happening, we could be trying to build on what happened at Cairn Fields, go forward.'

She took a shuddering breath.

'Every one of those people in that town, everyone who dies tomorrow in Airdrossa is my death, a death against my name

357

on the sky. I've been sitting here for hours, just thinking about it, thinking about being here and listening to every single one, knowing I could have stopped it. All those deaths are because of me, and I can't stand it. I won't stand it. You have to help me get a message to them.'

Terise knew what she should say, but couldn't. She took refuge in sarcasm.

'To the Chi!me? Yes, because we can just call them up any time. How would we even get through?'

'I can tell you the frequency to use, the codes. I know you have equipment, Du'Fairosay must have called you on it enough times setting the meeting up.'

'And we'll just announce to the world where we are, shall we? We only use that equipment when we have to, for the very good reason that we don't want to be tracked and killed. We can't use it for this.'

'You said yourself you've had the screen on, can't that be tracked too? You're not taking your normal precautions, you've left yourselves wide open because there is no one tracking you any longer, you know that as well as I do. And who is there to betray you to? My people already know where you are.'

Terise felt something strike once inside her, like the first tolling of a bell. *The Chi!me know where we are…* She said, desperately, 'Alright, I accept we could send a signal. But why do you think it would do any good? You're the excuse, not the reason, now. What do you think they're going to say when they hear from you? "Oh sorry, honest mistake, we'll just take our envoy and go home"? You know they're coming for Desailly and they're coming for Airdrossa and even if you were there right now on the bridge of the lead ship there is nothing you could say that would stop them. There's no point trying.'

It sounded weak even in her own ears. It was Quila's turn to be scornful.

'You don't believe that. There's always a point in trying, even when your cause is lost. Why else are you here? But you're wrong. I'm not a fool, I know there's other aims now, that they wouldn't just turn round because I'd appeared. But they can only have got UP on board because of me, I can't believe they would have got a vote otherwise. If some of the other planets start saying that they should pull out now I'm safe, they might have to think again, maybe just topple Desailly and then leave straight after, leave the rebuilding to Benan or something, not come for the north at all? That would be something, something worth trying for, wouldn't it?'

'I can't let you.'

'I can't sit here and do nothing while people die in my name! I don't understand why you won't even attempt it. What is it, are you afraid? Or do you just enjoy death that much?'

Terise shrugged, not rising to it. 'I live with it. But it's not because I want people to die that I don't think you can stop the Chi!me, I really don't think you can.' Out of the tolling inside, she added, 'I think they were waiting for us all along. I think they were always coming, whatever we did or didn't do, whatever we were. Whatever roads we took, whether they were true or not, they always ended here, with them.'

Quila made an impatient gesture, a swoop of dark arm on lighter dark. 'That's ridiculous. They're not some force, they're people. People, Terise. People who make decisions, who can change their minds. If I could talk to them, I could change their minds. You have to let me. I insist that you let me, I don't care what you do to me, I'll scream the place down if I have to.'

Terise could hear the determination in her voice, knew she would do it. Knew it would bring the others running, Ladyani with the *I knew she'd be trouble* look in his eye, and his blaster... Knew she had run out of prevarication.

'You don't have to do that,' she said. Her voice sounded oddly calm to her, still like the spaces between bells. 'Quila. Quila, listen to me. You can't call the Chi!me, you can't tell them where you are. There's something you don't know, about when you were shot.'

She imagined her face turned towards her, guileless eyes widening with the foretaste of comprehension. *Don't look like that*, she wanted to say, *defend yourself. Please*.

'It was your aide.'

'My *aide*?' It was more incredulous than shocked, still safe for one more moment in innocence. 'What do you mean?'

'Your aide. Fairo something, I don't remember his name. The one that was with you when I met you in Airdrossa, when I went to your hotel. He was the one who shot you.'

'You must be wrong. It can't have been.' Her voice rose, fast, panicky. 'Or, or he was shooting at you, that's it, he was shooting at you and it went wrong, I got in the way, I moved and got in the way, it was my fault, I'm always so clumsy, *it can't have been him!*' She stopped. 'He didn't mean it.'

'I saw his face. He aimed at you. He meant it.' She added, uselessly, 'I'm sorry.'

'I see.' Raindrops pattered on the roof. Quila said, 'I thought he liked me.'

Incongruously, Terise wanted to reach out to her, hug her, make it all not true. She walked across the room and sat down on the bed. 'I don't think it was personal. Really. I saw his face. It was a job he had to do, maybe a job he didn't want to do. It wasn't because he didn't like you, it wasn't about you, not to him.'

'No,' echoed Quila, 'not to him.' Her hand found Terise's on the bedspread. 'Do you know, I hadn't had an aide before. I thought it was an honour when they sent him with me, because I'd deserved it. I thought they were looking after me. But instead... I wondered where he was. I thought he must have gone on the flyer with Par'Lennan but I didn't know. I even worried. But you know what happened to him, don't you?'

'I shot him.' Quila let go of her hand. 'I'm sorry I didn't get there sooner. But if I hadn't spoiled his aim he would... you'd be dead.'

'I should thank you, then.' She didn't sound very thankful. 'Ai'Amadi didn't want me to come. He was my boss, back at IntPro. He tried to talk me out of it, I thought he had some other protégée he wanted to get the assignment. But all along it wasn't that, it was because he knew I wouldn't be coming back. Do you think they all knew?'

Terise shook her head. 'I don't know how it works.'

'No, you wouldn't. Obviously I don't either. I thought it was about freedom, and justice and something right. I knew that round the edges there were other things, things about trade and interests and all the murky stuff we pretend doesn't exist, but I thought at its centre there was something good and true, that wasn't there to be bought. It's ironic, isn't it? You could almost think it was funny. Such a good joke. There I was, prancing around telling everyone how we were the good ones, how we weren't just lawful but the very epitome of law and order. No one was better, no one was more principled than us, while all along we were the biggest criminals of all. Stars, they must have thought I was so *stupid*.

'Because I was, wasn't I? I was stupid and I was meant to be stupid, I was meant to look so idealistic and foolish that when I died, that when they killed me in their games it would be the death of an innocent, a poor stupid girl who didn't have the sense to know when she was being played with. I just don't know why it was me out of everyone else that they picked. Were they training me for this? Even on Iristade, in the Academy, was this all they wanted me for? I thought I was valuable, but if they could just throw me away…'

Her voice broke. Terise said, gently, 'When it comes down to it, we're all expendable. It's no reflection on us.'

'So back home I'm a dead hero, is that how it works? But I'm not dead. I can't live and I'm not dead. What am I? What do I do now?'

'I don't know. I really don't know.' Dubiously, she added, 'If you can think of anywhere you could go, I could try and help…'

'Because space is wide and has no memory? Yes, I could go anywhere, any place my people haven't civilised yet, anywhere that's still beyond their reach. I could tell people, listen, this is what they've done, this is what they do, I have risen from the sea and the stars to tell you to rise up indeed. But my people aren't like you Terrans, we don't believe in resurrection. We know our end, we say, and we meet it. It's just that mine seems to have gone on by. Maybe if I sit still it will realise it's missed me, and come back. What do you think?'

She couldn't answer the question. 'I'm sorry,' was all she

could say. 'Look, I have to get back, I've been gone too long as it is. You'd better not go out into the camp - what with the bombing and all, feelings are running pretty high against the Chi!me just now - but you can stay here, I'll make sure you get fed. Well,' in the spirit of belated honesty, 'for as long as I can.'

In reply, Quila managed a watery smile. 'As long as you can.'

Part 23

The Invasion

When Mario arrived to open the bar, he found old Pedro sitting on the second from bottom step, waiting for him.

'You're late,' he complained as Mario got the shutters up. 'There's some as would give their best customers a free drink for that.' He collected his grubby coat around him as if it were a king's cloak, sullied by the basement dust. Mario wondered how many days he'd come to see if the bar would open and how long he'd waited, but sensed that it would only lead to further discussion of free drinks if he asked. He grunted in reply and flicked up the last shutter with a practised hand. He hadn't seen the bar since the day before the attack started, but beyond a slightly thicker layer of grime it seemed untouched. Pedro settled on a stool at the counter, sipping on his first beer while Mario switched lights on and put the chairs back out. Not that anyone would sit in them.

Every day was money, of course it was, and with his wife pregnant again he couldn't afford to miss one credit. If anyone had asked that was the reason, he even believed it himself. Sitting in his friend's cellar for the three days of the bombing, in their one-room flat for the five days of perpetual curfew, he let the children climb, screaming, over his knees and told himself that he was going to open up as soon as he could. For the money, of course.

In the long lines at the Chi!me checkpoint, beside the rubble that used to be the station, it had occurred to him to wonder how many of his tattered regulars would never appear again. By the time he reached the bar his hands were sweating. When he had seen Pedro there'd been a moment he was so glad to see him he could have hugged him. It would have been unsavoury, but then, after upwards of two weeks with no water he wasn't too fragrant himself. He'd heard there was a broadcast saying that the water would be back on soon, but so far it hadn't been.

There was no power either, but the power in the basement had always been erratic and he had a cylinder left for the generator. The beer in its fridge would be warm, but his customers were rarely discerning enough to care. He waited for the generator to chug noisily into life, then turned on the screen above the bar. It was set to one of the national channels, that had been showing sport from Benan on the night the Chi!me came. He thought, as he let the switch go, that it would just be static, but to his surprise it wasn't.

The screen was almost black, but out the darkness came a low, urgent voice. 'The snipers are over there, just behind that rubble pile, and over on the other side, is the Chi!me transport. They have the weapons, but the resistance has the willingness to fight and the knowledge of the ground, and so far they're even. In the ruins of Nuerio, this is far from over…' Feet sounded on the stairs outside. Mario dived for the controls and switched it over at random.

'Hey!' Pedro protested, 'I was watching that!'

'You'll be watching it in jail if you're not careful,' Mario retorted, a response which lost its sting as he realised that the newcomer was not police but Beni, another one of his regulars.

'Ha, Beni.' Pedro greeted him vindictively. 'Still alive? You're not dead but you ain't quick neither, you could have got a free drink if you'd been here sooner.'

Surprising himself, Mario reached into the fridge and pulled out another warm bottle. 'There you go, Beni. I'm feeling generous.' Beni looked at him incredulously, so grateful he felt shy. 'I've got to see to the stockroom,' he added quickly. 'Don't pinch anything.'

Beni pulled himself onto the stool beside Pedro and slowly divested himself of his coat. For a while they sat in silence, watching the flickering grey that was all Mario's panicked channel-changing had found. Pedro finished his bottle, and since Mario was still in the back, helped himself to another one from the open fridge.

'Still got your head on your shoulders, then, Beni?'

'Oh, aye. Just about.'

Pedro shot him a look. 'Bad?'

'Bad.'

'You stay in the house?'

'No, not us. We went down St Mary's. Fifty of us, from all up and down the street, all packed in the crypt and nothing to drink but water out of the font.' He took a long gulp of his beer, remembering. 'There was kids screaming and crying, all the women carrying on for something they hadn't brought, or they hadn't locked the door, or something. We had to carry Juanita Delterro down there, me and old Eddy Marguiles one on each side of her chair, and her carrying on and hollering she weren't going to move, she'd stay behind and die before she moved, and her Nadia following on behind and screaming at her just as loud. We put her back in her house after, it weren't hardly touched, and the look on the old bat's face… Come off better than mine, anyway.'

'Oh yeah?'

'Something took half the wall down, everything got blown around.'

Pedro nodded as if this was familiar, but didn't offer any information about his own home. Beni didn't know where he lived, anyway. Instead he joked, with an edge of malice, 'Surprised you noticed the difference.'

'Very funny.' Beni drained his beer and gestured to the screen. 'Is there anything on?' he asked. 'We've not got power at home.'

'Let's see.' Pedro reached for the terminal and started hitting saved stations at random. The static changed under his finger from grey to green to sparkling blue, crackling, shiftingly, up and down the screen. He pressed it again and the sharp pink lines swirled and resolved themselves into a face. 'Here's something,' he said.

The young woman looked Terran, though she had a blue tunic buttoned in Chi!me fashion and her glossy hair was set in an unfamiliar style. She wore bright red lipstick and a general air of prosperity.

'And now,' she was saying, 'another chance to see those inspiring pictures of the moment Airdrossa knew it was free. I don't know about you, but I just don't get tired of seeing these.' Her Ty Terran was impeccable except for her accent, an odd, singing ending to her words that betrayed her as a foreigner. 'This was the joyful scene in Airdrossa, five days ago.'

The screen flicked to the main shopping street. Some of the buildings, it could be seen, were burnt out. All had their windows broken and the shop displays had clearly been looted. Beni leaned forward, interested. 'That's that jewellers, isn't it? What's it called? They used to have all those necklaces in the window, my daughter was always on at me to get her one, never mind the price. Fair bothered me about it, she did.'

'Well if you'd been quicker,' rejoined Pedro unsympathetically, 'you could have got her one for free, couldn't you?'

In front of the shops was a line of people, one or two deep, looking back towards the camera. The faces were a mixture of anger, fear and a sort of defiant expectation. 'Yeah, they look joyful,' Pedro said. The first Chi!me carrier appeared at the bottom of the screen, making its way slowly up the road. The tops were open and the soldiers inside, five to ten in each, stared grinning around them. One of them waved and as if pulled by invisible strings the crowds burst into wild cheering. Flowers like torn paper rained down over the Chi!me convoy and a group of young men, breaking away from the main group, ran up alongside it, beating the sides of each carrier as they passed.

The soldiers inside redoubled their smiles but you could see, Beni thought, that they did not particularly relish this. It was clear that the youths were hitting quite hard. A group of women leant from an upper window, stretching out their arms to the carriers and shouting something. The camera caught their pleading faces but not what they said. In the building next door, a sign in an unoccupied window, miraculously uncharred, read 'Hooray for Chi!me,' Terran first then Chi!me characters underneath. Handfuls of petals, as the camera dwelt on it, drifted across it like snow.

'This is the Chi!me 47th battalion, one of their elite squads justly famed for their peacekeeping all round the galaxy. They've been everywhere, but they can hardly have had a more rapturous reception. Just listen to that crowd! I hope you can hear me over the noise!' The voice was male and Ty-accented this time. 'That's the sound of freedom on the way and, let me tell you, it feels good.'

The picture returned to the female announcer. 'There'll be another chance to see more of that incredible footage later in our programme,' she said. 'But I'm now joined on the link by General Ta'Briel of the Chi!me Liberation forces and in the studio by Dr Hans Bremmer, the former professor of politics at Airdrossa University, who was dismissed last year for what was called "political unreliability." General, if I can start with you, what is the situation in Airdrossa now?'

The General's face under his helmet was darker than most Chi!me and wide at the chin as if he favoured plain speaking. He spoke in Chi!me, the Ty Terran translation emerging from a device on his shoulder. 'The situation in Airdrossa is very good. The city is calm, there has been a limited lifting of the curfew for essential business and life is getting back to normal.'

'That's great news, I'm sure. And you have good news on the water and power supplies too?'

The General lifted his palms in assent. 'The power and water are back on for all but a few districts and we are hoping to get them also restored within the next two to three days.'

'Yeah, right,' Beni muttered. 'Believe that when I see it. Do you know anyone, anywhere, who's got it? All meant to think you're the last, that's all that is.'

'And the streets are peaceful? There has been some talk of

insurgency, has that been a problem?'

'There are a few diehard adherents to the old regime, criminals who know they'll be taken to justice if they're caught, but they are very few. We have the situation under control.'

'Thank you, General. Now, turning to you, Professor, as someone who saw more than many, perhaps, the nature of the previous regime, what has made you happiest about the last few days?'

The Professor leaned back in his chair, palms spread upwards as if to underline the new honesty. 'I think it must be the fact that civilian casualties have been so few, and that the Chi!me were able to free Nuerio, Airdrossa and the other towns without bloodshed. Before they arrived there were many doom-mongers, supporters of the criminal Desailly and his cronies, who were telling us that we'd all be bombed to bits and that the army would fight to the death outside the city.

'We were all supposed to be preparing, weren't we, for a long fight and the fact that that didn't happen is, I think, one of the very best aspects of this liberation, that it is possible to have justice without fear. I think some of us always knew that the troops would have no heart to fight for Desailly's gang, that they would just disappear, but,' he smiled, modestly, 'it's good to be proved right.'

'And what do you think has been the Chi!me's most impressive achievement in these last few days?'

'Well…'

'There's got to be something better than this on,' Pedro snarled. 'Where's the terminal, let's try this one.'

The screen flickered into static.

'There *is* nothing else, man,' Beni objected. 'You can see for yourself, they're the only ones doing any broadcasting. Got to watch what we're told, haven't we? D'you suppose he'll notice if we get another beer?'

'Be his guest. Hang on, here's something.'

There was no picture save for a steady blue background, but the voiceover was clear. 'This is Ty broadcasting, Kayro division,' the voice said. 'We don't know how much longer we can stay on the air, but as long as we can keep evading the jammers, we'll keep on telling the truth about what's happening out there to Ty. Keep your footage coming in, pictures, eyewitness stories, whatever you've got. If you can get it to us, we'll show it. The link is at the bottom of the screen. Next up, a Benan team have more pictures of the terrible casualties in Airdrossa as the full extent of the bombing is revealed. Keep refreshing.'

The blue gave way to a street, a straight road between two lines of tall houses. Those that were standing had an air of decay to them, peeling paint and crooked pediments as if they had fallen on hard times much longer than five days before, as if this was merely the final indignity among many. It could have been any southern town. The picture was grainy, shifting, occasionally half-obscured as if the camera was concealed.

'We're now in the outskirts of Airdrossa,' said a voice. It spoke Terran with a flat accent, long nasal vowels like the commentators on the Benan sports channels, with a tightness like just before a penalty. 'This is one of the major residential districts and it's been pretty badly hit, by all accounts. We're going in to see just how badly. We have to hide the camera because journalists still aren't allowed out without a Chi!me escort and we haven't got the right permits. We've all heard about that Gargarin crew yesterday, so we're pretty nervous, but we're hoping that there won't be many Chi!me around this time of day. We just have to keep a low profile…'

He was interrupted by a scream, off-camera. The picture swung wildly as they tried to find it. Another scream followed, more loudly.

'You screen? You screen?'

'Over there. Mike, over there, on that pile. Have you got her?'

A black-haired young woman, waving from among the ruins of one of the demolished buildings. She came slowly nearer as the team ran towards her.

'What's your name?' the main speaker asked.

'You journalists? You put this on screen? I show you. I show you, come.' She gestured to them to come round the back of the pile. The first journalist peered round after her, drew back suddenly with a hand over his mouth. 'Mike, get…'

Mike looked. 'God…' he exclaimed weakly. 'God.'

'Tell me you're getting this.'

'Yeah.' A long breath, shuddering. 'I'm getting this.' Behind the highest heap of rubble the woman had made a little shelter, a piece of metal balanced on two columns extending out from the main mass to make a roof. Underneath it was another woman, a girl a little younger with the same black hair and the same empty eyes. She was sitting on her feet, and resting across her, so that the head was pillowed on her arm, was a corpse.

The face was mostly gone, only one eye looked fixedly out of the mass of black blood. The left side of the body, nearest the screen, was also the worst hit; no arm, no hair, the stump of a leg ending in no foot. The girl looked up at the camera. Her face was splashed with old blood. 'This is our father,' she said. 'He brought us here for good life. He was out working for us, he drove his cab to make money for us. And this is what they did to him.'

'He lived three days like that,' the first girl added, her voice rising. 'We have nothing. Our house is gone, our father is gone, they have taken everything away from us. We have nothing, we have no power, we are little people. We cannot fight them. But you tell them, Mr Screen, you tell them for us. They will be punished for what they do.' She stared into the camera, screaming now, crying out. 'They think they are gods but they are not, they are nothing. God has instruments everywhere and God will punish them. He sees what they do. You tell them. He sees what they do.'

'I - ' the man filming began and was abruptly cut off as the signal dissolved into static.

'It's funny how you don't see any Jeba dead,' Beni remarked when the silence became oppressive. 'Plenty of 'em alive before the bombing, but now not a single one and no bodies. It's strange, like they're birds or something. You never see dead birds.' Pedro only grunted in reply. Trying again, Beni went on.

'D'you think they've caught Desailly yet? They must be pretty close to it.'

Pedro snorted into the dregs of his bottle.

'Oh, they'll make sure we know when they have.'

'I heard he's on Trentama.'

'And I heard he's fled to Terra. Can't you stop yammering and get me another beer?'

'Alright. By the way,' remarked Beni, his face in the slowly-cooling fridge, 'did you hear about his wife?'

373

Agana heard in the middle of the afternoon from one of the guards and thought he was going to have to tell him. He avoided him for as long as he could, but when he slunk onto the roof terrace after dinner, he saw he already knew. Desailly acknowledged him briefly then bent his head again over the note in his hand.

'Someone down in the town brought the message. An old school friend of ours, actually. Hadn't seen him for thirty years. He said he'd heard we were here and thought he'd tell me. Considerate of him.'

'I'm sorry, sir,' Agana said, woodenly professional. 'Shall I have the guards stop him leaving?'

'What? Oh, no. No. It was bound to get out sooner or later. We're hardly inconspicuous, are we? And I don't really think it matters.'

Agana couldn't think of an answer to that. He didn't have the knack for grief.

He had hardly ever spoken to Julia Desailly, for all he was her husband's aide. All he knew about her was what everyone knew, that she was plain, dumpy, provincial, shy in public and uncomfortable in politics. That she had been his girl from their schooldays, married as soon as he had come back home for the Chaireddan job. That whatever went on behind the quiet mask she had had something sufficient hold him, sufficient to be worth keeping for him despite the sniggers and the young women of whom she surely could not have been ignorant. That she was dead beneath the charcoal rubble of the palace, in the hulk of the bunker that was not, after all, Chi!me-proof, after they had left her behind.

She had not wanted to come. In the haste of their departure

for Chaireddan her accompanying them was not something that would have occurred to Agana, but he was sure that if she had protested he would have known about it. He remembered waiting, foot tapping, at the end of a dim corridor while she and Desailly said goodbye. There had been nothing anxious about her then, nothing out of the ordinary. He had even wondered then, impatient, what it would take to move her.

Desailly had said something to her, briefly; he couldn't hear what it was. She had replied as quick and low as he. No tears, no recriminations: they had been married a long time, those two, beyond passion. Only Desailly had taken her by the shoulders, kissed her, light and ceremonial, on each cheek, before he turned and walked away. Agana remembered how his words had echoed against the empty walls, as he'd called out to him, too loud, 'Come on, sir, we have to go. The transport's waiting.' How she hadn't watched them go.

There was one obvious place to fortify in Chaireddan: the hilltop overlooking the market square. By the time they arrived, on the morning of the Airdrossa bombing, the government buildings were largely abandoned and the local police were finishing the clearout of the shanties that had sprung up between them. They should be loyal to Desailly in Chaireddan. Agana, Desailly and his personal guard had moved into the biggest building, the former Office of Northern Trade, with its wide roof terrace on the edge of the ridge. Since the bombing they had had no communication from Airdrossa, no reports but snatched messages passed hand to hand. Anything else would be too dangerous, would give away their position without a doubt. Desailly had spent most of his time on the terrace. It had the advantage, Agana thought, that you always knew

375

where he was.

The evening was close and humid now that the clouds were drawing in, though to Agana's southern sensibilities it was hardly hot. Leaning on the rail beside Desailly he watched the café owners in the square taking the tables in, the rattles as they chained them together loud on the yellow evening. A little two-wheeled transport, puttering under the weight of three youths, careered unsteadily along a side street and skidded at the corner. Desailly played with a chip from the balustrade, digging it gently into the top of the rail.

'I used to do that,' he said, suddenly, nodding at the streets below.

'Sir?'

'Ride around on a two-wheeler, three or four of you all clinging to each other's shoulders, shouting at girls. I'm amazed they still do it. We always used to come off at that corner, too, couldn't take the angle. How about you? Did you ride?'

'Me?' Agana was taken aback. 'No, sir. I was… well, I suppose I was too busy studying.'

'Hah.' Desailly nodded. 'Maybe in the circumstances, not such a wise choice.' He paused. 'Do you think it's ever justified to torture torturers, Agana? I don't mean it as a plan for the future, just a moral question. What do you think? Is it just?'

'I… um… well… I don't know, sir. I suppose you could say it was a due return, but… I don't know. I can't say.'

'I suppose we're not at home with moral questions, are we? Morality, all you have to turn to in the aftermath of power. The sop of the weak-minded and the defence of the fool.' The stone chip clattered far below, but when Agana looked at him he was smiling. 'But we may as well indulge it, don't you think?

Since we have time for reflection?'

Agana collected himself. 'Sir, we had no way of knowing they would go after her, as far as we knew she was safest staying behind. Your wife hadn't done anything. She was innocent, just like everyone they've killed.'

'She didn't live in my palace, wear my clothes, eat my salt? She was not the slightest bit complicit?'

'She was not involved in politics, everyone knows it. Sir, she had nothing to reproach herself for, and neither do you.'

Desailly laughed. 'I think there are some who would disagree with you there, but we'll let it go for now. But we're missing the point, aren't we? She wasn't killed because of her deserts, she was killed for mine, because she was mine. This is a thing the Chi!me have done to me. So the question remains, is it justified to do bad things to a very bad man?' He was quoting a broadcast, Agana recognised the reference all too well. 'They don't know what they're talking about,' he rejoined, stoutly.

'But, hypothetically…?'

'Hypothetically, then… no. No, it's still not. It doesn't matter what someone's done. You can stop them doing it, you can punish them under the law, but killing their…' he broke off. 'Anything else,' he substituted, 'anything else, well, it's just vindictive, isn't it? When they could choose to do otherwise, when they picked a fight, created their excuse simply so that they would have a chance to attack in the first place, when it has nothing to do with… anything. It's not just, not unless you have no other choice.'

'Which is something of which no one could accuse the Chi!me, with all the resources of the galaxy at their command. So it's one law for the powerful and one for the powerless, is it? The responsibility of power? I can't say that's a concept I would have had any truck with before now, I think if anything I rather thought it was the duty of the weak to be good. It's funny how a little thing like an invasion makes you suddenly see things from the other side's point of view.'

'Sir?'

'Never mind. Too much time standing around here waiting, that's the trouble. Too much time to think.' He paused again. 'I wonder if it was the same for her.'

'I... that is, I'm sure she didn't have time to think anything,' said Agana awkwardly. 'She probably didn't know anything about it.'

'What? Oh, Julia. Yes, I'm sure. That wasn't actually what I was thinking of.' He moved away from Agana, along the terrace. Almost out of earshot, he added, as if to himself, 'It always does end here, after all. All you have to wonder is which side you'll be on.'

They came for Cico while he was finishing his breakfast. Later he found he resented that lack of style in them, that they had found him so negligible they had not even troubled to make it in darkness. His mother had answered the door. He'd heard her voice, the tone she used for door to door hawkers, then the melodic reply. He'd heard his name. He didn't know who had betrayed him; his mother had been so proud when he'd got the job it could have been anyone. His chief feeling then was embarrassment, that it was mid-morning and he was still in his nightclothes, his mother's broth still dripping off his spoon. Since the office had been bombed there hadn't seemed any reason to rise early.

'Cico, these soldiers say...' his mother quavered.

'You are Cicero Donato?' It was strange, the way such a pretty voice could be so brusque. He pushed back his chair, got to his feet. At least he could keep his dignity. 'That's me,' he said and held out his hands.

They seized his arms behind his back, tied his wrists with wire. His mother began to shout, 'Cico! Cico! Let him go, he's done nothing, he's innocent, what are you doing to him? Cico!' One of them took a step towards her, there was a snap and she screamed.

'Mama? Mama?' he couldn't turn his head, couldn't find her. 'Let me see, you bastards, is she all right? Mama!' As they dragged him out of the door he could hear her wailing. 'Mama!' One of the soldiers chirruped something to the other and they both gave a high, hissing laugh.

The transport was waiting outside the door. The street would usually have been busy; it was empty now but Cico felt the unseen eyes upon him. The Chi!me flung him against the back corner. He couldn't put his hands up to defend himself. Pain blossomed iridescent over his face and he felt the blood spurt from his nose as he landed. He leant on the metal, winded. They opened the back door of the transport and one of them leaned in and brought out something soft and black. He couldn't work out what it was.

The Chi!me turned back to him, brought his face so close to his that all he could see were his sharp-cornered features, the dark blue skin and opaque eyes so deep you could drown in them and still not know what they meant. He had a small cut across the bridge of his nose; an absurd thing to notice.

'You shit-faced fucker,' said the Chi!me to Cico in precise

Ty Terran. He smiled, jovially. 'Think of this as the last thing you'll ever fucking see.'

Cico felt the spit spatter his face, then the black hood slammed down over his head and there was only darkness.

They pushed him on to the floor of the transport, tied his feet together with wire. His trousers, loose for sleep, caught on the catch of the door and dragged down over his behind. He couldn't pull them up himself, not with his hands tied. One of the soldiers slapped him on his bare flesh, said something in Chi!me he didn't want to understand. They slammed the doors and, in a moment, he felt the transport move.

Lying on his front on the metal floor, every vibration seemed to go right through him. He crawled along the floor until, reaching out blind with his tied hands, he could touch the side wall and lever himself up to a sitting position, his legs bent beside him. The manoeuvre pulled his trousers even further off, but he couldn't do anything about that. He sat against the transport wall, panting with the effort, until he realised he could hear more than one breath.

'Is there anyone there?' he asked. 'I'm sorry, I can't see you, they put something over my head.'

'Yeah, I'm here.' The voice was low, as if very tired.

'Have they got you tied up too?'

'Tied, battered, hooded, you name it. I've been in this van so long, I don't know how long, feel like I've forgotten there's an outside.'

'What's your name?'

'Michel. You?'

'Cico. Well, Cicero really, but everyone calls me Cico.'

'What were you, CAS?'

He hesitated before answering, but after all, what could it matter now?

'Yeah. I worked the desk in one of the offices. You?'

'Army. Palace guard.'

'Oh.' They sat in silence, listening to the engine. He wondered what the other man looked like. It was so strange, talking to someone when you couldn't see anything. His voice sounded middle-aged, tough; he would have to be to be a palace guard. Tough enough to take anything they could do to him, they would have trained for it, in case they were caught by ViaVera, how to survive the torture and not talk. But he had not been trained and he did not have anything to say. The darkness pressed on him, stifling.

'Where are they taking us?' He'd meant it to sound calm, even cynical, but it came out as a plea. 'What're they going to do to us?'

'I heard they had a camp down at the spaceport, a big camp with wire and guards and guns round the terminal buildings, and they've got people there from all over that they've taken, keeping them there. And there are rooms in those terminal buildings you go into, but you don't come out. They've got all sorts there, electrodes and needles, wave machines and good, old-fashioned beating. Don't matter what you've got to confess, they'll make you do penance right off, no question. You'll be screaming every little thing you ever knew and you know what?' His voice seemed very close to Cico now, though he couldn't have moved, 'They won't even be listening.'

'I… I don't believe you,' Cico stammered. 'I don't believe you. I… they wouldn't. I haven't done anything. I just sat at a fucking desk, I did nothing, all I did was process fucking reports, what difference did it make? I didn't do anything!'

'Yeah? Well, they don't care. But, don't worry, kid. You with your bare arse, you're going to fit right in.'

'What? You said you're hooded. How did you know I…? Who are you?'

A different voice, high, mocking, answered him. 'Not your friend.' A fist, judiciously, slammed into his face. He slumped over his bound hands. 'Not your friend.'

They found a wood to hide in, that first night when they escaped the ditches, by the Santana road, close enough to the capital that each bomb seemed to shake the trees. Nothing flew overhead, which Iro said was a good sign, and he wouldn't let them move on until the bombardment stopped. 'We'll sit tight,' he said, 'they aren't fucking with us here.' Raffi and Juan went hunting for obeo, the small scuttling creatures of the plains, in the fields around, while Mario boiled roots for the pot.

They left their uniform jackets behind when they did this, but always picked them up afterwards. If asked, they would not have been entirely clear why. On the third night, Paulo went into the city to see what was happening and did not come back. They didn't know what had happened to him; the bombing was especially fierce that night and they had only the macabre hope that he had been hit rather than captured. Still, Iro said, everyone was too busy to look for deserters. 'It's when they've got their feet under the table we'll have trouble.'

On the fifth night they heard not only bombing but blaster fire, far away, and guessed that the Chi!me were storming the city.

'We'd better move,' Raffi said. 'They'll be coming for Santana soon enough, now, we don't want to be sitting right here in the middle.'

Mario piped up. 'Yeah, but where do we go? I mean, what are we doing? Shouldn't we just go home?'

They all looked at Iro, stretched against a tree with his hands behind his head.

'Go home? Yes, we could go home. They'll be looking for us, mind, might find us, too, if our neighbours don't like the look of our face. Might cart us off to prison, might put us up against a wall and shoot us, how can you tell?'

'They might not. Anyway, how're they gonna find us? There was thousands in the army, you telling me they're gonna round up them all? We go home, we keep quiet, they leave us alone. Simple. Anyway,' he went on defensively, 'my ma'll be worrying.'

Raffi snorted and Iro shushed him with a wave of the hand. 'You want your ma, son, you go home and welcome. You're right, they might not come for you. You could just take off your uniform, hang it in the back of the cupboard, do as you're told. But could you face yourself in the mirror in the morning? Because I fucking well couldn't.

'These Chi!me, they come here, bomb us to shit, take our land and we do what? Run away from them, sneak home and hope we don't get caught? I did that when I was seven, I'm too old to do it again now. Way I see it, we wanna be free we gotta fight for it. We owe it to the next planet they're planning on bombing to teach them a lesson now.'

'If you wanted to fight them, why didn't you stay in the trench, then?' Mario's tone was mulish. 'Why'd we all run away?'

'Because we were all gonna get killed, you little fuckwit!' Iro roared. 'You got to pick your time, pick your place, take them from behind when they aren't expecting it. You can't stand there in two feet of mud and expect them to stop for you. They'd've gone right over us and not even known we were there. But now, they're more vulnerable. We can hurt them, if we want to. Do we want to?'

Juan got slowly to his feet. 'You know my girl was in Nuerio when it fell,' he said. 'I don't know what happened to her, I might never find out. All I know is that she could be dead because of those bastards and yes, I want to hurt them. I'm with you.'

'Raffi?'

'What the hell, didn't fancy going home, anyway. What d'you reckon, head north? Best cover's on the Biterra road.'

'Alright.' Iro stood up. 'North it is then. You coming, or what, Mario?'

Mario heaved a sigh. 'Yeah,' he said. 'Of course I'm coming.'

They took two days to get round to the Biterra road. They travelled only at night, the better to dodge the Chi!me patrols, but still the world was replete with running shadows, a whispering darkness, full but unseen. It was on the second night that they met them. They had been moving faster than usual, pressing on through open fields to get into the trees by the road before dawn. There were no Chi!me north of the city yet and they'd been tired, not keeping an eye out. That was the excuse, later, for how they hadn't seen them, but at the time it seemed as if they had sprung fully-formed from the ground. There were perhaps ten of them, all armed with as varied a collection of weapons as possible. The leader, dark and heavyset, wore a green bandana tied over one ear.

'Stop,' he called, raising his blaster.

Iro mirrored the gesture. 'You stop.'

They stood still and looked at each other. Ferns, starlit, eddied in rustles around their feet.

'ViaVera?' Iro asked. The leader nodded. 'Desailly's men?'

'We're soldiers, yes.'

The leader's face split into a grin, showing very white teeth. 'Don't worry, we won't hold it against you. There's more than one with us has been on the other side, at one time or another. Where were you headed?'

'Biterra road. Good cover for ambushes, we were thinking.'

'We've just come from there. You're right, it is good cover, and we've got a few other ideas as well. We're camped just a mile or so down west, if you want to come with us.'

Iro turned to the others. 'What do you think?'

ViaVera, Juan was thinking. ViaVera, the only enemy he had ever fought, the enemy who were so bad they weren't even human. He realised that the men behind the leader were studying them, as if they were curious too to meet the enemy they had been fighting until death only a few days before. They were good fighters, everyone had always allowed them that. And they knew how to resist. He glanced at Raffi and Mario, saw them nod. 'We think yes,' he said.

Then the field was a confusion of back-slapping and introductions, too many names to keep track of after a long night march. Juan found his head swimming with it, all the more so when they got back to the camp and there was food, and drink and more stories until he could stand no more and had to crawl off somewhere to sleep. The camp was strangely familiar, he thought as he lay down, as if, if you didn't know, you could think it was an army camp and not ViaVera at all. Of course, they were not soldiers and ViaVera now, it was one of the things Iro and their leader had said. Like the bare patch on his jacket, he would have to get used to it.

The leader had introduced himself to Iro as soon as they'd agreed to join them.

'Marius,' he'd said, smiling. 'Pleased to meet you.' He was very polite for a terrorist. He'd held out his hand. Iro had wiped his palm down his army trousers, as if it was sweating. 'There's one thing first.' He'd reached up to his shoulder, where the badge of his regiment was sewn, and with one, brutal movement, tore it off. 'We're not Desailly's men,' he'd said, and Juan behind him had felt that every word was suddenly true. 'We're not fighting to get that bastard back, or his kind. We're fighting for us.'

The shiny young woman on the Chi!me Free Ty station was enthusing about the interim government. The new head of state had already been appointed, as there was one very obviously suitable candidate. Stevio Gonsales was not only a wealthy businessman but had known and worked with the Chi!me for many years through his involvement in several companies, particularly space transport and ore extraction. He was open to the intergalactic community, he would not pursue isolationist policies that would damage the people.

Mr Gonsales was not able to come into the studio, but they had a picture of him, looking smooth and slightly pleased with himself in a side-buttoned navy suit. Of course, as soon as possible they would hold elections, but Ty had to get used to democracy after having been without it for so long, it would take time. And there were the rogue elements, the insignificant little resurgencies that followed in the Chi!me's wake.

These would soon be put down, but the liberating forces would also have to deal with the ViaVera problem that the previous regime had allowed to go unchecked for so long. There was a long way to go but, the young woman said, smiling, the people of Ty could be assured of UP and through them the Chi!me's full support in this difficult period of transition. Because the Chi!me, of course, had only justice at heart.

On the Kayro channel, the Benan team were approaching the cathedral.

'This was one of the centres of the bombardment,' one of them whispered into his hidden mike. 'Here, on the north side of the cathedral close, was a nightclub that was hit on the first night. It was full of people. No one knows how many died, the ruins are still too hot for any clear-up to begin. They haven't been able to recover any bodies, but looking at it, there are probably none to find.'

The camera regarded the pile of charred debris, faintly smoking like the aftermath of a volcano. In amongst the concrete, pathetic pieces of possessions could be seen; a bag, a snatch of glittering cloth, a silver shoe, dried blood caking its high heel.

'And, of course, in the later bombardment, the cathedral itself was also hit. The top half of the spire fell down onto the nave; no one has been able to tell us how many people were sheltering there. It's odd, if you look at the stump you can see that the force of the explosion actually made the spire twist round before it fell. You can make out the stretch marks where it pulled itself around. This jagged remainder can be seen all over the city and you know, it seems to symbolise everything we've witnessed over the last days here. It must have been a terrifying sight when it moved and fell, like the end of the world.

'It reminds me in fact of a Terran story I once heard. There is a famous twisted spire somewhere in the north on Terra and the story went that it was so because the spire cared so much for its people that it leant over whenever there was something interesting happening, so that it could watch. I look at these ruins now and I wonder what Airdrossa's spire watched those nights while the city burned around it. I wonder if it thought those flames were just and necessary, when all these uncounted people were dying. I wonder if it was surrender or relief when it made its final turn and fell down to join them. A symbol for a new age of Ty, for those who lived to see it, and the end of the world.'

Part 24

Quila and Terise

'The word is they've taken Biterra,' Terise said. She stood with her back to the hut door, feeling the wood rough against her hands like comfort. 'We just heard. They've got a division in Santana now and a mixed division from some of the other UP planets in Camino, going down to Terra Nueve in the east. I don't know about the islands; someone said all the guards had run away from the prison on Worm Island and left the prisoners there locked in to rot, but I don't know if it's true. They're still fighting in Airdrossa, there's resistance there and all over Drossa province, but they're not leaving all that many troops behind to deal with it. Most of them went to Biterra, and from there, they'll be going north. They'll be coming along the tracks to Santos, for Desailly in Chaireddan, and for us.'

It was Ihanakan who had brought them the news. Since Airdrossa had fallen the screen had been nothing but pictures of cheering crowds from the Free Ty station and shaky-shot atrocities from Kayro; no use for information. Their network of supporters was gone, destroyed in a welter of blood and dust, it was only the Jeba, coming through the mountains in ever-larger numbers, who could bring them any reliable news of the campaign.

Terise had first noticed them a day or so after the Airdrossa bombardment started, but since then it seemed that every day there was another group. Ten or twenty Jeba, mixed in age from gnarled elders to babes in arms, two or three in front carrying the long poles, higher than their heads, that they used as walking sticks, and the rest following behind with bundles on their backs.

Sometimes the leaders would be men, sometimes women. Terise had never been able to work out how Jeban leadership worked. They would stalk into the camp, confer briefly with Ihanakan, then leave through the north gate. She would watch them plodding steadily up the road into the mountains, till they were hidden by the trees. They never stopped for food or even water, when she asked Ihanakan why he would not answer. She wondered if the Jeba, like Terrans, would prefer not to picnic in a graveyard.

Ihanakan always had something for them after they had left: the interim president chosen; the Kayro TV station bombed; Santana burning and the air full of the phantasmagoric scent of a thousand roasting flowers. The righteous wrath of UP, wielded by the Chi!me, coming at last to end ViaVera once and for all. That last time, he'd come up to the palace as he always did, asked for Issa with nothing in his voice to show that he had anything unusual to say to her.

She had been sitting with Ladyani in one corner of the hall, while Terise was settled opposite mending a jacket. Terise was too far away to hear it, what Ihanakan said or what they said to him in reply. She never did know precisely how he'd announced the end; she hadn't had to ask. She'd got to her feet, jacket and needle falling unheeded to the floor before her, when she'd seen their faces, the same sick excitement on both of their faces, shining in their eyes like joy.

Then they'd called the council and told them and the planning had started for the last stand. It was only at the end, when it was all worked out and the full futility of anything they could do was laid bare, that any of them had dared to suggest what they had been thinking all along. Terise had stayed in the room, since it didn't seem to matter now whether they knew she heard or not, although she still sat rather apart from the circle. She'd seen the look go round, from Roberto to Sario to Wolf, *it needs to be said, but not me, not me to say it*, and surprisingly, it was Wolf who gave in.

He'd been sprawling in his chair as he always did, giving that air of inattention that Terise had always imagined him practising in his hut to get right. Now he pulled himself up, cleared his throat. 'If you'd go, we could get you away, Issa,' he said. 'A few of us could get you to safety, if we went now. It's worth considering.'

Her face froze. 'Oh, really?' The words were mild enough, but for the bite in her voice. 'And where were you thinking I'd go? Zargras, perhaps? Chi!me itself, have a holiday, why not? Worth considering, indeed.' She pushed her chair back, signalling that the meeting was over, but Wolf refused to be put off.

'You could go to one of the islands,' he said, doggedly. 'Corio, Aiga perhaps. We've got support there, we know places you could stay.'

'Yes, stay in comfort till they catch me!'

'They don't know you exist! You're a myth, a story to them. They don't know who you are! Roberto and Sario, Ladyani and I...' 'Leave me out of it,' Ladyani interjected. '...We're the ones on their list, we're the ones they'll chase, not you. We can get you to the coast tonight. Terise can go with you.' Terise said immediately, 'I'm not going without Lad,' but no one paid her any attention.

'You've got it all worked out.'

'Someone has to think about your safety, since you won't.'

Issa grinned at him, showing her teeth. 'No, I won't,' she echoed. 'I won't and I don't and I'm not going. Try and make me.'

He stood up. 'You don't want to see me make you.'

'Oh, I don't know.' Ladyani stepped between them. 'I might be interested.'

Wolf's tone was immediately conciliatory. 'Lad, I'm only saying for her own good…'

'I think she knows what's for her own good.' Ladyani patted him on the shoulder. 'Why don't you go organise your squads?'

'I suppose…'

'Yeah, Wolf,' Issa added inopportunely from behind Ladyani's shoulder. 'Stop trying to save people and get back to killing them. It's what you're good at.'

She smiled at him again from safety and enraged, he shouted at her.

'You bloody Karnes, you're all the same. You're exactly like your bloody father and your bloody sister! Why do you always have to be the martyrs? Why do you think it's your fucking God-given right to kill yourselves while the rest of us stand around and watch? When Mara…'

'Yes, what about Mara?' Issa snapped back, 'what about my sister who's everyone's property but mine?' She flung up her arms, her voice rich with sarcasm. 'My wonderful, caring sister, who never did anything for me.'

'That's not fair, she saved you!' That was Sario, shocked into response. 'She got you away from the government.'

'She got me away? She saved me? Is *that* what you think? What makes you think I asked to be saved? Especially by you?'

'You were a child…'

'Beppe the head guard used to give me rides round the garden on his back. There were flowers, big, pink flowers all round the walls, I remember. I was happy there. I liked it there, it was quiet. Then she came and took me and there was nothing but dark and screaming and then I was here and *then she left me here*. She left me here, with you.'

To Terise, her voice was as real as she had ever heard it, stripped of pretence and all her usual chill naivety, and somehow familiar. The tone caught at the edge of her mind, reminding her of something, what was it? A girl's voice, harsh with crying, smoky light and a fish half-gutted on the table, 'I hate you, you never let me do anything, I wish you weren't my mother!' She had been thirteen then. Her father had been out on the boat, she would never have dared to say anything like it to her mother in his hearing. She couldn't remember what she had been angry about.

'She left me here with you,' Issa repeated. 'She told you to take care of me, didn't she? Or maybe she didn't and you just assumed she would have meant to, as if she would have remembered me at all. So you took care, such fine care of me, and what did you teach me? A hundred ways to kill, a hundred ways to die. How to make a weapon of pain itself, how to forge yourself so that everything that did not serve the cause melted away.

'You taught me this and I learned. I learned so well that now,

393

Wolf, you stand there and say, as if you were accusing me of something, that all I know is death. What else did she leave me? What else is there?' The sharpness was back in her voice, the dangerous smile on her face. 'I'm staying here,' she said. 'You know you can't make me do anything else.'

She turned on her heel and strode out of the room. The councillors went, muttering, about their duties, trying not to catch each other's eyes. Ladyani and Terise were left alone.

'I should go and check on her,' Terise said, 'she was pretty upset.'

'Leave her. She'll be better by herself.' He stood still for a moment, regarding her.

'Do you regret it?' he asked.

She looked at him in puzzlement. 'Regret what?'

'Coming here with me. That I came and told you, brought you.' He shrugged, smiling. 'It.'

'Oh. It. That's a funny thing to ask. Why d'you think I would?'

'Oh, I don't know. You could have been a professor.'

'Dottore again? I thought I'd got away from that.' She laughed. 'I don't think I ever would have been. A civil servant, that would have been me, with a tiny flat and a frilleh for company, what a life.' A man with grey streaks in his red hair, a girl and a boy in front of their house by the sea. Walking away. 'No,' she'd pronounced with decision. 'I can't think of anything better I could have done with my life. I don't regret it.'

And Ladyani had leaned over to her then and planted a kiss on her brow. 'I always said you were mad,' he'd said, and he'd laughed with her.

'It's strange,' she said now to Quila, 'now we know they're coming, it's almost like it's a relief. The air is different, it's more like it used to be, when we were preparing for a big operation, everyone busy and knowing that they were making a difference.'

'I know. I can hear them singing when they walk past the wall, like they're happy.'

'I'm sorry.' Terise sat down on the end of the bed. 'I haven't done well by you. I should have left you in the cairn field, someone might have found you who could have taken better care of you than I have. Or I should have been quicker, then you never would have been wounded at all. I am sorry about that.'

'I don't think it would have made any difference.' Her voice was toneless. 'I'm dead already, didn't I tell you that? I've been dead since I boarded the ship on Zargras, since Ai'Amadi tried to talk me out of it and I didn't understand. I was just hiding it well.' She tried to smile, but Terise was undeceived.

She said, gently, 'I think it will only be days. From what Ihanakan says, they won't be long in Chaireddan, or Ultima. We'll go out to fight them, but... well, you know. We aren't exactly as well-equipped as them.'

'No, you get your weapons from the Gargarin, don't you? I recognise the style. We made sure they never got the best blaster tech. Got to keep them in the right suit, haven't we? Stars above, I never thought I would be wearing it too.'

'And that's for the ones who actually have the Gargarin rifles. There are a few Chi!me blasters and some Terran stuff, but the way things have been going, if there's a big engagement some of us have to have Espada and to be honest, we'd be better off throwing rocks at them. What I wouldn't give for a decent weapon! But there was never the money to equip all of us properly, we all have to take what we can get.'

Quila regarded her with an air of discovery. 'You like it, don't you? Fighting, I mean. You enjoy it.'

Terise shrugged. 'Some of it, sometimes, I suppose. I suppose I always liked having fought, you know? Having been brave, having won a battle, having everything complicated come down to something that's so simple, just you and the enemy and your weapon in between. It's like innocence, that moment. I suppose I like that. Not so much the rest of it.'

'So not the train to Santos, then?'

'No. Not that.'

There was a pause.

'You know I cried when Mara died?' Quila went on. 'I told you I used to have pictures of her. I admired her so much. When I was young, I used to look up at her on my wall and it was like she knew me, you know? I was older than that when she was killed, maybe four cycles, but it still hurt. It seemed like that was when it all started to go wrong, though even with Mara there were things...

'You don't know how difficult it is to support a group that uses violence. Even when Mara was alive, it was difficult for people on Chi!me to say they sympathised with ViaVera, even though no one has ever trusted the Benanist government, even though most people condemned Sept Karne's murder. There was so much support you could have had, so much goodwill. But, after a while, it just became too hard. And after the train to Santos...Why did you do it? Why, after everything good that ViaVera had stood for, did you just throw it all away? You didn't have to, you didn't need to, why did you? Did you just want the blood?'

Terise's mouth twisted. 'It was a mistake.'

Her tone was so bitter that Quila looked up sharply.

'Were you there?'

'What makes you think you have the right to ask?'

'I didn't think it mattered, now. Were you?'

Her eyes were wide in her thin face, unwavering. Terise sighed.

'Yes, I was there and yes, I still do hear the screams, even over all the others. It was a mistake. We thought the explosive would break the tube, that it would stop the train, destroy the goods wagons in the middle, hit some of the big corporations, you know. Mara always said, it's not about ideology, it's about money. Get the Benan companies pulling out, that's when we'll see some difference. We were going to ransom the passengers, we never thought that the tube wouldn't shatter and the train would just sit there, burning.'

'Five hundred people died in that train.'

'Four hundred and ninety-seven, including twenty-three children, and I've listened to every single one. Don't you think I know?'

She waved her hand, as if to dispel the memory.

'I don't know why it went wrong, God knows we'd spent long enough working it out. It was Issa's first mission, if you want to know, she planned it. It was all her idea, every detail, she was so insistent it would work. I suppose we must have been too busy worrying about her.'

'And after that, were they all mistakes?'

Terise grimaced. 'It would be so easy to say yes, wouldn't it? So much simpler to pretend we never meant to hurt anyone, we're little saints up here on our pyre. Well, we aren't. You know the answer as well as I do.'

'But did you never think of passive resistance? Why does violence have to be the answer? As I said, there were many, many people on Chi!me who were sympathetic to Mara, to your cause, but they couldn't support the sort of indiscriminate violence they saw from you even when Mara was alive, let alone after. You made yourselves outcasts, you must see that.'

'Of course I do, but what other choice did we have? You talk about peace, about finding non-violent solutions as if that ever works, as if the best way to stop soldiers with guns from burning your home is to sit down in the street and sing songs while they do it.

'You know what they did to my village, to my family and Ladyani's. You know what they did to Mara's family, what they did to her, what they do to any of us when they catch us. You've never had to think of your comrades tortured, of friends locked up in the dark for the rest of their lives and now starved when their guards run away. Are you telling me that we should let them get away with that? That we could ever have won by letting them do whatever they pleased? Disobedience, passive resistance, making a face at the policeman when his back is turned, the peasants do these all the time and they don't make any difference. They aren't free. You can't reason with a state, you can't appeal to its better nature. You can only fight it and kill it.'

She paused. An image of the wooden cross outside Three Trees flickered in her inner eye.

'You don't understand anything,' she went on. 'You talk as if we should be ashamed of our victories, apologise for fighting back, while the things we maybe should be ashamed of you don't even see.'

There had been strips of black cloth fluttering from the cross-piece, she remembered, left behind when the villagers had taken the priest's body down. They had shot the man who'd organised the burial, too.

'You don't care what we do when you don't hear about it, the unspectacular violence that the screens don't show. But in public you want us to be the bearers of your conscience, parrot your principles so that you can say to yourself in your soft bed far away, "oh, I do hope ViaVera are alright" and go to sleep. So you couldn't support us. Well, we did what we had to do, and we didn't ask for your help.'

Quila looked rueful. 'No. Well, I suppose I asked for that. I'm sorry. It's just… I find it so difficult to understand. I've been here for a long time now and it seems so normal, so… domestic. I talk to you and I could be talking to anyone I've known, as if we were, well, friends. But then I remember what you do, what you all do and I don't understand it. How do you do it? How do you kill someone?'

'I don't think we have a monopoly on it,' Terise rejoined. 'Why don't you ask your people when they get here?'

Quila ignored the jibe. 'I mean face to face. How do you do it? How do you bring yourself to it, to be close enough to feel them living and then make them stop?'

Terise considered. 'Well, it helps if you don't remind yourself that they are living. It becomes like a contest, fighting, you know. You just have to get through it, you don't think about it. But, I suppose sometimes, when it's harder, you find the person inside who knows. Someone who knows how to kill,

399

who knows it's necessary. They're there all the time, watching, all you have to do is let them out. You don't even know what they're doing, it all goes past in a haze, as if you weren't there at all, and when you come back to yourself you're surrounded by corpses and you think, *is this what I did?*

'So you make a killer, something you're not responsible for. Something that's not you, or not the real you. Is that what you've all done?'

'No,' Terise answered. 'I told you, you *don't* understand. The person inside, the killer, they're what's real.'

She stood straighter against the door. The afternoon sun shone through the cracks around her, catching in her hair and the threads of her ragged jacket, crowning her in golden light.

'You think this is real, this home, this comfort, this life? It's all pretence, it's all nothing. We are what we are made to be, you think we could live in the heart of the flame and not be touched? We struggle and we are the struggle, there's nothing else. Whatever else we were was burned away, on the train to Santos, on a rooftop in Chaireddan, on a thousand different pyres. We are the blast, we are the blot, we are the blood and the carnage and the death. That's the truth, it's always been the truth. Everything else is just transitory.'

Part 25

Desailly

Desailly stood on the terrace, watching the transports come.
It was colder than that day twenty years ago, a raw morning with a gusting wind. No yellow heat that threatened to burn
out the fuel cells with every hill, no sweat trickling down the
back of his collar as he waited. The market started later, too;
they had to wait for dawn on windy days in case the lamps set
fire to the nets.

The black-clad women were the same, scurrying away with
three days' food on their heads, and the market traders frantically packing up the stalls behind them. He had grown up
among them, he had been further and learned more than they
had ever dared to hope, but he had still never worked out
how they knew when something was about to happen. It was
something his mother had bred out of him, perhaps, to fill its
place with dreams of glory. She had always thought he was
better than everyone else.

Far below, the first transports edged into the market square,
squat and black against the wet grey buildings. He remembered
how the mission on the hill had seemed to glow with golden
light, clouds massed around it like a halo, and he had been so
sure he would prevail.

'Never fight a battle unless you know the outcome,' he said

to himself, half laughing. 'Well, at least I'm sticking to that.'

Footsteps pounded on the stairs and Agana emerged breathless behind him.

'Sir, I told you, the Chi!me are in the city, their transports are nearly at the square! We should be away from here. What are you still doing here?' He panted, shifting from foot to foot in his urgency. 'Come on, we have to get out!'

Desailly kept his voice calm. 'And go where?'

'Sir? I don't know, Kayro…'

'They're bombing Kayro.'

'Well, then Santos, or Corio or Aiga. What does it matter as long we get away?'

'You forget yourself.' He drew himself up, stiff and tall against the rail. 'I have no intention of running. What, you thought I'd follow along with you, run till you've all left me and I'm left like a rat cornered by frilleh?'

Agana wailed, 'but I told you, we have a transport standing by!' and he overrode him.

'I intend to make a stand while I still have the troops to do it and this is as good a place as any to do it. Station the men to cover the front entrance. You'll need a few at the back but not many, I shouldn't think they'll try to get in that way. They're just clearing the square now, I would say you have twenty minutes.'

'And what are you going to do?'

'I am going to stay here. Any questions?'

Agana regarded him as if looking for some way to talk him out of it, then despaired.

'No, sir!' he snapped.

Desailly could hear him bellowing orders all the way down the stairs.

'Right, Gonsales, you and Morio go to the back door, yes, I said the back door... I don't know, find a plank of wood or something, break down a door... for God's sake, man, use your initiative!' Something crashed to the ground and broke, unforgiving little tinkles bouncing down the steps. 'For fuck's sake, pick that up!... Yes, you!... You three, come with me... yes, bring that! And that!... Good, thank you Nico, nice to know someone's paying attention. Alright, let's go...' The front doors were only wood and glass, not anything that had been made to withstand assault. Not that anything else could stand against the Chi!me. It was all only symbolic now.

The lead transports were past the square, winding slowly through the narrow streets that led up to the hill. As he watched, one of them misjudged a corner, clipping the side of a building. The frontage fell away with a roar, too loud to hear if there were screams. There were no people on the streets, the women had disappeared and the last few stalls in the square were empty and abandoned. In the settling dust there was a thick, breathless hush; no traffic, no voices, nothing but the faint drone of the transport engines and the soft howl of the wind around the hill. As if they had all run away and left him, all his people, and really, why shouldn't they, for all he had done for them?

He came from their town, he had used it as a training ground, a battlefield to propel himself to power, then he had left and never come back. It had been poor and down-at-heel when he knew it and it was still poor and down-at-heel now. There was no loyalty, no romantic belief, no ideology that would lead the people of Chaireddan to fight for him, not the ideal of Benan nor the hopeless dream of another Terran empire. They knew him better than that.

He had used these time and time again to win people to his side, to convince them that he somehow stood for them when his intentions were the opposite, but clearly it hadn't been fooled, his Chaireddan. Strangely, he found he liked it better for that. It was a shame, in a way, that he would never see the resistance. He would like to have watched how they fought the Chi!me.

He supposed he should be helping Agana get the guards into position, that he should possibly have allowed Agana to get him away in the transport, but he didn't seem to be able to. He would not have called himself fatalistic; he was a modern man with modern ideas, he had always believed that he could change the world and nothing was beyond his control. It was against inevitability that he had fought on this hilltop twenty years before, against all the people who had said that police could do nothing against the might of ViaVera, and he had won. He could win again, if he would just try. Take hold of his mood, march down those stairs, take charge. Fight his way out, wipe the superior smiles off their smooth blue faces... He raised his eyes to the horizon and saw the black shape that had appeared on the south-eastern sky. In the end, all he could do was laugh at himself.

The shape was rather larger before the guards noticed it, rather more identifiably a flyer. He heard someone calling in one of the lower rooms, 'Sir? Sir? I think you'd better come and have a look at this,' then Agana's voice, loud and hoarse with tension. 'Fuck! Fuck! It's a flyer, it's a fucking flyer! Get the anti-aircraft! Get it right now... well, where the hell is it?... building like this's got to have some... well fucking well find it!

You, Morio, you and Peters help him look, the rest of you, up to the roof. Come on!' Several feet pounded up the stairs and Agana emerged on to the roof with a group of guards. There were, Desailly couldn't help noticing, rather fewer of them than there had been earlier. 'Take position!' Agana screamed at them. 'Sir, can you at least get into cover?' Desailly shrugged, remaining by the edge, and after a moment, Agana turned away.

There was no cell housing hiding his view this time. The flyer loomed above him, its black shape covering the sky. It didn't have the folding wings that ViaVera's had had, instead they seemed to retract almost into its body. It lowered itself over the farthest patch of roof, bolts from the guards bursting around it in swirls of colour like a welcome. He remembered how, when he had levelled his blaster at her, Mara had turned around and greeted him smiling.

'We can't get at them,' Agana yelled. 'It's just bouncing off, the blasters can't do any damage. Where's the fucking anti-aircraft, those useless bastards...' He sounded almost tearful. 'Fuck this, we're sitting ducks out here!' He stood up, blaster in hand. 'You won't do anything, you won't save yourself, there's a limit to what an aide can do for you!' He didn't look at Desailly. 'I've done my best for you and I've done enough. Just because you want to sacrifice yourself doesn't mean I have to! I have a life to lead! I'm going.' He looked for a moment as if he wanted Desailly to dissuade him, and when nothing came he ran for the door and plunged down the stairs.

The flyer touched gently down. Two of the guards followed Agana as it landed; one made it to the stairs. Leisurely, the blasters picked off the others, so easily it was clear they didn't have to try. Down below, the ground troops blew the main door in. Somewhere in the building there was a brief exchange of fire, then silence. Desailly stayed by the rail, by the edge of the roof. The blaster ports opened their black mouths towards him but didn't shoot. He waited.

A ramp slid out from the underside of the flyer and anchored itself on to the roof. Two soldiers marched down it, blasters held ready in front of them, followed by a Chi!me in civilian dress, a side-buttoned jacket with gold lacework on the shoulders and along the lines of the lapels. The three of them walked across the roof and stopped a few feet away. The civilian chirruped something to one of the soldiers. The soldier waved a bleeping gadget in Desailly's direction, then handed it to the civilian, who nodded.

'You are Petrus Desailly?' His accent was stilted but understandable enough.

Desailly nodded. 'I am.'

'And you are not armed. So.' He pulled a small screen from his jacket and started reading from it. 'Petrus Desailly, formerly known as President of Benan Ty, you are charged with crimes against sentience. By the authority of United Planets and at the behest of the peoples of the galaxy I hereby take you into custody pending your trial for these crimes at a court to be determined. Do you have anything to say?'

Did he have anything to say? He would like to think of something cutting, some phrase that would show them that he despised all of it, how the serpentine pretence of virtue made him gag. The last words of Petrus Desailly, to be told to wide-eyed children for decades, centuries to come. He couldn't think of anything.

'No. You Chi!me, you're so loquacious you leave all the rest of us speechless.'

They didn't bind his hands. They allowed him to walk to the flyer with them almost as if he was still President and this was a state visit, except for one light steel touch on his arm. He didn't think they would mistreat him, not physically. They would want him to show to an audience eventually, even if the trial they promised never actually took place. They would lock him up somewhere and feed him and clothe him and keep on talking at him in their persistent voices until one day he would be converted, he would renounce his past, accept their way and they would bring him blinking into the light to proclaim it. The prospect of it scared him almost more than anything else they might do.

They let him sit by the window as they took off. The pilot had to circle the building to face back to the spaceport. Desailly looked out at the northern mountains, hazy with distance, the huddled grey roofs of Chaireddan in the rain; the flat expanse of the terrace, wreathed now in smoke from the lower floors burning and stained, here and there, with blood. He thought, suddenly, that there should be something more, as if the husk of his Presidency could lie there crumpled on the roof behind him, but of course there was nothing. The flyer completed its turn and sped away into the clouds.

Part 26

Quila and Terise

'I won't pretend it will be victory,' Issa said. 'I won't lie to you and pretend we'll win.' She stood in the centre of the square on the makeshift platform Jaiyro had spent all night building, addressing the assembled crowd of all that remained of ViaVera. She looked very small in her camouflage jacket, framed against the lightening sky as the sun rose over her head.

Beside her, Ladyani leaned on the railing, his blue bandana marking him out from even the back of the throng. To most of them he would have appeared sensibly controlled, the leader being responsible, not panicking. To Terise, at the front, he seemed genuinely calm, a smile echoing around his mouth. It was the same smile with which he had greeted her when she had woken and found him dressing, because word had come that the Chi!me were only hours away. The smile of a child on his birthday, as if a wish had come true.

'You know the strength of the Chi!me, how great are the forces that we're up against. You know our plans, you've all been told what you must do. We don't have much time so I won't go over them now. I only want to say one thing.' She paused momentarily, letting the beat go, timing it until they were all waiting with her.

'It hasn't always been easy, what we've done here. We've

always known that we were on the true road, but the way to stay there, what to do for the best, hasn't always been so clear. There've been mistakes, disagreements, you know that, but we can let them go now. We don't have to think about them any more, because that's over. Remember that. The hard part is the planning, the deciding, the endless work of holding this movement together every day, over and over again, and that's finished. It's done. There are no more questions to answer, no more decisions. It's simple now, it's easy, because all we have to do now is fight and we know how to do that better than anyone else. We've all fought every day of our lives and we have only to do that for one day more and we will be a name that will never, ever be forgotten. And we will have lived without fear, which is the best thing of all.'

She stopped and into the silence that followed, Ladyani added, 'You've almost all of you served with me at some time and I just want to say that I'm proud of all of you, and Mara would have been too. Now, let's do it.'

'Three cheers for *la dona*, our Caduca,' someone at the back shouted and the rest, freed suddenly from silence, joined in. Amid the calling and clapping, Issa seemed more Terran than she ever had; an almost imperial air like a leader from the great old days with a Roman title, a sheathed smile and a laurel wreath on her head. She should have given the speech from a chariot, Terise thought, like Roman generals did before their triumphs. Issa raised her outstretched arms to them as the cheers continued and, for a moment, caught Terise's eye and winked.

They knew the Chi!me would bomb the camp before the ground troops got to it, so there was no point in staying. 'The one advantage we have,' Ladyani had said, 'is that we know the ground better than they do. They'll have to come up the track from the Ultima road, they won't be able to find any other way. They'll be expecting ambushes, but they won't know exactly where, so if we stake out several groups along the path we should at least be able to hurt them.' He, Terise and Issa were to join the last group, closest to the camp, the group that would make the last stand after the others had fallen. They were under no illusions that they would.

The rendezvous was set for two hours after dawn; Terise had just time to fetch her rifle from her hut before she had to get in position. The hut was a mess, her clothes and Ladyani's strewn over the unmade bed from their hurried rising earlier that morning. She had an absurd urge to tidy it, to put everything away and straighten the bedspread as if that would mean something, as if the Chi!me bombs would notice. She resisted it and closed the door firmly.

Her route back through the camp took her on a long loop past the point where the path to the kitchens struck off up the hill. She hesitated at the bottom. She knew she didn't have time to go up to Quila, knew there was nothing she could do for her in any case, but it still seemed wrong to leave her. If she told her to get away, she could maybe run into the forest, die of starvation and exposure if the Chi!me didn't find her. Or she could stay in the hut until the bombs came, waiting. She knew that if she was Quila, she would prefer not to know the choice she had, since it was no choice at all, but ridiculously she still wanted to tell her, if only as an excuse to say goodbye. She was making herself turn away when footsteps came running down the path.

'Terise!'

She turned back. 'Elenore! Where are you going? Are you going down to the road? Because we could…'

Elenore shook her head. She had six of the kitchen girls with her, clustered around her with wide, silent eyes. 'I'm not going,' she said. 'I'm going to get the girls out.' Terise didn't say anything but she went on defensively, as if she had seen something in her expression. 'They don't know how to fight, they're no loss and, really, why should they? We brought them here, they never asked for this. They haven't done anything. They don't deserve to die.' Her eyes searched Terise's face. 'If I thought you would I'd ask you to come too.'

'I can't. Lad…'

'Yeah. I know. And you know all my arguments on that one, you've heard them often enough.' She paused. 'I am sorry they didn't work, though, Terise.'

Terise nodded, acknowledging. 'What will you do, after you've seen them home?'

Elenore shrugged. 'I don't know. Stay and bake bread for them, perhaps, at least I've got the practice. Or maybe I'll go home, surprise my cousins, throw those slates off the roof after all.' She grimaced, as if admitting the futility of both of those options. 'I don't know. I don't really think it matters. At least I'll have something to put on the other half of the scales, something to show for it all, that it wasn't all death.' She swallowed, collecting herself. 'I wish you could come. I'll miss you.'

'Yeah.' Terise's throat was constricting, it was suddenly difficult to speak. All the times sitting in the kitchen with Elenore; gossiping in whispers beside an ambushed road; her arms dragging her back to safety from a burning transport while bolts whistled over her head. She had a sudden vivid memory of the first time she had seen her, standing thin and pugnacious in the middle of the square, carefully swearing at the lads mocking her with every syllable precise and expensive as glass. It seemed impossible that their conversation could really be over, but at the same time there wasn't anything left to say.

'Take care of yourself.'

She heard herself offer it, limply, and half to cover the banality of it put out her hand. For a moment she felt Elenore's palm on hers, her other arm light over her shoulders as it had rested so many times on campaign, in the camp, by a hundred stolen fires. She closed her eyes, smelling her scent, then there were only footfalls on packed earth, hurrying away. The skin on her palm was tingling, as if looking for the touch it could remember but no longer feel. She clapped her other hand over it, blinked until her eyes were clear, and carried on.

The first flyers came into view as she reached the square, black against the clouds to the south. Running down the path to the main gate she almost collided with Ihanakan; she had apologised and run past before she realised that he was going the other way. She turned and hurried back after him.

'Ihanakan! Ihanakan, could you do something for me?'

He stopped and looked at her steadily. 'I cannot take you. You will not be empty enough.'

'What?' She had no time to think about it, brushed it off with an impatient hand. 'No. It's about Quila, the Chi!me woman? She's up in the hut. She's all alone. I think she could walk a bit now, if she had help, but she doesn't have anywhere to go. I haven't got time to see her, I have to…' She gestured to the gates, 'You know. Can you get her out, Ihanakan? It's not her fault, she doesn't deserve… and I brought her here. She'll just sit there in the hut till the bombs come, and then she'll… She needs someone to help her, but I can't. Could you save her?'

'I will.'

Terise let her breath go in relief. 'Thank you. Now I have to go. Ihanakan…' She studied him. 'I think… we've been friends, haven't we?' She tried to keep the plea out of her voice, not knowing quite what she was asking.

His expression, as far as a Jeban ever had expressions, was kind.

'I will tell her you were thinking of her,' he said, 'and, in memory of friendship, I forgive you for your father taking the fish.'

When Ihanakan entered the hut, he found Quila sitting on the bed, facing into the dark. She had woken just before dawn to shouts and footsteps outside. She could tell something was happening, but she could not understand their Ty Terran, let alone the dialect, well enough to understand what it was. She had not seen her own clothes since she came, she assumed that they were too torn and bloodied to be of any use, but two days before, without comment, Terise had brought her a pair of trousers and a jacket in dusty green. She had no idea what she was going to do, she knew there was nothing she could do, but whatever was going to happen she knew she would feel better facing it dressed and not lying in bed like an infant. She had dragged the clothes on, grimly fumbling with the unfamiliar fastenings, then subsided back into the corner to wait.

'Your people are here,' Ihanakan said. 'They will be bombing the camp very ssoon now. They are going out to fight them, but they will losse.'

Quila pulled herself up straighter in her corner, adjusted the edge of her jacket. 'I was expecting them,' she said. 'I am ready.'

'Terisse assked me to take you away with me. She goess out to die now with the otherss, but she wass concerned for you.'

'That was kind of her, but I don't want to go.' Her tone was dull, expressionless. 'There is nowhere to go. There is no point in anything.'

Ihanakan went on, relentless. 'She wishess it. She wishess to do one good thing before she diess.'

'I can't…'

'She doess not know that I wass coming here without her assking. I would have come here anyway for you. To take you away.'

There was something intent in his face Quila had not seen before. She was aware that if she had had anything more to lose, she would have been afraid. 'Why?'

'I told Terise once of *kabila*,' he replied obliquely. 'The dance that iss danced when you do not know it, except that through all the dayss of waiting ssomething iss guiding your stepss. This is *kabila*, Ar'Quila of the Chi!me, and thiss iss the mosst important sstep of all.'

'Isn't it the last step?' she asked sourly. She was not interested any more in his culture. It was not her work any more.

He ignored her question. 'All your peopless, you Chi!me, the Terranss, government and ViaVera both, you are all trapped in your mazess,' he said. 'Running round in your spiralss never knowing that your path growss more and more twissted, never able to look outsside. You think your maze iss the whole of the world, when in fact it iss only a trap. They fight, you fight, you

414

all trick each other and for what? The rule of the prison? At the centre there iss only emptiness and you know it iss sso. But we Jeba, we are outsside the maze and we can ssee it clearly.

'Ssince the Terrans came to our planet we have been disspossessed, pushed out, ignored. Our land hass been taken from uss, our ssea, and we have been left only crumbss. We clean their buildingss, we sserve their rich and they do not ssee us. They do not ssee us, but we ssee. We ssee. A long time ago ViaVera were fighting for freedom, but true freedom iss only when the oppressed, all the oppressed fight together against the oppressorss. Who iss more oppressed than the Jeba? Mara knew thiss, she talked to uss, she came to uss and ssaid, your sstruggle iss our sstruggle. She wass a great woman, Mara. When we sspeak of her it iss ass a Jeba and not a Terran. It wass she who taught uss that we cannot do thiss alone, that when we fight we musst not fight the poor Terrans, but with them.

'We cannot drive them off our land. Just ass we are oppressed by them, sso they are exploited by the rulerss of thiss land, and their rulerss and theirss; your people, the lordss of the world. Compared to them the peassantss are innocent. They do only ass they musst and they have almost ass little ass we. We could kill them, but if we did there would be sso much blood that we would never be free of it. We have sseen that blood here, we have sseen how it runss and we do not wish it. We are wisse enough not to wish it. We will join with them and take back with them what iss ours and what iss theirss. We will share it fairly and it iss enough.

'We are the oness who can do thiss, the only oness. Who can read the messagess we leave for each other, undersstand the words we exchange right besside their earss? We do not have to hide away in the foresst, we can have our ssafe place right in the heart of the capital and they will not know.'

'And do you?' It was strangely compelling, the way he spoke of his revolution as if it were more than a dream, as if it really were something they could do.

'Not yet. Not yet. We were waiting for the dance to lead uss to the moment. It iss almosst here, almosst here now. We will return to the capital ssoon, many of uss, and to the other townss, and we will continue to organisse. We will find the resisstance and make common causse with them. It will take a long time, our work, it iss the work not only of a sseasson but of all our livess. But we have made a beginning. All our calling hass not been in vain and we know that we will make an end. Once the ceremony iss done.'

She asked because, chillingly, she realised she already knew. 'Ceremony?'

'To thank the ssun and the ssea that after all these long yearss at lasst we have a Caduca again.'

Terise found Issa and Ladyani by the main gate, deep in conversation. The flyers were getting closer now, droning on the edge of hearing like an insect in the next room. Issa glanced at her as she ran up.

'You coming with us then, Terise?' Her tone was carefully surprised, artificial.

'Of course I am. Where else would I go?'

'Well, I don't know what to think, with you. You never know.'

Terise looked at Ladyani, puzzled, but his expression was blank, giving nothing away.

'Issa, what are you talking about? We'd better get to our position, we don't have much time. Come on.'

Issa didn't move. 'After all, I don't know what you might have arranged with the Chi!me, do I? You might have decided with them to signal to them from the square, I wouldn't know.'

'What? Issa, I don't know what you mean. If you mean the Ambassador, she can't…'

'Because since you were talking to the CAS all that time, who else might you have been betraying us to?'

It seemed to Terise that the whole world became very still. 'What are you talking about?'

Issa's voice was silky. 'I mean your little trips to Airdrossa to see your friends in the CAS, of course. All the little secrets, just tumbling out. Did you think I didn't know?'

'But…' She wanted to deny it but somehow she couldn't. Ladyani still hadn't moved.

'You know? How do you know? How could you have found out? I haven't been to Airdrossa for ages, what reason would there be…' Suspicion, curling inside like a shell. 'What reason would there be?' she repeated slowly. 'You mean you always knew? You always knew, Issa? But then…' She felt her way through realisation, every word stepping further and further out over the void. 'You kept sending me to Airdrossa. You kept encouraging me, making me go. Why did you do that, if you knew? Why didn't you stop me? Did you *want* me to do it? Is that it? Did you want me to, let me do it? Why wouldn't you have stopped me, otherwise? Why wouldn't you? Why didn't you stop me, Issa? *Why did you make me go?*'

'Oh Terise.' Issa looked at her kindly, as if to a stupid child. 'You never could keep up, could you? I needed you to go because you would betray us, of course. How can you end, if they can't stop you? How can you die if they can't kill you? You have to have a Judas, Terise, if you are to be God. In the end, of course, the Chi!me came to do it for me, but without them I would have had you lead us here eventually, all gone in one glorious burst... You were very useful.' She smiled at her, her frank, innocent smile. 'Thank you.'

'I...' She couldn't think, couldn't breathe, couldn't do anything but stare at her. 'Oh, God, Issa, you can't mean it. You can't, you can't, I don't believe you!'

'But I know, so it must be true, mustn't it? You all taught me to reason. You taught me well.'

'Oh, God...'

'Well, it's been nice knowing you, Terise, and as I said I'm very grateful. But you are a traitor, and traitors have to be punished. To encourage the others, you know, I'm sure you taught me that, too. Lad?'

Obediently, impassively, Ladyani turned his blaster towards her. Terise screamed. 'No! No, please! You said I did what you wanted me to! It can't matter now, it's the end anyway, let me come with you! Let me fight with you, please. Don't...'

Issa shook her head. 'It's about choosing the company you die in. I'm sure you understand.'

'Lad! Lad, you understand. Please don't do this.' She started to gabble, clawing frantically at any words that might reach him. 'I know I was wrong, I know I shouldn't have done it, but I did it for you. They told me they'd let me get you out, in the end. They told me you could have an amnesty, that you'd be free to go. I know it was wrong, but I only wanted to save you.'

She was crying now, helplessly, tears splashing disregarded

on to her jacket, stumbling on. 'I know you never wanted to be saved, I always knew really this was what you wanted, but I couldn't. I couldn't want this for you. I'm sorry, I know that makes me weak, not good enough, but it's how I felt. I couldn't ever help loving you; God, if I could have done I would have stopped. You don't know what you did, you don't know what it was like, every day, over and over. I just couldn't bear that one day I would have to watch you die!'

She stopped. She had sworn she would never tell him that.

Ladyani regarded her, head on one side as if curious. The light behind him smoothed his features into the boy who used to throw pellets at her in class, scouring away the years between. She made one movement towards him; one hand, swiftly stilled.

'Lad...'

'I'm glad for you then, my dear,' he said. He was smiling. 'You got your wish.'

'We have not had a Caduca ssince the Terranss came, sso it iss fitting that when we have found one, it iss an alien alsso. It iss fitting that it iss one of your people.'

Quila waved her hands frantically. 'No. No, you can't mean...'

'You know what you are. You know thiss. You are the Caduca.'

'No. I won't, I won't be...'

'It iss not a choice to be. It iss not a cloak to be put on, it iss what you are. And you are.'

'I can't...'

'Yess, you cannot and sso you are. You are the empty one,

you are the one with nothing, for whom everything hass losst all meaning and to replace it iss only void. You are the Caduca. You cannot choosse otherwisse when it iss what you are.'

She wanted to keep denying it, but somehow she couldn't. She couldn't do anything. She asked instead in a small voice, 'What will happen to me?'

Ihanakan looked pleased. 'I will take you now to my people and there will be the ceremony. Then you will enter the place that iss prepared for you, the Caduca's housse that hass not been lived in for sso many years, and food and everything elsse you wish will be brought to you, all the dayss of your life.'

'And?'

'And there iss nothing else,' he said gently. 'You are. You do not have to do anything. It iss enough for uss to be free.' He put out his hand to her and after a hesitation she took it and let him help her to her feet. 'We musst go now, or the bombing will catch uss,' he said. 'There are ssome otherss of uss waiting outsside to help you, but we musst hurry. We have a long way to go.' He looked her in the eye. 'You think this iss a terrible thing that hass happened to you, and it iss indeed terrible to be Caduca. But it iss also greatness.

'Thiss hass been our long night, our long night that iss nearly at itss end. All Caducass bring a time of greatness, but for uss you are already ssomething more: our omen, our presage of the dawn. The one who iss Caduca doess not have a name among uss, it iss one of the thingss that must be losst. But before it iss, I thank you, Ar'Quila of the Chi!me, for the great sservice you have done for uss and for all the people of Benan Ty. For what we will do with you behind uss, I thank you.'

A memory of voices in an echoing hall, her name caught like

moths in her hair, far, fading away. His hand on hers was cool and smooth. A word whispered once more, breathily, 'Quila;' falling back into void. She bowed her head and let him lead her from the hut.

The flyer pilot made one last sweep low over the terrorist camp, the burning huts and the one body lying on the ground just inside the gates. The rest of the bodies were a little way down the track where the last ambush had been defeated, a fallen circle around a small woman sprawled together with a big man in a blue headscarf, so close they might have been embracing. Beyond the camp a movement caught his notice, a group of what looked like the native people hurrying away north through the tall ferns to the shelter of the trees. The pilot considered blasting them, tapping his finger idly against the trigger, but decided against it. It seemed a waste of good bolts and, after all, they couldn't be very important.

No one noticed when exactly the Jeba returned to Airdrossa. Everyone was talking of the big bomb outside the army headquarters that killed forty Chi!me guards, and of the reprisals that had ripped through every street. It seemed that everyone had a son or a brother or a cousin lifted by the blue bastards and everyone who ventured near the now-forbidden river reported seeing bodies in it. If there were more Jeba than there had been before no one gave it much thought either. Who knew why the Jeba did what they did? There had been no warning for the bomb and no one contacted Free Ty to claim responsibility. Free Ty blamed it, as they always did, on Benanist insurgents; the government on Benan was getting rather anxious these days.

They didn't report the note the investigators found pinned, strangely pristine, to a charred beam. Around the outside was a pattern of short lines, like the scratches you sometimes saw on the walls, and in the centre was one word: Dawn.

On Zargras

On his way upstairs after supper he stopped by his daughter Felia's room. She was out with her age-mates, re-bonding after half a cycle away on Chi!me Two, and would not be back until late. The night lights shone in over a confusion of half-unpacked trunks; clothes and shoes, discarded, spilling out over the floor. They would have taught her to be as neat as long ago they had taught him, but however well he had done at the school, as soon as he had got home he had strewn his things all over his floor just the same. Cast onto the wall, slightly crooked, was a new picture; a grainy image of a young Terran woman, white-faced beneath dark hair, with an ancient gun. Now ViaVera were gone, Mara Karne was fashionable again.

On the terrace the lights were low, the sinking sun a thin line beneath the clouds on the distant horizon. A fine rain fell, pattering like dust, on the dome above his head. The houses at the edge of the dome were at a premium on Zargras but he had been happy to pay it. It didn't do, he had always said, to be too cut off from the universe.

It was also the most fashionable district, of course, and that was important too. Even in his position you had to be seen with the right lifestyle, even Felia keeping up with the latest trends was part of that. He was pleased to see she had listened to him. It was strange, how the young responded to Mara Karne, this Terran rebel dead half a galaxy and five cycles ago, but an interest in Benan Ty was always going to be useful, these days.

He was always careful, but even he should be able to allow himself to feel pleased about Benan Ty. It had gone well, despite the resistance and Ai'Amadi's long face there was no denying it. They would crush the insurgents, they always did. It was just a matter of time and it needn't concern him, it was an army matter. He had had some very useful talks with some of the major traders, the business in Airdrossa was booming.

Once they had control, they could open up the rest of the continent, get some of the land under proper cultivation, start using it profitably instead of allowing this foolish peasant agriculture. There was always a better use for peasants; judging by his current housekeeper they could do with some on Zargras. No, he had been right when he had said, cycles ago, that Benan Ty was the true road to Terra. It never did to gloat, but he could enjoy vindication.

There was the question of the Desailly trial, of course, but the longer they left that, the less of an issue it became. Everyone knew Desailly was guilty, there was no need for a performance when they could keep him secure for the moment when they might need him again. He had been a determined man for a Terran, Desailly, but everyone always broke in the end. There was no reason for Ai'Amadi's doomsaying; he was upset about his protégée, that was all, and had to learn a long-overdue lesson about attachment. This doubt he claimed about what had happened to the woman was just silly, as if she might still be wandering about down there, waiting to save or to accuse.

She was dead, dead as she was supposed to be from the very first. All the ends were tied.

As he thought that, he realised he had the oddest sense that it was not so, the faintest image of a line flapping free, but that was ridiculous. What else could there be? The rain splashed louder on the dome. He was not going to dwell on it, this unease that must be the product of fatigue, nothing more. He knew there was nothing wrong. He would go down and sit with his terminal for a while, tidy up a little, drop a note to his assistant to check he was still awake. Maybe he would look into a few things, get rid of this absurd worry before it became a habit. Wasn't there something about some other people who weren't Terrans, in the mountains? He was never one for details.

He clicked his fingers at the terminal screen. He had a new message from the second representative that he really should answer, three from his assistant that he would have to review, another from a source he didn't recognise at all and piqued his curiosity. He worked on, immersed, and in the blue hum of the terminal, the thing he was going to check slipped quietly from his mind and disappeared.

The lights in the house went off at around midnight, then on briefly again a little later when En'Felia came home. Her voice drifted outside in laughter, doors slid shut, then again there was silence. Over the darkened terrace, beyond the orange-lit dome, on Zargras and Ty, on Chi!me and Jeba the rain went on falling; falling gently, patiently, to the end of the night.

Acknowledgements

Thanks are due to many people. To the members of the Bounds Green Book Writers Group – Susie Helme, Rajes Bala, Lynda Brennan and Ann McTaggart – for support and advice. To the editors who have supported my short fiction, in particular Stephen Theaker and John Greenwood at *Theaker's Quarterly*, Ian Redman at *Jupiter* and Michael R Colangelo at *The Harrow*. To James Essinger at The Conrad Press. And to Dominic Alexander, who has had to hear far more than anyone should about possible future histories, and without whom, none of them would ever have been possibly going to happen.

About the author

Elaine Graham-Leigh is an activist, historian and qualified accountant (because even radical movements need someone doing the books). She is the author of The Southern French Nobility and the Albigensian Crusade (Boydell and Brewer 2005), A Diet of Austerity, Class, Food and Climate Change (Zero Books 2015) and Marx and the Climate Crisis, (Counterfire 2020). She speaks and writes regularly on a range of political issues and her science fiction stories have appeared in zines including Jupiter SF, The Harrow, Bewildering Stories and Theaker's Quarterly Fiction. Her website is www.redpuffin. net. She lives in north London.